✔ KU-323-929

WITHDRAWN

BETRAYAL

BY AARON ALLSTON

Galatea in 2-D

BARD'S TALE Series (with Holly Lisle)
Thunder of the Captains
Wrath of the Princes

CAR WARRIORS Series
Double Jeopardy

DOC SIDHE Series
Doc Sidhe
Sidhe-Devil

Star Wars: X-WING Series
Wraith Squadron
Iron Fist
Solo Command
Starfighters of Adumar

Star Wars: NEW JEDI ORDER Series
Enemy Lines I: Rebel Dream
Enemy Lines II: Rebel Stand

Star Wars: LEGACY OF THE FORCE Series
Betrayal
Exile

TERMINATOR 3 Series
Terminator Dream
Terminator Hunt

STAR WARS

LEGACY OF THE FORCE

BETRAYAL

AARON ALLSTON

arrow books

Published in the United Kingdom by Arrow Books in 2007

1 3 5 7 9 10 8 6 4 2

Copyright © Lucasfilm Ltd. & ™ 2006

Excerpt from *Star Wars: Legacy of the Force: Bloodlines* copyright © 2006 by Lucasfilm Ltd. & ® or ™ where indicated. All rights reserved. Used under authorisation.

'In His Image' copyright 2005 by Lucasfilm Ltd. & ® or ™ where indicated. All rights reserved. Used under authorisation. 'In His Image' by Karen Traviss first appeared in *Vader: The Ultimate Guide*, in April 2005. 'Two Edged Sword' copyright 2006 by Lucasfilm Ltd. & ® or ™ where indicated. All rights reserved. Used under authorisation. 'Two Edged Sword' by Karen Traviss first appeared in *Star Wars Insider*, Issue 85, in January 2006.

Aaron Allston has asserted his right under the Copyright, Designs and Patents Act, 1988 to be identified as the authot of this work.

This novel is a work of fiction. Names and characters are the product of the author's imagination and any resemblance to actual persons, living or dead, is entirely coincidental.

This book is sold subject to the condition that it shall not, by way of trade or otherwise, be lent, resold, hired out, or otherwise circulated without the publisher's prior consent in any form of binding or cover other than that in which it is published and without a similar condition, including this condition, being imposed on the subsequent purchaser.

First published in the United Kingdom in 2006 by Century

Arrow Books
The Random House Group Limited
20 Vauxhall Bridge Road, London, SW1V 2SA

Addresses for companies within The Random House Group Limited can be found at: www.randomhouse.co.uk/offices.htm

The Random House Group Limited Reg. No. 954009

A CIP catalogue record for this book
is availabe from the British Library

ISBN 9780099491136

The Random House Group Limited makes every effort to ensure that the papers used in its books are made from trees that have been legally sourced from well-managed and credibly certified forests. Our paper procurement policy can be found at: www.randomhouse.co.uk/paper.htm

Printed in the UK by CPI Bookmarque, Croydon, CR0 4TD

acknowledgments

Thanks are due to my partners-in-plotting Troy Denning and Karen Traviss, to my Eagle-Eyes (Chris Cassidy, Kelly Frieders, Helen Keier, Bob Quinlan, Roxanne Quinlan, and Luray Richmond), to Shelly Shapiro of Del Rey, to Sue Rostoni and Leland Chee of Lucas Licensing, and to my agent, Russ Galen.

THE STAR WARS NOVELS TIMELINE

1020 YEARS BEFORE
STAR WARS: A New Hope

Darth Bane: Path of Destruction

33 YEARS BEFORE
STAR WARS: A New Hope

Darth Maul: Saboteur*

32.5 YEARS BEFORE STAR WARS: A New Hope

Cloak of Deception
Darth Maul: Shadow Hunter

32 YEARS BEFORE STAR WARS: A New Hope

STAR WARS: EPISODE I
THE PHANTOM MENACE

29 YEARS BEFORE STAR WARS: A New Hope

Rogue Planet

27 YEARS BEFORE STAR WARS: A New Hope

Outbound Flight

22.5 YEARS BEFORE STAR WARS: A New Hope

The Approaching Storm

22 YEARS BEFORE STAR WARS: A New Hope

STAR WARS: EPISODE II
ATTACK OF THE CLONES

Republic Commando: Hard
Contact

21.5 YEARS BEFORE STAR WARS: A New Hope

Shatterpoint

21 YEARS BEFORE STAR WARS: A New Hope

The Cestus Deception
The Hive*

Republic Commando: Triple Zero

20 YEARS BEFORE STAR WARS: A New Hope

MedStar I: Battle Surgeons
MedStar II: Jedi Healer

19.5 YEARS BEFORE STAR WARS: A New Hope

Jedi Trial
Yoda: Dark Rendezvous

19 YEARS BEFORE STAR WARS: A New Hope

Labyrinth of Evil

STAR WARS: EPISODE III
REVENGE OF THE SITH

Dark Lord: The Rise of Darth
Vader

10-0 YEARS BEFORE STAR WARS: A New Hope

The Han Solo Trilogy:
The Paradise Snare
The Hutt Gambit
Rebel Dawn

5-2 YEARS BEFORE STAR WARS: A New Hope

*The Adventures of Lando
Calrissian*

The Han Solo Adventures

STAR WARS: A New Hope
YEAR 0

STAR WARS: EPISODE IV
A NEW HOPE

0-3 YEARS AFTER STAR WARS: A New Hope

Tales from the Mos Eisley
Cantina
Galaxies: The Ruins
of Dantooine
Splinter of the Mind's Eye

3 YEARS AFTER STAR WARS: A New Hope

STAR WARS: EPISODE V
THE EMPIRE STRIKES BACK

Tales of the Bounty Hunters

3.5 YEARS AFTER STAR WARS: A New Hope

Shadows of the Empire

4 YEARS AFTER STAR WARS: A New Hope

STAR WARS: EPISODE VI
RETURN OF THE JEDI

Tales from Jabba's Palace
Tales from the Empire
Tales from the New Republic

The Bounty Hunter Wars:
The Mandalorian Armor
Slave Ship
Hard Merchandise

The Truce at Bakura

dramatis personae

Aidel Saxan; Prime Minister, Corellia (human female)
Ben Skywalker (human male)
Brisha Syo (human female)
C-3PO; protocol droid
Cal Omas; Chief of State, Galactic Alliance (human male)
Cha Niathal; admiral, Galactic Alliance (Mon Calamari female)
Gilad Pellaeon; admiral, Supreme Commander of the Galactic Alliance (human male)
Han Solo; captain, *Millennium Falcon* (human male)
Heilan Rotham; professor (human female)
Jacen Solo; Jedi Knight (human male)
Jaina Solo; Jedi Knight (human female)
Kolir Hu'lya; Jedi Knight (Bothan female)
Leia Organa Solo; Jedi Knight; copilot, *Millennium Falcon* (human female)
Luke Skywalker; Jedi Grand Master (human male)
Lysa Dunter; ensign, Galactic Alliance (human female)
Mara Jade Skywalker; Jedi Master (human female)
Matric Klauskin; admiral, Galactic Alliance (human male)
Nelani Dinn; Jedi Knight (human female)
R2-D2; astromech droid
Syal Antilles; ensign, Galactic Alliance (human female)
Tahiri Veila; Jedi Knight (human female)
Thann Mithric; Jedi Knight (Falleen male)

Thrackan Sal-Solo; Chief of State, Corellia (human male)
Tiu Zax; Jedi Knight (Omwati female)
Toval Seyah; Galactic Alliance scientist-spy (human male)
Tycho Celchu; general, Galactic Alliance (human male)
Wedge Antilles; general, Corellian Defense Force (human male)
Zekk; Jedi Knight (human male)

chapter one

CORUSCANT

"He doesn't exist." With those words, spoken without any conscious thought or effort on his part, Luke Skywalker sat upright in bed and looked around at the dimly illuminated chamber.

There wasn't much to see. Members of the Jedi order, even Masters such as Luke, didn't accumulate much personal property. Within view were chairs situated in front of unlit computer screens; a wall rack holding plasteel staves and other practice weapons; a table littered with personal effects such as datapads, notes scrawled on scraps of flimsi, datachips holding reports from various Jedi Masters, and a crude and not at all accurate sandglass statuette in Luke's image sent to him by a child from Tatooine. Inset into the stone-veneer walls were drawers holding his and Mara's limited selection of clothes. Their lightsabers were behind Luke, resting on a shelf on the headboard of their bed.

His wife, Mara Jade Skywalker, had more personal items and equipment, of course. Disguises, weapons, communications gear, falsified documents. A former spy, she had never given up the trappings of that trade, but those items weren't here. Luke wasn't sure where she kept them. She didn't bother him with such details.

Beside him, she stirred, and he glanced down at her. Her

red hair, kept a medium length this season, was an unruly mess, but there was no sleepiness in her eyes when they opened. In brighter light, he knew, those eyes were an amazing green. "Who doesn't exist?" she asked.

"I don't know. An enemy."

"You dreamed about him?"

He nodded. "I've had the dream a couple of times before. It's not just a dream. It's coming to me through currents in the Force. He's all wrapped up in shadows—a dark hooded cloak, but more than that, shadows of light and . . ." Luke shook his head, struggling for the correct word. "And ignorance. And denial. And he brings great pain to the galaxy . . . and to me."

"Well, if he brings pain to the galaxy, you're obviously going to feel it."

"No, to me personally, in addition to his other evil." Luke sighed and lay down again. "It's too vague. And when I'm awake, when I try to peer into the future to find him, I can't."

"Because he doesn't exist."

"That's what the dream tells me." Luke hissed in aggravation.

"Could it be Raynar?"

Luke considered. Raynar Thul, former Jedi Knight, presumed dead during the Yuuzhan Vong war, had been discovered a few years earlier—horribly burned during the war, mentally transformed in the years since through his involvement with the insectoid Killik race. That transformation had been a malevolent one, and the Jedi order had had to deal with him. Now he languished in a well-protected cell deep within the Jedi Temple, undergoing treatment for his mental and physical afflictions.

Treatment. Treatment meant change; perhaps, in changing, Raynar was becoming something new, and Luke's presentiment pointed toward the being Raynar would someday become.

Luke shook his head and pushed the possibility away. "In this vision, I don't sense Raynar's alienness. Mentally, emotionally, whoever it is remains human, or near human. There's even the possiblity that it's my father."

"Darth Vader."

"No. Before he was Darth Vader. Or just when he was becoming Vader." Luke's gaze lost focus as he tried to re-capture the dream. "What little of his face I can see re-minds me of the features of Anakin Skywalker as a Jedi. But his eyes . . . as I watch, they turn a molten gold or or-ange, transforming from Force-use and anger . . ."

"I have an idea."

"Tell me."

"Let's wait until he shows up, then crush him."

Luke smiled. "All right." He closed his eyes and his breathing slowed, an effort to return to sleep.

Within a minute the rhythm of his breathing became that of natural sleep.

But Mara lay awake, her attention on the ceiling— beyond it, through dozens of floor levels of the Jedi enclave to the skies of Coruscant above—and searched for any hint, any flicker of what it was that was causing her hus-band worry.

She found no sign of it. And she, too, slept.

ADUMAR

The gleaming pearl-gray turbolift doors slid open side-ways, and warm air bearing an aroma that advertised death and destruction washed over Jacen Solo, his cousin Ben Skywalker, and their guide.

Jacen took a deep breath and held it. The odors of this subterranean factory were not the smells of corrupted flesh or gangrenous wounds—smells Jacen was familiar with— but those of labor and industry. The great chamber before them had been a missile manufacturing center for decades, and no amount of rigorous cleaning would ever be quite able to eliminate the odors of sweat, machine lubricant, newly fabricated composite materials, solid fuel propellants, and high explosives that filled the air.

Jacen expelled the breath and stepped out of the turbo-lift, then walked the handful of steps up to the rail overlooking the chamber. He walked rapidly so that his Jedi cloak would billow a little as he strode, so that his boot heels would ring on the metal flooring of this observation catwalk, and so his apprentice and guide would be left behind for a moment. This was a performance for his guide and all the other representatives of the Dammant Killers company. Jacen knew he was carrying off his role quite well; the company officials he'd been dealing with remained properly intimidated. But he didn't know whether to attribute his success to his bearing and manner, his lean, brooding, and handsome looks, or his name—for on this world of Adumar, with its history of fascination with pilots, the name of Jacen's father, Han Solo, went a very long way.

His guide, a slender, balding man named Testan ke Harran, moved up to the rail to Jacen's right. Contrasting with the dull grays and blues that were common on this factory's walls and its workers' uniforms, Testan was a riot of color—his tunic, with its nearly knee-length hem and its flowing sleeves, was the precise orange of X-wing fighter pilot uniforms, though decorated with purple crisscross lines breaking it down into a flickering expanse of small diamond shapes, and his trousers, belt, and scarf were a gleaming gold.

Testan stroked his lustrous black beard, the gesture a failed attempt to conceal the man's nervousness. Jacen felt, rather than saw, Ben move up on the other side of Testan.

"You can see," Testan said, "ar workars enjoy very fan conditions."

Ben cleared his throat. "He says their workers enjoy very fine conditions."

Jacen nodded absently. He understood Testan's words, and it had taken him little time to learn and understand the Adumari accent, but this was another act, a ploy to keep the Adumari off-balance. He leaned forward to give the manufacturing floor below his full attention.

The room was large enough to act as a hangar and maintenance bay for four full squadrons of X-wing snubfighters. Tall duracrete partitions divided the space into eight lanes, each of which enclosed an assembly line; materials entered through small portals in the wall to the left, rolled along on luminous white conveyor belts, and eventually exited through portals on the far right. Laborers in gray jumpsuits flanked the belts and worked on the materials as they passed.

On the nearest belt, immediately below Jacen, the materials being worked on appeared to be compact visual sensor assemblies. The conveyor belt brought in eight such units and stopped. Moving quickly, the laborers plugged small cables into the units and turned to look into monitors, which showed black-and-white images of jumpsuited waists and worker hands. The workers turned the units this way and that, confirming that the sensors were properly calibrated.

One monitor never lit up with a view from the sensor. The worker on that unit unplugged it and set it on a table running parallel to the conveyor belt. A moment later, the other workers on this section unplugged their sensor units and the conveyor belt jerked into motion again, carrying the remaining seven units to the next station.

One lane over, the conveyor belt remained in constant motion, carrying sensor unit housings along. The workers on that belt, fewer in number than the sensor testers, reached out occasionally to turn a housing, to look inside, to examine the exterior for cracks or warping. Some workers, distributed at intervals along the line, rapped each housing with a small rubber-headed hammer. Jacen assumed they were listening for a musical tone he could not possibly hear at this distance over the roar of noise from the floor.

Another lane away from him, the workers were clad not in jumpsuits but in full-coverage hazardous materials suits of a lighter and more reflective gray than the usual worker outfit. Their conveyor belt carried white plates bearing irregular balls the size of a human head but a nearly luminous green. The belt stopped as each set of eight such balls entered the lane, giving the workers time to plunge needle-like sensors into each ball. They, too, checked monitors for a few seconds before withdrawing the needles to allow the balls to continue on. Jacen knew that poisonous green—it was the color of the high explosive Adumari manufacturers used to fabricate the concussion missiles they exported.

While Jacen made his initial survey, Ben kept their guide occupied. "Do you wax your beard?" he asked.

"I do not."

"It just seems very shiny. Do you oil it?"

Testan's voice was a little more irritated in tone. "I do not oil it. I condition it. And I brush it."

"Do you brush it with butter?"

Jacen finally looked to the right, past Testan and at his cousin. Ben was thirteen standard years of age, not tall but well muscled, with a fine-featured freckled face under a mass of flame-red hair. Ben turned, his face impassive, to look at Jacen, then said, "The Jedi Knight acknowledges that this factory seems to meet the minimum, the absolute minimum, required safety and comfort standards of a Galactic Alliance military contractor."

Jacen nodded. The nod meant *Good improvisation.* He was exerting no Force skill to communicate words to Ben; Ben's role was to pretend to act as his mentor's translator, when his actual function was to convince the locals that adult Jedi were even more aloof and mysterious than they had thought.

"No, no, no." Testan drew a sleeve over his brow, dabbing away a little perspiration. "We are wall above mini-mam standards. Those duracrete barriars? They will vent any explosive farce upward, saving the majority of workars in case of calamity. Workar shifts are only two-fifths the day in length, unlike the old days."

Ben repeated Testan's words, and Jacen shrugged.

Ben imitated his motion. The gesture caused his own Jedi robe to gape open, revealing the lightsaber hanging from his belt.

Testan glanced at it, then looked back at Jacen, clearly worried. "Your apprentice—" Unsure, he looked to Ben again. "You are very young, are you not, to be wearing such a weapon?"

Ben gave him a blank look. "It's a practice lightsaber."

"Ah." Testan nodded as though he understood.

And there it was. Perhaps it was just the thought of a thirteen-year-old with a deadly cutting implement at hand, but Testan's defenses slipped enough that the worry began to pour through.

It was like the game in which children are told, "For the next hour, *do not think about banthas*." Try as they might, they would, within minutes or even seconds, think about a bantha.

Testan's control finally gave way and he thought about the banthas—or, rather, a place he wasn't supposed to go, even to think about. Jacen could feel Testan try to clamp down on the thought. Something in the increased potency of that worry told Jacen that they must be nearer to the source of his concern than during previous parts of their factory tour.

When Testan turned back, Jacen looked directly at him and said, "There is something here. Something wrong." They were the first words he'd spoken in Testan's presence.

Testan shook his head. "No. Evrything is fan."

Jacen looked past him, toward the wall to the far right of the chamber. It was gray and regular, a series of metal panels each the height of a man and twice as wide stacked like bricks. He began a slow, deliberate scrutiny, traversing right to left. His gaze swept the walls, the assembly lines, the elevated observation chamber directly opposite the turbolifts by which they had entered, and continued along the wall to the left.

As his attention reached the middle of the left wall, along the observation balcony, he felt another pulse of worry from Testan. Ben cleared his throat, a signal; the boy, though nowhere near as sensitive in the Force as Jacen, had gotten the same feeling.

Jacen set off along the balcony in that direction. This time the ringing of his boots and billowing of his cloak were a side effect of his speed rather than an act.

"You wish to see the observation chambar?" Testan hurried to keep up. His anxiety was growing, and there was something within it, like a shiny stone at the bottom of a murky pond.

Jacen reached into that pond to draw out the prize within.

It was a memory of a door. It was broad and gray, closing from above as men and women—in dark blue jumpsuits, the outfits of supervisors in this facility—scurried out ahead of its closing. When it settled in place, it was identical to the wall panels Jacen saw ahead of him in the here and now.

Jacen glanced over his shoulder at Testan. "Your thoughts betray you."

Testan paled. "No, there is nothing to betray."

Jacen rounded the observation balcony corner, took a few more steps, and skidded to a halt in front of one of the wall sections.

It was here. He knew because he could feel something beyond.

Conflict. He himself was there, fighting. So was Ben. It was a faint glimpse of the future, and he and his apprentice would be in peril beyond.

He jerked his head toward the wall.

Ben brought out his lightsaber and switched it on. With a *snap-hiss* sound, its blue blade of coherent energy extended to full length.

Ben plunged the blade into the wall panel and began to drag it around in a large circle.

Testan, his voice pained, said, "He told us it was a practice weapon."

Jacen gave him an innocent look. "It's true from a certain point of view. He does practice with it." In his nervousness, Testan didn't seem to notice that Jacen was understanding him clearly now.

Ben completed his circle and gave the meter-and-a-half-high section he'd outlined a little kick. It fell away into a well-lit chamber, clanging on the floor beyond; the edges still glowed with the heat the lightsaber had poured into them.

Ben stepped through. Jacen ducked to follow. He heard Testan muttering—doubtless an alert into a comlink. Jacen didn't bother to interfere. They'd just been within clear sight of hundreds of workers and the observation chamber. Dealing with Testan wouldn't keep the alarm from being broadcast.

The room beyond Ben's improvised doorway was actually a corridor, four meters wide and eight high, every surface made up of the same dull gray metal rectangles found in the outer chamber, greenish white light pouring from the luminous ceiling. To the left, the corridor ended after a few meters, and that end was heavily packed with tall plasteel transport containers. They were marked DANGER, DO NOT DROP, and DAMMANT KILLER MODEL 16, QUANTITY 24.

To the right, the corridor extended another forty meters and then opened up; the rail and drop-off at the end suggested that it opened onto another observation balcony above another fabrication chamber.

Now making the turn from the balcony into the corridor and running toward them were half a dozen troops armed with blaster rifles. Their orange jumpsuits were reminiscent of X-wing pilot uniforms, but the green carapace armor over their lower legs, torsos, lower arms, and heads was more like stormtrooper speeder bike armor painted the wrong color.

And then behind the first six troops came another six, and then another eight . . .

Jacen brought his lightsaber out and snapped it into life; the incandescent green of his blade was reflected as highlights against the walls and the armor of the oncoming troops. "Stay behind me," he said.

"Yes, sir." Ben's sigh was audible, and Jacen grinned.

The foremost trooper, who bore gold bars on his helmet and wrists, shouted, his voice mechanically amplified: "Stop whar you are! This saction is restricted!"

Jacen moved forward at a walk. He rotated his wrist, moving his lightsaber blade around in front of him in a pattern vaguely reminiscent of butterfly wings. He shouted back, "Could you speak up? I'm a little deaf."

Ben snickered. "Good one."

"You may not entar this saction!"

They were now twenty meters from the ranks of troopers ahead.

Jacen continued twirling his blade in a practice form. "Fewer people will be hurt if you just get out of my way." It was a sort of ritual thing to say. Massed enemy forces almost never backed down, despite the reputation of the Jedi—a reputation that became more widespread, more supernatural, with each year the Jedi prospered under Luke Skywalker's leadership.

The phrase was ritual in another way, too. Once upon a time, Jacen would have felt tragedy surround him when his actions resulted in the deaths of common soldiers, common guards. But over time he'd lost that sense. There was a wearying inevitability to leaders sending their troops to die against more powerful enemies. It had been happening as long as there were violent leaders and obedient followers. In death, these people became one with the Force, and when Jacen had accepted that fact, his sense of tragedy had largely evaporated.

He took another two steps and the trooper commander called, "Fire!"

The troopers began firing. Jacen gave himself over to the Force, to his awareness of his surroundings, to his sudden oneness with the men and women trying to kill him.

He simply ignored most of the blaster bolts. When he felt them angling in toward him, he twirled his lightsaber blade in line and batted them away, usually back toward the crowd of troopers. In the first few seconds of their assault, four troopers fell to blasts launched by their friends. The smell of burned flesh began to fill the corridor.

Jacen felt danger from behind; felt Ben react to it. Jacen didn't shift his attention; he continued his march forward. He'd prefer to be able to protect the inexperienced youth, but the boy was good at blaster defense practice. Hard as it was to trust a Jedi whose skills were just developing, he had to. To teach, to learn, he had to trust.

Jacen intercepted the next blaster shot that came his way and batted it toward the trooper commander. It struck the man in the helmet and caromed off, burning out against the ceiling; a portion four meters square of the ceiling's illumination winked out, darkening the corridor. The commander fell. The shot was probably not fatal—protected by his helmet, the man would have forehead and scalp burns, probably a concussion, but he was unlikely to die.

The strategy had its desired effect. The troopers saw their commander fall. They continued firing but also exchanged looks. Jacen never broke pace, and a trooper with silver stripes on his helmet called "Back, back." In good order, the troopers began a withdrawal.

Behind him, Jacen heard more blasterfire and the distinctive *zap* of a lightsaber blade intercepting it, deflecting it. Within the flow of the Force, Jacen felt a shot coming in toward his back, felt it being slapped aside, saw and felt it as it hit the wall to his right. The heat from the shot warmed his right shoulder.

But the defenders continued their retreat, and soon the last of them was around the corner. Jacen's path to the railing was clear. He strode up to it.

Over the rail, a dozen meters down, was another assembly-line pit, where line after line of munitions components was being assembled—though at the moment all the lines were stopped, their anonymous jumpsuited workers staring up at Jacen.

Jacen's movement out of the corridor brought him within sight of the orange-and-green defenders, who were now arrayed in disciplined rows along the walkway to Jacen's left. As soon as he reached the railing they opened fire again. Their tighter formation allowed them to concentrate their fire, and Jacen found himself deflecting more shots than before.

He felt rather than saw Ben scoot into position behind him, but no blaster bolts came at him from that direction. "What now?" Ben asked.

"Finish the mission." Jacen caught a too-close bolt on his blade near the hilt; unable to aim the deflection, he saw the bolt flash down into the assembly area. It hit a monitor screen. The men and women near the screen dived for cover. Jacen winced; a fraction of a degree of arc difference and that bolt could have hit an explosives package. As inured as he was to causing death, he didn't want to cause it by accident.

"But you're in charge—"

"I'm busy." Jacen took a step forward to give himself more maneuvering and swinging space and concentrated on his attackers. He needed to protect himself and Ben now, to defend a broader area. He focused on batting bolt after bolt back into the ranks of the attackers, saw one, two, three of the soldiers fall.

There was a lull in the barrage of fire. Jacen took a moment to glance over his shoulder. Ben stood at the railing, staring down into the manufacturing line, and to his eye he held a small but expensive holocam unit—the sort carried by wealthy vacationers and holocam hobbyists all over the galaxy.

As Jacen returned his attention to the soldiers, Ben began talking: "Um, this is Ben Skywalker. Jedi Knight Jacen Solo and I are in a, I don't know, secret part of the Dammant Killers plant under the city of Cartann on the planet Adumar. You're looking at a missile manufacturing line. It's making missiles that are not being reported to the GA. They're selling to planets that aren't supposed to be getting them. Dammant is breaking the rules. Oh, and the noise you're hearing? Their guys are trying to kill us."

Jacen felt Ben's motion as the boy swung to record the blaster-versus-lightsaber conflict.

"Is that enough?" Ben asked.

Jacen shook his head. "Get the whole chamber. And while you're doing it, figure out what we're supposed to do next."

"I was kind of thinking we ought to get out of here."

With the tip of his lightsaber blade, Jacen caught a blast that was crackling in toward his right shin. He popped the blast back toward its firer. It hit the woman's blaster rifle, searing it into an unrecognizable lump, causing her green shoulder armor momentarily to catch fire. She retreated, one of her fellow soldiers patting out her flames. Now there were fewer than fifteen soldiers standing against the Jedi, and their temporary commander was obviously re-thinking his *make-a-stand* orders.

"Good. How?"

"Well, the way we came in—no. They'd be waiting for us."

"Correct."

"And you never want to fight the enemy on ground he's chosen if you can avoid it."

Jacen grinned. Ben's words, so adult, were a quote from Han Solo, a man whose wisdom was often questionable—except on matters of personal survival. "Also correct."

"So . . . the ends of those assembly lines?"

"Good. So go."

Jacen heard the scrape of a heel as Ben vaulted over the rail. Not waiting, Jacen leapt laterally, clearing the rail by half a meter, and spun as he fell. Ahead of and below him, Ben was just landing in a crouch on the nearest assembly line, which was loaded with opalescent shell casings. As Jacen landed, bent knees and a little upward push from the Force easing the impact, Ben raced forward, reflexively swatting aside the grasping hand of a too-bold line worker, and crouched as he lunged through the diminutive portal at the end of the line.

Jacen followed. He heard and felt the heat of blaster bolts hitting the assembly line behind him. He swung his lightsaber back over his shoulder, intercepting one bolt, taking the full force of the impact rather than deflecting the bolt into a neighboring line.

No line workers tried to grab him, and in seconds he was squeezing through the portal.

chapter two

In the next chamber, racing between and across assembly lines while workers ducked to get out of their way or, occasionally and more foolishly, lunged at them, Jacen and Ben spotted turbolift doors. It took a moment to get to them, and another moment to realize that the sensors indicated no movement of the turbolift beyond even when they'd pressed the SUMMON button multiple times. With a sigh of exasperation, Jacen cut his way into the turbolift shaft and he and his apprentice leapt through the hole, its edges still glowing, to grasp the diagonal support spars on the far side of the shaft. Clinging there, they could see the turbolift car roof about ten meters below . . . but this shaft was side by side with another, and the car in that shaft was only a few meters down and rising fast.

Jacen swung over the second shaft and readied himself for the shock of impact when the turbolift car reached him. He could feel Ben following his motion, could even feel it as Ben also began focusing on aspects of the Force that would allow for the absorption of kinetic energy . . .

Then the rising car hit them. They absorbed the shock with their knees and with control over the Force, and suddenly they were hurtling upward along the darkened shaft.

Jacen estimated that they'd risen three hundred meters or more before the car executed a rapid deceleration and locked into place a mere three meters before the top of the shaft. Jacen and Ben both grabbed at support spars at the shaft's side. After a moment's noise from beneath—hissing of opening doors, tramping of feet, conversation, closing doors—the car dropped away out of sight, leaving them alone in comparative silence at the top of the shaft.

"I think we're aboveground," Ben said.

"Well aboveground." Jacen ignited his lightsaber and plunged it into what he assumed was the back wall of the shaft—the direction opposite that of the turbolift doors lining the shaft below them. He dragged the blade around in a circle, and just before the end of the burning circuit met the beginning, the plug he was cutting was yanked violently away into daylight brightness, spinning out into open space. A tug of air nearly yanked Jacen after it, and more air roared up the shaft to flee through the hole he'd cut.

Outside the hole was a skyscraper vista of the city of Cartann, part of the nation of Cartann and government capital of the planet of Adumar. The Jedi could see forty-story apartment buildings thickly lined with balconies, many of those balconies serving as small landing pads for personal fighter craft, as well as taller business spires, circular defensive towers whose featureless exteriors hid gun emplacements, and tall flagpoles from which streamed government, neighborhood, sports team, and advertising banners dozens of meters in length.

Jacen leaned out. The building wall beneath them sloped away at an angle rather than straight down. Far below, he could see skyspeeder traffic in tightly regulated streams through the air.

Ben stuck his head out just under Jacen's. "Lubed. I know how to do this."

"Don't say *lubed*."

"Why not?"

"It's generational slang, invented to distinguish between your generation and every other one by making use of superfluous and irritatingly precious vocabulary, and I'm not from your generation."

Ben turned up to look at him. His mouth worked as he sought to come up with a cutting reply.

Jacen continued, "Do you have a grapnel and line in your utility belt?"

"Sure, but I won't need it. I know how to do angle building drops like this."

"Get it ready anyway."

Ben grumbled but pulled the grapnel from his belt and dragged out a few meters of slender, strong cord.

"All right, Ben. You first."

Ben grinned and leapt outward. Jacen clipped his lightsaber back onto his belt and followed.

They fell a few meters, but Jedi acrobatic training and their control over the Force allowed them to come down with their heels against the angled building wall. From that point, it was a simple matter of reducing their inertia, keeping friction maximized between heel and wall surface.

They ran and occasionally slid down the side of the skyscraper along duracrete strips set between broad, high transparisteel viewports. On the other side of those viewports, they saw faces with mouths open in surprise or disbelief.

Jacen sensed the wind gust a moment before he felt it. He braced himself against it with foot placement and the Force before it hit.

Ben, less experienced, didn't. Jacen saw the boy's cape flap, then Ben was whirled away from the building face, yelling.

Jacen reached out for him, but the boy, still mostly clear-headed, was already hurling the grapnel hook toward him. Jacen snatched it out of the air and wrapped the cord several times around his wrist before the cord hit its maximum length. Jacen braced his arm against the shock of the impact and withstood it without being dragged off the building front.

With cord control and an extra tug against Ben himself through the Force, he dragged Ben back to the building face. Now Jacen was in front on the descent, Ben meters above and behind. He heard Ben shout, "You can let go now." The boy's voice sounded appropriately abashed.

Jacen released the grapnel. "You know how to do angle building drops like this, huh?"

"What?"

"I said—"

"Can't hear you. Too much wind."

Jacen grinned.

"Up ninety degrees!"

Jacen looked up in the direction Ben indicated. Above, just over skyscraper level, a blue-green flying vehicle was banking at them over a tower dome. It wasn't shaped like the split-tail Blade series of starfighters produced on this world and flown recreationally, and for duels, by so many Adumari—this was shaped roughly like a starfruit, one central body and five arms protruding from it. The arms ended in stubby housings that, Jacen could see, held thrusters, repulsor vents, and weapons muzzles. He decided that the vehicle would be slow but highly maneuverable—and capable of attacking in any direction, perhaps several directions at once. The arms rotated as a unit, but independent of the vehicle's central body, where Jacen could see a darkened transparisteel canopy protecting the pilot's seat.

Not that this was likely to be a threat to the Jedi. Unless the vehicle was armed with antipersonnel weapons systems, something capable of piercing flesh but not penetrating typical building construction material, the odds of it making an actual attack were low—

The vehicle's foremost pod fired. Jacen saw the smoke trail of a missile headed their way.

He felt an exertion in the Force from Ben, the boy leaping laterally. He added some kinetic energy to his own downward motion, reduced friction to his heels and buttocks—he sat down and slid faster.

The missile impacted dozens of meters above his head. He heard the explosion, felt the building shake beneath him, but was not hit by any heat or debris. The warhead must have penetrated into the building before detonating.

A little part of him went cold, infuriated at his enemy's callous willingness to risk and kill civilians to bag the targets, but the rest of Jacen remained analytical. He put on the brakes, stepping up heel friction and coming more upright again.

The enemy fighter spun closer, then dived past him and out of sight.

Out of sight? Jacen leaned forward. Yes, the building surface did seem to come to an end only a few dozen meters below him, but still well above street level. That meant the angle had to change at that point, becoming a vertical drop. The attacker was below the drop point, waiting.

Jacen turned his attention to reflections in the spacescrapers in the distance ahead of him. There, he could see the enemy fighter. It was flush against this building, its central body still and its legs rotating, four stories below the drop-off point, several meters to the right of where Jacen would go over the edge.

If he kept his current angle of descent, of course.

As the distance to the drop-off point shortened, he bounced across one bank of viewports, then another, ending up on a duracrete strip headed straight for a point above the enemy fighter. Then he reached the lip.

He was now only about twenty stories above the ground. Below, he could see a main avenue thick with traffic and, for the first four or five stories above street level, heavily crisscrossed with cables—private communications cables strung across streets all over Adumar to give neighbors secure communications access with one another.

Directly below Jacen was the fighter craft. Jacen somersaulted as he went over the lip, then came down straddling one of the fighter's arms just beside the vehicle's main body. The fighter jolted from the impact and dropped a couple of meters. Through the transparisteel canopy, Jacen could see a helmeted pilot, her body language showing alarm at the sudden proximity of her enemy.

She jerked the control yoke. The fighter spun away from

the building. In his peripheral vision Jacen saw a grapnel and white cord wrap around another of the vehicle's arms.

They angled away from the building, roaring out high above the avenue—then dived straight toward the ground.

Jacen grinned. It was a smart enough tactic. All those cables crossing the street would cut an average attacker—assuming an average attacker could end up in this situation—to pieces without doing significant harm to the fighter.

But Jedi weren't average attackers.

Ben pulled himself onto the arm his grapnel had grabbed. His face looked flushed with windburn, and his red hair had been whipped into an unruly mess.

"Cut your way in," Jacen invited.

Ben perked up. Holding the vehicle arm with both legs and one arm, he got his lightsaber into his hand and ignited it.

Jacen leaned over and looked at the ground, so much closer than it had been just seconds before. He gestured toward it, fingers flexing . . . and the comm cables directly beneath him suddenly wavered like alarmed serpents. He exerted himself more and they parted, some separating completely from one side of the street or the other. The fighter craft plunged into their midst but hit none of them. Just before hitting the street, and below where the cable layer ended, the fighter angled to join the groundspeeder traffic.

The pilot looked at the Jedi, obviously expecting to see limbless torsos or mere gouts of blood remaining. She had just enough time to register alarm before Ben plunged his lightsaber blade into the side of the canopy. As he dug around, trying to find the release catch or hinges, the blade almost grazed the woman's thigh.

She panicked. That was the only explanation Jacen could come up with. She wrenched her control yoke off to the side, at an unnatural angle, and the canopy suddenly blew clear, shooting up into the sea of comm cables above, nearly knocking Ben clear as it went.

An instant later, the pilot's seat ignited and shot her straight up. Into the cables. Half blinded by the ejection seat's propulsion, Jacen still saw her hit the first set of cables.

They held. She didn't. She and her ejection seat separated into two pieces, each headed a different direction. Jacen saw the upper half of her body hit yet another cable, and then her remains were out of sight behind them.

Jacen glanced ahead. The pilotless fighter was rising. In another few seconds, it would hit the cable layer again, this time at an angle that would keep it within that layer for long seconds or even minutes. "Let's go," he said.

Ben nodded, deactivated his lightsaber, and dropped clear. Jacen followed suit.

He saw Ben drop into the back of a groundspeeder, bounce out of it as though it were a trampoline, angle over to bounce onto one end of a dinner table on a streetside second-story balcony—the spray of food dishes catapulting off the table was quite impressive—and then drop down to street level. Jacen contented himself with one bounce from a heavy transport speeder and a tuck-and-roll as he reached the sidewalk beside Ben. Adumari pedestrians gave the two Jedi curious looks but seemed unalarmed. Most of them were watching the fighter plow through the cables overhead.

Ben had a well-cooked leg of some avian in one hand. He'd already taken a bite out of it and was chewing furiously.

"What, don't you get enough Jedi Temple food to eat?" Jacen commented.

Ben shook his head. "What's next?"

"Transmit."

"Don't you want to do that? You're the Jedi Knight."

"I'm not the one who needs to learn how to do it." Jacen turned and led the way through the sidewalk traffic. If his bearings were correct, this direction would lead them to the hangars where his shuttle waited.

With a long-suffering sigh, Ben discarded his improvised meal and pulled the little holocam, a datapad, and a comlink from pouches on his belt. Awkwardly, handling three items with two not-fully-grown hands, he began manipulating controls and keyboards, entering commands. "All right. The data package is being compressed and encrypted."

"While it's doing that, check to see if the shuttle's holocomm is still live. Remotely activate it and bounce a comm echo off the old lunar New Republic station."

"Yes, sir." This time, Ben didn't sound as put-upon. This was more of a challenge, something he'd never done before on his own authority. He typed commands into his datapad, relayed them through the comlink. "Holocomm is . . . live."

Kilometers away, the communications system aboard Jacen's shuttle—a full-fledged holocomm unit, capable of transmitting through hyperspace and thus communicating faster than light—would have just awakened from its power-down status.

"Querying automated comm systems on Relay Station ADU-One-One-Zero-Four through to Coruscant," the boy said. His voice, though no deeper, sounded more confident, more mature when he was engrossed in a task like this. "Successful echo." Another message popped up on his datapad. "Package encrypted."

"Transmit it," Jacen said. He kept a close eye on the pedestrian traffic, but he didn't anticipate any problems at this point. It would be some time before the operators of the Dammant Killers firm figured out where the Jedi were. "Await confirmation of reception. Request confirmation of decryption."

"Yes, sir." Ben typed in another set of commands, then tucked his holocam back in its pouch; it would no longer be needed. "So how do we get offworld?"

"We go back to the shuttle and take off."

"But the planet's full of starfighters! One shuttle, even an armed shuttle, isn't going to be able to fight its way through all of them."

"Correct. But why would they attack us?"

"To keep—to keep—" Understanding dawned in the

boy's eyes. "To keep us from getting offworld with what we found out."

"Correct."

"But we just holocast it, so it's too late." Ben checked the screen on his datapad. "They got the package. They're decrypting." His expression turned suspicious. "But what if the Adumari attack us for revenge?"

"Think it through, Ben. Take your time." They reached a broad plaza, and Jacen knew his bearings were correct; they were headed back toward the proper hangars, which should only be a couple of kilometers distant.

"If the package decrypts, and the spies see what we saw, they'll start talking to the government here."

"Military Intelligence. Not spies."

"Oh, they're spies." Ben sounded scornful of Jacen's correction. "Mom's a spy. What we just did makes us spies."

"Your mother's a Jedi. We're Jedi."

"Jedi spies." The datapad beeped, and Ben looked at it again. He snapped it shut. "The message decrypted. Our spy bosses say 'Well done.' So . . . they'll talk to the Adumari government, who know that if anything happens to us, things will be worse for them."

"Correct."

"So we can leave."

"And go on to our next assignment."

A look of unease crossed Ben's features. "Do we have to?"

"Yes, we do."

"There are going to be a lot of them."

"Not as many as we just encountered."

"It's going to be noisy."

"Not as noisy as that assembly line."

Ben heaved a sigh, defeated.

A few minutes later, Jacen and Ben boarded Jacen's shuttle—an armored variant on the old *Lambda*-class model, fitted with a turreted laser cannon and a holocomm unit—and lifted off. The shuttle's upswept wings lowered into horizontal position after liftoff, and Jacen oriented the craft toward Adumar's sky.

A flight of four Blade starfighters, Adumar's distinctive split-tail fighter craft, escorted the shuttle until it left the planet's gravity well and entered hyperspace. Nothing came close enough to fire a shot at the Jedi craft.

chapter three

CORUSCANT

Leia Organa Solo, one-time Princess of the world of Alderaan, former Chief of State of the New Republic, now a Jedi Knight, stood dressed in all-white robes, suitable to either a Jedi or a politician in informal surroundings, before the portal. It was not an ordinary door; though in appearance it was identical to billions of dwelling exterior doors found on the world of Coruscant, in reality it was not. In the recent past, the original low-cost, composite-material door had been replaced with this innocuous-appearing thing of armor. It would hold against blaster assault—for a while, anyway. The cool blue it was painted belied its defensive function.

Leia's husband, Han Solo, one of the most famous men in the galaxy, moved up beside her. He was wearing his favorite clothes: dark military trousers decorated with the red Corellian Bloodstripes he had earned when he was a younger man, light long-sleeved shirt, black vest, practical black boots. Except for the lines in his face and gray in his hair, honestly earned through deeds as well as accumulated over the passage of time, he was indistinguishable from the man she'd met aboard the first Death Star so many years ago.

Her spirit lifted. No matter how badly things went, they were always better with Han at her side.

Not that she'd necessarily tell him that. His ego hadn't diminished in all those years, either.

Han looked gravely at the door. "You figure that's how they're going to come at us?"

She nodded. "That's the only approach that makes any sense, and you know it."

"Well, the only *strategy* that makes any sense is for us to just open the door for them. They're less likely to attempt some sort of sneaky side entry if the front is open. We can pick them off as they're framed in the doorway. Once their numbers become too great for us, we can manage a staged retreat through the inner chambers."

Leia considered. "I don't know. Maybe I should be up front and center to bat back their blaster assaults while you fire on them from the side."

"Oh, my." This third voice was higher-pitched than Han's and carried just a hint of alarm. "If I may ask, has there been some change of plans?"

Han and Leia turned. Entering the outer chamber was C-3PO, the gold-toned protocol droid who had served them faithfully—if fussily—for four decades.

C-3PO moved up to them, his every action accompanied by the barely audible sound of whining servos, and added, "I thought that the plan was to admit them, then feed them the appetizers I have labored for so long to assemble. Appetizers that are laid out in the kitchen. Was I wrong? Will there be shooting?"

Han and Leia exchanged a glance. "Appetizers would be easier," Han admitted.

"Fewer blaster bolts hitting the walls, fewer repairs," Leia said, nodding. "We could do it that way."

"All right, Goldilocks." Han clapped C-3PO on one shining shoulder, rocking the droid in place. "We'll do it your way. This time."

"You're toying with me again, aren't you, sir?" C-3PO's sigh was audible.

Han nodded. "It's more fun and less destructive than hanging meat around your neck and letting the war-dogs loose on you."

"Humpf." The droid turned back toward the door through which he'd entered. "Not very sporting, I must say."

A chime filled the air—the delicate first five notes of "Path to the Sky," a ballad from Leia's homeworld of Alderaan.

Han heaved a sigh. "Not too late to change your mind. We could hold them off for days."

Leia smiled at him. "Hush."

First through that door were Luke Skywalker and Mara Jade Skywalker. For this occasion, Luke wore his black Jedi robe and accoutrements, a stark contrast to his still-fair complexion and bright blond hair. Mara wore more traditional Jedi robes in browns and tans, and a red belt that set off her red hair.

With them was R2-D2, the plug-shaped astromech who had variously served Luke and the Solos for decades, and the little droid made as many musical, wheeling noises of appreciation during their tour of the Solos' new quarters as the humans made verbal comments.

Next to arrive, just a few minutes later, were Jacen and Ben. Led from room to room by C-3PO, Jacen made non-committal noises about the antechamber, living chamber, master bedroom, bedrooms for Leia's Noghri bodyguards Meewalh and Cakhmaim, guest bedrooms, library, refreshers, furnished balcony, kitchen, dining room, and communications center, all but the last decorated and furnished in warm-colored hardwoods, some with dark carpets and some with pebbled flooring. The communications center, where the majority of the household's computers and electronics repair equipment was kept, was more modern, all steely surfaces and blue metal rolling racks.

Ben's only comment was, "Where are the secret chambers?"

C-3PO stopped short and leaned awkwardly to look at the boy-man. "I don't quite understand, young sir."

"C'mon." Ben grinned up at the droid—not far up, as he'd grown centimeters since the last time he'd seen the protocol droid. "Uncle Han is a smuggler. I bet this place is stuffed with secret chambers. They'll all have blasters in them. Some of them will have identicards in fake names, and credcards, and secret electronics gear, and maybe a disassembled scoutspeeder. Some of them will be hidey-holes for the Noghri."

C-3PO's voice was stiff, even for the droid. "I can assure you, sir, that there are no secret chambers."

"Aha!" Ben held up an accusative finger. He sounded as though he'd just found the essential clue to solve a murder. "*I can assure you* isn't the same thing as *There are no*. C'mon, Threepio, say it. Say 'There *are* no secret chambers.' "

"I can assure you, sir, that there—"

"Aha!"

The droid shot Jacen a look that, as far as Jacen could interpret droid body language, looked hurt. "I say, sir, must every generation of Solos and Skywalkers act like this?"

Jacen nodded. "Pretty much, yes."

In the living chamber, as C-3PO held out his carefully arrayed tray of geometrically shaped cheeses and fungus crackers to Mara, Leia said, "Jaina just called in. She and Zekk are just a few minutes out."

Han straightened, irritably, on the couch. "And Zekk. Who, may I ask, invited Zekk? He's not family."

Luke and Mara managed to say "Not yet" simultaneously.

Han glared at them.

"I invited him," Leia said. "Just now. Otherwise, he would have gone off to the Temple, been alone in whatever tiny chamber they gave him, been eating bland Jedi cafeteria food, all alone—"

"While rain poured on his head wherever he moved and

sad synthesized music filled the hallways." Han shot her a scornful look.

Leia merely smiled at him, the maddening smile of a politician who won't be budged from her position. "Han, he's her partner. Her Jedi partner. If he were her, say, smuggling partner, would you send him off?"

"Depends on how he looks at her. Y'see, here's the problem. A father's got a right to terrorize any young bantha who's following his daughter around."

Leia shook her head. "Jaina says they're friends. Just friends."

Han's scowl deepened and became almost comic. "Jaina's got herself blinded. It's got to be one of those Force abilities—they say the Force can have a profound effect on people who don't want to believe the truth."

Luke snorted. "No, they don't."

"Anyway, it's my right to scare Zekk out of his hide, but Zekk's a Jedi. He doesn't scare easily. So what do I do?" Han considered, then looked around. In corners of the room, motionless, inconspicuous, stood Leia's bodyguards, Meewalh and Cakhmaim, members of the Noghri species—gray-skinned, no taller than R2-D2, shrouded in concealing cloaks. Like hold-out blasters, they were small, hard to detect, and deadly. "Maybe we could get Meewalh and Cakhmaim to rattle him."

"Give it up, Han," Mara suggested. "Leia, I like your quarters."

"Thanks." Leia settled on the couch beside her sulky husband. "It's really nice to have someplace that's permanent, not the hotel of the month, or quarters aboard some political ship, or the living compartment on the *Falcon*. It's the first place we've been able to really call home since Coruscant fell." A shadow crossed her face. Coruscant had fallen to the Yuuzhan Vong at almost the same time the Solos' youngest son, Anakin, had died. Those had been dark times.

"We almost decided on Corellia," Han said. "A planet where you can move more than three meters without hit-

ting a wall. But we have too many family and friends here."
The door chime rang again. "Speaking of which . . ."

This time it was Jaina and Zekk. Jaina, too, was in standard Jedi robes, hers made of hard-wearing cloth suited to
travel and styled to be less conspicuously those of a Jedi
Knight. She was of about the same height as her mother,
and more slender of build, with dark eyes and delicate features. Zekk, her partner, was in his late twenties, slightly
younger than Jaina, but was otherwise her opposite in almost every way—tall enough for his scalp to scrape the top
of the doorway as he entered, his long black hair pulled
back in a ponytail, he would stand out in any crowd regardless of the cut and color of his traveler's robes, and so
made little effort to conceal his cheerful, energetic appearance. But he was, in contrast with his good nature, quiet almost to the point of shyness during the tour he and Jaina
received of the quarters. His one comment was to Leia: "I
take it that the Vongforming has pretty much been beaten
back from this area?"

At the height of the Yuuzhan Vong war, when Coruscant
had fallen, the Yuuzhan Vong had used their arts to alter
the very nature of the world, installing a World Brain to coordinate the reshaping of the planet. Under the brain's
guidance, they introduced overwhelming quantities of
fauna and flora to erode the construction that nearly covered Coruscant's surface and replaced indigenous species
with Yuuzhan Vong species, attempting to eradicate every
sign that any species but the Yuuzhan Vong had lived here.
The process, called Vongforming, would have been complete within a few standard decades, save that Jacen Solo,
who had befriended the World Brain during his captivity,
convinced it to turn on its makers and help the newly
formed Galactic Alliance recapture the world. Now, the
Vongforming was slowly being reversed by the aggressive
use of technology and toxins, but everywhere on Coruscant there remained signs of the World Brain's influence—
alien molds that lived in cracks and gaps and culverts,
insect species that had become a part of Coruscant's eco-

system, odd and dangerous life-forms who now dwelled in the darkness of the sewers and other subterranean infrastructure.

Leia shrugged. "A few kilometers from here, you get weirdly overgrown ruins and some areas I can only think of as alien parks. It's much more normal around here," she said. "The nearby areas that were, before the change, dangerous after dark or too deep for sunlight to reach are just slightly more so now. It's like Coruscant used to be . . . except the shadows have a little more in them, you know what I mean?"

Zekk nodded, smiling slightly. "I know all about that."

The argument began over spiceloaf.

Spiceloaf was not the cause of it. The traditional Corellian dish, a dense ground meat spiced to the heat tolerance of the diners, was, as Leia had prepared it, both mild and savory, and was not likely to cause disagreement all by itself. It was merely the course that was on everyone's plate at the point Han decided to become argumentative.

He set his fork down and looked suspiciously at his nephew Ben. "You were doing what?"

"Making sure they did what the government said." The boy returned his uncle's stare, unintimidated. "Stopped making weapons except for the government."

"Well, that's an oversimplification," Jacen said. "This Adumari company was producing explosive ordnance beyond what was permitted for delivery to the Galactic Alliance armed forces or otherwise legal as per Order GAO-eleven-thirty-three-B—that is, beyond the amounts necessary for their own planetary defense. In other words, they were assembling proton torpedoes and other missiles for sale to other planets, not for delivery to the GA."

"So?" Han asked. "That's not business for the Jedi. That's a problem for politicians with nothing better to do. Next thing you know, we'll have Jedi walking the government halls on Corellia and telling *us* what to do."

Leia smiled. Han hadn't lived on Corellia for decades,

but in his heart, he was all Corellian, embodying the swagger, the cockiness, the carefree attitude that the citizens of that system considered essential elements of their culture. His exploits during the Rebellion and up through the present day had made him dear to the hearts of the people of that system. The second best-known Corellian hero of the same era, Wedge Antilles, did live in the Corellian system, but he was more reserved, less brash, and simply hadn't captured the public's affection as Han had.

But Luke wasn't as amused. "Han, the Corellians are playing a dangerous game. They're demanding all the advantages of Galactic Alliance membership—trade benefits, use of the GA communications and travel infrastructure, citizenship rights, all of it—but not contributing their fair share of Alliance overhead. They're dragging their heels on supplying ships and personnel to the military, on providing tax revenues—"

"See, that's the thing." Han pointed his fork at Luke's chest as if intending to jam it in and probe around the heart and lungs. "We can maintain our own military, and not the tiny peacekeeping and police force the new laws are calling for. When the time comes for military action, the Corellians have always brought our forces up, under our own colors, even when we weren't members of whatever government was swinging the biggest stick at the time. We did it for the Old Republic and the New Republic. We did it in the Vong war."

Jaina grimaced. "Not a good example, Dad. How many lives, how many whole systems were lost in the Yuuzhan Vong war because governments couldn't work together, didn't have standardized weapons, communications, tactics?"

Han turned his scowl on his daughter. "How many lives, how many whole systems were lost," he asked, his tone mocking hers, "because the New Republic government was so bloated, impersonal, and stupid that it couldn't see when it was getting its rear end kicked and didn't care when millions of its people got killed? How many members of Borsk's old Advisory Council ran off to their home-worlds with personal yachts packed with treasure and left people behind them to burn?"

"Which is exactly what Corellia is doing," Luke said, his voice soft but his expression unrelenting. "They're trying to pack up their treasures and avoid the economic toll that rebuilding civilization is taking on the rest of the Galactic Alliance, while they're throwing up a shield of planetary pride to convince people that their decision is based on something other than selfishness and irresponsibility. And other systems are starting to look to Corellia in a leadership role. It's foolish to cast the Galactic Alliance as the Empire and Corellia as the Rebel Alliance. Because that's what it might come to, a rebellion—a stupid and unnecessary one."

"Luke," Mara said. Her voice was a whispered note of caution.

"Is that the position of the Jedi order?" Han asked, voice rising. "What the galaxy needs is one language, one system of measurement, one uniform, one flag? Should we just cut the word *no* out of the language and substitute *Yes, sir, right away, sir* instead?"

"Han," Leia said. "Not nice to argue in front of a guest."

"Zekk's not a guest. He's the man chasing my daughter all over the galaxy."

"*Dad.*"

"*I* think—" Han paused and looked around the table, finally aware of all the eyes on him. He plunged his fork into the last piece of spiceloaf on his plate and hurriedly swallowed the piece of meat. "I think I'm done. I think I'm going to wash some dishes."

"Please," Leia said.

Han rose and took his plate and utensils with him.

When the kitchen door slid shut behind him, Mara asked, "Is he all right?"

Leia shrugged and took a sip of wine. "It's been getting worse as things have been heating up between Corellia and the GA. On the one side, the fact that his own cousin is Chief of State of Corellia and is playing this slippery, deceptive political game bothers him a lot. On the other hand, Han doesn't really trust any interplanetary government anymore, not since the Yuuzhan Vong war. Not that he ever did, but it's worse now. And since Anakin died—" She stopped, shot Luke a regretful look.

Luke sat back. Years ago, during the worst days of the war with the Yuuzhan Vong, Han and Leia's youngest son, Anakin Solo, named for his grandfather, had led a unit of fellow Jedi on a mission to a Yuuzhan Vong world. There, they'd exterminated the queen voxyn, preventing the creation of any more of the Force-sensing, Jedi-killing beasts. There, Anakin had died.

Luke, however reluctantly, however regretfully, had signed off on that mission. "Ever since Anakin died," Luke said, "Han has never really trusted the Jedi order, either. Has he?"

Leia shook her head. "It's strange. He trusts *you*, his old friend Luke. But Master Skywalker, head of the Jedi order? Not so much." Then her smile returned. "Not that he can talk too much about Jedi, not with every member of his immediate family *being* a Jedi."

Jacen smiled, too, and raised his wineglass in the direction of the kitchen door. "Here's to irony, Dad."

chapter four

Jacen, Leia, and Mara relaxed on the living chamber furniture. In the kitchen, Han, maintaining his self-imposed exile, was riding roughshod over C-3PO in the act of cleaning the dinnerware. Luke was alone in the sealed-off communications room, borrowing the Solos' comm gear for some sort of official Jedi business call. Ben and R2-D2 were out on the balcony, matched in a musically noisy but bloodless hologame. Jaina and Zekk, too, were out there, but the occasional glimpses caught of them suggested that they were at the railing side of the balcony, watching the endless streams of multicolored traffic flow by in the night-time sky.

"Ben," Mara said, "is more open. More trusting." Her words, directed at Jacen, were as much question as statement.

Jacen nodded, thoughtful, and took a sip from his wineglass. "I think he is. He's coming to understand the Force . . . and people. The fact that he's inherently a bit suspicious of both of them is working in his favor. He's progressing slowly and cautiously. He's not as likely to give in to temptations of the dark side of the Force . . . or even to teenage hormone rushes."

As a small child during the tragic Yuuzhan Vong war, Ben had become fearful and suspicious of the Force, retreating from it despite his own inherited facility with it.

Only as Jacen's unofficial apprentice had he begun to over-come the emotional damage of that time.

Mara shuddered. "Don't bring up the specter of teenage hormone rushes."

Leia snorted. "Not ready to become a grandmother yet?"

"I think I'd throw myself on my lightsaber first."

Leia smiled. "I think I'm ready. I plan to be the sort of feisty, bad-example grandmother who teaches her grand-children deplorable habits." She turned her attention to Jacen. "How long should I expect to wait?"

He gave her an admonishing look. "If you're trying to embarrass me, you're talking into a dead comlink."

"Not embarrass. I'm just trying to get a timetable."

"Ask Jaina."

Leia's expression soured comically. "She said to ask you."

"Then ask Zekk. I'm sure he has things planned out. He probably just hasn't informed Jaina yet."

Leia shook her head over her own wineglass. "I have to find some sort of appropriate punishment for Han. For giv-ing our children smart mouths and unhelpful manners."

"All joking aside," Mara said, "Jacen, thank you. Ben is doing so much better. I spent years being afraid that he'd never be at home with himself, with his Jedi legacy, with things he could never escape. You've given me reason to think I can stop worrying."

"You're welcome. Though, as Mom put it, I have to find some sort of appropriate punishment for *you*."

Mara looked surprised. "What do you mean?"

"Well, if, as Mom asserts, the smart mouths and unhelp-ful manners of the Solo children come only from Dad, it means they come not at all from the Skywalker family. Right? So Ben's smart mouth and unhelpful manners have to come from *you*. I'm going to have to figure out some sort of appropriate revenge, someday."

Mara grinned, her good humor restored. She tapped the

lightsaber hanging at her belt. "Do you have a favorite prosthetics manufacturer? I can preorder you one."

"Jacen." Luke stepped into the main living area from the hallway leading to the communications chamber. "Care to take a walk with me?"

"Of course." Jacen rose. All of them knew that as simple a request as *Care to take a walk with me?* under these circumstances probably meant, *Time to talk Jedi business*.

They left through the door that not so long ago Han and Leia had spoken of defending with blasterfire. A dim side corridor led them away from the main access corridor toward an oversized door that occasionally vibrated; beyond it, though muted, was the hum and roar of Coruscant nighttime traffic. The door lifted out of the way as they approached, revealing a swirl of colors outside—the running lights of flying vehicles, from two-person speeders to small lumbering freighters, hurtling by outside, a high aerial traffic lane that passed mere meters from the pedestrian balcony outside the door.

As the door slid shut behind them, they paused for a moment at the balcony railing, looking down two hundred stories toward Coruscant's ground level. At night, despite the fact that windows on every floor between their position and the ground were illuminated, that advertising signs and banners glowed and gleamed brilliantly, ground level was too dark and distant to be glimpsed.

As a child, Jacen had once become lost at Coruscant's bedrock level along with Jaina. The depths held no terror for him; even now, more than twenty years later, they seemed to be a place of mystery and exploration.

But it wasn't really the same Coruscant as the one of his childhood. The Vongforming had reshaped much of the world into the Yuuzhan Vong image. Now, years later, huge tracts of what had once been continuous pole-to-pole cityscape still remained black at night, overgrown with fauna, and places like the bedrock levels of the planet and the infrastructure beneath were still home to the crawling and slithering life-forms the Yuuzhan Vong had introduced, some of them deadly.

Still, that reminder of the beating Coruscant and the old New Republic had suffered was not visible from this viewpoint. Here, it looked like the Coruscant of old, with swirling streams of air traffic, and high-rise dwellings outlined and illuminated by millions of viewports.

This balcony ran the length of Han and Leia's building along a canyon-like drop. Bridges, some of them canopied and some open to the sky or to overhanging spacescrapers above, spanned gaps between buildings. This elevated pedestrian roadway changed appearance, surface texture, and lighting every few hundred meters, intersecting other walkways. Had someone no need to work a job, had he an infinite credcard and feet as tough as duracrete, he could probably walk entirely around Coruscant's circumference at this altitude.

Most of the men, women, and who-knew-whats traveling this path—Jacen counted only thirty or so within a hundred steps in either direction—were probably on less ambitious errands. Jacen saw wealthy businessbeings, many of them accompanied by bodyguards both overt and covert, on strolls; there were young lovers and families, chiefly belonging to the higher income brackets, walking apparently unprotected. Some of them probably didn't worry about the dangers that they might face walking so far from protection. Some were probably better defended than they looked.

Luke gestured to the left, where the walkway rose in a series of short steps some five meters across a distance of fifty, and they began walking in that direction.

"Your father surprised me," Luke said. "With his mention of Jedi walking the government halls in Corellia."

"Surprised you?" Jacen thought about it. "Not because he's being paranoid. Because he's *not* being paranoid. Because there are plans along those lines."

Luke nodded, his expression glum. Then he put up his

hood and wrapped his cloak more closely around himself, the better to conceal the presence of his lightsaber.

Jacen did the same. A young human couple pushing a repulsor-assisted baby stroller, trailing two dark-clad security men, one human and one Rodian, were walking in their direction. Luke and Jacen would still be slightly conspicuous in their cloaks, which had the anonymous appearance of travelers' garments but were seldom worn by the sort of people who lived at these altitudes . . . then again, the residents of these heights did often go slumming in inappropriate clothes, so they weren't too unusual. Their features shadowed by their hoods, the Jedi passed unrecognized by the oblivious couple and their alert guards.

Once they were past, Jacen continued, "It seems like an extreme action. Has the GA given up on negotiation with Corellia?"

"The GA is aware of some facts that haven't made it to the holocomm news feeds," Luke said. "Such as, the Corellians aren't really negotiating in good faith—just stringing the GA negotiators along while making no internal effort to edge toward compliance with the new regulations. Such as, the Corellians are secretly encouraging other systems to follow the same sort of resistance. Such as—"

Luke looked troubled. "What I'm about to tell you is for your ears alone."

"Understood."

"The Corellian government, or someone inside it, appears to be constructing a planetary assault fleet. In secret."

Jacen frowned. Historically, there was only one reason ever to build a planetary assault fleet, and to do so in secret: to launch a sneak attack on another system. "For use against whom?"

"That's a good question. And it's a question military intelligence hasn't been able to answer yet." Luke shrugged. "But there are dozens of possibilities. Most of the recovery loans Corellia made after the Yuuzhan Vong war are in default, and the Corellians have no shortage of trade disputes. They might even be considering a resource-grab. There are just too many possibilites at this point to guess."

"Why did you say the Corellian government or 'someone inside it'? Do we not know who's responsible?"

Luke shook his head. "The truth is, this intelligence is based primarily on analyses of procurement patterns, plus a long history of suspicious personnel assignments."

"Wait. The existence of the fleet is based on the reports of *accountants*?"

Luke grinned. "What do you have against accountants?"

"Nothing, I guess."

"The problem with the data we have, though, is that it gives us no idea where they're building the fleet—only that it's been under construction for almost a decade, and our logistics people think it's nearing completion."

Jacen grew thoughtful for a moment, then asked, "And you want me to find the shipyards and confirm the intelligence?"

Luke shook his head. "I wish it were that easy. Admiral Pellaeon is confident that military intelligence will soon pinpoint the base. We need you to handle a more pressing matter."

"More pressing than a planetary assault?"

"Yes." Luke took a deep breath. "The Corellian government is close to making Centerpoint Station operational again."

That stopped Jacen where he stood. He stared at Luke, his surprise earning him a nod of affirmation from his uncle.

Centerpoint Station was a relic, an artifact of an ancient civilization that had, in a sense, constructed the Corellian star system—by dragging several inhabitable planets to the system and sending them into beneficial orbits. Several hundred kilometers in diameter, bigger even than the Death Stars that the Empire had wielded against rebellious planets decades ago, it had, over the centuries, been the object of internal and external attempts at control by political and military forces that had never quite learned how to utilize it.

At the heart of Centerpoint Station was an apparatus that could focus gravity and move planets or even affect the orbits of stars. It could move them, it could affect them; used more aggressively, it could destroy them. At times, the Corellians and others had been close to being able to utilize this as a reliable, devastating weapon. But it had for years been restricted by biometric data to operation by only one person—Anakin Solo.

The last it had been used was during the Yuuzhan Vong war. After years of being essentially nonfunctional, it had been brought to operability by the simple realization that it had imprinted on Anakin Solo and could be activated only by him. Jacen had argued that it should not be used against the Yuuzhan Vong or anyone—it was too terrible, too unpredictable a weapon. Anakin Solo had argued for it, his reasoning being that its use would prevent the Yuuzhan Vong from destroying millions of lives.

Anakin had activated it. Thracken Sal-Solo had fired it. Its use hadn't gone well. It had destroyed much of the mighty war fleet of the Hapes Cluster, one of the New Republic's allies. Later in the war, of course, Anakin had died, apparently eliminating the likelihood of it ever being used again.

Jacen felt a moment of dissonance. His younger self refused to utilize Centerpoint Station. His current self, in the same circumstances, would use it, his qualms having evaporated across the intervening years. The recognition of the changes in himself surprised him. They had crept up on him while he wasn't paying attention.

The Jacen of more than a decade ago was gone, as dead as the Anakin of the same era was. He took a deep, slow breath and wondered why he no longer mourned either loss. "How have they made it operational again?" he asked.

Luke shrugged. "The information we have suggests that they've figured out how to duplicate crucial elements of Anakin's biometrics—probably handprint, retinal patterns, and brainwaves, in the absence of surviving tissues—to pull it off."

Jacen felt anger swell within him. Use of his brother's identity for such a purpose smacked of disrespect for the dead. There was a ghoulish quality to it he did not appreciate. Still, he recognized his reaction as illogical, irrelevant, so he dismissed it. "And the GA is afraid the Corellians will actually use it as a weapon against them?"

"Not directly . . . not at first. But if the Corellians use their new fleet to launch an assault against some system, they could then keep the GA at bay with the threat that Centerpoint Station poses. And even if this theoretical sneak attack turns out not to be their plan, Chief Omas is concerned that if the GA continues to enforce its current mandates, the Corellians would be able to use the station to preserve their independence, their autonomy."

"That—" Jacen stopped before he spoke further. He'd been about to say, *That wouldn't be too bad*. But no, the prospect of the Corellians, a notoriously independent planetary culture, possessing the single most potent weapon in the galaxy, and not being obliged to use it for the greater good of galactic civilization—in fact, being able to use it to assert their own agenda—*would* be bad. Very bad. He let his mind drift for a moment into the future—into one possible future, one most likely to result from the actions Luke was describing—and caught just a vision of vast fleets at war, of planetary surfaces suffering bombardment, of brother and sister firing on each other. The brief glimpse turned his stomach. "So the Galactic Alliance is calling on the Jedi order."

Luke nodded. "More specifically, Admiral Pellaeon sees outright rebellion across many star systems as a direct consequence of continued inaction by the GA. Several of his computer-modeled outcomes point that way, as apparently his instinct does. Other admirals he's consulted agree, and so Cal Omas has signed off on this plan."

Jacen took a deep breath, considering. Admiral Pellaeon, for decades the leader who had kept the Imperial Remnant proud, independent, and ethical, had been chosen as Supreme Commander of the Galactic Alliance a few years earlier, sure sign of the Imperial Remnant's growing status and importance within the GA. If he saw continued Corellian reticence as a sure path to civil war, Jacen would have a hard time arguing with that conclusion. "So what's the plan?"

Luke circled in around his answer. "Among the scientists and support crew who have been studying Centerpoint Station for Corellia there are GA spies, of course. They would have a very hard time smuggling in squadrons of elite soldiers to damage or disable the facility. One or two infiltrators they could manage. And packing squadrons' worth of effectiveness into one or two people . . ."

"Means Jedi."

"Yes."

"What do you want me to do?"

"Travel to Centerpoint Station and disable or destroy it."

Jacen tapped the hilt of his lightsaber. "Disable or destroy a moon-sized installation with just what I can smuggle in?"

"Others have been destroyed with just a proton torpedo and the right knowledge. We'll try to get you the right knowledge. And the GA will be initiating an operation elsewhere in the system that should attract the defenders' attention. Will you do it?"

"Yes, of course. But why me?"

"A few reasons. First, unlike most Jedi, you've been there. Second, because of who raised you, you can put on an authentic Corellian accent when you want to—that, and the fact that you've inherited a bit of the Corellian look from your father, will make it easier for you to move unobtrusively through the installation. Third, your specialized training in alternative philosophies of the Force makes you more versatile than many other Jedi—than some Jedi Masters, in fact—making it harder to stop you."

"And what about Ben?"

Luke was silent for a long moment. He and Jacen turned

onto a bridge spanning the chasm between two long rows of spacescrapers. It was made of transparisteel embedded with brightly colored sand and gravel, its railing high so that the occasional ferocious gusts of wind that coursed through Coruscant's duracrete canyons would not toss a pedestrian over the side. Pedestrians could look down through the transparent surface beneath their feet into the two-kilometer depths below them, and they felt the slight sway of the bridge as a gust of wind pushed it. A dozen meters down, a stream of traffic coursed by like a river made of multicolored lights.

Luke's tone was impassive, artificially so. "That is a matter for you, as his teacher, to decide."

Even on dangerous missions, Jedi Masters often took their apprentices—it was how those apprentices learned. Sometimes the apprentices died with their teachers. And Luke had considered the question of whether Jacen should take Luke's own son and put the decision entirely on Jacen's shoulders.

Luke had responded as a Jedi Master should, not letting his relationship with the apprentice in question cloud his judgment. Jacen would have to do the same.

Ben was bright, inventive, and largely obedient. At the flip of a switch he could act like any precocious thirteen-year-old, as un-Jedi-like as it was possible to be. He'd be an asset on a mission like this. "He'll come with me."

Luke nodded, apparently serene in his acceptance of Jacen's decision.

"It's going to get ugly when this happens," Jacen continued. "The Corellians—this is going to infuriate them."

"Yes. But the other part of the operation, which is in part distraction for your mission, is a show of force. All of a sudden, an entire GA fleet will materialize within Corellian space. Between that and the loss of Centerpoint, Military Intelligence thinks the Corellians will realize that they can't continue to adopt a *we-do-whatever-we-like* stance."

Jacen shook his head. "Whose brilliant idea is that?"

"I don't know. It was presented to me by Cal Omas and by Admiral Niathal, one of Pellaeon's advisers."

"She's Mon Cal, not Corellian."

"Well, she indicated that the psychological warfare experts had evaluated the Corellian planetary mind-set and were certain that this operation would have the desired effect—assuming the destruction of Centerpoint Station was effective."

Jacen snorted. "What do you want to bet that they based their evaluations on old data? Pre-Vong-war data? Maybe even diktat-era. I don't think they've factored in what surviving the war did to the Corellians. It stiffened their pride."

"I'm sure they're using up-to-date information. Regardless, that part of the operation is one I don't have any influence on. It's going ahead regardless of the opinion of the Jedi order." Luke's expression was still serene, but Jacen detected a flicker of regret. "Let's get back."

"I think I'll walk awhile longer. Settle my thoughts. Figure out what I'm going to say to my father when the time comes."

"Don't overplan." Luke clapped Jacen on the shoulder and turned back toward Han and Leia's building. "The future is to be lived, not prearranged."

As he reached the door providing access into the Solos' building, Luke felt a little tickle of awareness, as though someone had materialized just behind him and brushed him with a feather. He turned to look.

No one actually stood behind him. But across the avenue, perhaps thirty meters away, standing on a pedestrian thoroughfare at about the same altitude, someone was watching him.

His watcher stood a few meters away from the nearest light source, wrapped up in a traveler's cloak not dissimilar to the outer garments he and the other Jedi wore. Its hood was up, and the garment masked the wearer's build. Luke could tell little more than that the wearer was of average height or taller and looked lean.

But something in this being's posture reminded Luke of the image from his dream, and caused him to wonder if the watcher had features similar to long-dead Anakin Skywalker, with eyes turned a liquid yellow by anger and Sith techniques.

As Luke watched, the watcher turned, walked the few steps to the nearest doorway into its own building, and entered, vanishing into darkness.

Luke shook his head. He could go over there, of course. But it would take time, and he'd find nothing. Either the watcher was unrelated to Luke's dream, or it was someone deliberately making contact as a warning or greeting. Either way, no evidence would remain.

Luke entered the Solos' building.

After all the guests were gone, most of them returning to quarters at the Jedi Temple, and the Solo quarters were dark, Han and Leia lay wrapped in each other's arms in their bedchamber.

That chamber was against an exterior wall of the building, just below the pedestrian walkway outside, and featured a broad transparisteel viewport that afforded them a view of the traffic lanes outside—or, if Han and Leia were close enough and ducked low enough, of the skies. It was a much thicker plate of transparisteel than most dwelling viewports featured, as was appropriate to a former Chief of State and her equally famous husband, either of whom might become the target of assassins or kidnappers. It was armor suitable to a naval vessel and one of the more expensive features of these quarters. But it was as clear as any more ordinary viewport, and, with the blinds opened, they could watch through it the endless, brilliantly colorful streams of traffic.

"You were pretty hard on Zekk," Leia chided. "All evening long."

"You think so?" Han considered. "I didn't challenge him to any drinking games or ask him about all his failed relationships."

"Good." Leia nodded against his chest. "But you could have been . . . nicer."

"Nicer to the man who's chasing my daughter around? What sort of example would that set? I'm her *father*. Besides, he's taking advantage of her."

"That's ridiculous."

"No, listen. Since she doesn't believe that he's after her, since she's maintaining her *we're-just-good-friends-despite-anything-that-might-have-happened-before* self-delusion, he can stay close and operate without her being aware of it."

"He's a good boy."

"Where my daughter is concerned, nobody is a 'good boy.' Besides, nobody that tall should be referred to as a boy."

"Well, if she likes taller men, it's probably a preference she picked up from her upbringing."

"Oh?" Han considered. "You think she's more comfortable with taller men because of me?"

"No, because of Chewbacca."

Han looked down at her. A sliver of blue light crossed over the bed and illuminated her eyes, which were open, her expression somehow both merry and artificially innocent.

Chewbacca, Han's Wookiee copilot and best friend, had died more than a decade ago, at the onset of the Yuuzhan Vong war. After that, it had been years before Han could hear or speak his name without feeling a stab of pain in his heart. Now, of course, there was still sadness at his loss, but with it were years of more glad memories.

"You," Han said, "should not mock Han Solo, hero of the galaxy."

"I would never. I was mocking Han Solo, meddling dad and supreme egotist."

"Now you're in trouble."

She laughed at him.

chapter five

CORUSCANT

Two days after the Solo-Skywalker family dinner, Han Solo
sat on one of his living chamber sofas, a portable terminal
in his lap, scowling at the display screen. Every so often he
typed in a series of commands or used the voice interface,
but each attempt he made was eventually greeted with a
red screen indicating failure.

Leia materialized behind him, leaning over his shoulder,
and read aloud the text on the screen. "OPERATION FAILED.
YOU MAY BE USING CONNECTION INFORMATION THAT IS
OUT OF DATE. Trying to straighten out your taxes?"

"Very funny." Han didn't sound amused. "Do you remember Wildis Jiklip?"

Leia frowned. Wildis Jiklip was a mathematics prodigy
about Han's age. Well traveled, with a Corellian mother
and a Coruscanti father, she had been educated in both systems and had been licensed to teach at the university or
academy level by the time she was in her early twenties.
Then she'd disappeared for two decades, and only a few
people knew what she'd been doing during that time.

She'd become a smuggler under the name of Red Stepla.
She ran unusual routes, carrying unusual cargoes, and had
an uncanny ability to get forbidden goods to their markets
at a time when they'd be most valuable. Her record for suc-

cess was unrivaled. Where most smugglers led a hand-to-mouth existence, spending their earnings in port on gambling binges and other recreations, retaining barely enough for fuel and to acquire new cargoes, Red Stepla and her crew led very unobtrusive lives, investing their earnings in a variety of ports all over the galaxy.

A few years before the start of the Yuuzhan Vong war, Red Stepla and her crew retired—by the simple expedient of disappearing. Wildis Jiklip then reappeared, an independently wealthy theoretician who occasionally taught university-level courses on Coruscant and Lorrd, focusing on interplanetary economics, supply-and-demand trade economics, systemic economic reactions to widespread warfare, and related subjects.

Han knew the secret of her dual identity, and Leia had learned it from Wildis herself, who trusted anyone Han would trust enough to marry.

Leia nodded. "Sure. What about her?"

"She's supposed to be on Coruscant, doing one of her lecture series. I tried to get in touch with her to talk about Corellia. I thought maybe she could give me a hint about the official GA reaction to what's going on there. But she discontinued her lecture series in the middle, just a few days ago, and all the ways I have to get in touch with her are out of operation—reporting that she's on leave of absence due to a family emergency."

Leia shrugged. "So?"

"Well, she has no family. Yeah, I know, that's not suspicious in and of itself. But I still wanted to talk political shop with other Corellians. So I arranged for a holotransmission to Wedge Antilles."

Leia felt a moment of surprise but kept it from her face. She knew she was spoiled when it came to finance—she'd lived as a planetary princess, albeit one from a financially responsible family, as a child and young woman; she'd commanded the resources of a rebel government and then a legitimate one. Expenditure had seldom been a consideration for her. Han, who had been reared in poverty and had lived in difficult financial circumstances for the first half of his life, was more stingy, and the fact that he'd been willing to pay for a live, instantaneous conversation with a friend light-years away was quite a concession for him. It told more about the state of his concern over Corellian politics than anything he'd said over the last few days. "And how *is* Wedge?"

"Well, I couldn't get through to him via HoloNet. They say there's some sort of equipment breakdown causing intermittent connections with the Corellian system."

"So you sent him a message by standard record-and-transmit."

Han nodded. "Just a heads-up, how're-you-doing sort of message."

"And?"

"And it got there, and I got a reply . . . but it was delayed by several hours. Long enough for my message and the reply to have been intercepted, decrypted, scanned, and analyzed before being passed on."

Leia didn't say, *Now you're being paranoid.* They were the first words to leap to her mind, but in truth Han *wasn't* being paranoid. The GA government was probably keeping a close eye on comm traffic to and from Corellia in light of that system's ongoing defiance of government edicts. "All right," she said, "so communications to Corellia are under close scrutiny."

"So I kept looking around." Han looked troubled. "Activated some false identities. Bounced message packets to Corellia via Commenor and some other worlds. Checked with some old friends still in the trade, found that antismuggling patrols by the GA are intensifying right now . . . in the vicinity of Corellia and a few worlds that have spoken out in support of Corellia. I'm really beginning to think something's up."

Leia moved around to the front of the couch and settled beside her husband. "Something more than just mild harassment by the GA to inconvenience a system that's not playing by the rules, you mean."

"Yeah. But I don't really know how to confirm it. How to take my hunch and make it into a fact."

Leia considered. As a Jedi Knight her primary responsibilities were to the Jedi order and the Galactic Alliance. If the Galactic Alliance was indeed planning some sort of action against Corellia, her duty was to support it.

But that was only one of her loyalties. She couldn't just ignore her loyalty to Han, even if he was supporting a foolish cause. Suddenly she grinned. Had he ever supported a cause that, from some perspective, wasn't foolish, including the Rebel Alliance?

"What's so funny?"

"Nothing. I was just thinking about . . . other ways to figure out what's going on."

"Such as?"

She began counting off on her fingers. "One. If the GA is planning some sort of action against Corellia, then a number of people in the GA government know it. Particularly self-serving ones with economic interests on Corellia are going to be doing whatever they can to protect those interests. If they're sloppy, it would be possible to spot their activities, their transactions.

"Two. If the action against Corellia is going to involve the military, determining which military forces are called up would be very informative. Different forces would be used for an assault or for a blockade, for instance. Now, it's tricky to find out that sort of information—without being spotted as a spy, especially—but it's possible, and we have a slight advantage in that it's been a good while since we've been at war. Security won't be as tight as it was at the height of the Yuuzhan Vong war or the war against the Empire, for instance."

Han nodded. "Good, good."

"Three. We could formulate some likely plans for action against Corellia, determine the resources needed for those plans . . . and then attempt to determine whether those resources are actually being moved into place. That would give you some sense of what's actually going to happen . . . assuming that your plans are accurate ones."

"Right." Han smiled. "I don't care much for data work or number crunching, but it looks like I've just assigned myself a lot of it."

"I'll help you."

"Thanks."

"After breakfast."

Han's smile grew broader. "You're just not the same tireless, selfless woman I married, are you?"

"I guess not."

"I've corrupted you."

She sighed dramatically. "Well, you're the same tireless egotist *I* married."

The CorSec officer, trim in her brown and burnt orange uniform, her face hidden behind the blast shield of a combat helmet, leapt into the doorway and raised her blaster rifle. Before it could line up against Jacen, he lashed out with his lightsaber, slicing through the weapon, through the woman. She fell in two smoking pieces, making a resounding bang against the metal floor.

Jacen cast a quick look back the way he'd come, down endless halls packed with twisting cables and mechanical extrusions whose functions no one had been able to discern or divine even after decades of study. Somewhere back there, Ben lay, victim of a blaster shot to the chest, part of a barrage that had been too fast, too heavy for Jacen to compensate for . . .

He shook his head. He couldn't allow himself to be distracted by irrelevancies, not with the success of his mission so close. He reached out with the Force, a casual sweep that would reveal to him the presence of living beings beyond the portal, and, feeling none, he stepped through.

Here it was, the control chamber for the Centerpoint Station weapon. The room was surprisingly small, considering the incredible power it harnessed—it was large enough for a medium-sized crew of scientists to operate in, but something this grand should have been enormous, with monumental statuary commemorating the times in the past it was used. Instead there were seats, and banks of lights, switches, and levers, an upright joystick control at the main seat—all of it exactly as he'd last seen it, years before.

Shortly before Ben's birth, in fact. He'd last seen it before the boy was born; now he was seeing it just after the boy had been cut down.

Irrelevancies. From a pocket within his Jedi robes, he plucked a peculiar datachip. Unlike a standard data card, which would fit within the slot readers of the billions of datapads, computers, high-end comlinks, or vehicular control panels that were equipped to scan and utilize the memory devices, it had rounded ends and spiky protrusions of gold, allowing it to conform to exactly one known port in all the galaxy.

But where was that port? Jacen scanned the banks of switches and other controls. Nothing seemed suited to the datachip, not even on the exact section of control board he'd been told to look for. He was aware that there were distant shouts out in the corridor, signs that Corellian Security forces were rushing his way, that he had only seconds left to complete his mission.

He closed his eyes and probed with senses that could not be so easily fooled.

And he found, almost instantly, what he was looking for—a slot shaped in the reverse image of the front end of his datachip. Eyes still closed, he stepped forward, extended the chip, and felt it being gripped by, then drawn into the machinery below the control board's surface. He released it and opened his eyes.

The chamber's thousands of indicator lights went dead and the sounds of shouts and onrushing feet from the corridor stilled. A female voice announced, "Simulation ended. Success ratio seventy-five percent, estimated only."

Jacen grinned sourly. Anything over 51 percent was sufficient for the success of the mission—it meant that one of the several techniques intended to damage or destroy Centerpoint Station had been initiated. But even 75 percent wasn't good enough: it meant that either he or Ben had fallen. Fifty-one percent and both would have died.

Ben moved into the doorway and carefully stepped over the bisected body of the droid wearing CorSec armor. He rubbed his chest and looked embarrassed. "Stun bolts sting," he said.

Jacen nodded. "More motivation for you not to be hit by them."

The wall behind the main control board slid upward, revealing a monitoring chamber beyond—several computer stations, one central chair with four viewing monitors mounted on spindly, adjustable bars around it. The man in the chair—stout, gray-bearded, a trifle overweight—offered the two Jedi a faint smile. "You're getting there," he said, his voice deep, rumbling.

"This one seemed pretty easy, Doctor Seyah." Jacen gestured around. "*One* guard in the final chamber—"

"Easy?" Ben sounded outraged. "They shot about a thousand blaster bolts at us!"

"Jacen's right," Dr. Seyah said. "This one is easier. Easier than restarting the station's centrifugal spin and sabotaging the artificial gravity counterspin to tear the station apart, easier than introducing the station's own coordinates into its targeting computations and having it destroy itself, easier than hijacking a Star Destroyer and crashing it into the proper end of the station—"

Ben's face brightened. "We haven't done that one yet."

"Nor are you going to. That's not a mission for Jedi. It's for crazy old naval officers."

"Oh." Ben's expression fell. "I would have liked that one."

Dr. Seyah pushed aside a couple of obtrusive monitors and rose from his chair. "The problem is, we don't know what the main weapons control chamber looks like now. This is how it was three weeks ago, when everyone but a core crew of scientists—carefully vetted, very pro-Corellian scientists—was pulled out and reassigned elsewhere. They could have replaced all the equipment with string cheese or encased the room in duracrete—we don't know. But we have no reason to think they did." He shrugged. "So long as you have that datachip intact, and so long as that receptacle slot is still in existence on the control board—even if you have a wobber of a time finding it—then this approach could work."

"*Could* work?" Jacen repeated.

"We think it will. The commands in that datachip should initiate a ten-minute countdown and then activate a complex repulsor pulse that will tear the station apart. Assuming that they haven't reprogrammed their systems sufficiently to overcome the programming on that chip. Assuming that my team and I did our jobs right all these years. Assuming a lot of things." Dr. Seyah sighed, then placed a hand on the shoulder of each Jedi. "This is the only thing I can guarantee you: come with me to the cafeteria, and I can treat you to lunch."

"Sometimes the simple answers are best," Jacen agreed, and allowed himself to be turned toward the door.

But inside, worry tried to gnaw at him. Ben had faltered or died in eight out of ten of the simulations they'd run, suggesting that he should not, after all, be along on this mission . . . but Jacen's own sense of the future, day after day, told him that the boy would be crucial to its success, if success were to be found at all. Perhaps both outcomes were correct. Perhaps the mission would succeed, but only if Ben fell during its accomplishment.

If that were so, how would Jacen face Luke?

"So what's it like to be a spy?" Ben asked.

Jacen murmured, "Doctor Seyah is not a spy, Ben. Be nice."

"Oh, of course I'm a spy. Scientist and spy. And it's very nice. I get to study ancient technology and learn how the universe works. And every so often, I get to go on vacation to learn how to plant the newest listening comlinks, to subvert or seduce enemy spies, to use the latest blasters and fly the latest airspeeders—"

"Have you ever broken anyone's neck?"

"Well, yes. But it was before I was technically a spy . . ."

Across a span of days, Han and Leia put together facts, numbers, disappearances, reappearances, ship movements, personnel reassignments, things said, and things not said into a complex computer projection, carefully maintained— though scarcely understood—by C-3PO.

Fact: elements of the Galactic Alliance Second Fleet were being diverted from their missions of record. As an example, the Mon Cal heavy carrier *Blue Diver* was supposed to be heading out to the Tingel Arm of the galaxy on an annual fleet mission to retrace the Yuuzhan Vong's entry route into the galaxy in order to spot any lingering manifestations of their passage. Yet when it had reprovisioned, it had not taken on the sort of provisions appropriate to a months-long solo mission.

Fact: communications between Coruscant and Corellia continued to be problematic, in a fashion suggesting that comm traffic was being heavily monitored and analyzed— but no anticipated boycotts or economic sanctions had been put in place against the increasingly independent system.

Fact: civilian experts on Corellian government, military, and economics were increasingly unavailable. None had technically disappeared; all were "on vacation," on leave of absence, on recent intergallactic assignment. The same was not true of experts on other worlds that had united with Corellia in agitating against the GA—Commenor or Fondor, for instance.

Fact: Corellian corporate properties belonging to Pefederan Lloyn, chair of the GA Finance Council, had recently been sold or traded in kind for properties in the Kuat system. In theory, because of the active role she played in GA government finances, Lloyn was not exerting any direct control over her business holdings, having assigned that control to business officers for the duration of her government service . . . but Han Solo put no faith in theories heavily involving the integrity of government officials.

These were only a representative sampling of the data Han and Leia found and loaded into C-3PO's new analysis routine. But all the facts supported Han's growing conviction that something very bad was about to happen in the planetary system where he'd grown up. His conviction wasn't eased when C-3PO, during one of their analysis sessions in the Solos' living chamber, said, "To all appearances, Corellia is about to experience a—a pasting, I believe the term is."

Han snorted, an irritated noise that caused the protocol droid to lean back, away from him. "Does your newfound analytical skill give you any idea as to exactly what form this *pasting* is going to take?"

"Oh, no, sir. I'd have to be loaded with extensive military planning applications, not to mention extensive databases, in order to offer you a useful prediction on that matter. Which would, of course, interfere with my primary function as a protocol droid. Why, the memory demands alone would force me to remove millions of language translators and inflection interpreters. That would be disastrous. I might even become"—the volume of the droid's voice dropped—"more aggressive."

Leia kept her face straight. "That would be terrible. What form would this aggression take? Would you strangle security officers and kick children?"

"Oh, no, Mistress. But I might become . . . more sarcastic. Even verbally abusive."

"Goldilocks, go get us some caf," Han said.

"Yes, sir." The droid rose. "I don't believe any has been brewed. Would you like instant?"

"About as much as I'd like a blaster burn on my knee-cap. Go ahead and brew some." Han waited until C-3PO was in the kitchen and the door closed behind him. He turned to his wife. "So what do we do to keep this from happening?"

Leia drew in a breath to answer, but held it for several

long moments. Han stared at her curiously. He could tell that she was framing her reply, but she was so well practiced at doing so that she could normally compose a speech as she was beginning to recite it. This sort of delay was unusual for her.

"Perhaps," she finally said, "the best thing to do would be to not interfere." The look she turned upon him suggested that she expected him to transform into a rancor and go on a rampage.

"Not do *anything*," he said.

"Han, what happens if Corellia continues doing exactly what it's doing . . . and gets away with it? Suffers no consequences?"

"Corellia becomes independent again." Han shrugged. "So?"

"And other worlds follow Corellia's lead."

"Again—so?"

"The Alliance will be weakened. Things will become more . . . untidy. More opportunities for crime. Black markets. Corruption."

For once, Han spent a few moments considering his reply. A flip answer would have come easily to him, but good government and a stable galaxy were important to his wife, and he couldn't casually dismiss them. "Leia, there's got to be room in this galaxy for independence. For chaos. In a galaxy as tidy, as sanitary, as controlled as you're talking about, I never could have happened. I'd really prefer to live in a galaxy where there's room for someone like me."

Leia looked away from him, and in her expression Han could see the dawning of a regret that amounted to mourning. Once again, she was mourning the loss of a system, a government that had always existed only in the abstract—one so fair and reasonable, it could never endure when implemented. "Then the thing to do is warn Corellia," she said. "Preferably without alerting the GA that you're doing it. Because it would be nice for you not to be thrown in jail."

"You'd just rescue me. If I took too long to escape on my own, that is."

She smiled sourly, still keeping her attention on the viewport and the sliding door out onto the balcony.

"I need your help, Leia. I can't do this alone." It took an effort to speak those words. Admitting that he couldn't perform some ordinary task—such as saving a world from invasion or conquest—all by himself was painful enough. It was worse to ask a woman devoted to order and lawfulness to set those considerations aside for him.

"I know." Leia looked back at him. "I'll do it, Han. But only if you'll help *me*. Corellia can't play both sides of the field. If the system is going to be independent, it has to be *independent*. It can't continue to accept all the benefits of GA membership *and* defy GA law. If you tell them the GA is coming in to compel them to obey, you have to tell them to stop playing games. They have to grease the whole bantha."

Han blinked at her. "They have to grease—they have to *what*?"

"To grease the whole bantha. It's an expression. From Agamar, I think."

"Sure it is."

"It *is*. And you're just trying to keep from responding to what I just said."

"No, I'm not. You're right, Leia. No more games for Corellia."

"Then I'll help."

"And more grease for the bantha."

"Don't make fun of me, Han. There are consequences."

"We could grease the protocol droid."

"Han, I'm warning you . . ."

chapter six

CORONET, CORELLIA

Wearing only shorts and a blue undershirt bearing the symbol of the original Rebel Alliance in black now fading to gray, Wedge Antilles moved to the front door of his quarters and activated the security panel on the wall beside it. The screen flickered to life and showed a man and a woman standing in the hall outside. Both were young, in their midtwenties, and despite the fact that they were in the gray jumpsuits and overcoats that constituted one form of anonymous street dress on Corellia, their haircuts—military short rather than slightly shaggy—and an indefinable quality about their body language and facial expressions marked them as outsiders.

They shouldn't have been able to reach the front door of Wedge's quarters without him knowing about it. His housing building was given over to military retirees such as himself. Some were retired from the New Republic, some from CorSec—Corellian Security—some from other Corellian armed forces. There were very basic security measures in place at all the entrances into the housing complex, so if these two were here without having been announced by complex security, it was because some other resident had let them in.

Wedge shrugged. The complex's security was designed to

keep ordinary folk out of their building, not to prevent agents with contacts from getting in.

He glanced over his shoulder. His wife, Iella, stood in the doorway to their bedroom. She wore a simple white robe and her hair, normally a wavy, gray-brown cascade, was a tousled mess, including one tuft protruding almost straight up. She had one hand cupped over her mouth as she yawned; the other held a full-sized blaster pistol at her side. Yawn done, she gave him a questioning look, one eyebrow raised.

He shrugged, then turned back to the door and activated the exterior speakers. "What is it?"

The female visitor, a well-muscled blond woman who looked to be at least as tall as Wedge—not that this was unusual, as Wedge stood slightly shorter than the average human male—said, "General Wedge Antilles?"

"He moved," Wedge said. "I think he's over in Zed Block. He left the carpets a mess, too."

It was a test, of course. If the visitors showed confusion or retreated, then they were simply admirers, or children of colleagues, people who could stand to contact him through ordinary channels and during daylight hours. If they didn't—

They didn't. The male visitor, a broad-shouldered, dark-haired man who looked as though he'd probably represented his military unit as wrestling champion, merely smiled. The woman continued, "I'm sorry for the late visit, General, but we really need to speak to you."

Wedge flipped on the living room lights and looked back over his shoulder again. The door was open, but Iella was no longer in sight. She'd be hanging back in the darkness, wearing something far less visible than the white robe, the blaster in hand . . . just in case.

Wedge flipped another switch on the security panel. Now the door leading into the side hall would be sealed, preventing Wedge and Iella's youngest daughter, Myri, from wandering into the living room if she awoke. An intelligent and stubborn girl, Myri had inherited her mother's inquisitive nature; it would not be beyond her to try to eavesdrop on a late-night conversation if she was aware one was taking place.

Finally Wedge pressed the switch to open the front door. It slid down and out of sight, revealing the two visitors.

The two straightened, an ordinary at-attention courtesy for a retired general, but they couldn't quite keep dubious expressions from their faces. He knew they were looking at a skinny, graying man with knobby knees, a man wearing a sentimental-value undershirt older than either of them. It was a vision that did not match his reputation.

Wedge kept any annoyance out of his voice. "Come in."

"Thank you," the woman said. The two moved in and Wedge tripped the door just as soon as they cleared the threshold. The door tugged at the man's shirt cloth as it rose into place.

"I apologize for waking you," the woman said. "I'm Captain Barthis with Intelligence Section. This is my associate, Lieutenant Titch."

"Identification?" Wedge said.

Both reached into inner pockets of their coats. Wedge willed himself not to tense. But their hands emerged with identicards. Wedge held out a hand—not to take the identification, which by regulation these two would not have yielded in any case, but so that a green scanning light from the security panel would fall across his palm.

Captain Barthis waved her card across his hand, and Lieutenant Titch followed suit. Now Wedge's computerized security gear would be processing their card information, comparing it with Corellian data sources and a few databases that Wedge was not officially supposed to be able to access.

He waved the visitors toward the cream-colored stuffed furniture that lined one wall of the room. "Have a seat."

Captain Barthis gave him a little shake of the head. "Actually, we've been sitting for hours, on a shuttle—"

"Of course." Wedge waited.

"The Galactic Alliance needs your help, General," the woman said.

Wedge offered a faint snort. "Captain, the Galactic Alliance is teeming with officers who were compelled to retire after the war with the Yuuzhan Vong, for the simple reason that a peacetime military doesn't need as many of them. Some of these folks are quite brilliant, and, unlike me, they're anxious to get back into uniform. Me, I'm anxious to sit around in comfortable clothes all day, give my wife all the time my military career wouldn't allow me to give her, and complete my memoirs. You're looking for the wrong man."

"No, sir." Captain Barthis shook her head in vigorous denial. "The GA needs you and your specific help."

The male visitor finally spoke, his voice softer than Wedge would have suspected. "It has to do with the events of nearly thirty years ago when Rogue Squadron did so much work preparing for the taking of Coruscant from Imperial forces."

"I see. And it's something that requires my presence instead of a simple holocomm call."

"Yes, sir," Captain Barthis said.

"And if you're here in the middle of the night, it's because you need me in the middle of the night."

The captain nodded, the expression on her face regretful.

Wedge flipped a switch on the door-side panel, and the entryway opened again. "Wait for me in the building lobby. I'll be down directly."

Now, finally, the two of them glanced at each other. Barthis said, "We'd prefer to remain here, sir."

Wedge gave her a frosty little smile. "And will you be making a holocam recording of my good-byes with my family? Or perhaps you'd prefer to hug my daughter *for* me."

Barthis cleared her throat, thought the better of it, and moved out into the hall. Titch followed. Wedge shut the door behind them.

Iella moved into the bedroom doorway again. She was now wearing a green-black rain drape. She looked annoyed. "What do they need that they couldn't have asked you decades ago?"

Wedge shrugged. "*Retired* is such an imprecise word . . . Did they check out?"

Iella nodded. "They're the genuine article. In fact, I worked for a year with Barthis's father. The family is Corellian." She moved up to put her arms around Wedge's neck. "Sometimes I wish you hadn't been as influential as you were in your job. So that they'd stop coming for you anytime the military discovers it's forgotten how to coordinate an X-wing engagement."

Wedge wrapped his arms around her waist and pulled her to him. "And who was it they came for last time? An hour before dawn, sweeping the hallway for listening devices before they even rang the chimes?"

"Well, me." Iella had spent her professional career as a security officer, first for CorSec and then for New Republic Intelligence, and the demands on her postretirement time matched the demands on Wedge's.

Wedge kissed her. "Wake Myri up so I can say good-bye. I'll grab my go-bag and get dressed."

She reached past him to unlock the hallway, then turned toward that door. Not looking back, she said, "I don't like Titch."

"Yeah." It was a bit of verbal shorthand. She didn't mean she didn't like the man; she didn't know him. But Titch was the sort of intelligence officer brought along to ensure security—to ensure that the person being transported didn't cause trouble. It led to the question—Was Titch actually Barthis's regular partner, or had he been brought in because someone anticipated Wedge causing trouble?

CORUSCANT

Han and Leia crowded in close, side by side, so that the holocam on the terminal before them could capture both their images. "Luke," Han said.

The lights on the terminal flickered, and after a few seconds the face of Luke Skywalker swam into view on the terminal screen. He was wearing a cold-weather wrap in black, with jagged decorative lines on it in subdued gray, and behind him was an anonymous white wall. He looked surprised to see the caller. "Hello."

"We were wondering," Leia said, "if you were planning on seeing any X-wing action in the near future." Her tone was light and conversational.

For the merest instant, Luke looked startled, but his features settled into an amused grin. "Why do you ask?"

"Well, we're planning on a vacation," Han said. "In the *Falcon*. Dashing around, seeing old friends. Me, Leia, Goldilocks, the Noghri—do you see what I'm getting at, conversationally?"

Luke's grin broadened. "I think so."

"Leia and I can talk. The Noghri can keep each other occupied. But if See-Threepio doesn't have Artoo-Detoo to talk to, he'll talk to *us*." Han mimed putting a blaster barrel to his own temple and pulling the trigger. "Save me, Luke Skywalker, you're my only hope."

Still cheerful, Luke shook his head. "I wish I could. But Mara and I are about to do a quick training tour with a bunch of Jedi Knights anxious to learn about adapting their Force-based abilities to X-wing piloting tasks. In other words, I'm about to head out with Artoo."

"Oh." Han gave his brother-in-law an unhappy stare. "All right, then. Doom me to day after day of listening to dithering obsequiousness."

"Nice word choice," Luke said. "By the way, where will you be heading on your vacation?"

Leia shrugged. "We're not sure yet. We may visit Lando and Tendra and get a tour of their new manufacturing complex, but don't tell them, since we want it to be a surprise if it happens. We're thinking hard about a trip through the Alderaan system, and then planet-hopping along the Perlemian Trade Route."

"Lots of shopping," Han offered, his tone suggesting

that such a fate was only one step above death as a matter of preference.

"Ah, good. Have fun. And sorry I couldn't help with Artoo."

"That's the way it is sometimes," Han said.

The polite smile remained fixed on his face after Luke reached forward to break the comm connection. But Han's posture failed him; he sagged into his chair as if beaten. "He's part of it," Han said.

"We can't be sure—"

"Don't try to kid me, Leia. He was wearing a weather wrap indoors. Either he just got out of the 'fresher—and his hair was dry, you'll note—or he threw it on to cover over something else he was wearing, like a pilot's uniform. You saw the wall behind him? White, curved. A bulkhead on a vessel. He's already shipped out."

Finally Leia nodded, reluctant. "Probably."

"He's on *their side*."

"As the Master of the Jedi order, he has taken oaths to support the Galactic Alliance." Leia let a little sternness creep into her voice. "And don't pretend this is a simple situation, where everyone on one side is smart and sensible and everyone on the other side isn't. It's more complicated than that. It's more complicated than that for *me*."

Han reached over to hold her for a moment. "Yeah. I'm sorry. It's just—it's just like he hit me when I wasn't looking." He buried his face in her hair, took a deep breath. "All right. It's time for us to go."

In the foremost passenger seat, Wedge sat up, startled, as his shuttle came in for its landing and a familiar-looking Corellian YT-1300 leapt up past his viewport, headed for the skies. "That," he announced, "was the *Millennium Falcon*."

"If you say so, sir." Across the aisle between seats, Captain Barthis looked dubious. "There are thousands of those old Corellian transports still flying, though."

"Oh, that was definitely the *Falcon*. I'm intimately familiar with her lines . . . and her rust spots. I had to replicate them once on a decoy vehicle, decades ago. No matter what Han does, paint the hull, anodize it, those rust patches come back after a few months or years."

Barthis cocked her head, a *whatever-you-say* gesture that left no doubt in Wedge's mind that she was humoring him, and returned her attention to her datapad.

Half an hour later the two of them, Titch, and a droid porter swept into the government facility Barthis had said would be Wedge's home for the next several days at least. It was deep within a gray pyramidal building at the edge of what had once been the Imperial government district. The dark corridor from the turbolifts led into a large outer office laid out in rows of monitoring stations; most of the stations were empty, their viewscreens unlit, but Wedge could see two that were active, both showing holocam views of long rooms with dormitory-style accommodations for four at one end and office equipment at the other.

Barthis led Wedge and the others to a door, which *whooshed* upward and *thumped* into place with the speed, air displacement, and echoing sound of an armored portal. The chamber's overhead lights flickered on as they entered, revealing a room very much like those shown on the monitors: closest to the door were four desks, facing one another, laden with computer material; the far side of the room held four bunk beds and oversized equipment lockers. Wedge could also see a door that he presumed led into a refresher.

The porter droid moved in to drop Wedge's bags on the nearest of the bunk beds. Barthis and Titch stayed near the door and gestured at the accommodations. "A bit plain," Barthis admitted. "I'm sorry."

"They're luxurious compared with some of the places I've been quartered." Wedge glanced over the computer equipment, noting brand names and designs. "These terminals have to be thirty years old."

Barthis nodded. "Almost. This facility was installed by Intelligence just after the New Republic conquered Coruscant and drove Ysanne Isard into exile. The equipment is original . . . but it has been serviced and upgraded."

"What's the facility for?"

"It was what we called a pressure cooker," Titch said. "The idea is that in times of crisis, you get teams of civilian coders, technicians, and specialists together in combined living and work quarters. They're the sort of people who are going to be working sixteen, twenty hours a day anyway. More convenient for them to be packed in together, exchanging ideas, keeping one another's spirits up, and so forth, rather than in separate offices and with quarters minutes' or hours' travel time away."

"Ah." Wedge grabbed the rolling chair before the nearest desk, swung it around, and sat. "So. You wouldn't tell me on Corellia, you wouldn't tell me on the shuttle trip— now, in the heart of your own secure facility, maybe you can tell me what this is all about? What am I supposed to be doing?"

Barthis and Titch exchanged a look. Their faces remained impassive, but Wedge read it as a *here-we-go* exchange. Barthis returned her attention to Wedge. "Just, um, *waiting,* General."

Wedge blinked. "Waiting for orders?"

"No." Barthis looked regretful, and waved for the porter droid to leave the chamber, which it did. Wedge noticed that, though his posture looked relaxed, Titch was ready for action, and had positioned himself in the doorway so that he could draw the blaster at his hip and fire without endangering Barthis.

"No," Barthis continued, "you have no orders. Our orders are to keep you as comfortable as possible during your stay here."

Wedge refused to allow the alarm that was beginning to well up within him to show on his face. "The duration of my stay?"

Barthis shrugged. "Unknown."

"Its purpose?"

"Can't say."

Wedge closed his eyes and offered up a slow, silent sigh. Then he looked at the two of them again. "I said no, you know."

They looked confused.

"When officers of the Corellian military came to me and said, 'There could be trouble between us and the GA,' I said, 'Sorry, fellows, I'm retired. You can get advice as useful as mine, and much more up to date, by looking at other Corellian officers.' And so they left me alone. Why didn't you?"

Barthis opened her mouth, evidently realized that she could offer no answer without somehow compromising her orders, and closed it again.

"Because, you see . . ." And this time Wedge couldn't quite keep the pain he was feeling from being reflected in his voice, as a hoarseness he could not control. "You see, that way I'd be with my family if something happened. And now, someone, somewhere, at the GA end of things has decided I need to be out of the way for what's going to happen. *And has separated me from my family.*" He fixed Barthis and Titch with his stare.

Barthis actually leaned back. She shook her head. "I'm sorry," she said—not an admission that she or her team was doing what Wedge was speculating, but her voice carried emotion, and it sounded genuine. She turned away and walked into the outer office.

Titch seemed unaffected. "You approach this door anytime it's open, it closes," he says. "Meaning it won't do you any good to make a sudden dash for the door when we bring you food or drink. Besides, if you do make an attempt to escape, I get to kill you." He patted the blaster pistol at his side. "This model can be set to stun or burn. I always leave it on burn." He nodded as though he thought the gravity of that action would impress Wedge.

He also glanced after his partner, apparently making sure she was out of earshot. He turned back to Wedge. "Let me add this," he said. "I'm sick of hearing the Rebel Alliance generation brag about how they stomped the Empire and then whine about how the galaxy owes them a living, or special favors. The Empire would have kicked the Yuuzhan Vong in the teeth, and I wouldn't have lost almost everyone I knew when I was a kid, if you hadn't 'won.' Well, the higher-ups seem to think they owe you a little dignity, so here it is. Eat your meals, get in some quiet exercise, keep your mouth shut, and when all the shouting's done, you can go home and finish your self-serving memoirs about how you single-handedly won half a dozen wars. That's the deal. Got it?"

Wedge studied him. "If you'd been a little smarter, I might have left you some shred of a career when I leave here. But I won't. You'll be cleaning refreshers for the rest of your life."

Titch snorted, unimpressed. He backed out of the doorway, and the door slid shut.

chapter seven

OUTER SPACE, NEAR THE CORELLIA SYSTEM

A few light-years from the star Corell, a vessel dropped out of hyperspace, winking back into existence in the physical universe.

In design it was something like the old *Imperial*-class Star Destroyers, and was just as long, though where the ISDs looked more like narrow, armor-piercing arrowheads, this ship was broader, massing half again what an ISD did.

It was the Galactic Alliance Space Vessel *Dodonna*, the second capital ship named for the Rebel Alliance–era military leader who had plotted and executed the destruction of the first Death Star, and it was the first completed vessel of its type, the *Galactic*-class battle carrier—a designation chosen to avoid unpleasant reminders of the old Star Destroyers, of which this new ship was little more than an elaboration and update.

On the bridge, on the broad walkway that looked over technicians' pits and stations, Admiral Matric Klauskin, commander of *Dodonna* and leader of this operation, stood staring out through the high viewports into space. In his peripheral vision, to starboard, another vessel of war, one of the Mon Calamari star cruisers with hull designs that suggested a successful blend of technology and organic design, popped into existence.

Over the next several hours, many elements of the Galactic Alliance's Second Fleet would be arriving here to form up with *Dodonna*. Once everything was in position, Klauskin would give the word and send this operation into motion.

He knew that, on the surface, he appeared calm, rock-steady. Had there been a course at the academy in maintaining appearances of coolness, he would have placed first every time. But inside, his guts knotted.

With the correct few orders, the correct few maneuvers, he could prevent a war. The galaxy might not reexperience the sort of horrors it had within living memory—the agony of worlds being besieged, families torn apart, homes and histories *erased*.

He could prevent it. He had to succeed.

Had to.

CORONET, CORELLIA

The diminutive woman was dressed in the flowing gowns and profanely costly jewelry strands of a noblewoman of the Hapes Consortium; a semi-transparent veil concealed the lower half of her face. Her bodyguard stood in contrast to her in every way possible: tall, primitive, and brutal of appearance, he wore the dusty robes and carried the crude blaster rifle of one of the Tusken Raiders, the Sand People of rural Tatooine. His features were concealed behind the dust-storm-resistant mask that such beings usually wore in their own environment.

Five World Prime Minister Aidel Saxan watched the two of them enter the hotel suite's outer chamber. Saxan, a handsome, black-haired woman of middle years, wielded considerable political power, but in the company she was about to receive she did not feel at a political advantage. She was, as such things could be measured, the peer of her guests, and it was in recognition of that comparative equality she had agreed to meet them here, in this relatively ill-protected hotel away from the prying eyes of others.

When, years after the end of the Yuuzhan Vong war, the Galactic Alliance had decided to reward the Corellian system with removal of the appointed governor-general position, Corellian-born politicians had been swept into the new offices created by the change. Each of the five worlds had elected its own Chief of State, and together they had created the office of the Five World Prime Minister, charged with coordinating budgets, resources, and policies of the five worlds, as well as representing the system in negotiations with other multiplanetary bodies. Aidel Saxan was the first and, so far, only person to occupy that post.

Saxan waited until the outer and inner doors had shut behind her two visitors, then rose from the spindly decorative chair that served temporarily as her seat of power. She offered her visitors a nod. "Welcome to Coronet," she said.

"Thank you," the woman replied. "Before we continue— the chamber has been searched for recording devices?"

Saxan looked back over her shoulder at the CorSec officer. He stepped out of the shadows in a curtained corner of the chamber. "Thoroughly," he said. "And there were some. Of considerable vintage. The sort a hotel security office might plant for purposes of blackmail or peacekeeping. I removed them."

"Thank you," the female visitor said. She reached up to unhook one side of her veil, letting it drop away from her face—the face of Leia Organa Solo.

To his credit, the CorSec officer made no noise of surprise or recognition. He simply returned to his shadowy nook.

The presumed Tusken Raider, less graceful or delicate of motion than his companion, pulled the sand-mask from his face and tossed back his hood, revealing the craggy, somewhat flushed features of Han Solo. "Yes, thank you, Your, uh—"

"Excellency," Leia supplied.

"Right, Excellency."

"For one of Corellia's most celebrated heroes, of course,

an audience is in order at any time . . . in any place. Though I'll admit that your requests for secrecy are unusual. Please, come with me." Saxan led her visitors into an adjacent chamber, a windowless dining room by the look of it—but the dining table, a massive thing topped with black stone inlaid with gold wire, had been rolled against the shimmering blue wall, leaving behind only well-padded chairs arranged in two semicircles. Saxan sat in the central chair of one semicircle, with her CorSec man taking up position behind her; Han Solo took the seat opposite her, with Leia sitting to his right.

Interesting, Saxan thought. *So this is to be Han Solo's speech, or request.*

"I'll get right to the point," Han said. His features were returning to their normal color; out from under the Tusken Raider mask, he had to be cooling down. "I believe that the Galactic Alliance is going to take military action against Corellia within the week, maybe within the day."

"Why would they?" Saxan asked, keeping her voice controlled, impersonal. "Negotiations between us and Coruscant are still cordial. Still in developing stages."

Han shrugged. "I don't know why. Just that they are. There are political, financial, military movements going on that all point to action here, and soon."

Saxan considered. Could the Galactic Alliance have finally uncovered the Kiris shipyards? It seemed unlikely. She had been Prime Minister a full year before her budget auditors discovered that the secret appropriations authorized by Thrackan Sal-Solo and his political allies were being used to build a secret assault fleet. Her auditors had had direct access to the Corellian budgetary records; the GA investigators, impeded by Corellia's formidable counterintelligence service, *should* not have been able to uncover the same facts.

It seemed more likely that the GA's premature action had been prompted by the reactivation of Centerpoint. Despite everything, all the vetting and counterspying that had taken place at that facility since the Galactic Alliance had reluctantly surrendered its control to Corellia, some word must have reached Coruscant of the facility's status.

She said nothing of this. Instead, she asked, "And why are you telling me this?"

"Well, let's just say it galls me," Han said. "If Corellia wants to be independent, I'm all for it."

"Would you be willing to say that publicly?" Saxan asked. "In speeches to the Corellian people?"

"Sure," Han said. "If you resign as Prime Minister and Thrackan resigns as Corellian Chief of State."

This time, Saxan couldn't keep the surprise off her face, out of her voice. "I should resign? Why?"

"I don't like the game you're playing," Han said. "Whining 'independence' out one corner of your mouth and 'benefits' out the other."

"That's just strategy," Saxan assured him.

"No, it isn't. Not when a lot of people are listening to you and agreeing. People who don't have the time or energy or brains to think it through. People who trust you because your father was famous or because you're good looking." Han finally looked disappointed, perhaps even faintly disgusted. "You need to be showing Corellians the lives they'll be living if they do become independent. Planetary pride is one thing, and I'm all for it. Planetary pride with an assumption that the economy's going to thrive and everyone's going to love us is another thing. It's a lie."

Saxan kept the anger and, yes, hurt she felt at Han's rebuke from showing. She turned to Leia. "And what about you? You're a Jedi Knight. The Jedi are sworn to defend the Galactic Alliance. In coming here, aren't you committing treason?"

Leia blinked at her. "How's that again?"

"Your husband wants me to commit to a politically dangerous position. And yet here you are, straddling two positions, too. I think perhaps you and your husband should stay here in Corellia and lend us your support. It would be safer for you. If Coruscant learned you'd come here on

your errand, it could do irreversible damage to your reputation."

Leia smiled, showing teeth. "I *am* a Jedi Knight. And I
am sworn to defend the Galactic Alliance. Even from itself,
sometimes. But coming here with my husband and listening to him speculate on the future of political relations isn't
treason. It's just something you do when you're married."

"Speculate?"

Leia nodded. "Speculate."

"Meaning that you won't have any hard data to hand me
supporting his speculations."

Han smiled, the knee-weakening, cocky smile Saxan had
seen so often on holonews and occasionally in person.
"What data?"

"Of course."

"And, by the way"—Han lost his smile—"it wouldn't do
for Coruscant to learn we'd been here speculating. We'd
take it personally. You might think about going through
the historical records and seeing what happens when we
take things personally."

Saxan didn't ask whether that was a threat. Of course it
was. And it was the sort of threat they'd proven again and
again they could make good on.

Well, this meeting was still a success. She'd learned two
important things: that the Galactic Alliance probably knew
about developments at Centerpoint Station, and that Han
Solo could be just as hard and ruthless as his cousin,
Thrackan Sal-Solo.

Saxan let a gracious smile return to her face. "Never fear,
Corellia knows who her friends are," she said. "By the
way, how long will you be staying insystem?"

Leia shrugged. "A few days."

"Excellent. Perhaps you will do us the honor of paying
us an official visit sometime. Whether it's wartime or peacetime, your husband is one of Corellia's favorite sons."

"That would be most agreeable." Recognizing Saxan's
words as a conclusion to the audience, Leia rose and

pinned her veil back in place. Han followed his wife's lead
and began wrestling his sand-mask into place.

"Oh, Han . . ." Saxan smiled as she saw the tiniest of
frowns mar Leia's brow, reaction to her inappropriate use
of Solo's first name. "If I see Thrackan, do you have any
message for him?"

Mask in place, Han pulled his hood up. "Sure. How
about, 'Look out!' "

"I'll pass that along."

OUTER SPACE, CORELLIA TRADE SPINE,
PASSING YAG'DHUL

The passenger-seating compartment was not ideal. It was,
in fact, a cargo container, the sort used to transport bulk
goods from one port to another. But it had been fitted with
reclinable seats from decommissioned passenger shuttles.
Every row was a different color, and some of the seats
smelled bad.

Jaina's smelled bad. If she'd been in a self-destructively
contemplative mood, she might have speculated that at
some time in the distant past, it had been occupied by a
Hutt with a digestive disorder. Every so often, an injudi-
cious movement on Jaina's part would compress the padding
she was sitting on and an odor, half bitter, half sweet, all re-
pulsive, would cause her nose and the noses or equivalent
equipment of the other passengers in the vicinity to twitch.

Those passengers were an interesting collection, Jaina
decided. Most looked and acted like beings on the run, eyes
alert to anyone who might be giving them too much attention, clothes bulky enough to conceal the blasters tucked
away underneath, bags and satchels containing who-knew-
what always close at hand. Some were humans, some
Bothans, some Rodians. Jaina spotted one Bith at the rear
of the compartment. It appeared that one passenger was a
beaten-up YVH 1 combat droid traveling without a companion.

And of course there were Jedi, though they didn't look

like Jedi. Jaina was dressed in a fashion that would have let her fit in with her father's old friends—tight-fitting trousers and vest of black bantha leather, a red silk shirt with flowing sleeves and a matching hair scarf, a blaster holster on her belt. Half her face bore an artificial tattoo, a red flower on her cheek with green leafy tendrils spreading across her jaw and up to her forehead, and her hair was blond, a temporary dye job.

Next to her, Zekk, eyes closed in sleep, wore a preposterous tan jacket of fringed leather. Beneath it was a bandolier holding eight vibroblades. Two false scars marked his face, one a horizontal gash across his forehead, the other down from the forehead to the right cheek; an eye patch with a blinking red diode covered that eye.

The two compartments directly aft were sectioned into small, claustrophobic sleeping berths. The compartment aft of that held luggage.

And they were surrounded by containers holding Tibanna gas, harvested on Bespin, where this cargo vessel had begun its journey. If the vessel was attacked, incoming damage could ignite the cargo, and Jaina and all her Jedi friends would be vaporized.

This was, despite its size, a smuggling vessel. The Tibanna gas it carried boosted the destructive power of blasters. Its mining and export was carefully limited by the Galactic Alliance government, which was why a daring smuggler with a large cargo of the stuff could make a substantial profit by taking it to a system whose industries wanted it—for instance, Corellia, this vessel's destination. And since the cargo was intended for weapons manufacturers receiving the tacit blessing of Corellia's government, this vessel would, upon reaching the Corellia system, be ignored by customs inspectors . . . meaning that its passengers, many of whom were lightsaber-carrying Jedi, would also be unmolested. Mara, Jaina's former Master, had prevailed on her oldest friend, smuggler Talon Karrde, for a way by which a unit of Jedi could enter Corellia with their lightsabers and other gear unnoticed, and he had offered the name, flight route, and departure time of this vessel.

And its smelly seats.

Zekk's eyes opened. "Are we on Corellia yet?" His voice was pitched as a whisper.

Jaina shook her head. "Not for several hours."

His eyes closed. Then they reopened. "Are we on Corellia yet?"

Despite herself, Jaina grinned. "Why don't you go play outside for a while?"

CORUSCANT

There was a lot of open floor space between the office and dormitory portions of the room, and Wedge made use of it, taking his rolling chair there and playing a new game. Sitting facing one wall, he would suddenly stand, propelling his chair backward with his knees, and then turn to see how close he'd come to placing the chair near a mark he'd made on the floor.

At exact six-hour intervals, Titch came in with Wedge's meals. When at the office desks, Wedge habitually sat at the one closest to the outer door, with his back to the door; he thought of it as the number one desk. Every six standard hours, morning, noon, and evening, Titch brought Wedge's food and drink to the next desk to the left, the one Wedge thought of as the number two desk, and set the meal down there.

The first time Titch entered while Wedge was playing his rolling-chair game, Titch paid him no special attention. This was exactly what Wedge expected; Titch, Barthis, and possibly more security officers had to be watching his activities on hidden holocams, and so were already aware of Wedge's new preoccupation. Titch merely set Wedge's meal down in the usual place, then gave the older officer a condescending, pitying shake of the head before walking out the door and letting it slide shut behind him.

Wedge grinned after him.

Six hours later, minutes before the evening meal was due to arrive, Wedge sat at his usual desk, the terminal alive before him. Of course, it didn't give him access to the worldwide datanet; that would defeat the purpose of his captivity. But it did apparently sample the datanet once or twice a day, allowing Wedge to follow Coruscant and galactic news, and offered a wide variety of thirty-year-old games and battle simulation programs. Now he brought up one of those simulations—this one allowing him to re-create, at squad-action level, the ambush of Rebel Alliance ships at Derra IV, an action that had taken place before either of his captors had been born—and began playing it through from the Rebel side.

The little chron at the top right of the terminal screen told him that he had five minutes to wait before his next meal would arrive.

He took a sip from his tumbler of water, untouched since his noon meal arrived. It was still almost full. Slowly, his attention still apparently full on the battle simulation before him, he lowered the hand with the tumbler to his lap. He positioned it under the lip of the desk until it was beneath desk number two, and then, with excruciating, silent care, poured most of the water out onto the floor there. It broadened as a slowly spreading, all-but-invisible pool.

Three minutes left. He couldn't cut things too close. Titch might vary his schedule by a few seconds. Young officers weren't that dependable.

He held the tumbler over desk number two, inverted it as close to instantly as he could, and set it down rim-first. To observers, it would—well, *should*—look as though he were merely setting aside an empty drink container. Water began pooling out from under the rim and spread out in all directions—toward that desk's chair, toward the lip adjoining Wedge's desk. Like the water on the floor, it should be all but invisible to the sort of low-resolution holocams used to monitor prisoners.

Wedge typed in the next turn's series of commands to the simulation program and leaned forward to watch the turn's results. While locked in that pose, he groped around carefully under the desk and located the power cable that ran from the system's main processor up to the monitors around the desk.

Two minutes left. He watched the Imperials on the screen slaughter the Rebels at Derra IV, as they had more than thirty years before. He made an exasperated noise. With his free hand, he powered down the terminal. Then, with his other hand, he pulled the power cable loose and drew it to him, gathering all the slack he could obtain. Only then did he lean back in his chair.

The door behind him slid open. Titch entered—Wedge recognized him by the sound of his heavy, confident stride—and asked, "Not going so well, is it?" Then the man moved into view, Wedge's meal in his hands, and walked up to desk number two. He set the tray down. For a brief moment, he looked confused as his fingers contacted water on the desktop.

Wedge powered up his monitor and tossed the power cable onto desk number two.

Titch jerked and began to shake, trapped in the spasms of electrocution. The overhead lights dimmed.

Wedge stood quickly, propelling his rolling chair back and away from him. He glanced behind him. The chair came to a halt a hand span from where he'd aimed it, dead in the center of the open doorway.

Wedge watched the security man being electrocuted. It was now a waiting game, duration measured in seconds. If Barthis did not act before Titch suffered irreparable damage, Wedge might have to—

Finally it came, Barthis's voice from the next chamber: "Power down Block Forty-five-zero-two. Do it now!"

Nothing happened. Wedge waited. He heard running footsteps, a single individual approaching—Barthis. He could imagine her with a blaster pistol in her hand, and he was still armed with nothing.

Then the lights went out. Wedge heard a gasp from Titch, a metallic *thud* as the man hit the floor. This was followed within half a second with a *whoosh* as the depowered door slid down and slammed into Wedge's rolling chair.

Wedge located Titch by touch. The man moved feebly. Wedge found his belt, removed the blaster from its holster, and switched it from its burn setting to its stun setting. He said two words: "Remember, refreshers."

Then, on hands and knees, he scooted over toward the chamber doorway. Just before he reached it, he could feel air flow into his makeshift prison, and then his free hand encountered one wheel of his rolling chair. Carefully, quietly, he slid past the chair, which creaked under the weight of the door it held.

He listened and could hear Barthis's voice, a few meters away: "Send a security detachment to Forty-five-zero-two. The prisoner was contained when the power cut dropped the door, but he has Lieutenant Titch as a prisoner. No, for the moment, we're secure."

Then the emergency lighting, dim orange glow rods installed where the ceiling met the walls, came on. Wedge could now see the desk stations here in the outer chamber, could see Barthis where she stood a few meters away, a comlink in her hand.

And she could see him, too. Her eyes widened.

He shot her. Nerveless, she hit the floor with a much less resounding noise than Titch had.

He appropriated her comlink, blaster pistol, identicard, and other effects, stuffing them in his pockets. In seconds, he hauled her over to the door to his prison, shoved her through, and then kicked at his chair until it was forced back out of the doorway. The powerless door slid down into place with a *thump*.

Beginning on the far side of the chamber, beside the door by which they'd entered this complex of offices, Wedge methodically smashed the emergency glow rods with the butt of Titch's blaster. Completing the circuit of the room, he smashed the last rod, then situated himself under a desk beside the exit.

Sixty seconds later, there was a whine from that door as the temporary power supply someone had attached outside was activated and lifted it out of the way. Four armed and armored security officers rushed in. The first shouted, "Captain Barthis?"

Sliding quietly out from his desk, Wedge eased out through the doorway and into the dimly lit hallway beyond. He grabbed the temporary power supply now attached to the doorway control console and yanked it free. That door came down with a *thud*, trapping the security detail within.

So far, so good, he told himself. Now all he had to do was find a locker room, shed the clothes he was wearing— whatever sensor they'd been using to make sure the door would close when he came near it had to be in his clothes or gear somewhere—and substitute a local uniform, then find his way to a hangar and steal some hyperdrive-equipped starfighter or shuttle, with Intelligence Section crawling all over the place looking for him.

Easy.

chapter eight

The shuttle was not elegant; it was just an oblong mass
with thrusters and hyperdrive at one end, a viewported
bridge at the other, and plenty of room for passengers in
between. But in the passenger compartment, the seats were
well spaced and well padded. In the back of each one was
a monitor allowing the passenger behind to watch Corellian news or entertainment holocasts, or to see what the
holocams spaced around the shuttle's exterior were viewing.

Dr. Seyah kept his monitor switched to the bow view. In
it, he could watch, as he always did, Centerpoint Station
first appear, then grow larger and larger and larger. Just
now, there was nothing to see but stars; the shuttle hadn't
performed its final hyperspace jump to drop it into the
vicinity of the station.

Seyah wore a plastic shirt. It was comfortable enough
that it didn't always feel plastic, but plastic it was, and embedded with circuitry. Just now it was orange, with violent
purple flames crisscrossing it, a design suited to someone
wandering around in a warm and sandy vacation paradise,
which was precisely what Dr. Seyah's documentation said
he'd been doing for the last few weeks. The spray-on sun-

tan he sported, covering the fact that he'd only become paler while training Jedi to destroy Centerpoint Station, supported his cover story.

But the thing about the shirt, sold to wealthy tourists, was that whenever it was poked with sufficient energy, it would make an audible *boop* noise and change both color and design.

The little human boy in the next seat, dark-skinned like his mother and perhaps three standard years of age, had discovered this when he'd kicked Dr. Seyah, minutes after they'd taken off from Talus. He'd been persuaded by his apologetic mother not to kick Dr. Seyah anymore, but couldn't be restrained from reaching over and poking the scientist-spy, causing the shirt to make its pleasing *boop* noise and change its color scheme. And the little boy would chuckle, and look at the new colors, and about a minute later reach over to poke the shirt again.

Dr. Seyah barely noticed. Inside, he was sick. As long as he'd been assigned to Centerpoint Station, he'd known that the sheer power and destructiveness it represented might someday result in it being destroyed. It could destroy entire stars, and the only thing that could ever keep it from being civilization's greatest weapon of terror was the wisdom of its controllers . . . or its destruction.

And wisdom was in increasingly short supply.

Boop. Now his shirt was pink, with frothy clouds on his shoulders and upper chest, recreational seaspeeders skimming across red waters at his waist.

He didn't want Centerpoint Station to be destroyed. Like almost everyone who'd worked there, he was desperate to learn more about the long-vanished species that had built it and used it to drag habitable planets to the Corellia system. It was a rare system that had two worlds lush enough to sustain life; Corell was orbited by five. If the station's secrets could be cracked, the intelligent species of the galaxy could re-create that feat, engineering whole systems to please or accommodate the beings who would live there.

More importantly, in harnessing the very forces that held

the universe together, the station promised an improved scientific understanding of how the universe itself worked. If Centerpoint was lost, that opportunity might be gone forever.

But perhaps it wouldn't come to that. Dr. Seyah had stressed to the Jedi again and again his belief that destroying the computer controls the Corellians were installing throughout the system would be sufficient to keep control out of Corellia's hands. With any luck, they'd listen. With any luck, they'd agree.

Boop. Now his shirt was a deep blue, with a stylized rancor rearing up on the front, arms outstretched. The little boy chuckled.

Dr. Seyah looked over at the boy's mother. "Will you two be debarking at the station?"

She nodded, sending into motion her blue-frosted black hair, so fine that every little breeze from the shuttle's life-support system stirred it. "I'm a cartographer, a member of the station-mapping project. Loreza Plirr." She extended a hand across her boy.

Dr. Seyah shook it. Words bubbled up inside him. *Don't get off at the station. In hours, you could be superheated gas. Go back to Talus.* Instead, he said, "I'm Toval Seyah."

This was his job. This was the dark side to being a scientist and spy, something he'd never even tried to explain to the boy Jedi. He might just have to let a pretty young woman and her innocent son die.

Blast it.

"And this is my son, Deevan."

"Hello, Deevan." Gravely, Dr. Seyah shook the little boy's hand.

Deevan chuckled.

On the monitor screen, the stars twisted and elongated. Of course they didn't in reality—but that was the visual effect of entering hyperspace. The ship left hyperspace almost as quickly, the duration of the greater-than-lightspeed portion of this flight mere seconds . . . and when the stars were returned to normal, in precisely the same positions as before, Centerpoint Station occupied the center of the monitor screen.

The station wasn't pretty, wasn't even elegant like the Death Stars whose size it exceeded. A gray-white blob with axial cylinders protruding at two opposed points, it was merely impressive in its scale and in the potential damage it could do.

At this distance, of course, its scale was not apparent. What looked like a smooth surface would, as they got closer, be revealed to be a rough, scaly exterior of towers, spires, antennae, parabolic dishes, conduits, traffic tubes, ports, spacescraper-sized battery arrays, shield generators, and other apparati, something like the surface of Coruscant in its busiest sectors but without that world's feeble attempts at maintaining a consistently pleasing set of architectural standards.

Home, to Dr. Seyah, was an ugly spot in space.

He tugged at his shirt collar, and as he did so he squeezed a chip embedded there. The pressure activated the chip, causing it to transmit a single coded pulse on a single frequency. The transmission lasted a few thousandths of a second.

Boop. This time the shirt changed without the boy poking it. It was the shirt's acknowledgment that it had received a countertransmission. The boy chuckled anyway.

Dr. Seyah settled in to watch the station grow larger on his monitor, and to compose himself for the struggle, and perhaps tragedy, that was to come.

In the shuttle's cargo hold, in a cargo container the size of an average groundspeeder, Jacen Solo was awakened by a melodious alarm chime. His eyes flickered open.

There wasn't much to see. The interior of the compartment was dimly lit by the device to the left of his head, a combination computer and life-support system. It blew cool air on him.

The air wasn't cool enough. The heavy enviro-suit he

wore kept him too warm. He'd been sweating as he slept, and the crate smelled like a rancor nest.

He glanced over at the computer monitor screen. Text there indicated that Dr. Seyah had just transmitted that they'd completed their final hyperspace jump before arriving at Centerpoint Station.

Jacen reached over and switched the computer off, plunging the crate interior into darkness.

By touch, he located the valve knob just inside the collar of his bulky suit. He turned it until it locked in the open position. Gas hissed out from the valve—breathable atmosphere. Half an hour's worth was contained in the bottles he'd be carrying with him.

He reached up to the right of his head and found the suit helmet waiting there. He pulled it into place over his head and twisted it against his collar until it locked. Only then did he reach down to the latch beside his waist and trip it.

The top of the cargo box lifted away from him, revealing a dimly lit cargo-hold roof only a couple of meters above him.

Awkward in the enviro-suit, Jacen struggled into an upright position, dragged his atmosphere bottles to lock them into place against his back, and clambered out of the box.

His box was situated atop a stack of cargo containers the size of refresher stalls. One stack over, another box was opening identically, and Ben, similarly suited and helmeted, was struggling upright.

It had taken some careful bribery of cargo porters to make sure that these two boxes were situated at the tops of their respective cargo stacks. If they hadn't been, of course, it would have been harder to exit. The Jedi could have done so, by igniting their lightsabers and cutting their way out, but the damaged cargo boxes would then have been noticed, potentially endangering the mission. Fortunately, the porters had stayed bribed.

And the enviro-suit . . . Jacen encouraged himself to be patient, refrained from cursing the suits even as he stepped out of his cargo box and pushed the lid down into place.

The suit was the heaviest, most awkward thing he'd ever worn.

All its radiation shielding lay in physical materials, none from electronic screens or energy fields. The atmosphere supply came from bottles opened and closed by hand. There were no electronic sensors, no servomotors designed to assist in movement and ease the burden of the suit's weight. The helmet had no comm gear, no visual enhancers.

There were, in fact, no electronics whatsoever installed in the suit. The only electronic items within were the lightsabers, datapads, data cards, and comlinks the two Jedi carried—and for the time being, those items were switched completely off, their power supplies physically disconnected.

Slowly, clumsily, Jacen finished climbing down from his cargo stack and observed that Ben was beginning his own descent.

The advantage to the crudeness of the suits was that they were essentially immune to the varieties of security scanning performed by Corellian Security customs units at Centerpoint Station. With no detectable electronics, the suits would simply not register on CorSec scanners. Of course, life scanners would pick them up . . . but CorSec customs chiefs, in a cost-saving effort, had decided long ago that it was sufficient to scan for electronics. What life-form could move around on the station's exterior without electronic support? Only mynocks and other unintelligent space parasites.

So Jacen and Ben would be mynocks this day, and that's why their portion of the operation's forces had been code-named Team Mynock.

He helped Ben down to the floor, and together they moved to the aft air lock. There, on the hull beside the control panel, almost invisible in the dim cargo-hold lighting, there was an X-shaped mark scratched into the paint, a sign that someone else had remained bribed—that the security sensors on this air lock had been disabled. Jacen pulled open the air lock door; he and Ben crowded into the tiny chamber beyond, and Jacen awkwardly punched the buttons to cycle the air lock.

A minute later, the cycle finished, and Ben impatiently pushed the exterior door. It opened onto a starfield of dizzying beauty; Jacen could see stars, distant nebulae, even a comet whose tail was just beginning to be illuminated by the star Corell.

Jacen poked his head out and turned toward the shuttle's bow. In the distance ahead, he could see Centerpoint Station, now close enough for its moon-like immensity to be evident and its convoluted surface to be obvious.

CORONET, CORELLIA

The conveyance, a ten-meter-long airspeeder that seemed to be mostly windows and standing room, deposited Jaina and half her team on the street outside the Prime Minister's official residence. It drifted away, carrying with it the remaining heavy load of commuting workers, tourists, and people on errands.

Jaina took a deep breath and looked around, wary for signs of too much attention being directed their way. There shouldn't be any. After having made planetfall hours ago, she and her team had had time to check into a hostel, clean themselves up, sleep, and eliminate disguise elements that would cause them to stand out. Jaina now wore a cumbersome Commenorian traveler's robe; her hair was back to its natural dark color; her false tattoo was gone.

"I miss the tattoo," Zekk said. He was now dressed in Corellian common citizens' garments—dark pants and open jacket, a lighter, long-sleeved shirt, knee-high boots in black. His long black hair hung in a braid.

A passerby, a young woman with orange hair and a green, filmy dress, flashed Zekk a smile as she passed. Jaina felt a stab of irritation, pushed it from her mind.

Zekk grinned at Jaina. "What was that I felt?"

She scowled at him. "We're on duty. Concentrate on your mission."

"Yes, Commander." The grin didn't leave his face, but he turned his attention back to the ministerial residence.

A few years earlier, Jaina and Zekk had bonded, a union of mind and personality that went beyond even a Force-bond. It was something that had resulted from their inter-action with the Killiks, a hive-mind species. Eventually the intensity of that union had largely faded, but Jaina's and Zekk's thoughts and feelings remained intertwined to a de-gree unusual even for Jedi. Sometimes it was comforting, even exhilarating. Other times, like now, it was uncomfort-able and distracting.

Nothing suggested to Jaina that she or her companions were attracting attention. The broad, multilane avenue be-fore her was thick with groundspeeder traffic—and the Corellians were such maniacal speeder pilots that anyone near the street with any sense kept his or her attention on their lane-changing, position-jockeying antics. The huge, gated building behind them was, by contrast, inert, some parts of its grounds in deep shadow from trees and creep-ing vines. Even the guards at the sidewalk gates and main doors were still.

The other two members of their team, female Bothan Kolir Hu'lya and male Falleen Thann Mithric, moved up to join them. Kolir, the youngest member of the team, having completed her trials and achieved Jedi Knight status only weeks before, wore an abbreviated dress in white that con-trasted nicely with her tan fur and would not overheat her on this warm day. Thann, dressed in a traveler's robe, looked the most Jedi-like of the four of them but was still thoroughly unremarkable of appearance in this cosmopoli-tan city; he had his hood up over his long black topknot and was maintaining his skin color at a light orange, mak-ing him virtually indistinguishable from a human.

"I don't see any problems," Kolir said.

Not that reassuring coming from someone who'd been an apprentice a few days ago, Jaina reflected. She heard Zekk snicker. Kolir looked curiously at him, but Jaina said, "Transmit that we're onstation."

Kolir nodded. She dug around in her white carry-bag, the same bag that held her lightsaber and an array of other destructive weapons, and brought out a comlink. She smiled as though she were calling a boyfriend and spoke into it: "Team Purella here, just checking in."

OUTER SPACE,
NEAR THE CORELLIAN SYSTEM

Luke, dressed in what looked like standard brown-and-tan Jedi gear but which actually had all the equipment and functionality of a pilot's suit, sat on the rolling staircase that was meant to give a pilot or mechanic access to the X-wing's top surfaces. It wouldn't be needed for that purpose. The mechanics were finished for now with his XJ6 X-wing, and Luke wouldn't need any assistance in getting to the cockpit—for a Jedi, it was just one quick leap away.

The bay where his squadron's X-wings waited was frantic with activity. A broad expanse, all scuffed and burned permacrete flooring and pristine glow-white ceiling, it was the size of a sports arena, with room for Luke's squadron, a squad of Eta-5 interceptors, two squads of shield-equipped TIEs from the Imperial Remnant, and a half squad of B-wings for support. Mechanics fueled some starfighters, made last-minute repairs on others. Pilots arrived to perform inspections of the craft they'd be flying. Commanders moved from pilot to pilot, machine to machine, issuing orders, offering advice.

Luke didn't feel the need to do so. His pilots were all Jedi, all calm in the face of the storm to come, in the face of possible death.

One X-wing over, Mara, similarly garbed, made some final ratcheting motions with her hydrospanner, finishing adjustments to her laser cannon positioning, and slapped closed an access panel on her craft's S-foil underside. She dropped the hydrospanner in a toolbox and moved over to join her husband. "Any word about Ben?"

Luke shook his head.

"You're very quiet." Mara leaned over to stroke his forehead. "Is everything all right?"

"I meditated earlier," he said. "And I had a vision of Ben talking to the man who doesn't exist."

"Not a dream," Mara said. "A vision."

He nodded.

"Could you tell when?"

"The future. Ben was a little older, a little taller."

"At least," she said, "that argues well for what he's up to today."

Finally, he smiled. "Thanks for not killing me."

"When we met?"

"When I told you that I left it to Jacen to decide whether Ben would go on this mission."

"Oh." She didn't return his smile. "I might have been tempted . . . if I had any sense of what the right answer was. I've fouled up in the past, clinging too tightly to him, trying to protect him. What's the right amount?"

Luke shrugged. "You're asking a Jedi Master. Not a Parenting Master."

"Is there one, somewhere?" Finally, she did smile. "I've spent more than thirteen years worrying about him. Which has given me great wisdom about why the Jedi of old didn't allow marriages within the order, discouraged attachments, that sort of thing. If they hadn't, it wouldn't have been Sith or alien empires or natural disasters that killed the Jedi. It would have been worrying about their kids."

"I think you're right."

"Master Skywalker?" The voice, female, emerged from the vicinity of Luke's chest.

He reached under his robe and pulled out a comlink. "Skywalker here."

"Bridge here. Team Purella reports onstation."

"Thank you." He put the comlink away. "Jaina's ready. And that's one more check on the checklist to start this operation."

Mara looked over to the hangar's far wall, where chrono displays showed the time at local hours for CORUSCANT

GOVERNMENT CENTER, CORELLIAN CITY OF CORONET, CENTER-POINT STATION DAYCYCLE, and elsewhere. "We should be getting a bunch more notices like that, if everything goes to plan."

The others in the hangar knew it, too. Activity was increasing. Mechanics withdrew from the starfighters. Several pilots were already clambering into their cockpits.

Luke glanced around the pilots of his squadron. Some were talking with one another. Three were stretched out in the shadows of their X-wings, sleeping, wrapped up in Jedi robes they'd be stowing before takeoff. Two sat cross-legged, meditating. He nodded in approval at this calmness in the eye of the storm.

"Master Skywalker? Team Mynock reports in position."

Luke almost sagged with relief. The lack of any sort of "complications" notification meant that Ben, Jacen, and Dr. Seyah were aboard Centerpoint Station and standing by.

He reached for his comlink to offer thanks to his bridge contact, but she spoke up again. "Team Tauntaun reports in position. Team Slashrat reports no new activity in target zone. Team—wait a moment—"

Then over the hangar's speakers came a different voice, male, that of *Dodonna*'s flight control officer. "All pilots to their craft. Group enters hyperspace in five minutes. All pilots to their craft."

All around Luke and Mara, Jedi pilots rose to their feet. Mara leaned in for a final kiss before launch. "Time for you to do one of the six or eight things you do best."

He smiled at her. "Wait, where's my traditional put-down? You're going soft, Jade."

"Sure I am." She turned, smiled over her shoulder at him, and walked with a jaunty stride back to her X-wing.

Luke looked around at his pilots. "Hardpoint Squadron," he said, "mount up."

chapter nine

CORONET, CORELLIA

Kolir gestured down the avenue, then glanced at the chrono embedded at the snap closure of her bag. "Right on time," she said.

The other Jedi turned to look. In the middle distance, approaching at a high rate of speed even for Corellian drivers, was a convoy of closed-canopy airspeeders. The two in front and two in back were CorSec vehicles painted in brown and burnt orange, and warning lights of the same color flashed atop their forward viewports. The middle vehicle was a somber crimson, its viewports tinted to prevent those outside from viewing whoever might be inside.

"Jedi," Jaina said, "meet Aidel Saxan, Prime Minister of the Five Worlds. Aidel, meet your captors. Thann, alert Control that we've made visual contact. It's on."

The convoy, floating in from above the fluid streams of groundspeeder traffic, merged with the incoming stream and slowed to the groundspeeder travel rate as it neared the Jedi. Kolir stretched the carry-straps of her bag and then stepped into them, allowing them to shrink around her waist, transforming the bag into a pouch. She reached into it and, making no show of the motion, drew out her silvery lightsaber.

The convoy was now meters away and still closing,

though it had slowed to make a left-hand turn over cross-traffic into the gate entrance to the residence compound. "Just like we practiced it," Jaina said. "Three—two—one—Now!"

In unison, the four Jedi leapt up and over the cross-traffic, each arcing toward one of the speeders in the convoy.

Jaina whipped off her traveler's robe as she leapt, leaving her dressed in a close-fitting black jumpsuit. Her lightsaber was at her belt when the robe flew away, in her hand before she cleared the lane of cross-traffic groundspeeders, and lit as she came down on the forward portion of the lead CorSec vehicle. She plunged its glowing blade into the metal surface beneath her and wrenched it around, cutting through the vehicle's engine compartment. There was a *pop,* and the speeder immediately began to lose speed and altitude.

The next CorSec speeder in line angled upward and came on straight over Jaina's speeder, trying for a close fly-over that would hammer Jaina clean off and possibly kill her. She wrenched herself down, flat onto her speeder's hood, and lashed up with her lightsaber as the pursuer passed overhead. Her blade sliced into its bottom armor, plowing through the engine compartment and dragging partway back into the passenger compartment, straight down the center. This speeder didn't *pop*—it coughed, emitting a great cloud of blue-black smoke from the gash she'd made, and immediately pitched over to the left and dived straight down toward the street.

All four CorSec speeders were now shrilling an alarm, a high-pitched, rapid-pulsed tone that hammered Jaina's ears and told Corellians for a kilometer around that there was trouble.

Jaina felt the blow as the speeder she rode hit the avenue. But the pilot was good, retaining control. The speeder bumped once, hard, slewed to port, slewed to starboard, and came to a skidding, shower-of-sparks stop not far from the Prime Minister's residence gates. The other airspeeder she'd cut was mere meters ahead, still moving, rolling bow-to-stern toward traffic that angled frantically in all directions to get out of the way.

Two up, two down, Jaina thought. Then she felt the pulse of shock and alarm from Zekk.

Zekk came down atop the Prime Minister's speeder and drove his lightsaber into the canopy over the passenger compartment. It was a shallow thrust, followed by the traditional circular swirl, and it was a slow maneuver. The airspeeder was heavily armored, and from the instant Zekk landed it began a series of swerves and climb-and-dive bucking maneuvers all designed to throw him free.

He just grinned, relying on the Force to keep him rooted firmly in place. Meanwhile, every maneuver, every extra moment of full-speed travel drew the Prime Minister's vehicle farther from its now crippled escort of CorSec vehicles, farther past the gates to the Prime Minister's residence and all the guards waiting there.

The airspeeder was upside down and fifty meters above the avenue when Zekk finished transcribing his circle with the lightsaber. The impromptu hatch he'd cut fell past him. He leaned upward, the awkward position and angle pulling muscles like an abdomen-firming exercise, and stuck his head into the passenger compartment to confront his quarry. "Madame Minister," he said, voice jaunty and raised a bit to carry over the whistling of the wind, "I apolo—"

He wasn't looking at the Five World Prime Minister. The only individuals in the passenger compartment were droids. A skeletal figure with a CorSec uniform loosely fitted to it was in the forward position, piloting. And in the spacious, crimson-velour-lined main compartment sat a battered old protocol droid wearing a cumbersome ball gown and matching wide-brimmed hat of blue velvet. Only its face and arms were visible, their silvery finish worn off in places with rusty brown showing beneath.

It held a rectangular object that looked like a double-thick portable computer terminal in closed position. On the top surface was a blinking red light. In friendly but officious tones, the droid said, "I have been instructed to play this for any unexpected visitors." Then it pressed the button.

Zekk straightened, yanking his head and shoulders free of the hole, and leapt clear—straight down.

He was a bare two meters from the inverted airspeeder when it exploded.

Kolir and Thann, riding their respective crippled CorSec vehicles to shuddery, sliding stops on the avenue, heard the *boom* and looked up.

The reddish flash of the explosion was enough to blind Thann for a moment; he threw his free arm over his eyes and concentrated on maintaining his balance.

Kolir didn't look at the explosion straight-on. She saw chunks of disintegrated airspeeder flying out of the explosion cloud, and, to the lower left, Zekk—limp, on fire—plummeting.

She raised her hand, an instinctive gesture, and exerted herself through the motion, feeling the Force swell from her, feeling it intermix with the unique set of sensations and memories and textures that were Zekk.

There wasn't a question of not being able to move a mass of less than a hundred kilograms. Under the right circumstances, Kolir could telekinetically lift tons. But the right circumstances meant having a moment to compose herself, to channel the Force through her, to eliminate all distractions . . .

She did what she could. She focused entirely on the task at hand, abandoning the attention she had been paying to the Force-based adhesion that kept her feet firmly planted on the slewing, skidding airspeeder beneath them, on the lit lightsaber in her hand, or the honking, beeping, screeching groundspeeder traffic roaring toward her and veering aside at the last second.

She found Zekk and slowed his descent. A speeder bus passed between her and her unconscious charge, but she was not relying on eyes; she continued to slow his plummet in the brief moments she could no longer see him.

Now he was fifteen meters above the pavement outside the Prime Minister's residence. His back was still on fire, and smoke curled up from his shoulders.

Then Kolir's airspeeder hit the rear of one of Jaina's downed airspeeders. Kolir, catapulted forward, smashed into the rear of that vehicle's passenger compartment, ricocheted off at an angle, hit the pavement of the avenue itself, and rolled a dozen meters before coming to a halt, bloody and unconscious.

Jaina's eyes cleared of the explosion afterimage in time for her to see Zekk suspended in the air not far from her—and Zekk suddenly plummeting again. She leapt free of her airspeeder, hurtling between oncoming speeders in the next lane, and landed on the sidewalk outside the residence. Drawing on the Force with more speed and confidence than Kolir could have employed, she caught Zekk five meters off the ground, lowering him quickly but safely to the walk beside her. She slapped at the flames dancing across his back, smothering them.

Through the Force, she could feel life pulsing strongly within him. Through her other link with him, she could feel his pain—skin and joints jarred by the explosion, burns across his back and shoulders, piercing hurt scattered across his body where fragments from the destroyed airspeeder must have hit him.

She didn't have time to determine whether any of those fragments had penetrated vital organs, to find out whether Zekk's life would soon begin to fade. The doors of the airspeeder she'd ridden and downed *whooshed* open and its two passengers stepped out.

They weren't CorSec agents. They were tall and angular, their skins gleaming and metallic. Brandishing oversized blaster rifles, they advanced on Jaina's position with a confidence born of aggression programming and a lack of concern for their own welfare.

They were YVH droids—Yuuzhan Vong Hunters, produced by Tendrando Arms during the Yuuzhan Vong war,
designed to match those fearsome alien warriors in deadli-
ness and determination.

"We," Jaina said, "are in trouble."

The doors of Thann's airspeeder opened and the YVH
droids within emerged, swinging their blaster rifles up
toward where he stood on the roof.

Thann leapt off to the right, flipping over the head of one
of the combat droids and just ahead of its stream of
blasterfire. He landed on his feet in a low crouch, putting
the body of the airspeeder between him and the far combat
droid, and lashed out with his lightsaber. It caught the midsection of the blaster rifle as the weapon was being lowered
into line with his body. The rifle crackled and detonated, a
small explosion by comparison with that of Zekk's airspeeder, but sufficient to blow the weapon into two pieces
and send stinging hot metal fragments into Thann's chest.

The droid, undismayed, unconfused, kicked at Thann;
the blow connected with his midsection. Thann twisted at
the last moment, reducing the impact, but what was left
was like being hit by a pneumatic ram. The blow catapulted him back and off his feet. His shoulders hit the
groundspeeder avenue; he continued into a backward roll,
coming up on his feet, his lightsaber at the ready.

The second combat droid leapt atop the airspeeder, giving it a clear line of sight on him. Thann gestured, catching
up the closer droid with a wave of telekinetic force, hurtling
it up and back into the farther droid. Both droids went
backward off the airspeeder roof together, the second firing, its shots wildly inaccurate, as it went.

Thann's tactical sense kicked in. *Break line of sight.
Contact superiors. Evaluate friend-and-foe resources.* He
leapt up, caught the side of an open-topped airspeeder with
his free hand, and used the Force to propel him in its direction of travel so that the sudden impact would not dislo-
cate his arm. He looked over, saw the frightened features of

the pilot, a dark-haired boy of late teenage years, and smiled reassuringly. He got one foot up against the side of the airspeeder and catapulted himself off and up, cart-wheeling as he went, then landed cleanly atop the forward engine housing of another speeder, this one at the top of the traffic current. Its pilot, a middle-aged man in business dress, waved angrily at him and shouted, words lost in the wind.

Now Thann was ten meters in the air and traveling away from the scene of the conflict in the direction from which the Prime Minister's convoy had originally come.

Traveler's robe flapping in the wind but voice unruffled, he pulled out his comlink and said, "Purella to Tauntaun, Purella to Control. Purella situation a trap, target not ac-quired. Be advised."

OUTER SPACE, CARRIER **DODONNA**

Lysa Dunter sat cursing her bangs and waiting for launch.

A pretty blue-eyed young woman with dark blond hair, she never lacked for attention but got slightly more when she kept her hair in a short cut with bangs. But if she didn't sweep her hair back absolutely correctly in the split second before donning her flight helmet, her bangs would drift down again and hover at the top of her peripheral vision . . . as they did now.

She could take her helmet off in the cramped Eta-5 inter-ceptor cockpit and try to adjust things . . . but if her squadron commander, whose interceptor rested on the *Dodonna*'s starfighter hangar floor one row up and just to the left of hers, were to see her do it, he'd mock her. Lysa didn't like being mocked.

So she sat there, irritated with her hair, anxious to launch, her right leg bouncing up and down to help her vibrate away her irritation and impatience.

Her speakers *popped,* then she heard her squadron com-mander: "V-Sword Lead to pilots, report status." The commander's wingwoman immediately replied, "V-Sword Two, tip-top, ready to go."

Lysa's breathing grew faster. They were right on the verge of it, her first combat launch. If they were lucky, the commander had said, they wouldn't even see combat now . . . and anyone who wanted to be lucky could put in a request for a transfer. Lysa didn't want to be lucky.

She heard the pilot before her in sequence complete his acknowledgment. "V Seven," Lysa said when it was her turn. "Two green, weapons lit." Then the roster was on to her wingman.

Moments later, once the last of ten pilots had reported in, the squad leader said, "V-Sword Seven, we're hearing a strange vibration over your comm."

Guiltily, Lysa froze her right leg in place, willing it to keep from bouncing. "Sorry, sir," she said. "Had to dog down a loose rocker arm."

"You sure it wasn't a rocker leg, Seven?" The squad leader's voice sounded amused.

Lysa closed her eyes and bit back a curse. She wouldn't reply; she wouldn't give the man any more verbal ammunition. She ignored the faint laughter she heard over the squadron frequency.

Then a new voice: "Hyperspace jump complete. All squadrons, prepare to launch. Hardpoint Squadron, Shuttle *Chandrila Skies*, first in queue." Straight ahead of Lysa's position, but obscured by the ranks of Eta-5 interceptors ahead of her and X-wings ahead of them, a dark line appeared in the floor, then broadened into a yawning starfield.

Lysa saw the X-wings complete their power-up procedures, some of them activating repulsors and floating up a meter or two off the hangar floor. She felt a stab of irritation that the Jedi squadron would be the first fliers off *Dodonna* in this operation, but she forced it back.

Her own father had told her, *All through your flying life, you may have to face the fact that pilots who use the Force will be able to react more quickly, aim more accurately, get*

*the better starfighters, get the greater fame. But those of us
who can't use the Force—well, when we manage to make
it to the top of our profession, we can look the Jedi in the
eye and remind ourselves that we got there without any
crutches.*

The thought soothed her. She activated her repulsorlifts
with a delicacy and precision that had to impress any Jedi
looking her way—she floated exactly a meter off the
hangar floor, not drifting—and turned her attention to one
last check of her instrument readings.

The burners of the Jedi X-wings kicked in and they
launched forward, diving down into a starry black gap
leading to space. A squat armored shuttle lumbered along
in their wake.

"VibroSword Squadron, launch."

On the bridge of *Dodonna,* Admiral Klauskin stood near
the bow viewports, taking in the view and trying to recon-
cile it with the words his aide spoke to him.

To starboard hung the world of Corellia, close by. They
had winked in out of hyperspace on the night side, close
enough that the planet blocked out the sun. The ships belonging to the operation had arrived pointed straight down
at the planet and had executed a simultaneous maneuver to
port, swinging into high orbit and hurtling toward the
planet's sunlit side.

To port cruised the dozens of capital craft belonging to
his operation—cruisers, carriers, destroyers, frigates—and
streaming from them were hundreds of starfighters and
support vehicles. Every one of them cruised with running
lights ablaze. Down on Corellia, all eyes would be at-
tracted to the gleaming beauty of the GA military, to the
flowing formation whose very presence said, *Do not defy
the most powerful authority in the galaxy.*

Klauskin tuned back in to the words of his aide, Fiav
Fenn, a female Sullustan. She was saying something about
the accuracy of their arrival pattern, which had apparently
been pleasingly within the parameters he had set down in

the previous day's staff meeting. He gently shook his head and waved to brush the topic aside. "Ground response?" he asked.

She paused as if to change gears. "None so far."

"None?" Klauskin frowned. "How long since we dropped out of hyperspace?"

"Four minutes thirty-eight seconds," she said. "Thirty-nine, forty, forty-one—"

"Yes, yes." Klauskin blinked. The Corellian armed forces must be very sloppy not to have their first fighter squadrons off the ground after more than four and a half minutes.

Then the other fleet winked into existence.

He saw the flicker of green running lights in his left-side peripheral vision even as the bridge's threat alarms began howling. The admiral spun to look and stood there, transfixed.

Stretched thin as a veil, a formation of spacecraft now occupied space between Klauskin's formation and every reasonable exit path away from Corellia. It was on the same course as Klauskin's fleet, a higher orbit, its vehicles and vessels traveling much faster than Klauskin's in order to maintain the same relationship to the world below and Klauskin's fleet in between.

The admiral could not tell, just by eyeballing, the makeup of the intruder fleet; at this distance, all he could determine was that each of the scores or hundreds of vehicles and vessels had green running lights, an impressive visual formationwide show of unanimity. He wished he'd thought of it for his own formation.

He became aware that his bridge crew was talking, shouting over the threat alarms, doing their business. Words intruded on his shock: ". . . formed up on the far side of Crollia or Soronia and jumped in . . ." ". . . no hostile moves . . ." ". . . communicating among themselves, but haven't opened comm with us . . ."

Klauskin finally regained control of his voice. "Kill the

alarms," he said, his voice, to his own ears, sounding weak. "We already know they're there. Composition?"

"Working on it," his chief sensor operator said. "They have nothing in the size class of *Dodonna*, but they have *Strident*-class Star Defenders and a large number of frigates, corvettes, patrol boats, gunships, and heavy transports. Mostly Corellian Engineering Corporation, of course. They must have lifted every half-finished frame, every rusted hulk, and every pleasure boat insystem to have pulled this off."

Klauskin smiled mirthlessly. "Our sensors can't tell us which are the rusty hulks and which are the shipshape vessels of war, though, can they?"

"No, sir, not at this range. We also count at least a dozen squadrons of starfighters, possibly more—a tight grouping at a distance will sometimes return a signal as a single medium-sized ship. We suspect they're mostly older fighters. Kuat A-Nines and A-Tens, Howlrunners, various classes of TIE fighters."

"With crazed Corellian pilots at the controls," the admiral said.

"Yes, sir."

Klauskin's unobtrusive aide Fiav decided to become more obtrusive, stepping up beside the admiral. "Sir," she whispered, "have you revised orders for the operation?"

"Revised orders?" Klauskin's mind went oddly blank as he considered that question. It was an unsettling feeling, especially in one for whom decisiveness had always been a career hallmark.

Ah, that was the problem. Revised orders should be issued to enable his formation to accomplish its goals despite the complication that the Corellian formation posed. But that was now impossible. The overriding goal of this operation was to use a show of force to induce fear, awe, and consternation in the Corellians.

But he could not do that now. They had matched his first move with an equal move. At this point, they could not be awed by the forces arrayed against them. They could be defeated . . . but a bloodless victory was out of the question.

He had failed. Less than five minutes into his operation, he had failed. His thinking processes became attached to that notion and could not pull free of it.

"Orders, sir?"

Klauskin shook his head. "Continue with the operation as per existing orders," he said. "Redeploy half our starfighter squadrons to positions screening the capital ships. Do not initiate hostile actions."

He turned his back on the Corellian fleet and stared down at the planet's surface, at the gleaming star-like patterns of nighttime cities, at the brightening crescent ahead of the daytime side of the world. Dimly, he was aware that his new orders hadn't accomplished much, and certainly wouldn't do if the Corellians had any more surprises for him.

This was a problem he had to address. He'd get right on that.

VibroSword Squadron launched, a typical fast-moving stream of Eta-5 interceptors. As they poured out of *Dodonna*'s forward-port-flange starfighter hangar, Lysa saw the distant thrusters of Luke Skywalker's Hardpoint Squadron far ahead. Already the Jedi X-wings were roaring down toward the atmosphere for their mission, which would begin on Corellia's day side.

Then Lysa became aware of all the green running lights in the port-side distance. She turned and stared. "Leader, we have a problem . . ." Her voice mixed with others, a sudden babble of alarm across the squadron frequency.

"Maintain course and speed." V-Sword Leader's voice, as ever, was calm, reassuring. This time, at least, it wasn't mocking. "Correction. Stay on me." With that, V-Sword Leader and his wingmate rolled over and looped back almost the way they'd come, heading back toward *Dodonna* but swinging out a bit from the carrier. Once they were parallel to the carrier but out several kilometers, he brought them around again on a course paralleling the capital ship. "This is our new station," he said. "Keep your eyes open for aggressive action by the Corellians."

"Leader, Seven," Lysa said. "Sir, doesn't their just being here constitute aggressive action?"

"They're probably asking the same thing about us, Seven. And the answer to both questions is yes."

"Thank you, sir." Lysa's leg began twitching again. This time she didn't bother to try to control it.

chapter ten

CENTERPOINT STATION,
CORELLIAN SYSTEM

Jacen brushed aside the cloth over his head and peered out—out, up, back.

The conveyance he lay upon was one open-topped car of a repulsor train. The cars, connected end-to-end, floated along a containment track laid years earlier along Centerpoint Station's long axis. Jacen could tell from the way the ceiling was no longer kilometers away but only hundreds of meters above, and getting closer, that they were heading out of the vast open central area known as Hollowtown and into a narrowing choke point toward the station's "top"—the region where the greatest number of significant control chambers had been found, the region where the majority of the investigating scientists' new installations of equipment and computer gear had been made.

Far overhead, Jacen saw a cluster of buildings, blocky apartment residences in subdued brown and green tones that seemed very out of place in this ancient technological artifact. Despite the urgency of his mission, he grinned. He was staring up at the apartments' roofs, which were upside down to him. It had to be disconcerting to emerge every morning from sleep and stare up at a distant floor, one across which turbolifts and repulsor trains were always moving.

He lay alone in the midst of a mound of supplies for the station residents—bolts of cloth, preserved foods, crates full of entertainment data cards, deactivated worker droids. Ben was also aboard the repulsor train, several cars back, maintaining his own hiding place. Jacen had settled on this method of operation as the mission planning entered its final stages. "You'll trail me at a distance of not less than fifty meters," he had said. "Practice stealth techniques and make no effort to contact me unless your life is in danger. If I'm disabled, defeated, sucked through a malfunctioning atmosphere containment shield, or otherwise distracted from my goal, you set out on your own to accomplish it." And Ben had nodded solemnly, perhaps finally being convinced that things were serious by the prospect of performing a mission alone.

The ceiling continued to get closer, until it was a mere thirty meters overhead, and then Jacen lurched as the repulsor train took a sharp turn and a plunging descent into a tunnel. The tunnel was three times the width necessary for the repulsor train and lit by pastel green glow rods at intervals; protruding from the walls every hundred meters or so were box-like metal extrusions. Jacen decided that the tunnel had not been intended by the station's creators for the purpose to which it was now put—the station's new masters had simply discovered it and decided that it would be a convenient way to keep the homely repulsor train out of sight as it entered the station's more sensitive areas.

Someone had marked the metal extrusions with huge painted numbers. Dr. Seyah had explained their meaning—they corresponded to hatches providing access to specific sets of chambers and accessways above and below. Often that access was suitable only for workers or athletes—it was common for it to be no more than a crudely installed, open-sided winch turbolift, the sort found on building construction sites all over Coruscant.

At the box extrusion marked 103, Jacen swung aside the

cloth concealing him, took a careful look around to make sure there were no observers present, and leapt free of his car. He landed beside the box extrusion and moved toward the nearest wall hatch—an access helpfully, if inelegantly, emphasized by splashes of orange paint.

It was a depression in the wall, nearly oval but with more squared-off corners, about two-thirds the height of a human male. The hardened durasteel door plugging it was of modern manufacture, as was the computer control panel mounted on the wall beside it.

Jacen tugged at the bar that indicated the hatch was dogged closed. Only the handle portion of the bar was accessible through an arc-shaped slot in the doorway, and pulling it from the left to the right position should have opened the hatch.

The bar didn't budge. The hatch was locked.

He gave the control panel a look. He knew the combination required to open the door—Dr. Seyah had given it to him. But if CorSec's Intelligence Section mandated different access numbers for different personnel and then tracked their use, using that number would compromise Dr. Seyah.

He ignited his lightsaber and drove it into the hatch toward the base. This was slower going than many obstacles he cut through; the hatch metal was thick and treated against heat. Slowly he pushed it through, and even more slowly he pulled it laterally.

Half a minute later, the edges of the cut glowing gold from the lightsaber's heat, there was an audible *thunk* and the metal bar swung free. Well above the area of overheated metal, Jacen gave the hatch a push and it swung open.

Beyond was a cylindrical metal shaft, almost featureless, lit by green glow rods affixed at intervals. Dangling at head height were four heavy metal cables ending in loops and four lighter cables ending in small two-button controls, standard for industrial lifting and lowering. Jacen nodded. In ordinary use, a worker would attach a personal safety hook to one of the loops and activate the corresponding

LIFT button. Jacen merely put his lightsaber away, grabbed a loop with his left hand, and punched the LIFT button with his right. The winch controls at the top of the shaft activated and raised him with arm-jarring swiftness.

Moments later, forty meters up, the ride came to an end. A circular side tunnel led away from the shaft. Jacen gave himself the most fleeting push with the Force and swung over the floor of that tunnel, then dropped noiselessly. A few meters down, a ramp led up to another modern-era hatch.

The dogging bar on this hatch was already in the right-hand position, and the control panel beside the hatch was not lit. Jacen stared at it for a moment. Dr. Seyah had given him the access code for this hatch, too, but apparently it wasn't needed now.

Apparently.

Jacen took his lightsaber in hand again and pushed the hatch open.

It required a little more push than its mass would ordinarily have called for. The atmospheric pressure on the other side of the hatch was higher than on Jacen's side, and once he got the hatch more than a hand span open cool air began to pour across him. He shoved the hatch open far enough to see through—there was only darkness beyond—and then wider yet. Once beyond, he slowly shut the hatch, not letting the air pressure differential slam it shut.

Here, the only sounds were his own breathing and echoes from the air-conditioning system. He could not see anything, but the chamber felt large, very large. He nodded. That matched what Dr. Seyah had told him; this was supposed to be a featureless oval chamber, big enough to host small-scale groundspeeder races, its purpose unknown. On the far side would be a set of ramps allowing access to a higher walkway level, which would, in turn, give him access to Centerpoint Station's control room governing the station's artificial gravity generators. Those generators had been installed over several years and only recently made completely operational.

The hatch by which he'd entered went *thunk*. The control panel next to it lit up, the red and yellow glows from the numbered buttons providing Jacen with just enough light to see himself and the floor.

Jacen cleared his throat. He raised his voice so that it would carry. "Am I about to endure a speech?"

Far overhead, banks of white light came on, dazzlingly bright. Jacen shaded his eyes, focused his attention on the Force—on incoming danger, on malevolent intent.

There was none.

But a voice came from those walkways high on the other side of the chamber. "Is this somebody's sense of humor? Sending *you*?"

As Jacen's vision cleared, he saw a man in deep blue civilian dress—boots, pants, ruffly tunic, and open overcoat—and a dozen armored CorSec agents up on the balcony that was Jacen's route out of the chamber. Though Jacen knew the man, he still felt a momentary shock of a different sort of recognition.

For the man wore the face of Han Solo—but bearded, a little leaner, a little grayer, and possessed of a confidence that looked like political arrogance rather than Jacen's father's cockiness.

"Thrackan Sal-Solo," Jacen said. "I thought you were spending all your time groundside on Corellia, telling the population what to think and pretending not to be a convicted felon."

"Little Jacen." His father's near double gave him a condescending smile. "I'm also still in charge of restoring Centerpoint Station. And when word reached me that the GA intended to execute an offensive in Corellian space, an offensive that was premature by almost every political measurement—*unless* you factored in the possibility that they knew just how close I was to restoring the station to full operability—I decided I needed to be here. To prepare against strike teams. And commandos. And Jedi."

Jacen gave his cousin an admonishing look. "You can never prepare against Jedi."

"Yes, you can. And I must admit to being offended. For a target as important as Centerpoint Station, shouldn't they have sent Luke Skywalker? Are you stronger than he?"

Jacen offered a humorless smile. "No, just educated in different directions. Besides, it's been my experience that anyone who claims to be stronger than Luke Skywalker receives a lot of grief from his admirers."

Thrackan gave Jacen an expression of sympathy. "I understand that. Just as they criticize one who claims to be more Corellian than Han Solo."

"So." Jacen held up his lightsaber but left it unlit. "Would you and your troops do me a favor and get out of my way? There will be fewer severed limbs that way. Or heads."

Again, Thrackan offered him a pitying look. "Jacen, we can't afford to let you damage or destroy this station. It's not going to happen. Surrender now and you won't be killed. You won't even be hurt."

"Uh-huh." Jacen began walking toward the foot of the closest ramp below Thrackan.

Thrackan, nonchalant, held a hand out to his side. One of the CorSec officers there handed him what looked like a flight helmet. With slow, deliberate motions, watching Jacen all the time, Thrackan donned it. Then he snapped his fingers. Two droids, looking much like R5 astromechs but with their top halves removed and replaced by naked machinery, rolled up from behind the CorSec officers to the rail.

And the sound began.

Jacen didn't even experience it as sound at first. It hit him like a windstorm, blasting him to his knees, bringing pain to every millimeter of his skin as though he were being scorched by a gigantic blowtorch. His lightsaber fell from his lifeless fingers and rolled away.

Even as the attack convulsed him with pain, Jacen, in some dim portion of his mind that still functioned, recognized it—a sonic assault, something that did not have to be aimed or tracked to bring a Jedi down.

Moving from shadow to shadow with the noiselessness of a ghost, Ben reached the hatch Jacen had entered just in time to hear it *thunk* to a locked position, to see its control board light up. He stared at it in momentary confusion. Why would Jacen have locked him out?

Then he heard voices approaching from the tunnel's other end—voices and footsteps, some of them ringing heavily on the tunnel's metal floor. Ben sprinted back the way he'd come, to the lip of the vertical shaft.

There he hesitated. If he leapt for one of the cables and rode it back down, his presence would be detected—the *whir* of the winch, the swinging of the cable would give him away.

Instead, he moved to the side of the tunnel and swung over the lip of the vertical shaft, holding on by one hand, his other hand on the lightsaber at his belt. Four motionless fingers would be much less likely to be detected than a swinging winch cable.

He held his breath while the footsteps, seemingly more and more numerous, approached. They halted meters away, though—at Jacen's hatch, he assumed.

A woman said, "Set up here. Keep your eyes on the entire corridor. The Jedi have a nasty habit of cutting through walls where you don't expect them. Nine-two-Z, position yourself here." That command was followed by heavy, clanging footsteps.

Ben dared to pull himself up and peer over the lip.

A detachment of armored CorSec soldiers was set up outside the hatch. There were two unliving things with them—Ben recognized YVH combat droids, machines of war designed to fight the Yuuzhan Vong. Shaped roughly like humans but taller and thicker in the chest, they packed immense firepower and combat programming.

These two also carried backpacks huge enough to hold a full-grown human male. One of them, approaching, came to a stop before the CorSec woman at the door. She continued, "All right, troopers. At the first sign of intrusion, draw back to form a firing line and open up on the enemy. Nine-two-Z, at the first sighting of a Jedi, approach it. When you've gotten as close as you think you can get, trigger your load."

The droid nodded. "Acknowledged," it said, its voice artificial, emotionless.

The woman continued, speaking to the others: "You hear that? You see the droid go into motion, *run*. Once it's detonated, return and mop up."

Ben lowered himself below the lip again.

This was bad, bad, bad. That backpack had to be full of explosives or something worse. And the woman's instructions meant that if the droid detected Jacen *or* Ben, it would attack. Ben didn't think he could take out a YVH combat droid—certainly not before it detected him and blew up.

He let go of the lip of the tunnel.

With the Force, he pressed himself up against the wall of the vertical shaft, the friction of his cloak on the metal slowing his descent. He slid almost noiselessly back down the forty meters he'd so recently ascended. As he approached the last five meters, he let go completely and dropped naturally, going into a tuck-and-roll as he hit, rolling away from the shaft. Now he'd be out of sight if any CorSec soldiers heard something and came to investigate.

He was on his own now. He had to try to complete the mission by himself.

He'd just abandoned his teacher, his cousin. A sort of numbness tried to creep its way into his thoughts. He shook it off and ran back toward the hatch to the repulsor train tunnel.

CORONET, CORELLIA

Jaina stood over the injured and unconscious body of Zekk, her lightsaber lit and in a ready position. Four YVH combat droids, situated behind crashed CorSec airspeeders, poured near-continuous blasterfire at her. She'd been able to deflect it all, mostly into the permacrete or back toward the firers, but none of her return shots had done them any significant damage, and the high intensity of their blasters and rapid rate of fire were tiring her. She needed just a second of rest to compose herself, to sweep the droids away—but they weren't giving her a second.

Then a line of concentrated blue light leapt into existence behind the most distant of the combat droids. Jaina saw it flash around in an arc, and the combat droid's head leapt from its shoulders with a shower of sparks.

The other combat droids turned to look. Jaina took the opportunity to move forward, a little to the side, and could see Kolir. The Bothan Jedi, incongruous with her party-girl dress, her lightsaber combat stance, and the blood streaming from the right side of her mouth, kicked the droid's remains off its feet and turned to face the other three.

Their blasters swung around—but Jaina had had her second of composure. She reached up and tugged at a large cargo drone, causing it to gain a few meters' altitude, then to plummet—right onto two of the droids. It smashed down on them with the weight of tons of cargo. Jaina had a brief glimpse of plastic and metal crates leaping up from the drone's cargo bed, spilling out in all directions. Not all the drone's momentum was down—it continued bouncing forward, and then, its computer programs demonstrating considerable skill, became airborne again. It roared away from the scene at full speed, three-quarters of its cargo still skidding and rolling along the avenue.

Jaina launched herself forward. An impact like that would kill most living beings—might kill an armored bantha—but would only delay YVH droids. In midair, she twisted aside and missed being hit by a veering blue airspeeder; as she did, she saw Kolir advancing on the last upright YVH as it fired at her.

She landed beside a permacrete crater that had been the last location she'd seen one of the combat droids. As she came down, she saw that it wasn't a crater; it was actually a hole punched through into sewers or storm drains beneath.

The YVH droid came leaping up through it, facing her. Jaina flashed her lightsaber across its midsection as it rose. She felt the considerable drag that the droid's combat armor caused even to a lightsaber blade, but the blade emerged from the other side and the droid crashed to the pavement in two pieces.

One of those pieces was still dangerous. It rolled over and began to bring its blaster rifle up. Jaina stepped in and whipped her blade across the blaster, cutting it in two just forward of its power supply. Then she drove her blade into the crippled droid's chest, dragging it around to wreak as much damage to the droid's internal weapons systemry as possible.

Another YVH head landed a meter from her feet. She chalked that up as a second Kolir kill and spun toward the last known location of the fourth YVH droid.

It was rising, its back to Jaina, so much permacrete adhering to it that it appeared to have a new layer of badly installed armor. Jaina glanced over her shoulder, saw another high-mass drone speeder approaching—this one, she noted with satisfaction, a small tanker carrying a load of uncured duracrete. She yanked at it through the Force and brought it down atop the last droid, driving and grinding it forward along the avenue. She saw pieces of the droid severed by the high-mass attack—here an arm, there a leg. Once it was well past her, there was a muffled *boom* from beneath the nose of the airspeeder as something in the droid's chest exploded.

Jaina spared a glance back at Zekk. He lay unmoving where she'd left him. A passerby, a man in green business dress, was kneeling over him, but his intent did not seem hostile; he was reaching for Zekk's wrist as if to check his pulse.

Jaina turned to Kolir. "What's your status?"

"My teef are looshe on the right shide." With each word

Kolir spoke, more blood dribbled from her mouth and down her side, but she seemed unconcerned. "There'sh Thann." She pointed with her lightsaber.

The Falleen Jedi was indeed headed their way, bouncing from speeder to speeder in the oncoming traffic lane like a hyperkinetic insect.

And no wonder—blasterfire from two streaming sources was dogging him. Jaina saw him ducking under one stream, batting the other away, the second stream moving him laterally because he was in midleap when it reached him.

From her position, Jaina could distantly see the second YVH droid. The duracrete tanker she'd used to crush her last opponent was still moving forward, even picking up speed as it tried to get clear of the combat zone. Jaina reached out for the tanker again and diverted it from its intended flight path; it came down hard on top of the combat droid, grinding it to pieces as efficiently as it had the previous one.

Kolir's tactic was similarly subtle. She picked up the blaster rifle of the first combat droid she'd destroyed. It took her a moment to swing the weapon, oversized and ungainly for her small frame, into line; then, bracing herself, she fired off a stream of blasterfire at the second distant combat droid. Jaina saw at least two of the blasts hit the droid and glance off.

But the assault was enough to get the droid's attention. It swung around and focused on Kolir. Thann dropped from the sky to land beside it, severing its legs at the knees, then hacked at what remained until it was in too many pieces to do anyone any harm.

Moments later, running at Jedi sprint speed, the Falleen warrior rejoined them at Zekk's side. The passerby who'd taken Zekk's pulse took a look at the three lightsabers and stood up and away from Zekk, his hands half raised. "I didn't do anything."

"I know," Jaina said. "You'd better go."

He turned and was gone. Jaina knelt beside Zekk, put

her hand on an unburned portion of his neck. He still felt strong.

"This operation's a bust," she said, "and from the looks of things, the guards down by the gates are massing for a run at us. Let's deprive them of the opportunity to get themselves killed. Thann, secure us some transportation."

"Done." The Falleen pulled something from a belt pouch. It was an identicard in the same basic gold tone as CorSec investigators carried, though it correctly identified him as a member of the Jedi order. He stood and walked toward oncoming traffic, one hand holding the identicard high and the other raised to encourage someone to stop.

And as he walked his skin rippled in color from its near orange to a deeper, huskier red.

Jaina's pulse quickened, and not just from an intellectual recognition of what Thann was doing. The Falleen had tremendous control over emission of pheromones, chemical cues that dictated many types of emotional response, chiefly affecting members of the opposite sex. Thann was using both the Force and his pheromonal powers to attract, confuse, and overwhelm someone in the oncoming traffic lane, probably also using the Force to make his identicard look like something of local significance . . .

In her peripheral vision, Jaina saw Kolir sway. The Bothan Jedi reached out and Jaina caught her hand, steadying her. "He shouldn't do that while I'm injured," Kolir said.

A red groundspeeder, its driver a dark-haired human female wearing red-tinted racing goggles, pulled up beside Thann. Her features, angular and distinct, relaxed into a blank lack of expression. "Is there a problem, Officer?" she asked.

Thann's voice was as smooth as that of an actor in a holodrama. "Two of my fellow officers are hurt," he said. "We need to get them to medical care and to chase some bad guys. Can we borrow your speeder?"

"You can borrow my speeder," she said.

Thann waved Jaina and Kolir forward. "You'd better

hop out," he told the driver. "This is going to be danger-ous."

"I'll hop out." The driver exited the speeder on the side-walk side.

"And don't tell anyone who you are or the details of your speeder. They're all spies trying to catch us," Thann said.

"I won't tell anyone."

Jaina exerted herself and Zekk floated up a meter into the air. In moments she had him laid out faceup in the backseat, his head in her lap, while Thann and Kolir took the front.

Thann blew a kiss to the dazed driver, then set the speeder into motion, fearlessly merging with traffic. "Con-trol acknowledged my transmission," he said. "But Team Tauntaun didn't. I suspect they ran into a trap."

"Right." Jaina rapped her knuckles against the speeder's side. Nothing had gone right, and now the three Jedi of Team Tauntaun—Tahiri Veila, Doran Tainer, and Tiu Zax—were incommunicado.

"You shouldn't do that, you know," Kolir said.

Thann spared her a glance. "Do what?"

"Use Jedi mind tricksh and pheromonesh at the shame time. Not fair."

Thann shrugged. "I should perhaps use the mind tricks alone and maybe fail?"

"Well, no."

Thann changed the subject. "How's Zekk?"

Zekk said, "Ow." His eyes opened.

"Better," Jaina said.

chapter eleven

ABOVE CORELLIA

Luke's Hardpoint Squadron made a high orbital crossing over to Corellia's day side and then a fast descent into the atmosphere. The squad's speed was hampered by its having to shepherd the shuttle *Chandrila Skies,* an Uulshos space-capable light assault vehicle. Not much longer than an X-wing, the LAV had a horizontal chisel-shaped bow and was much broader across the fuselage than a starfighter, giving it enough interior room to carry a dozen or so passengers . . . making it a good choice for the extraction of the teams of Jedi now operating down in Coronet.

Despite the fact that the Corellian fleet continued to pace and, by its very presence, taunt the GA fleet, no units had moved out against Luke's X-wings. But now Mara's voice came across squadron frequency: "We've got some distant activity, looks like fighter swarms rising to meet us from Coronet."

Luke checked his own sensors. They did show a couple of fuzzy signals from ahead, but to his eye they could have been two cargo craft launching, or a swarm of airspeeders punching up above approved travel routes. Mara, designated sensor officer for this mission, had a more capable set of sensors than Luke did.

Mara's voice came back: "Confirmed two squadrons.

Probably some class of TIE, based on their movement patterns. We'll be within maximum laser range in two minutes."

A pity. Luke looked off to port, down at the planetary surface. Here, it was all green forest separated from blue sea by thin lines of sandy golden beach. Such a pretty world. It was a shame that they had to send flaming starfighters and their pilots crashing down onto it.

A new voice came across the comm: "Attention starfighter flight approaching Coronet from course three-five-seven. This is Corellian Defense Force Headquarters in Coronet. You are classed as a hostile. Identify yourself or return to space."

Luke switched his comm unit to broadcast on the same frequency. "This is Hardpoint Squadron of the Galactic Alliance Second Fleet, Luke Skywalker commanding. If your transponder hasn't recognized us as a legitimate GA unit by now, it's faulty. I'm transmitting you our ID . . . and your orders. Stand down." He switched off the speaker and added, "Artoo, send the package."

Artoo wheedled, the sound emerging from the cockpit speakers, acknowledging that the data package was away.

The land below was becoming less forest, more irrigated fields. Luke could see sailing craft, excursion boats, out on the water.

The Corellian comm officer's voice came back after a moment. "I'm sorry, but Corellia does not recognize the authority claimed in these orders. Turn back or be fired upon."

Luke shook his head and did not reply; he reset his comm board to squadron frequency. On his sensor board, squadrons of incoming craft were clearly visible, arriving from two different vectors. Ahead, he could see the near edge of the city of Coronet . . . and, above it, the two units of incoming fighter craft that looked like Corellian attack fighters. He counted eighteen of them on his sensor board, and that just wasn't enough to pose a serious threat to a squadron of ten Jedi pilots.

Then the incoming squadrons turned aside, one to starboard and one to port, at right angles to Hardpoint Squadron's course.

Luke felt a trickle of alarm. "Roll out!" he shouted, and followed his own orders, snapping his X-wing into a port roll. He was aware of Mara keeping close to him, just behind and to starboard.

An explosion shook his snubfighter and rattled his teeth. R2-D2 howled but immediately began putting diagnostics up on Luke's data screen.

Luke ended his roll a quick kilometer lower than his original position. Explosions continued to batter at his eardrums, but nothing as close as the first one. He glanced between his sensor board and the skies above.

The skies were filled with puffy gray clouds. They looked benign, but each was the lingering evidence of an explosion— results of a ground-based antispacecraft barrage.

Luke counted ten X-wings still flying. He breathed a sigh of relief. Then his breath caught. There should be eleven craft. *"Chandrila Skies?"* he asked.

"Took a direct hit," Mara said. "She's gone."

The skies ahead of Hardpoint Squadron began to fill up with gray clouds, and beyond them two squadrons of Corellian attack fighers danced around, waiting.

"Three, inform *Dodonna* of our situation," Luke told his communications specialist. "See if they have updated orders to offer. Meanwhile, we're going in. If we can't get another shuttle, we'll bring our Jedi off Corellia if we have to land one by one and stuff them into our cargo hatches."

"We have telemetry on CEC-One," Fiav said to Klauskin, giving this operation's designation for the nearest of the Corellian Engineering Corporation's orbital shipyards. The course followed by *Dodonna* and the rest of her group would eventually bring her up on CEC-One. "It's protected by a large number of starfighters and a handful of frigates. And there's the likelihood that, as we approach, units from the main Corellian fleet will close."

"Acknowledged," Klauskin said. He kept his attention on space dead ahead, where, eventually, CEC-One would be close enough for him to make visual contact.

Fiav paused, as if waiting for a more comprehensive response, then continued. "Corellian starfighter squadrons are crowding our squadrons. They're just jockeying around, but eventually somebody's going to cut loose with a laser shot and it's going to be a fight."

Klauskin nodded briskly. "Understood."

Fiav paused again, then finally said, "Luke Skywalker reports that his squadron has been fired on, and that their shuttle has been lost. They request an additional shuttle, but he also says he'll extract his ground team individually in the X-wings if he has to."

"Ah, good. I'm glad he has a plan."

Fiav's voice sounded pained. "Sir, do you have any order revisions?"

"Yes." Klauskin was pleased with the decisiveness he could hear in his voice. "Bring the group down to half forward speed."

"Yes, sir. Um, do we provide the Jedi with another shuttle?"

"Oh, no. Skywalker sounds like he has everything in hand."

"Yes, sir." The words hung there for long moments, then Fiav turned away to implement Klauskin's orders.

Klauskin felt his brain revving like an overtuned thruster engine. Slowing the group to half speed would give him more time to decide, to think his way out of this dilemma.

He needed the time. He thought and thought, but nothing seemed to happen.

He had to turn the group toward space, batter his way through the Corellian screen if they decided to hinder his progress, and make it far enough out from Corellia's gravity well to activate hyperdrives.

But that wasn't enough. He couldn't just run. He had to do something to salvage this mission. He had to intimidate or embarrass the Corellians, decisively. Somewhere. Somehow.

"V-Swords, heads up." That was the voice of VibroSword Leader. "We have a unit incoming."

On Lysa's sensor board, the swirl looked like a small formation of Corellian attack fighters. They weren't headed straight in; they had detached themselves from the Corellian fleet and were angling in, a course that was the counterpart of the interceptors', bringing them closer and closer to VibroSword Squadron.

"They're daring us." That was V-Sword Eight, Lysa's wingman, a Quarren male from Mon Calamari.

"That's right," Leader said. "So keep it under control. Remember, first one to twitch loses."

Eight asked, "And the first one to blink?"

"The first to blink will be Corellians, Eight. Now pipe down."

The attack fighters got closer and closer. Soon Lysa could count them on the sensor board—a full squadron dozen— and not long after that she could make them out visually as, now only a kilometer distant, they crossed in front of the stars. And on they came.

Lysa said, "Leader, Seven. I think they're going to continue their course straight through us."

"Seven, you're probably right. Squadron, they're going to move through our position as if they don't see us. Trying to make us flinch. Bring your shields up only if it's a sure thing you're going to be hit and announce the impact. If you hear me say *Incoming,* break by wing pairs, bring shields and weapons up, and attack at will. VibroSword Squadron doesn't flinch."

Lysa heard a chorus of affirmatives from her fellow pilots, added her own to it.

Inside, she felt sick. This wasn't a clean fight; it was confused and tense, and about nothing but playing a game of dominance. She hated it. Her father would have hated it.

She waited.

CORONET, CORELLIA

As the Jedi's commandeered groundspeeder hurtled along one of Coronet's main avenues in thinning traffic, a howl of distant space raid sirens filled the air, and tiny gray clouds began to pop up in the skies to the east, the direction of the groundspeeder's destination. Thann handled the speeder yoke with one hand, keeping his comlink pressed up between ear and mouth with the other.

Zekk, still stretched out on the backseat and Jaina's lap, had his eyes closed again. He hadn't passed out—he had sunk into a short-term Jedi healing trance, one that would help him deal with the damage of the burns and shrapnel, so that his injuries would not hinder him as much when the time came for action.

Thann put his comlink away.

"What's the situation?" Jaina shouted to him.

Thann pointed toward the distant gray antispacecraft clouds. "That? That's your uncle Luke and the Jedi coming to take us offplanet. But they've lost their shuttle and he doesn't think they're getting another one."

"Ah," Jaina said.

"Team Tauntaun was ambushed the way we were, except that they got inside Sal-Solo's mansion. They were attacked by troops and probots."

"Where are they now?"

"They're stealing a speeder and will rendezvous with us. They're thinking of stealing some payroll credit chips, or kidnapping a holodrama star so we won't come back empty-handed."

"Good of them. Anything else?"

"The fleet jumped in and was ambushed, too. Nothing much is going right."

"We need a spaceport," Jaina shouted. "We'll have to steal a shuttle."

"All nonmilitary air and space travel will be shut down until things are settled. And the Coronet spaceport is going to be crawling with CorSec."

"There are smaller ports. Private spaceports, spaceports for outlying communities. And they'll have charter shuttle services," Jaina said.

"I'm on it." Kolir's right cheek bulged with the cloth she'd stuffed in there to stanch the flow of blood. She reached into her blood-spattered bag and drew out a datapad. Opening it, she began searching the Coronet database she'd loaded into it.

"Find one with a female manager on duty," Thann said. Kolir grimaced at him.

"It'll speed things up," he said.

"If I ever find out you do that to get datesh," she said, "I'm going to cut shomething off you."

"I am an ethical Jedi," Thann said. Jaina couldn't tell whether the indignation his tone expressed was real or affected. Thann showed more emotion than most Falleen, but often it was a deliberate display, an attempt to put others at ease, rather than what he was truly feeling. "I only twist people's minds in the line of duty."

CENTERPOINT STATION

Jacen rolled sideways, kicking the metal floor to propel himself, and managed to be a meter away when the first blaster bolt hit the spot where he'd been kneeling. He continued the roll, awkward because of the pain that racked him, but came up on his feet. Despite his blurring vision, he saw his lightsaber rolling across the floor, extended his hand toward it—

Two white egg-shaped canisters hit the floor near him. He leapt backward away from them, rotating through the air as he went, and came down on his feet, but his legs buckled as he landed and he crashed to the floor.

He could still see his lightsaber. He exerted his will toward it. It wobbled on the floor and began rolling toward him.

The egg-shaped canisters detonated, filling the air around them with white smoke. It rapidly spread, obscuring everything. But Jacen managed to maintain his focus, and his lightsaber flew to his hand before the whiteness closed down all vision.

Jacen rolled to the side again, heard and felt the heat from blasterfire hitting where he'd just lain. *So they can see,* he thought. *Optics in their helmets.* There had to be sound bafflers, too.

Well, he had a couple of tricks remaining, and they had nothing to do with specialized gear.

He knew more about pain than his opponents realized. At the height of the Yuuzhan Vong war, he'd been a prisoner for months, subjected to their tortures and customs of self-inflicted agony. He had learned to function within their Embrace of Pain and other rituals that would break beings not accustomed to such hardships.

A sudden infliction of pain could surprise him, surely. But it couldn't keep him down.

He let the pain flow through him as though it were the Force. He internalized it, experiencing it as an old friend— albeit an old friend he didn't necessarily want visiting him too often.

He stood and moved forward. His first few steps were awkward and slow, his later ones sure, and once he was in full mastery of his body and the pain that suffused it, he put on a burst of speed in traditional Jedi fashion, outracing the blaster bolts that tailed him.

Pain-racked, unslowed, he neared the wall and leapt high up on it, landing on one of the ascending ramps. Now he was still within the smoke cloud from the canisters but shielded from blasterfire from above. Moments later he reached the walkway level where Thrackan Sal-Solo had stood.

He still could not see, but through the Force he could detect living beings ahead of him. They were changing their order, some retreating, some advancing, the foremost of them aiming . . .

The blaster bolts came, illuminating the canister smoke in curiously beautiful lines as they flashed toward him. He batted them back the way they'd come, mercilessly picking off the soldiers who'd fired them.

Then he changed tactics. There were curious gaps in the formation of the living ahead of them. Those gaps had to be where the droid generators of the sonic waves were situated. He began batting blasterfire toward them, and a moment later the pain-inducing shriek was reduced in volume by half. Three blaster bolts later, the sound and pain cut off entirely, and he could hear a mechanical cough as the motivator of the second sonic generator droid detonated dully within its housing.

"Ccase fire." That was the voice of Thrackan, coming from the rear of the unit of six remaining CorSec operatives. They obeyed. "Impressive, Jacen. But I'd like you to understand. We have more than enough troops, droids, and special surprises to deal with you. They're here or rushing here. You're never going to get anywhere you can do significant harm to this station."

"You may be right, cousin." *But you haven't mentioned Ben. You're not aware of him, are you?* "Still, I have to try."

The smoke was beginning to clear. Jacen could see the nearest three CorSec operatives, one kneeling, two standing, resolutely barring his way with their blaster rifles raised.

"I suppose you do. Resume fire."

The soldiers opened fire. Jacen advanced, hurling the blaster bolts back the way they'd come—but over the firers' shoulders, in the direction of Sal-Solo's voice.

CORONET, CORELLIA

Suddenly the explosions ended and the skies to port, starboard, and ahead were clear of gray smoke.

Luke checked his diagnostics board. His X-wing had suffered some shrapnel damage to its top-side starboard engine, but it was still running at 60 percent capacity.

There were only nine X-wings in his squadron now. The snubfighter of the Rodian, Toile Senn, had been shaken to pieces by three near hits. Toile had ejected . . . and at the apex of the ejection had disappeared in the center of another gray cloud. Luke had felt the sudden cessation of his life.

Now they emerged into the open skies where the Corellian attack fighters lived. "Keep sharp," Luke said, one eye to his sensor board. "S-wings to attack position. Break and attack at will. Continue toward original rendezvous position."

"They're coming at us from high, straight back," Mara said.

And they were, two streams of attack fighters roaring down at them. Luke dived, giving his X-wing more speed, more time before the foremost attack fighters reached him, and adjusted his shield strength to double rear; Mara stayed tucked in on his wing.

The attack fighters came on, green lasers battering at Luke's rear shields. R2 squealed a note of alarm—alarm for Luke and alarm for himself.

As the three attack fighters approaching from astern neared, as their laser barrage hit his rear shields with the strength of greater proximity, Luke cut his thrusters. He could feel Mara, through their link, understand his intent and do likewise.

Inexperienced fighter pilots would have overshot him and been easy targets for a moment or two. These Corellians weren't inexperienced. The moment Luke's X-wing began to grow too fast in their forward sights, they veered, two upward, one to starboard.

But Luke was far from inexperienced himself. Instinct and a touch, a glimpse of the future through the Force, had him hauling back on his control yoke and goosing his repulsorlift the moment he completed his deceleration maneuver. He was oriented upward as his pursuers banked. The only things he could see were blue sky and two Corellian attack fighters, one of them jittering madly in his targeting computer. He fired, red lasers closing on and hitting the port-side attack fighter, then traversed right again and fired even before the computer confirmed a lock.

Luke's first shot blew his target cleanly out of the sky. His second sheared the attack fighter's starboard wing off. The crippled fighter spun and plummeted, out of the combat.

These Corellian attack fighters were not equipped with shields. Luke shook his head over that, even as he looked with his eyes and his Force-senses for his wife.

She'd peeled off to starboard and vaped the attack fighter that had headed off in that direction. Now she was angled back his way.

Luke checked the sensor board. Nine X-wings and eighteen attack fighters had entered combat. Seconds later, nine X-wings and eleven attack fighters continued to occupy the field. He sighed. He was facing Corellians as brave, perhaps as skilled, as his friends Han, Wedge, and Corran, and he was obliged to purge them from the skies. Sometimes he bitterly regretted the oaths and traditions that bound the Jedi order to the Galactic Alliance.

He turned back in the direction of the conflict. Mara tucked in under his port side and matched his speed and course.

ABOVE CORELLIA

Lysa's sensor board lit up like a festival parade. She glanced at the readings. Someone had a targeting lock on her. She forced herself to ignore that fact. Her leg bounced even more frantically.

"Leader, Eight." Eight's voice sounded anguished. "They have a targeting lock on me. Permission to break and fire."

"Denied, Eight." VibroSword Leader sounded exasperated.

"They're just trying to rattle you, Eight," Lysa said. "Provoke a reaction."

"Seven's right, Eight. Concentrate on her. Do as she does."

Lysa perked up. That was one of the few completely un-sarcastic, unambiguously positive things Leader had said about her in the few months she'd been with the squadron—and he was saying it to a pilot with a year's worth of seniority on her.

Now she could see the oncoming attack fighters clearly in the light reflected from Corellia's surface. They glided toward VibroSword Squadron on what looked like an atmospheric arrival vector—as slow and unconcerned as if there were no interceptor unit in their direct path.

She eyeballed their approach. If they didn't vary their angle, they'd pass right through the center of the Eta-5 formation, coming closest to V-Swords Five and Six.

They did vary their angle. One wing pair of attack fighters adjusted, subtly, putting them on a direct intercept path with Five and Six. Another pair vectored slightly, putting them on a straight course toward the positions Seven and Eight would occupy in about ten seconds.

"Leader—"

"Shut up, Eight. Stay on Seven."

"Clamp down on it, Eight," Lysa said. She put her finger on the switch to activate her deflector shields. Minimal as they were compared with X-wing shields, they'd still provide some defense from an impact or an attack fighter's laser.

Five and Six would contact their opposite numbers first, she calculated. They were only a few dozen meters apart now. Lysa could have looked straight up and seen her own attack fighter opposition gliding toward her, closing slowly and implacably, but she didn't. She watched the sensor board, tracking Five and Six as well as her own opponent's progress.

And then the green blip representing V-Sword Five and the red blip of Five's opposite number merged for a moment.

"This is Five." Behind the woman's voice, Lysa could hear cockpit impact alarms ringing. "Impact."

"Incoming," Leader said.

Lysa snapped her shields on and kicked her maneuvering thrusters to point her nose down toward the planet's surface. Then she fired her main thrusters, putting the full thrust of its twin ion engines into the underbelly of the attack fighter just three meters away. Her Eta-5 leapt away from that fighter and its wingmate, hurtling toward the planet's atmosphere.

"Hey!" She saw Eight's green blip belatedly follow. "Where the wobber—hey, I'm hit!"

"How bad?" Now at full thrust, Lysa began a slow loop up from the planet, a maneuver designed to bring her around to the far side of what had been the attack fighter formation. An attack fighter taking a straight line to intercept her could do so, but one following in her wake would be left behind by the faster Eta-5 interceptor.

"No damage, shield took it. He's not pursuing."

"So why mention it?"

"Yours is a kill."

Lysa's eyebrows rose. She'd expected her thruster blast to do some harm to the fighter, perhaps surprise the pilot and cause him to bank away reflexively, but it must have penetrated the cockpit.

She felt—she wasn't sure how she felt.

Save up your feelings for later. Save your feelings for home. Her father's voice again, something he'd said to her fifty times over the years. She decided to listen to him.

Her loop completed, she looked down at the Eta-5/ attack fighter engagement with both eye and sensor. Her comrades and their opponents were stretched out in a rough line a couple of kilometers long, wing pairs circling one another in a dogfight.

A line—she liked lines. She oriented toward one end of it and continued her full-power thruster burn. "Get ready to do some shooting, Eight."

"I—yes. I'm your wing."

chapter twelve

Fiav stepped up to Admiral Klauskin. "Sir, there's been an incident. One of our starfighter squadrons has rubbed up against one of theirs, and they're fully engaged now. More squadrons from both sides are moving in to join the conflict."

Klauskin nodded. "Good, good."

"Sir, with all due respect, that's *not* good. It's not part of our operation goals." The Sullustan lowered her voice. "It would be a big help to officer morale if you'd let them know what our revised goals are. Are we going to assault CEC-One? Because as soon as we get to it, its defenders are definitely going to assault *us*. Are we going to punch back out of system? Are we going to take on the Corellian fleet?"

Klauskin considered her questions. He realized he was curiously without emotion on these matters. But that, at least, would allow him to make decisions logically.

No, assaulting the shipyard designated CEC-One was not part of their operation. They wanted it intact for the day when Corellia was back in the GA camp and everyone was friendly again. But that meant they'd have to alter their current orbital course, so some other plan had to be implemented.

Punch back out of system and go home with their tails

between their legs? Unacceptable. That would make this operation a failure. That would make *him* a failure.

Attacking the Corellian fleet seemed to be the best alternative of the ones presented to him. But he had insufficient information about the composition of the enemy fleet. The Corellians probably wouldn't be a match for his force, but they had the home advantage, might have some tricks standing by, and could seriously deplete his group before they were defeated.

He resented the fact that his alternatives were so few in number. He needed a new idea, a better idea. He wished he could return to his cabin for a while, lie down, and talk to . . . to . . .

"Edela," he whispered.

He should have remembered not to whisper near a Sullustan. Their big ears weren't just for show. "Edela?" Fiav said. "Your wife?"

"Yes."

"Sir, she's been dead for four years."

"Yes, I know."

Then the answer came. Yes, a rest, some downtime—a planetside station for some rest and recreation. That's what they needed.

He felt energy course within him again. "Which is the fifth inhabited planet here? Talus or Tralus?"

The Sullustan's big eyes blinked in surprise, perhaps at the admiral's sudden strength of tone. "Um, they both are. They orbit a common point in space. So one is fourth sometimes, and then the fifth the rest of the time."

"Which one is fifth *now*?"

Fiav raised a comlink to her lips, spoke, listened. "Tralus, sir."

"Set a course for Tralus. Communicate it to our entire force, but it's not to be implemented yet. Stand by to recall all non-hyperdrive-equipped starfighters and support vessels and to issue an optional recall to those with hyperdrives. Who's our best officer for planning city- and planetary-scale assaults on short notice—*very* short notice?"

Fiav blinked again. "I'll find out, sir."

"When you find out, put him or her in charge of planning an assault for the occupation of Tralus. I want the best plan we can get in fifteen minutes." Klauskin clamped down on a laugh that was trying to well up within him.

Suddenly he felt alive again, in charge of his destiny.

This operation would *not* fail. It would *not* be his fault.

A disc-shaped transport of Corellian design popped into existence ahead of *Dodonna*. "And blow that hunk of junk out of the sky," Klauskin said.

A sensor officer at a station on the lower level shouted, "That's a friendly, sir. *Millennium Falcon*."

Klauskin glowered over the edge of the walkway at the sensor officer. "So we can't destroy him?"

"That's, uh, right, sir."

"Well, tell him to get that deathtrap out of the sky. It's dangerous here."

"Yes, sir."

"What's *not* dangerous?" Han put as much put-upon aggravation into his tone as he could. "You're here, I'm reading Corellian forces ahead on this orbit and out from your formation, I'm getting reports of dogfights over Coronet—where do I go? I've got my wife here—how do I keep her safe?"

In the *Falcon*'s copilot's seat, Leia shot her husband an unamused look. *Keep me safe?* she mouthed silently.

Han shot her an apologetic glance.

"Solo, you've dropped your civilian vehicle into the middle of a military conflict," the anonymous voice from *Dodonna* said. "We just recommend you get to safety. Now. We don't have time to figure out where it is for you."

Leia tapped the sensor board, which showed a starfighter squadron, too far away for the sensors to analyze, break from the Corellian fleet and vector in toward the *Falcon*'s position.

"Hey, there's a whole squadron coming in at me," Han said. "You've sent me an escort?"

"They're not ours," *Dodonna* said. "Meaning they're probably coming in to blow you up."

"Oh. Look, I'm plotting an exit course back along your orbital track. I'll use your ships for protection. Tell 'em not to shoot at me. *Falcon* out."

"Wait—"

Han cut his comm board. "Strap in, sweetheart," he said.

Leia did so, grudgingly. "Han, you're playing a dangerous game."

"I'm sorry about the whole *protect-my-wife* thing, that was just to confuse them—"

"I don't mean that. I mean joyriding around in the middle of a battle."

"I want to see the composition of their forces. I want to see how they conduct themselves when they're assaulting my homeworld. Hold on."

Han set the *Falcon* into a tight, stomach-turning loop, sending her back toward the prow of *Dodonna*—but lower, a couple of kilometers below the carrier in orbit.

The sensor board showed the oncoming starfighters closing on the *Falcon*. Now it popped up a diagram of their pursuers: fuselage shaped like a beetle's body, two down-slanted wings stretching out to support lengthy thruster pods, a laser cannon turret under the fuselage main body.

"A-Nine Vigilance Interceptors," Leia said. "Speedy little things."

"Weak hulls," Han said. "I used to crack 'em with my teeth and suck out the meat inside."

"I'll grant that you have a mouth big enough to do it."

Dodonna flashed by to their port side. Her turbolaser batteries did not track the *Falcon* as they passed.

"Besides," Han said, "they won't fire on me. I'm a Corellian celebrity."

Leia snorted. "Make sure your transponder is sending out your real identity. Otherwise they have no reason not to blow you out of the sky."

"Good point." Han checked his comm board and nodded, satisfied. "Turn on the bow holocam, would you? I want to record what we're about to see."

Leia sighed and did as she was asked.

CENTERPOINT STATION

Ben lay atop a square-sided conduit a meter wide and tall. It was suspended five meters above the passageway floor, just a meter below the ceiling, and immediately below him CorSec agents were talking.

One said, "Any word?"

Another: "They've got him boxed in at one of the empty theater chambers."

"They've got him, then."

"I don't know. He's a Jedi. They're sneaky."

Ben grinned. *Sneaky.* He liked that.

Footsteps approached, and the first CorSec agent shouted, "Halt! Show your identicard."

A new voice, female: "Ables, Transportation."

"You need to evacuate this area. It's under lockdown."

"No, I'm excluded. Emergency personnel."

"So you are. All right, get to your station. And fast."

The footsteps left. The first CorSec agent said, "Back to the patrol."

"Don't get lightsabered."

"Very funny."

The CorSec agents moved away in opposite directions, leaving Ben alone.

His face fell as a realization hit him. He *was* sneaky, and he was really *good* at being sneaky, but being sneaky wasn't enough. Sneaky was slow. Skulking, crouching, hiding, crawling—it took forever. He was in the corridor that would take him to the station's repulsor control chamber. By his calculation, it was just a few hundred meters away. But moving stealthily along every centimeter of that distance might take hours.

And all because the enemy knew they were facing Jedi.

Ben sat up so fast he banged his head on the ceiling

above. He rubbed at the point of impact and considered. He didn't have to *be* a Jedi right now. Clumsy in his haste, he began pulling his boots off, pulling his Jedi robe and all its accoutrements free, and in a minute was left wearing just a black undershirt and black shorts. His lightsaber and all the electronic toys intended to make this mission a success went into his pouch.

Pouch in hand, he dropped over the edge to the floor beneath, rolling up to his feet, and began running in the direction of his destination.

ABOVE CORELLIA

Lysa ended her run along the length of the VibroSword/ attack fighter engagement. She would let her thrusters put her some distance away from the conflict before turning around for another run. She was certain that she'd scored some hits on Correllian attack fighters, but had flashed by so fast that she had no idea if any were debilitating, if any were kills.

Killing Corellians.

Eight was still on her tail, but sparks were shooting out and up from his port-side thruster. "Seven, I'm hit."

"How's it look?"

"Not good. It's overheating. Venting it to space isn't doing any good."

"Shut it down and get back to *Dodonna*."

"Will do." Eight sounded regretful. "You'd better hook back up with the V-Swords and see if you can pick up a temporary wingmate."

"You're right." Then Lysa's eye was caught by something on her sensor board—a lone enemy blip, its course taking it near her position and down toward the planet. "After this," she said.

"Lysa, don't do it alone."

"See you back at *Dodonna*." She peeled off and looped around to follow in the new starfighter's wake.

Her sensor board had it classified now—an X-wing. She

was surprised; she didn't think any of the Corellian units here were X-wing squadrons. But then, they hadn't seen everything the Corellians had to offer them. She smiled, the competitive expression her trainers had sometimes described as feral, and roared up after her new prey.

Yes, the X-wing's course was putting it into a lower and lower orbit, away from the GA fleet. Perhaps its pilot intended to join the battle against Skywalker's squadron. Perhaps it had been on a reconnaissance run and was now taking important sensor data back to the Corellians. She shook her head. Either way, it wouldn't get where its pilot intended to go.

She didn't bother trying for a targeting lock yet. X-wings were tough, and her sensor board indicated that this pilot had already put his shield strength to double rear.

As her range finder indicated that she was at maximum effective range for her interceptor's laser cannons, she swung her targeting brackets toward the X-wing. But the snubfighter suddenly jerked upward, sideways, to port and starboard, always in a direction opposed to her targeting bracket's approach to it. She had the eerie sensation that the pilot knew exactly when she was going to begin aiming.

She didn't know whether to curse or smile more broadly. This pilot was *good*. He jittered in her targeting brackets once, twice, three times, on each occasion long enough for her to pull the laser cannon trigger, but never long enough for the laser blasts to find a home in his fuselage. She missed with each shot, sometimes by only a few meters.

And suddenly he was going in reverse.

She overshot him, adrenaline jolting through her. It was a classic X-wing flying technique used against a faster pursuer, and it had been executed at exactly the moment she least expected it.

She pushed down on her control yoke, just long enough for her opponent to believe that she was going to dive and loop around, then she yanked back, coming up and into a port-side roll.

An inexperienced pilot would bite on that first, false-maneuver and dive to pursue. She'd be able to correct and dive after him. A more alert or experienced pilot would manage to stay on her tail, would have a few seconds of pursuit in which to obtain a target lock and fire lasers or even launch a proton torpedo at her starfighter, so much more fragile than the X-wing.

She heard no screech of a targeting lock alarm. She checked her sensor board. Her opponent hadn't dived, hadn't pursued. Apparently from the moment she made her evasive maneuver, he'd resumed his original course.

Lysa sat there in momentary shock. He hadn't even taken a shot at her.

Her comm board crackled and its scanner indicated that the broadcast was coming in across a general GA military frequency—but very low-powered, so faint that only she was likely to pick it up.

"Nice interceptor roll-out," her opponent said. "I'd swear you learned that from Tycho Celchu."

Again, Lysa froze. She *had* learned that maneuver from General Celchu, the celebrated officer who had flown an A-wing into and out of the second Death Star more than thirty years ago.

And she knew the voice of her opponent, even as altered as it was by the low-powered transmission and standard comm distortion. "Daddy?" she said.

"Hello, sweetheart."

She rolled again, sending her in a steep descent toward the X-wing. But her course wouldn't bring her up behind it in proper dogfighting fashion; instead, eyeballing it, she chose an intercept course . . . and switched her targeting computer completely off.

Her vector brought her in toward the X-wing's top side. She adjusted her course so they were parallel, her Eta-5 interceptor immediately above the X-wing. Then she rolled her starfighter over so they cruised canopy-to-canopy, a mere four meters separating them.

And she looked up into the face of her father, Wedge Antilles.

Corellia's second most famous pilot flashed her a toothy smile and he offered her a thumbs-up. He was wearing a standard X-wing pilot's helmet—not his own battered helmet with the distinctive wedges on it, but another, this one decorated with an arc of triangles along the rim.

"Daddy, you're *retired*. Get out of the skies." Lysa was suddenly aware of, and embarrassed by, the adolescent wail in her voice. But the realization that she'd fired on her own father made her feel drained, light-headed.

"I'll do that, sweetheart." Wedge waved an admonishing finger at her. "Don't get hurt."

"I won't, Daddy."

Wedge adjusted his course and was suddenly dropping more steeply away from her.

Lysa rolled back up to a more natural orientation, putting the planet beneath her keel, and pulled back on her control yoke, sending her higher. Slowly, she looped around back toward her squadron's last known position.

She'd really never before run up against the mythological depths of her father's reputation. Oh, yes, she'd grown up knowing of his fame, and it was a desire to have a career well out of the shadow of Wedge Antilles that had caused her to take academy training under the name of Lysa Dunter rather than that of Syal Antilles. She'd even chosen to train most in the high-speed, low-armor fighters such as the Eta-5 interceptor rather than the sturdy old X-wings her father loved, all in order to avoid invidious comparisons with him.

She'd never been aware of his reputation as a thing of legend rather than historical fact. Yet now, meeting him under the most unlikely of circumstances, in a place and time where history was being made, unable to do him harm though she'd tried with all her skill and will to do so, she felt it.

She had fired on her father. She had killed fellow Corellians . . . her duty, laid down on her the moment she'd sworn an officer's oath and not suddenly removed because her homeworld was now the enemy.

In just a few minutes, the universe had become an insane place.

She forced herself out of her reverie. She had enemies ahead, and daydreaming as she approached them would get her killed. "Focus," her father said, out of her memory, not out of the comm board. "Focus, and your odds of survival are improved."

She'd focus. She had promised him she would not be hurt.

Syal Antilles spotted enemy blips ahead, and her sensor board identified them as a pair of A-9 Vigilances. One was apparently shepherding the other, whose thrusters were spitting sparks. They swelled to occupy her whole mind, all other considerations forgotten, and she roared toward them.

chapter thirteen

CENTERPOINT STATION

Jacen sliced through the midsection of his last opponent's blaster rifle and followed through with a spinning kick that catapulted the man over the walkway rail. With a wail of fright, the man dropped two stories' distance to the metal floor—an impact that, Jacen calculated, would injure but probably not kill him.

Jacen turned to look back the few meters he'd just come. Eight of the CorSec agents lay on the walkway, unconscious, some bleeding, two of them missing their right forearms. Two sonic projectors installed on the lower bodies of R5 astromechs sat smoking and motionless.

The other four CorSec agents and Thrackan Sal-Solo had retreated through a heavy metal door—about four meters high, it looked like original Centerpoint Station equipment, though the security pad next to it was of more recent manufacture. Jacen could sense danger—and malice—on the other side of that door.

He reached for the OPEN button, not expecting it to work; doubtless Thrackan had locked it down. But a vision of the future, of one possible future, crossed Jacen's thoughts and he jerked his hand back. In his mind's eye, he saw himself depressing the button, an electronic signal passing along the security device's pathways to an odd device on the other side of the door, an explosion powerful enough to blow the door and a large section of wall around it to nothingness . . .

Jacen trotted down the walkway, putting a good distance between him and the door, then turned back to focus on the security pad. Barely visible at this distance was the tiny green glow of the OPEN button.

He put his hands over his ears and exerted himself against that button, the merest push with the Force—

With a brilliant flash and a punishing wave of sound, the door blew in, bending and crumpling as it flew through the space Jacen would have occupied. Smoke and shrapnel that had once been surrounding wall sections accompanied it. The walkway beneath Jacen's feet rocked, then quickly steadied itself. He ran back the way he'd come, putting on a Force-based burst of running speed, and leapt through the new opening in the wall.

Corridor, broad, dark. Left, away from the areas of the station he wanted to reach, open. Right, in the distance, a line of CorSec agents, twenty or more in a well-dressed pair of lines, the front line kneeling, curved transparisteel crowd control shields at the ready, while the rear line stood with blasters aimed. Behind the two lines stood Thrackan Sal-Solo.

Closer, ten meters away but floating toward him, scarred and still smoking from where explosion debris had hit them, were two probots.

No, not quite. These droids looked a lot like Rebellion-era probots—misshapen and bulbous, slightly less than two meters tall, they floated on repulsorlifts well above the floor, four mechanical arms dangling beneath, just like the old stealth droids. But these were bronze in color rather than black, and their arms seemed bulkier, sturdier, than old-time probots'.

And they ended in what looked like weapons pods.

As Jacen emerged into the hallway, they activated deflector shields, not a feature of the original probots, and flew straight at him.

They raised weapon pods and began firing—one, a blaster; the other, small oval canisters that had to be explosives.

Ben heard and felt the *boom,* distant and muffled, originating somewhere well beneath his feet, and was diverted enough to use the Force to seek out Jacen. Dimly, he could feel his Master, could sense movement and vitality from him.

But the distraction was long enough for Ben to run clean into someone. He banged into rigid body armor, bounced off, and hit the metal floor butt-first.

He looked up into the face of a CorSec officer glowering down at him.

"Back the way you came, son," the officer said. "This area is under lockdown."

"I've got to see my father," Ben said, swiftly improvising. "He's guarding the repulsor control room. I have to be sure he's all right."

"No, kid, it's off-limits."

"I have to know he's all right." Ben made the words a child's frightened wail. He darted around the CorSec officer, eluding the man's grab, and continued running down the corridor.

He couldn't keep his shoulders from riding up, tensing. He reached out with the Force, searching out the guard's response to his action.

Ben felt no intimation of danger—the guard didn't aim his blaster. The man's emotions were a mix of irritation and sympathy. Ben felt the man weigh a decision, and it took the boy a few moments to figure out what it was: whether or not to communicate with his fellows, warn them that the boy was headed their way. Then Ben felt the man choose against that course of action. The guard turned away.

Ben grinned to himself. *That was easy.* But then he sobered. If his mission was a success, that nice, sympathetic guard might die in the destruction of Centerpoint Station.

But if Ben *hadn't* tricked the man, even more people might die.

It was a small wrongdoing to prevent a bigger one. It was all in the interest of the greater good, the needs of the many. Ben had heard these words hundreds of times, mostly from Jacen, and finally he began to have a sense of what they meant.

Still, deep down, he remembered his father once saying, *There are times when the end justifies the means. But when you build an argument based on a whole series of such times, you may find that you've constructed an entire philosophy of evil.*

Troubled, Ben ran on.

With his lightsaber, Jacen batted away the blasterfire coming from the right-hand probot. He couldn't aim his deflections; that would require too much concentration. Instead, with his left hand, he reached out through the Force and found the projectiles being fired by the left-hand probot. He seized them and redirected them in two streams, one stream toward each droid.

They flew only as far as the droids' deflector shields, out about a meter from their bodies, and adhered there. Then, one after another, they detonated.

Jacen saw the deflector shields weaken with each explosion. He charged forward, relying on his speed and sudden motion to throw off the aim of the probot with the blaster. When the last of the projectiles had detonated, before the probot shields had time to strengthen, he lashed out, first right and then left.

Two probots, sliced in half at the narrowest portions of their bulbous bodies, crashed to the metal floor.

In the silence that followed, Jacen heard Thrackan say, "Open fire."

The rear rank of CorSec agents opened up with their blaster rifles. Each was set to full automatic fire and they filled the air with blaster shots.

Jacen went into a fully evasive mode—running, leaping,

dodging, spinning his lightsaber in a defensive shield that intercepted shot after shot.

It wasn't enough. He felt a burn against his left calf as a blaster shot grazed it. Another shot, almost as close, tugged at his right sleeve and left a char-lined hole in it.

He leapt up and back, cartwheeling, and as he cleared the zone of heaviest fire, before the security agents could adjust their aim, he reached against the ceiling with the Force. He yanked against that simple, immobile metal surface for all he was worth.

It came free, yielding to his pull. As he landed, a huge sheet of metal ceiling tore free from its housing almost directly overhead and crashed to the floor a mere two meters ahead of him. The far end of the same sheet remained adhered to the housing above, so what Jacen faced was a crude ramp leading upward—and acting as an angled shield between him and the blaster line.

He looked up and frowned. His ramp led nowhere. Above the area where it had rested was heavier metal, a full bulkhead. But at least the metal sheet would give him a few moments' rest.

Even now, though, it was shuddering under the blaster impacts, turning bright in one spot where some of the security agents were concentrating their fire.

Jacen peered out from around his impromptu shield, drawing fire, but gathering valuable information about his enemies' tactics.

He saw three of the blaster wielders changing out power packs simultaneously—obviously part of a scheduled rotation. So they were carrying enough power packs to maintain constant fire for a long time, to keep him pinned down.

Jacen moved across to the other side of his shield and paused a moment before peeking out again. His enemies' strength was also their weakness, and he'd use it against them—

His comlink bleeped, three quick musical notes. The signal jolted Jacen. It was Ben, and it meant *Target in sight*.

Jacen nodded. He wouldn't just march forward in an effort to reach his objective. He'd continue drawing the station's defensive resources toward him, giving Ben some time.

He closed his eyes and looked with other senses for sources of power, of heat.

There they were, several of them, so close together that they seemed to form a single line of energy: the blasters of his enemies. Rugged weapons doubtless kept in tip-top condition, they were doing a decent job of handling the tremendous heat demands of the constant fire.

Well, he needed to change *decent* to *poor*. He reached out to those glowing energy sources, finding one at the end of the line. He poured his own power into it, pushed around to find weak spots, cracks, exits . . .

He found one and exerted himself against it. It held against him for long moments. Then he heard a cry of alarm from one of the security agents . . . and the crack as the power pack of her blaster rifle exploded.

Jacen dared a look. The agent was down, injured, her body smoking, and two other CorSec agents, a shield bearer before her and a rifleman next to her, were down, too. Now there was a small gap at the right side of the blaster line. Before the CorSec agents became aware of him, Jacen drew back . . . and went searching for the next power pack in line.

The second one was even hotter and weaker. It took less of an exertion to make it detonate. He looked again and saw four more CorSec agents down, the rest slowing their rates of fire or switching to single-shot firing mode.

Behind the lines, Thrackan turned and began trotting in the other direction, a comlink held to his lips.

Jacen grinned humorlessly. Another few moments and this firing line would be a thing of the past . . . and he'd see what surprises his cousin had in store for him next.

At a distance of fifty meters, Ben began to make out what guarded the door into the repulsor control chamber: two CorSec agents, one male and one female, and a floating

ball-shaped droid with four arms dangling from it. Even as
Ben saw them, the floating droid drifted out from the doorway, its repulsorlift humming, into the middle of the corridor as if to bar his passage.

Two of its arms, ending in bulbous pods with barrels,
rose to aim at him. Ben raised his own arms and shouted,
"Don't shoot! I'm only a kid!"

Embarrassing words. He wanted to grow up so that he'd
never be able to use an excuse like that again. But for now,
it was useful.

He heard the female guard say, "Hold your fire," and
then she stepped out to beckon Ben forward. He moved
toward her at a quick walk. "I'm lost," he wailed.

"How did you get this deep into restricted areas?" she
asked. Ben moved nearly ten meters closer to her as she
spoke.

"I was exploring in the tubes, and I got tired and hungry,
and I fell asleep, and then there were explosions and alarms
and sounds of people running, and I finally found a real
corridor, but I don't know where I am." He made it most
of the way to the guards in the course of that speech; now
only five meters separated them. He tried to summon tears,
but they didn't come. He decided he needed more practice.

"Do you have a datapad?" the woman asked. "I can
transmit you a map out of here."

"No," Ben said. Now he stood in front of her and the
hovering droid.

It looked pretty sturdy, and he could see nodules on the
top surface that probably indicated deflector shield generators. But he didn't think its shields were up. Even without
them, its bronze-colored metal hide suggested that it could
withstand a blaster shot or two.

"You stay right here," the woman said. "I'll get a print-
out of the map."

Her companion, who hadn't budged from in front of the
door, finally spoke. "No," he said. "Protocol is we call it in
and they send someone to escort him out of the area."

"There's no one available to escort him," she said. There

was a slight edge of condescension to her voice. "Everyone's been pulled off for Target Alpha. So we can babysit here until they send someone, maybe hours from now, or we can send him off with a map."

Her partner sighed, exasperated, but didn't reply.

Ben felt his pulse quicken. If the woman agent got her way, she'd be opening the door for him—one less task for him to undertake.

Still, he'd have to take her out, and her partner, and the big floating ball in order to get into the room.

Prioritize your steps, Jacen always told him.

Priority One was the floating droid. It had to be some sort of combat model, so it was going to be tough, and maybe alert to attack, even from as unlikely a source as a redheaded urchin. Ben let his pouch gape open so he could look down at his lightsaber. If he reached for it, the droid might correctly interpret the motion as the herald of an attack. But he didn't have to reach. After the droid, he'd take out whichever of the human agents was more alert to him, then the one less alert, but he'd wait for the moment to decide which was which.

Another of Jacen's lessons was *Plan and time your steps*. The woman was stepping up to the doorway and preparing to insert her identicard into a security board slot. The man wasn't moving. It was a staredown.

That gave Ben a moment to plan. He'd need to wait until the door was just opening. Then he'd take out the droid. His next priority would be getting into the chamber before the door closed again, and any security monitor might shut it as soon as it was open. So he'd rush through the door and deal with the human guards as he passed.

After that—Jacen would be disappointed in him if he didn't figure out some way off this station, but Ben didn't have time right now. The staredown between the guards ended. Irritably, the man stepped out of the way and the woman inserted her identicard in the slot.

Everything began to move in slow motion, as though the entire corridor were suddenly submerged in thick, invisible fluid. Ben saw the door begin to slide upward. Doors like this opened almost instantly, but his time perception was so dilated that he watched it as it rose a meter.

He held his hand above his pouch and tugged through the Force. His lightsaber leapt up into his hand, and he snapped it on, swinging it at the hovering droid even as the distorted *snap-hiss* noise announced that the blade was coming live.

Instead of slashing, he leapt upward and thrust down, aiming for one of the deflector shield nodules. The point of his lightsaber blade sheared through the bronze hull there, punching into the droid's insides. Ben kept his hands on the lightsaber handle, letting his weight drag the weapon down through the droid.

The droid fell almost as fast as he did—with agonizing slowness—and Ben could see the male guard reacting to the attack, bringing his rifle barrel up.

Ben's heels hit the ground and he continued downward, going into a sideways roll toward the now fully open doorway. The male guard tried to track the boy with his blaster rifle. The woman, her face distorted in surprise, was punching the CLOSE button on the security panel. Her identicard was still in the panel's card slot.

Ben came up on his feet between the man and the woman, so close that the man's blaster barrel now protruded safely past him, and lashed out at the control panel. His lightsaber blade slashed into the controls and into the identicard, burning and fusing it into place. The blade came so close to the back of the woman's hand that he saw her skin blacken along a four-centimeter patch. Her knuckles still hit the CLOSE button, even as the near edges of that button melted from the lightsaber's heat. Ben continued his forward roll, going head over heels into dimness—and, as the door came slamming down behind him, into darkness illuminated only by the glowing blue blade of his weapon.

He couldn't make out much of the chamber's interior. There was a large mass in front of him, as if someone had parked a small groundspeeder on its tail there—it didn't correspond to anything Dr. Seyah had shown him in the simulations. There were little lights in various colors all over the walls.

First things first. He spun and lunged back at the door, thrusting with his lightsaber at the top, where the lifter mechanism should be. He shoved the lightsaber blade in well above his head, cutting upward and sideways, trying to sever the mechanism or, failing that, fuse it. This would give him time to accomplish his mission.

His mission. That thought almost made him dizzy. It was *his* mission now.

His cutting done, he slapped the light control on the door control panel. White overhead lights came on and he spun, lightsaber ready, in case enemies waited there in the dark.

No living enemies did. But the room was still not as it was supposed to be.

The banks of lights, computers, and secondary control tables, some original equipment and some installed by the Corellians, lined the walls as they had in Dr. Seyah's simulations.

But where the main control table was supposed to be rested something else entirely.

It was a mound of machinery as big as half a dozen Hutts engaged in a no-rules wrestling match. Roughly human-shaped, it had a desk-sized head that looked like a sensor node whose surface was thickly crusted with antennae, light monitors, and holocam lenses. Its torso was made up of mismatched modules, each at least as big as the head, connected with durasteel cables and light-bearing trans-paristeel fibers. Dangling torso units surrounded—perhaps incorporated—the control board Ben needed to access. The machine's arms appeared to be the heavy-duty cylindrical limbs from a wrecker droid, and ended in the same clumsy, destructive manipulator hands. Instead of legs it had a thick bottom plate whose skirted edges probably concealed repulsorlift machinery. All these components were of different colors, some black, some silver, some industrial green.

Fully upright, it would probably be four meters tall, but it sat hunched forward, like a lazy student kneeling with bad posture.

Its head turned to bring two oversized holocam lenses to bear on him, and it spoke from somewhere in that head unit, its synthesized tones strikingly reminiscent of Jacen Solo's voice: "Who are you?"

"I'm Ben Skywalker," the boy said. He didn't add, *I'm here to destroy this whole installation.*

"Wonderful," the droid said. "I'm so happy to meet you. I'm Anakin Solo."

chapter fourteen

CORONET, CORELLIA

The Behareh Spaceport, though a minor one by the standards of Coronet or any decent-sized city, still sprawled for many acres, even though it was located only a couple of kilometers from the urban heart. Unfortunately for Jaina and the team members, it differed from the city's main spaceport in a significant way: there was no central parking or hangar area for visitors' groundspeeders, no large common-arrival point where it would be comparatively easy to remain inconspicuous. Instead, Behareh was divided into dozens of smaller commercial properties, usually with the offices and hangars of three or four firms clustered around common launching and parking areas.

Kolir directed Thann to a cluster of businesses whose parking area was surrounded by tall trees. He landed. Here, the city's space raid sirens were not as loud as in the government districts, but continued to blare into the skies.

As the groundspeeder slowed to a stop, Zekk's eyes came open, alert, untroubled, unclouded by pain. "Are we on Corellia yet?" he asked.

"Quiet, you," Jaina said, but brushed a lock of his hair from his forehead, a gentle gesture robbing any sting from her words. "Thann, Kolir, status?"

"Skywalker's squadron is making a run over the government center," Thann said. "To disguise the real purpose of their arrival and to give us some time to get airborne. As soon as we are, he'll disengage and come over to escort us into space. Tahiri's speeder will be here in a couple of minutes." He frowned. "I think there's something she's not telling us."

"Like what?"

"I'm not sure. She wouldn't tell me."

"I have a likely proshpect," Kolir said, and held up her datapad; on its diminutive screen was a red-and-yellow company logo that read: DONOSLANE EXCURSIONS. "Female human manager on duty. The offishes should be over—" She looked around and spotted a curve-topped yellow duracrete building straight behind the ground-speeder. "Over there."

The others looked in that direction but were diverted—another groundspeeder, this one an inconspicuous blue, settled down on the parking pad adjacent to theirs. At the controls was Tahiri Veila, blond-haired and green-eyed, a few standard years younger than Jaina; she was dressed in a utility worker's gray jumpsuit. Beside her was Doran Tainer—tall, fair-haired, brown-eyed, square-jawed, and blandly handsome as any holodrama leading man, but incongruously dressed in brown grass-stained field-worker's garments. Both were Jedi. At the moment, neither looked like it.

In the speeder's backseat was something roughly the size of a grown human woman, wrapped in a brown cloak from its calves to the crown of its head. Only feet protruded, clad in brown leather boots.

Heart suddenly pounding, Jaina slid out from under Zekk and leapt over to that backseat even as Doran said, "It's not what you think."

Jaina whipped the cloak away from the head and shoulders of the body—and revealed the features of a brightly polished silver protocol droid, its photoreceptors dim. "What's this?" she asked. "Where's Tiu?"

Doran offered her a pained smile. "She's in Thrackan Sal-Solo's mansion."

"Captured?"

"No," Tahiri said. "Hiding."

"Hiding?"

"We ran into a trap," Doran said. "It sounds like you did, too. Lots of guards. Several combat probots. A couple of YVH droids. Not a tenable situation. So we decided to run away."

Tahiri gave him a reproving look. "There was nothing we could accomplish there. So I ordered a nice, clean withdrawal. Which would have been fine if Brilliant Notions here hadn't had his great idea."

Now Jaina fixed Doran with a hard stare. "Which was what?"

Doran shrugged. "We ran into this deactivated protocol droid in the room from which we decided to stage our retreat. And it occurred to me—I could dress it in my clothes, Tahiri and Tiu could carry it out, and it would look like they were taking the body of a fallen comrade to safety. They knew three of us had gone in, they'd watch three of us escape . . . and I'd hide there, see what I could find out in the wake of this disaster."

"And a naked man the size of a dwarf Wookiee is going to stay hidden for how long?" Jaina demanded.

Doran winced. "That's what Tiu asked. In almost those exact words, as a matter of fact. So I said, 'Forget it.' And she said, 'No, it's a good plan, except for the fact that, as usual, you introduced a fatal flaw. We pull out the fatal flaw and it's viable again.' "

Jaina nodded. "And fixing the plan meant substituting a tiny Omwati woman for a big slab of hanging meat." She seethed, but held her anger deep. She didn't want any member of her operation left behind on Corellia . . . but she had to admit that a resource, hiding out in Thrackan Sal-Solo's opulent home, could prove invaluable in the days to come. And Tiu, despite bearing the distinctive delicate blue skin and opalescent pale hair of her species, was very, very good at stealth and hiding games.

She covered the protocol droid's face and stood back from it, then pointed at Doran. "You. Get some bacta patches for Zekk's burns and whatever Kolir needs to deal with her mouth." Then her gaze fell on Thann. "You. Get us a vehicle."

CORELLIAN ORBIT

Han Solo sent *Millennium Falcon* down a course that was in a slightly lower orbit than Klauskin's formation of ships and back in the direction from which they'd come. In his wake came the squadron of A-9 Vigilances.

"They're not breaking off," Leia said.

"I can see that," Han said, his voice testy. "Do they not believe their transponders? Do they think I'm *pretending* to be Han Solo?"

Green laserfire flashed past the cockpit's starboard viewports. Then the *Falcon* shook as her stern took a hit from one of the pursuers' shots. Both Leia and Han could hear C-3PO's wail of "Oh, dear . . ." waft out from the transport's central areas.

Han added some side-to-side slew to their movement and rose, climbing into a higher orbit—almost into the path of a Mon Calamari heavy carrier, *Blue Diver.*

"Han, what are you doing?" Leia's voice conveyed a hint of worry.

"These vessels won't fire on me," he said, his tone cocksure even if his words sounded a bit unlikely. "I've already talked to *Dodonna,* remember? But they may fire on our attackers."

"They may."

Ahead, *Blue Diver*'s shields were already up—it was clear she was sustaining some long-distance fire from opportunistic Corellian starfighters—and now her bow and starboard turbolasers began to track the small-craft parade the *Falcon* was leading. At this distance, it was impossible to tell whether the turbolasers were aimed at the *Falcon* herself.

The *Falcon* shook again and again, harder, as the speedy A-9s came closer toward her stern. Two of them shot past the transport's bow and moved on ahead.

"In just a minute," Leia said, "they'll get far enough ahead that they can come around and head back toward us. Meaning you'll have to distribute your shield power equally all around, meaning some of those overcharged lasers might start punching through."

"I know," Han said. There was misery in his voice.

"Han, we have to return fire. Make them duck and scatter."

"I can't fire on Corellians, Leia. Not when I . . . when I . . ."

Leia didn't finish the statement for him. *Caused this.*

The *Falcon* and her pursuers reached firing range for *Blue Diver*'s weapons and those guns opened up, their energy flashing past the *Falcon*—and past the madly dodging A-9s, as well. Leia was relieved to see that the *Falcon* did not appear to be among the vessel's targets. But the battery fire came awfully close, and a single aiming mishap could put them square in the vessel's targeting brackets.

Then they were parallel to *Blue Diver*, blasting far too close along her starboard side, her guns tracking and firing.

The *Falcon* shot past *Blue Diver*'s stern. Six A-9 Vigilances continued to pursue her. The two that had gone ahead were intact and beginning their turn.

"Han," Leia said, "you're going to lose the *Falcon*."

It was unfair of her. Simple as they were, her words had additional, unspoken meaning. *You're going to lose your first love. You're going to lose your freedom.*

Han growled as though the sound were being pulled out of him with a fishhook. Then, through clenched teeth, he said, "Yeah. Hold on."

It wasn't just a command to wait. He threw the *Falcon* into a starboard turn that sent the transport shooting out past *Blue Diver*'s stern, up into the open space between the

Galactic Alliance and Corellian task forces, where starfighter squadrons were mixing it up in touch-and-go firing runs and dogfights. Then he said, "Get to the guns."

Leia unstrapped and headed back into the transport's main body. "Meewalh!" she shouted. "Bottom cannon turret." When she reached the tube and ladder accessing the laser cannon turrets, she climbed into the top-side turret and rapidly strapped herself in.

Syal and her temporary wingmate, a male Mon Cal flying VibroSword Ten, shot out one side of the ever-broadening starfighter combat zone and began a loop around to reenter from another angle.

Things were getting uglier. More squadrons from both sides had joined the furball accumulating halfway between the two vessel formations. Now other gunships, larger than starfighters but smaller than vessels of the line, were turning in to join the combat.

"*Dodonna* to VibroSword Squadron."

Syal spotted the gleam of a larger craft leaving the Corellian formation and heading in toward the combat zone. Even at this distance, she identified it by sight as a *Nebulon*-series light frigate—its ax-head-shaped bow, its cubical stern, and the spindly, lengthy spine connecting the two were giveaways at any visual range. It was the largest craft yet headed for the furball. Syal tapped its blip on her sensor board, causing it to flash there and on her wingmate's board. She adjusted her course for the frigate.

Meanwhile, *Dodonna*'s message continued to flare through her cockpit speakers. "Return to *Dodonna*. Upon arrival, do not stand down. Be ready for immediate relaunch."

Syal swore to herself. If she turned back now, she'd give up any shot at the frigate. If she didn't turn back now, she'd be disobeying orders. If she could stall by half a minute to a minute, she could adjust her current flight path . . .

She switched to task force frequency. "V-Sword Seven to *Dodonna*," she said. "Please repeat message." There. Five crucial seconds gone. And the comm operator probably wouldn't be able to reply instantly; he'd be fielding other confirmation requests, and higher-ranking pilots would get the information first.

It was ten more seconds before *Dodonna*'s message repeated, fifteen more before the message was completed. Syal acknowledged and began a slow loop back toward the carrier. Her course would take her through the middle of the combat zone . . . and across the frigate's path.

CORONET, CORELLIA

Luke roared in toward Mara's X-wing, which closed toward him, their combined speed causing the numbers on the snubfighter's range meter to scroll too fast to read.

As they reached the point where Luke could almost see his wife's face, a point at which most pilots would be unable to react in time to save themselves, Mara dived, flashing mere meters beneath Luke's X-wing . . . and revealing the attack fighter tailing her.

The attack fighter's pilot tried to vector out of Luke's way. He succeeded. He didn't succeed in dodging Luke's lasers. Red flashes converged on the cockpit, and suddenly the fighter was a cloud of smoke and shrapnel. Luke flew through it, pieces of attack fighter fuselage bouncing off his deflectors and scraping off his hull. He emerged into blue sky on the other side.

The maneuver was called the Corellian Slip. Fighter pilot legend had it that the maneuver had been developed here, by the madmen and madwomen who flew for this system. Luke shook his head, a little saddened by the irony.

On his sensor board, he saw Mara looping around to return to his wingmate position. The latest detachment of attack fighters was down to two viable starfighters—and now, realizing the depletion of their numbers, they suddenly veered off, leaving the dogfight. Nine Jedi X-wings, increasingly battered but all still in fighting condition, remained.

"Leader, this is Three."

"Go ahead, Three." Luke checked his diagnostics board. R2-D2 was reporting some increasing fluctuation in one of the X-wing's laser cannons, the port bottom cannon, and indicated that R2 himself was showing some damage, mobility-controlling circuits cooked by a grazing laser hit from one of the attack fighters.

"The landing party has reported in. They have a shuttle and are ready to launch. They're expecting heavy pursuit once they climb above the no-fly altitude."

Luke brought up a map of Coronet. It showed his squadron's location and, courtesy of Hardpoint Three, a blip indicating the location of Jaina's crew. Luke tapped the screen to designate a point much closer to the landing party's position than his own. "Artoo, designate that point as location Linkup. Three, tell the landing party to make their way to Linkup without attracting pursuit. We'll join them there and everyone will take off for space from that point."

"Acknowledged."

"Hardpoint, form up on me." Luke waited until seven more X-wings joined him in formation . . . and then dived, heading straight for the low, broad buildings that dominated this portion of Coronet.

A few hundred meters from the planet's surface, he began pulling up, but his rate of descent carried him low enough that he came horizontal slightly below the level of the surrounding buildings. Centering himself along the widest boulevard in the area, he shot off in the general direction of Jaina's crew, the Hardpoints maintaining formation behind him. "Artoo," he said, "plot a course to Jaina's position. Wide streets only, please."

R2 tweetled a cheerful acknowledgment.

Syal and VibroSword Ten hurtled into the furball at full interceptor speed. Syal's sensor board crawled with swirling red and blue blips; space outside her forward viewport was similarly crowded with the reflections, glows, and detonation patterns of a growing battle. Using every speed and maneuverability advantage the Eta-5 design gave her, Syal jittered her vehicle around, port, starboard, up, down, making it a maddeningly difficult target to get a lock on or hit with a spray of laserfire.

Ahead, growing in her viewport, was the *Nebulon*-series frigate. As she approached, it was moving from her port to starboard, from a relative higher to lower position, its forward laser cannon and turbolaser arrays flashing continuously.

"Ten," Syal said, "we're going for the deflector shield generator. Concussion missiles for maximum close-range results." They were now close enough that a schematic of the *Nebulon* frigates popped up on her sensor board; she tapped the top side of the rear nodule on the wire-frame image and it expanded on the screen, word labels and arrow-tipped lines appearing on the schematic to explain what was what. She tapped the words DEFLECTOR SHIELD GENERATOR to highlight them, dragged a targeting bracket from the corner of the screen over them, dragged an Eta-5 interceptor silhouette from the same corner to the same spot. Now her targeting computer would automatically seek out the shield generators and V-Sword Ten would receive a data transmission pointing to that target.

"Negative, Seven, negative," Ten said. "Even if we achieve fantastic results, all we do is knock down the shields—and someone else will get the kill before we can get back. I say we try to put our missiles into their squadron bays. The main hatches might still be open. We might get lucky."

"You can't plan for luck, Ten." It was weird to hear those words in her own voice, not her father's. "Plan smart and let luck land where it will. We're going for the shield generators."

"You don't outrank me, Seven."

"Yeah, but I'm in front." Syal diverted a quarter of her shield energy to her thrusters—a risky move. But she couldn't risk Ten using the same logic on her, overtaking her, screwing up her tactic. Ten did surge forward, briefly gaining on her, but dropped back, unwilling to devote as much shield power as she was using for thrust.

Syal grinned. *Lost your nerve, did you?*

They were now too close even to attempt a swerve and attack on the squadron hangars, which were in the bow module of the frigate. Syal returned the shield power to her forward shields.

A turbolaser attack flashed just over her, causing the interceptor's proximity alarms to howl. Syal drove in straight toward the deflector shield generator, as though her intent were to ram it, providing just enough side-to-side and up-and-down movement to throw off some targeting locks.

Her own targeting brackets found the frigate's shield generators, jittered around them, stabilized. Syal held her breath, held her focus, until the targeting computer indicated maximum efficient range for firing—and beyond, waiting until the computer flashed red for optimal range. At last, she fired. She saw white streaks as two missiles flashed away from her interceptor.

Even then she didn't change her course. *A lot of pilots bank and begin their run to safety the instant they launch missiles,* her father had told her. *A lot of gunners know this. You see a target coming in, you see him launch missiles, choose one vector for him and fire in that direction. One time in ten you'll choose right and you'll vape him. Unless you're Tycho Celchu, when it's one time in four.*

Syal didn't bank; she blinked as a red laser barrage suddenly filled space just above and to starboard of her course. As soon as the red streaks flashed by, she dived and banked to starboard, away from the frigate, back toward *Dodonna*.

The sensor board showed a detonation atop the frigate's stern nodule. The extent of the damage, if any, couldn't be displayed yet, but it looked close, closer than if the missiles had detonated against the shields.

Dodonna was free of enemy starfighter assaults as the two Eta-5 interceptors lined up on her, and word came in over the comm boards: V-Sword Leader had bagged the frigate, dropping his entire complement of concussion missiles into the engines, rendering the frigate dead in space, prompting a massive evacuation by escape pods.

"Profiteer," Ten said. "That's just what I was warning you about, Seven. We do all the work—he gets the prize."

"What's more important, Ten? A frigate silhouette on your fighter, or knowing that you're responsible for keeping units on your own side alive?"

"Silhouette."

"You're such a fish. You know you're broadcasting openly on the squadron frequency, don't you?"

"Sith spawn! I didn't—" Then Ten's voice went from shock and fear to anger. "No, I wasn't. You liar."

Syal laughed at him and lined up for her landing.

Leia aimed with the targeting computer, aimed with the Force. Her computer chattered to say she had a lock on her target, but she didn't feel her opponent yet. She moved slightly, a tiny adjustment with the quad-linked cannons she commanded, and felt heat, danger—the danger her target was experiencing.

She adjusted down a fraction of a degree of arc and fired. Blinding needles of light hit the Vigilance, shearing through its laser cannons and then the stern of the A-9. She saw the vehicle vent its atmosphere—then the canopy flew up and the pilot ejected, the dim glow of a life-support shield surrounding him as he hit hard vacuum. He was a couple hundred meters away from his doomed craft when it exploded.

A blip representing another A-9, hit by fire from Meewalh and the underside turret, disappeared from Leia's sensor board. Dimly, distantly, she felt the diminishment in the Force that heralded the pilot's death.

"Five down," Han called over the comm unit. "Four to—never mind. Four breaking off pursuit. I'm returning to our intended course."

Seconds later Leia was halfway back to the cockpit when Han announced, "Whoa. We're getting out of here." His sudden port turn threw Leia into a bulkhead, but she was prepared for it, cushioned it with body position and a little help from the Force.

Despite ongoing evasive turns, she managed to push her way back into the cockpit and strap herself into her seat. "What's happening?"

"We're not under fire," Han said. "We're not even *on* fire."

"That's a refreshing change."

"But we've had some hull-stress damage. And the GA starfighters are quitting the field." Han sounded jubilant. "They're running. The GA capital ships are turning out to space."

Leia glanced at the sensor board, then confirmed with direct observation. Out the cockpit's viewport, she could see the prow of an old frigate, built like a set of small exercise weights but a third of a kilometer long, turning away from its planetary orbit and pointing its bow toward space.

"Wonderful," she said. "Maybe now this catastrophe is over."

chapter fifteen

CENTERPOINT STATION

Jacen marched in Thrackan's direction, noting the silhouettes of more soldiers and possibly combat droids arriving from the distance beyond his cousin.

Thrackan turned to the side, activated a door, and jumped through. It slid closed behind him, leaving nothing between Jacen and the distant soldiers.

The enemy opened fire.

At this long range, even with as many enemies as were firing, Jacen had no trouble deflecting incoming blaster bolts. He charged forward, sending most of the bolts back toward the enemy line, where front-row agents caught them with their crowd-control shields, sometimes staggering from the strength of the blasts.

Jacen halted beside the door Thrackan had entered. Pressing on toward his original goal and drawing more and more enemies toward him—and, in all probability, Ben—would not benefit the mission. Keeping them well away from the centers where sabotage was to take place would.

He slapped the OPEN button on the doorway. The door slid up. Jacen grinned. Thrackan, certain that Jacen would charge the oncoming CorSec agents and droids, hadn't even bothered to lock the door down.

He found himself in a long hallway with a corresponding

door at the far end, forty meters away. That door was open and Thrackan was just on the other side of it, looking back at Jacen in some surprise.

Jacen stepped in, shut the door behind him, and shoved his lightsaber through the security board—all the way through, his blade emerging into the hallway he'd just left and ruining the control board on that side, as well. The oncoming enemy would have to run a bypass, a procedure that would take at least a couple of minutes.

He looked at Thrackan again. His cousin seemed frozen by Jacen's new tactic. Then Thrackan slapped the control board on his side of the doorway. The door slid down.

Jacen ran to it and slapped the OPEN button, but the door remained in place. Jacen grinned again. Thrackan did learn fast: he'd locked the door this time. Jacen drove his lightsaber into the top of the door, shearing through the machinery that held the door in place. In a moment he'd be through, and he could use the Force to lift the door out of the way.

Dimly, he heard the ringing of boots on metal flooring beyond the door as Thrackan ran away.

"No, you're not," Ben told the ungainly assembly of droid components. "Anakin Solo's dead. He died when I was little."

The couplings where the droid's torso units met its arm attachments lifted noisily, a gesture that looked like a human shrug. "Yes, I did die," it said. "And I became a ghost, and I was eventually drawn here to inhabit this mutated clone body, where I could help my ancestors, the Corellians."

"That's not a clone body," Ben protested. "It's a droid body."

The head swiveled so the droid could look down at itself. "You're wrong, little cousin. Or you're deliberately trying to confuse me. I suspect the latter. You're here to sabotage this station, aren't you? To destroy it, so the Corellians can never enjoy freedom and independence?"

"Boy, have they got you programmed." Ben took a step forward, his lightsaber up in ready position. With his free hand, he gestured at the droid's head. If he could use the Force to wrench it aside, he might be out of the droid's visual receptors, allowing him to jump in and attack without the droid seeing what was coming—

Ben convulsed and his vision blurred. He felt his entire body twitch and heard his lightsaber hit the floor and roll away, humming for a moment before its safety circuits switched the power off.

He shook his head and his vision began to clear.

He was a meter off the floor, the air around him shimmering. His legs still twitched.

The droid shrugged again. "I'm sorry about that. It's an anti-Jedi defensive feature installed by my other cousin, Thrackan Sal-Solo. It constantly monitors brain-wave activity in an area. When centers of the brain that tend to become active when Force powers are being utilized are detected, it turns on. Repulsors under the floor hold the Jedi safely above the ground, and electrical emissions— mostly painless—interfere with the Jedi's concentration. See, you've stopped using Force powers, and it has stopped shocking you. Efficient, isn't it?"

"Yeah, sure, whatever." Ben reached down to draw his lightsaber back up to his hand . . . and jerked and jolted again as the defensive system electrocuted him a second time. After a few seconds of recovery, he said, "I guess it really works."

"It does, doesn't it? So, what were you going to do here?"

"Destroy the station, or at least disable whatever they're using to regain control of the repulsor weapon." Ben looked dubiously at the droid. "I guess that's you."

Pounding began on the other side of the door. Ben winced. The guards outside would be calling for reinforcements. And even as badly as he'd damaged the door, it would still be only a few minutes before they had it open.

He'd failed.

Well, not quite yet. "They tell you they're going to use the station's weapon to stay independent," Ben said. "And that would be fine if that's what it was all about. But it's not. They're lying to you. The first, big lie is that you're Anakin Solo, and that you're in a living body. You're not. You're a droid."

The droid sighed. "Yes, yes. Of course."

"It's true! They needed Anakin Solo's bio- bio-whatsis—"

"Biometric."

"Yeah, biometric data to control the repulsor weapon. So they probably got his fingerprints from old records. They would have reconstructed his brain waves from whatever medical recordings they could find. Probably had to adjust them and mess with them until they could affect the station controls. And they installed them all in *you*, so they'd have an Anakin Solo who would think and behave like a human . . . but do whatever they say."

"I'm Anakin Solo. I'm a Jedi. I have control over the Force. See?" The droid extended an arm, and Ben's lightsaber flew from where it had rolled into its hand.

"That's not the Force. I would have felt it if it was the Force." Ben considered. "Since you can't have repulsorlift vents installed everywhere in the room, it was probably directed magnetics. You grabbed the metal handle of the lightsaber with magnetics." He tried to keep an expression of dismay and sadness from his face. He didn't think he was very successful. It wasn't just that his mission was in jeopardy; there was something grotesque about this situation, about dealing with a droid that honestly thought it was his cousin.

He'd have to find some way to destroy it.

"There are security holocams operating in here, aren't there?" Ben asked.

"Sure."

"What do you look like in them?"

"I'm a very big human teenager. With somewhat overdeveloped bones to handle the strain caused by my great mass."

"I'm going to open my pouch," Ben said. "I'm going to pull out a little holocam. Please let me record you with it."

"Go ahead."

Ben reached into his pouch and pulled out the holocam unit he'd used on Adumar. As soon as it cleared the lip of his pouch, though, the droid gestured and the holocam snapped across the room into the droid's other hand.

"Hey," Ben said. "You promised."

"No, I didn't." The droid held the holocam up to its head, scrutinizing it under a succession of sensors. "I have to be sure it's not a blaster disguised as a holocam."

"Well, it's not. You sound like someone who's afraid to get killed."

"I *am* afraid to get killed."

Ben felt a surge of accomplishment, as though he'd managed to take a step toward eventual victory. "Anakin Solo wasn't. You're not him."

"Quiet. I'm going to examine this thing's programming." A slot in the droid's head, approximately where a human mouth would be in relation to its eyes, slid open. It stuffed the holocam into the slot and it closed.

"Hey! What do you think just happened?"

"I'm using my Force interface with computer equipment to analyze the programming."

"That's not a Force power, you twit. And I mean, what just happened physically? You stuck my holocam into your own head!"

"You're crazy." The droid's mouth slot opened and deposited the holocam back into its hand. The hand twitched, and suddenly the holocam flew back across the room toward Ben.

Ben caught it. "So?"

"I'm satisfied it's not a weapon. Or programmed for any activity not part of a holocam's standard tasks."

Ben brought the holocam up, made sure that the droid's magnetics had not disrupted its operation, and began recording. "Do me a favor," he said. "Wave. Like you're on holiday. Do you have a message for your parents? Say something."

"That's a good idea." The droid waved awkwardly. "Hey, Mom. Hey, Dad. I'm working hard but having a good time. I hope I'll get to see you soon." It paused. "How's that?"

"Pretty good." Ben's feelings of dismay intensified. The droid's words, as banal as those spoken by any average teenager separated from his parents, hit him hard.

He stopped the recording and held out the holocam. "Now look at what you just recorded."

The holocam flicked out of his fingers and into the droid's hand. Once again the droid lifted it to the mouth-slot and internalized it.

Ben waited. There were more voices out in the hall, and the clanking of equipment being set down. The only other sounds were the hum of all the electronic equipment in the room and Ben's own breathing.

"It's a lie," the droid finally said.

"You looked at the holocam yourself. You said it had no weird programming."

"I missed something."

"No, you didn't. You know you didn't. That holocam is dumber than a mouse droid. It couldn't hide anything from you."

The droid turned its upper body as it looked at Ben again. The boy could swear that its posture sagged.

Tears sprang to Ben's eyes. He wiped them away. "I'm so sorry," he said. "But it's true. You're a droid who's been programmed to think it's Anakin Solo. But if you were really Anakin, you'd help me destroy the station now, because the people who made you can use it as a weapon and they could *destroy whole stars with it*."

"How would you have destroyed me?"

"I didn't come here to destroy you. I came here to destroy the station. I have a way to cause this control room to send a pulse through the station and wreck it."

"Killing everybody aboard."

"No, it sends an emergency evacuation code first and waits ten minutes."

"Ten minutes?" The droid sounded offended. "You think everyone on a station this large could get to escape pods in ten minutes?"

Guiltily, Ben shrugged. "I didn't come up with the plan."

"Give me the data."

Ben reached into his pouch and grabbed the spike-topped data card. As an afterthought, he also grabbed the other data cards, those that would have initiated self-destruct or shutdown sequences from other control rooms in the station. He held them up and felt the droid's magnetics yank them out of his hand. A moment later they went into the droid's mouth-slot.

"Analyzing," the droid said in its heartbroken tones. Then, "Oh, I know where that interface is. But I've been interpreting it as a candy dispenser."

"That's . . . wrong," Ben said.

"I have to reinterpet myself in light of what it really is. These commands . . . no. I won't take life unnecessarily."

"Unnecessarily? Think about what's going to happen if you don't!"

"It's true. Somebody is going to die. Them or me. Me or them."

"Except you wouldn't be dying," Ben said. "You're a droid. You're not really alive."

The droid leaned toward him, its posture suddenly menacing. "If I do this, I'll *end*. Everything I am will just stop and never happen again. Tell me that's not dying. Go ahead, tell me again."

Ben leaned away from the droid, ashamed. "I'm sorry."

The droid resumed its earlier posture. "Analyzing programming," it said, its voice distracted, almost droid-like. "Security bypasses. Passcodes. Hey, there's some brilliant stuff here."

"Our best spies have been working on it," Ben said absently. The clanking and voices from the hall were becoming louder. He heard a whining noise, and the door lifted enough that a centimeter of corridor light shone through.

"I'm going places I didn't know about. Seeing through security holocams I couldn't access before." The droid looked up and waved toward the ceiling. "Look, there I am." Its voice became dreamy. "There are places, intersections into the old systems. So old. Beautiful engineering. I can . . . *almost* . . . get in." It sighed, a sound of exasperation. "They won't let me in."

"Time's kind of running out," Ben said. "What are you going to do, Anakin?"

"I'm not really Anakin, am I?"

"You're . . . *an* Anakin. Not Anakin Solo."

"Anakin *Sal*-Solo." The droid laughed, but it was a humorless noise. "Thrackan's offspring. That's what I am."

Ben suddenly found himself falling. He landed in a crouch on the floor. He looked cautiously up at the droid.

"I'm not going to destroy this station," the droid said. "If you could feel it the way I do . . . feel its life . . . and there's so much knowledge here. But I'll keep my father and his friends from using it. I guess that means I have to die."

"I'm sorry," Ben said. And he truly was. He couldn't quite accept the droid as his cousin, but he abruptly realized he was thinking of it as a him, a living thing . . . a noble one.

"There it is, right at the human-builder interface," the droid said. "The code representing the station's imprinting on Anakin Solo. I'm installing a procedure to scramble what the station thinks Anakin Solo is. And another one to purge my memory—in me, in all my backups. Without those . . . files . . . I doubt they'll ever be able to deconstruct what I've done."

The door suddenly shot upward a meter. Without looking, the droid gestured toward it. It slammed shut again, so hard that the frame buckled. Ben heard cries of alarm and outrage from outside.

"There's my own code, my programming," the droid

continued. "Checks and locks in place. Let's get rid of that one." It sighed, a sound of tremendous relief. "There we go. No more fear of death. Take three steps to your right."

It took Ben a moment to realize the droid was addressing him. He obeyed.

The lightsaber flew from the droid's hand to him. He caught it out of the air.

"Straight down from where you are," the droid said, "there's an unguarded chamber. It leads to a corridor that parallels the one outside. You should leave now."

"Thank you," Ben said. He felt numb. He activated his lightsaber and pressed the blade tip into the floor. Smoke curled up as he began dragging the blade around in a slow circle.

"I think I'll activate that evacuation alarm anyway," the droid said. "You know why?"

"Why?"

" 'Cause it'll be funny to watch all the people run around." The droid laughed again, and this time there was real mirth in it. "Won't that be a good way to die? No pain, and watching people do silly things like in a holocomedy?"

"That's a good way, all right." Ben's circle was almost done. His lightsaber blade hissed louder as his tears fell on it, and little puffs of steam rose to join the smoke.

Jacen caught up to Thrackan in a corridor intersection. Against the long wall, flush with the floor, were two shiny silver discs more than a meter in diameter. Above them, transparent tubes emerged from the ceiling a short distance, no more than twenty centimeters. The tubes looked like some sort of escape access, but no ladders led up to them.

Thrackan was in the act of reaching toward a control panel on the wall when Jacen lashed out through the Force, hammering Thrackan into the wall. The older man bounced off, rolling painfully to his knees atop one of the silver discs.

And then Jacen reached him, holding the glowing tip of

his lightsaber just under Thrackan's chin. Jacen saw the tips of Thrackan's beard hairs blacken from the heat.

His cousin, panting and almost stunned, said, "I guess you win."

"I guess I—"

"Time to die, Solo!" The voice was Thrackan's but it came from behind. Reflexively, Jacen turned and began to bring his lightsaber up in a defensive posture.

There was a blaster retort from behind him. The shot hit his lightsaber hilt and catapulted the weapon out of his hand, sending it down the corridor.

He spun again. Thrackan, blaster in hand, finished rising and fired into Jacen's chest.

Jacen caught the shot—bare-handed, dissipating its energy before it reached his palm. He smiled and opened his hand, showing Thrackan his undamaged palm.

Thrackan fired again. Jacen twitched his hand over to the left, caught the second shot.

Then he crooked his finger with his left hand. The blaster flew from Thrackan's grip into that hand. Jacen glanced back to where his lightsaber lay and gestured for it. It flew the four meters between them and dropped into his right hand. He activated it again and positioned its tip in front of Thrackan's neck.

"Stang," Thrackan said. His expression suggested he was genuinely impressed. "I heard rumors that Darth Vader could do that. Can all Jedi do that?"

"No. What did *you* do? A recording?"

"Yes, a little sound recorder. It was triggered by me saying, *I guess you win.*"

"Time to die, Solo!" came the cry from behind Jacen.

Jacen snorted, amused despite the urgency of his mission. "I see."

"Except you really lose. In a minute, all the forces I've brought to bear will be here. They'll continue to follow you, to wear you down, until one of them drops you. And your plan to destroy this station will fail. In that sense, it already has failed."

A distant wail filled the air, a keening noise seemingly emanating from all directions at once, echoing and overlapping as though a city-sized droid were suddenly grieving for a slain offspring.

Thrackan paled.

Jacen grinned. "That's the evacuation alarm. It means we have ten minutes to get off this station before it destroys itself. Which means that my apprentice, who is fortunate enough not to share any blood with you, has succeeded in setting up the station's destruction." He leaned closer, the proximity of his lightsaber blade causing Thrackan to lean away. "I can still share in his success a little bit. I could kill you, remove your stain from the galaxy."

Thrackan shook his head. "Jedi don't kill prisoners who have surrendered."

"You haven't surrendered."

"I surrender." Thrackan raised his hands. "There."

A younger Jacen might have been offended by the older man's casual, even contemptuous manipulations. This Jacen merely met manipulation with manipulation. "Perhaps Jedi don't . . . but *I* might. You've done nothing but do damage to Corellia, to the New Republic, and to my family since I was a child. Wouldn't the universe be a better place without you in it?"

"Very funny," Thrackan said. Jacen could feel just the tiniest trace of increased distress in the man's emotions.

Distress and—no, he was feeling something else, from somewhere else. Pain. Death. From the future.

From *a* future, one of any number of possible futures. Jacen peered into it, letting the events of that potential time line wash over him, but kept one eye on his cousin, alert through just his sight for any treachery.

Events flashed past him too fast to absorb all their meaning. Starfighters launched lasers and missiles, raining death on the innocent. Why not the guilty? He could see no guilty. Pilot versus pilot, soldier versus soldier, no one was guilty. Neither side was more evil, more dark.

War spread out from Corellia like ripples from a rock

hitting the surface of a pond, and the rock was an image of Jacen and Thrackan. Jacen saw clouds of expanding gas where the brave had flown, corpse-littered fields where the brave had fought, near-unrecognizable ruins that had once been huge space vessels but were now crushed like beverage containers on the rocky surfaces of moons.

And pain—pain racking the Force like nothing had since the Yuuzhan Vong war. Pain twisting his kin. Shrieks of loss filled his ears.

He focused on the rock in the pond, the image of himself and Thrackan, and saw all these events unfolding from the point, the here and now, when he failed to kill Thrackan.

Shaken, he yanked himself back from the vision and stood there, breathing heavily.

"What is it, boy?" Thrackan asked, his tone almost kindly. "You've gone pale."

Jacen blinked at him. He felt as though he were hung on a hook. His mind told him that he couldn't do what his gut said he must. He couldn't cut down an enemy who had surrendered.

Trust the Force, Luke had told him, so often. *Trust your feelings in the Force.*

He couldn't *not* cut down this enemy, even if the man *had* surrendered.

Jacen slowed his breathing, his heartbeat. He got his voice under control. "I apologize," he said. "I actually *do* have to kill you now."

"You're insane. I've surrendered."

"That's not enough. You ruin the future, Thrackan." No, that wasn't quite right. But the future was ruined if he lived. "For the greater good, our Jedi traditions notwithstanding, I have to kill you."

"But my droids are here."

A blaster opened up from behind Jacen. He turned to intercept the bolt—and, partway into his maneuver, cursed himself for being tricked twice.

No one stood in the hallway. The sound of blasterfire

emerged from a small circular device adhering to the ceiling near a glow rod light fixture.

Jacen continued his maneuver into a full spin. His lightsaber, ending its 360-degree sweep, would cut Thrackan in half.

Instead, it hit a gleaming metal column.

Jacen glanced up. The column was rising out of the floor, propelling the metal disc Thrackan stood on up to the ceiling. The disc hit the edges of the transparent tube, and there was a tremendous *thoom* noise. Thrackan's feet launched up from the disc and disappeared from sight.

Jacen stepped onto the second disc and hit all four buttons on the control panel. The disc he stood on raised him rapidly into position, to the bottom of the second tube, and an instant later, a second ear-hammering *thoom* catapulted him upward.

Propelled by an energy he couldn't yet define—repulsors? pneumatic air currents? tractor beams?—he flew up through his tube, flashing past corridors, sometimes seeing open channels out to space, sometimes seeing lit passageways through which people were running.

The shaft the two tubes occupied was sometimes tight-packed with machinery or engineering supports, sometimes open. The first time it opened, Jacen looked up and could see Thrackan, a hundred meters or more above him, in his own tube.

Thrackan's tube twisted, a right-angled turn, and suddenly he was headed away. The turn would have pulped a human under ordinary circumstances. *Gravitics,* Jacen told himself. Only gravity manipulation could have allowed Thrackan to survive.

Jacen reached the same altitude. His tube turned the opposite direction. He felt his stomach lurch, and suddenly he was hurtling away from his enemy—away from the man he desperately needed to kill.

He howled, a noise of anger and distress he could barely hear over the wind noise whipping along the tube's interior.

Then he deactivated his lightsaber, clipped it to his belt, and tucked Thrackan's blaster into a pouch.

It was time to be calm, time to get off this station, time to find out Ben's status.

Thrackan was right. Jacen *had* failed. Not in his intended mission—but in his greater responsibility.

chapter sixteen

CORONET, CORELLIA

"On the datapad, it's See See See Thirty-nine," Doran shouted forward from the passenger compartment.

In the copilot's seat, Zekk twisted uncomfortably and shouted back, "I'm telling you, the signs read WEDGE ANTILLES BOULEVARD."

"Be quiet," Jaina snapped from the pilot's seat. "It's got to be the same route. Cities rename their streets all the time."

Their vehicle—a standard *Lambda*-class shuttle, its wings locked in the down position for flight—cruised down the center of the Coronet boulevard. Its presence was incongruous. Though no more massive than some cargo-carrying groundspeeders moving along the same avenue, it protruded in ways no groundspeeder did, its flight wings sticking out of the lane on both sides, its upper stabilizer rising well above the containment zone indicated for the traffic lane. Nor was it inconspicuous in any other way—colored the bright tan of desert sands, with a Corellian sand panther, twisting and lashing out, painted along each side, it was even more highly decorated than most Corellian personal vehicles.

Zekk twisted to face forward again. "This seat is too small for me—"

"It's too small for anyone," Jaina said. "I think it's built for a child."

"And it smells like fur."

Jaina glanced over. "Yes, there's fur coming off it and sticking to your clothes. Maybe a Bothan?"

Zekk leaned back to sniff at the seat top. "Doesn't smell like a Bothan."

"We don't all shmell alike!" Kolir's outraged shout floated up from the passenger compartment. "How do these rumorsh get shtarted?"

"Rest your mouth, you're injured," Jaina called back.

A groundspeeder rose from a lower lane and settled into place in front of the shuttle's bow, close enough that its proximity alarm sounded—precisely what the irritated Corellian pilot ahead intended. Jaina growled. All around, normal groundspeeder traffic was reacting negatively to the inappropriate presence of the shuttle in their traffic lane. They crowded the shuttle from behind, decelerated ahead to force Jaina to slow down, settled into place immediately above the shuttle's wings to aggravate her. "Rudest pilots in the universe," she said. "Where's Uncle Luke?"

"Soon, soon," Thann soothed from the main compartment.

A new sound cut through the shuttle's hull—the warbling alarm of a CorSec groundspeeder. Sighing, Jaina checked her sensor board and found the view showing the vehicle. It was right behind the shuttle, its flashers going, its pilot waving her to descend. Doubtless the pilot was also broadcasting a warning, but the shuttle's communications gear was set to Hardpoint Squadron and operation frequencies.

"Are we on Corellia yet?" Zekk asked.

"First chance, I'm going to space you," Jaina said.

They reached a point where Wedge Antilles Boulevard crossed under an even broader avenue, listed as Five Brothers Avenue on both the datapad and the ground-level glowsigns. Traffic on Five Brothers Avenue was higher than that on Wedge Antilles Boulevard, for the simple reason that this was an elevated trafficway, a thruster-scoured transparisteel bridge so broad that even the fastest-moving vehicles on Wedge Antilles Boulevard would be beneath it, in shadow, for long, long seconds.

But as Jaina's stolen shuttle neared the intersection, she and Zekk recognized some of the traffic up on the Five Brothers overpass—a formation of X-wings, tucked neatly among the groundspeeders, and also pursued by a CorSec speeder doubtless piloted by a very annoyed officer.

She keyed her communications board. "Hardpoint, this is Purella-Tauntaun. We have you on visuals. Over."

Luke Skywalker's voice crackled back instantly. "Are you spaceworthy—wait, I see you. Isn't that a little conspicuous? Sand panthers? Over."

"Best we could do on short notice. And we're ready for space. Over."

"Begin your ascent. Out."

"Belt in or hang on!" Jaina shouted. The jubilant tone in her voice came from being able, finally, to escape the restrictions of slow-paced traffic and a ruined operation. Not waiting to see if her teammates complied—they'd been told to belt in the instant they originally took off, after all—she used her repulsors to raise the shuttle's nose.

The pursuing CorSec vehicle crowded up on her rear a little too fast from a little too close. Jaina heard a *clang* of impact as the groundspeeder banged into her main drive unit. She fired her accelerators, just enough to splash thruster wash over the hood of the CorSec vehicle, and gave the pilot two seconds to get clear. Then she put her thrusters and repulsorlift units on full.

The shuttle leapt into the sky.

It didn't leap as nimbly as the X-wings on the bridge ahead. They stood on their tails and rocketed skyward. By comparison, her shuttle rose like a lazy balloon.

But it was better than being in traffic.

Four of the X-wings reduced speed and dropped into position behind her, forming a protective box beyond her stern. Three maneuvered into position around her, one above, one to port, one to starboard, a protective triangle. And Luke and Mara took point.

Jaina grinned. She'd prefer to be out there with them, in a nimble starfighter protecting a more vulnerable target . . . but if she had to be shepherded, to have Luke and Mara doing the honors was about as good as it could get.

CORELLIAN SPACE

The ships of Admiral Klauskin's task force pulled away from Corellia's gravitational attraction. It would be some time, long minutes, before they were far enough away from the gravity well to make the jump to hyperspace.

The vessels of the Corellian fleet moved in, forming up in small groups of four and five ships. "But they're not moving in for the kill," Fiav Fenn said. "They've recalled their fighter squadrons."

"We're just going to get harassment fire, then," Klauskin said.

"Probably."

"How's their frigate?"

"Floating dead in space. Minimal casualties as far as we can determine, but a confirmed kill. All their escape pods have been picked up by their side."

"Good, good." Klauskin nodded absently.

The forward elements of Klauskin's task force, including *Dodonna*, reached the leading edge of the reconfiguring Corellian fleet. *Dodonna* began shivering as she sustained long-distance laser battery fire. But as Klauskin had predicted, nothing heavier hit her; nothing threatened to batter down her shields.

Harassment fire.

The admiral grinned. "In about half an hour, they'll wish they'd tried to blow us out of the sky."

"Yes, sir." Fenn's voice sounded dull. Klauskin wondered what had happened to diminish her enthusiasm for her job.

As they passed through the harassment screen, *Dodonna* shook and vibrated, but Klauskin never felt genuinely threatened. Reports continued to flood into the bridge. GA ship after ship reached the point where they could enter hyperspace. Preliminary starfighter losses from the skirmish were assessed. The role of the accidental intruder, *Millennium Falcon,* in the action was evaluated. Hardpoint Squadron reported a successful departure from Corellian atmosphere.

The last, lagging vessel in Klauskin's task force reported readiness to enter hyperspace.

"All ships jump," Klauskin ordered.

A moment later the stars through the forward viewport seemed to twist and spin, an unsettling kaleidoscopic visual image. An instant later they straightened themselves, and the white-clouded blue-and-green planet Tralus wrenched into view in the distance ahead.

"All starfighter squadrons," Klauskin said, "launch."

Two hours later, it was done—a world was occupied and subjugated.

To be sure, this wasn't a tremendous military accomplishment. Tralus was lightly occupied, and its defense against invasion amounted to a few scattered CorSec units, plus a dangerous, well-armed commando unit holding the installation built around the repulsor unit associated with Centerpoint Station.

Klauskin's forces didn't bother with the repulsor defenders. They merely swept down on the city of Rellidir, whose population of one million made it a metropolis by the standards of Tralus, and took the city and planetary leaders into custody. Units of Klauskin's task force landed in the city and occupied several downtown blocks. A few assault shuttles full of elite soldiers surrounded the repulsor facility with orders to keep its garrison bottled up. The rest of the task force's ships remained in orbit, a defensive perimeter.

Units of the Corellian fleet began popping into nearby space—circling, reconnoitering, attempting to look threatening. It was evident to Klauskin that their commanders were confused, ill directed.

He smiled. He'd achieved his purpose by securing this beachhead. He'd confused the enemy. They were, at last, intimidated.

"Enemy reinforcements continue to arrive," he said, his tones ringing and military, "but take no action for fear of retaliation against or spillover damage to the civilian population." He thought for a moment, attempting to dredge up some further statement of hope and good cheer, then shook his head. "Operation Roundabout, Admiral Matric Klauskin, commanding." He nodded to Fenn to indicate she should cease recording.

She hit the appropriate button on her datapad. "Shall I clean it up before sending, sir?"

"No, send it raw. Let's not make Admiral Pellaeon wait for it any longer than he has to. He's getting on in years, you know."

"Yes, sir."

"I need a brief rest. I'll be in my quarters." Klauskin turned away from the bow viewports that had occupied his attention for the last several hours and began the long walk to his quarters.

Minutes later, the door into his quarters slid open and he strode through. Only then did his pace change, his step fading from energetic to slow and weary.

And weary he was, tired both physically and emotionally. To have his mission run head-on into certain failure, to have him wrest it back to a result that he could consider a success, had taken a toll on him.

An admiral's flagship quarters were large and could be dressed up in opulence, but Klauskin had never taken that route. His largest chamber, instead of being a living chamber full of entertainments and comforts, had been furnished as a conference room, one large oval table and numerous padded chairs, with viewports affording it a beautiful portside view of the stars. He walked past the table, seeing neither it nor the glorious view, and entered his bedchamber. He sat on the bed, remained upright long enough to pull his boots off, and lay back.

The air above him shimmered and Edela appeared.

She was a trifle overweight but dressed well to compensate for it, today wearing a green formal gown with a low neckline. Her long hair, brown streaked with gray, was piled high in a Coruscanti style that some considered out of date but Klauskin had always regarded as classic. She wore no jewelry. She despised jewelry.

In all the years they'd been married, she'd never looked more radiant. At the moment, she looked far happier and healthier than the month before she died.

He'd long since stopped wondering how he'd been so lucky to have her reenter his life. Now he just smiled up at her. "I'm glad you came."

"Shh." She put a finger to her lips, then lowered it to his. "You need to rest. You did so very well today."

"I did, didn't I?"

"Yes. Don't ever let anyone *ever* tell you that you didn't." Her tone was almost stern. "You just wait. Soon enough, they'll all be saying how you took impossible orders and sliced a victory out of them. You'll be famous. You'll be promoted to fleet admiral."

"Yes, dear."

"No other reward would be acceptable. Anything else would be an insult."

"Yes, dear."

"Sleep, Matric."

He did.

CORUSCANT

Two days later, Luke Skywalker, dressed in the full robe array of a Jedi Master, was escorted to a conference chamber within the densest government precincts on Coruscant.

Several invitees to the meeting were already there and seated. At the head of the table was Chief of State Cal Omas, a lean, fair man with thinning hair. The stresses of his office and late middle age had made the man gaunt, even frail looking, but determination kept him upright and lent him dignity. He wore garments cut in the fashion of a formal GA military uniform, but in nonregulation deep purple.

To his right sat Admiral Gilad Pellaeon, acting chief of the GA military. He had been a successful, ferocious space navy officer in the days of the Old Republic and even now, more than sixty years later, still commanded with wit, ingenuity, and uncompromising will. He and Luke exchanged glances, and the faintest of ironic smiles; more than thirty years earlier, the two had been enemies, Luke fighting for the New Republic, and Pellaeon for the remnants of the Empire, and now they served the same cause. Despite his advancing age, Pellaeon still appeared formidable: thick-chested, his white hair still bushy, his mustache still ferocious. His GA admiral's uniform was as crisp as his manner.

To his right sat Admiral Niathal, a female Mon Calamari. Unlike Ackbar, perhaps the best-known military Mon Cal officer in recent history, she was known for an icy disposition and cutting reprimands. Her outsized eyes followed Luke as he entered the chamber. He spared her a glance and a slight, friendly nod; he did not know her well and had neither affection nor disdain for her.

Elsewhere at the table sat advisers and aides for the three. The composition of meeting attendees told Luke that all the discussion would be about military affairs and their effects on political matters—and that meant the mess at Corellia.

Chief Omas gestured to the unoccupied seat to his left, and Luke took it. "Good to see you, Master Skywalker. Thank you for arriving so quickly."

"Happy to oblige, sir." Luke's arrival had indeed been quick—the transport carrying him, his Jedi teams, and others fresh from Operation Roundabout had landed less than an hour before.

"So." Omas glanced at Pellaeon. "Admiral, would you care to begin?"

"Yes." Pellaeon glanced at the datapad before him.

"Master Skywalker, how would you describe the Jedi operations that were part of Roundabout?"

"Successful," Luke said, "but not cleanly so. We had five operations. Slashrat, Purella, Tauntaun, Womp Rat, and Mynock."

Pellaeon managed a small smile. "Each creature being either bad-tempered or bad smelling."

"Yes, sir. Slashrat, commanded by Master Corran Horn, was a two-operative team observing Coronet's main starport for significant starfighter launch activities. Since most of Coronet's starfighter squadrons had apparently been pulled for Corellia's fleet action, of course, Slashrat's usefulness was largely nullified.

"Purella and Tauntaun, respectively commanded by Jaina Solo and Tahiri Veila, were assigned the task of kidnapping Prime Minister Aidel Saxan and Chief of State Thrackan Sal-Solo from their residences."

One of the aides toward the foot of the table, a male Bothan, cleared his throat. His fur rippled with what Luke interpreted as discomfort. "It's probably inappropriate," he said, "to use the word *kidnapping*."

Niathal's eyes twitched and her gaze pinned the speaker. "Master Skywalker isn't speaking to the public or the press," she said, her voice harsh and gravelly, "so he isn't obliged to mince words. In this company, we should be using precise terminology, not your public-relations pablum. Shouldn't we?"

The Bothan's fur rippled again, and Luke could sense it was from a combination of fear and anger at being rebuked. "Yes, Admiral," the man said.

"In the future," Niathal added, "try confining your remarks to useful ones."

"Yes, Admiral."

Luke suppressed a smile. He turned back to Pellaeon. "Their mission was an almost complete failure due to what appears to be foreknowledge on Corellia's part. Saxan and Sal-Solo remain on Corellia.

"Womp Rat, which I commanded, had the task of retrieving Tauntaun and Purella, and was successful, though not without loss; we lost a shuttle and its two-person crew, and an X-wing with its Jedi pilot.

"Finally," Luke said, "there's Mynock. The most important of the operations, and the one for which the other operations, as significant as they might have been, were also to act as a diversion. Mynock was, from both a short-term and long-term perspective, spectacularly successful. Centerpoint Station was removed as a threat through the elimination of the control mechanisms the Corellians had designed to make it completely operational. But the station itself wasn't destroyed, meaning that in the long run it can be further examined and investigated. There was some loss of life among Corellian Security Force members defending the installation, but neither of the Jedi involved in the mission was hurt—and this all despite the fact that the Corellians in charge of the station were fully aware that operatives were coming. That *Jedi* operatives were coming."

Pellaeon fixed Luke with a stare that could most charitably be described as unhappy. "You're certain they knew Jedi would be coming."

Luke nodded. "Yes, sir. According to Mynock's reports, they had developed tactics and brought in combat droids that were clearly optimized for action against Jedi. They used wide-effect weapons such as sonic attacks and explosives, very hard for Jedi to evade; they had fast-moving, very mobile units capable of sustaining action against powerful individual infiltrators; their holocam sensor network appeared to be set up to track individuals moving through the station. They even had a trap specifically designed to keep Jedi from using the Force. Also, a resource remaining in Corellia"—Luke didn't name Dr. Seyah, since all those here who were authorized to know that name would already be familiar with it—"reports discussions among the CorSec troops about the relative effectiveness of their brief anti-Jedi training."

"Ah." Pellaeon looked not at all surprised by the allegation that the Corellians had had not just advance warning of the operation but of specific details about the operation's composition. "I understand your own son was responsible for Mynock being a success."

"That's correct, sir."

"Your thirteen-year-old son."

Luke smiled. "Yes, sir."

"You're more ruthless than I realized, Master Skywalker."

Luke shook his head. "I simply don't swim against the currents of the Force."

Niathal asked, "Could General Wedge Antilles have been the conduit for all the advance knowledge the Corellians received?"

Luke frowned, puzzled. "I don't think so. Wedge is retired. I doubt he was involved at all, on either side."

"Oh, he was involved," Niathal said. "As an extension of the same governing principle that led to Operations Tauntaun and Purella, he was picked up and transported here prior to Operation Roundabout's commencement. To keep him out of trouble."

Luke covered his eyes with his hand.

"He escaped a short time later and apparently returned to Corellia," Niathal continued. "It's just been announced that Chief Sal-Solo has ousted the old Minister of War to assume the position himself, and Antilles has been assigned liaison between Sal-Solo and Prime Minister Saxan."

"I'm surprised," Luke said. He looked up at the Mon Cal officer again. "Surprised that he'd take a position like that."

"I'm not," Pellaeon said. "If I'd been subjected to that sort of treatment, I might declare a personal war on the government that had authorized it. I suspect Antilles isn't fighting for Corellia. He's against *us*—us personally." He indicated himself and Cal Omas, then turned to Niathal. "Find out the name of every officer who botched any portion of the operation against Antilles. Perhaps he'll remove himself from the picture if we bust every one of them down to floor sweeper."

"Admiral, it will be a pleasure." Niathal turned to Luke.

"I need you to be logical instead of sentimental when answering this: Could your sister have been the leak, informing the Corellians about the Jedi involvement?"

Luke shook his head. "Impossible."

Niathal made a wet, rubbery noise, the Mon Calamari equivalent of a snort of derision. "*Nothing's impossible*, Skywalker."

"I'll explain, with logic, why I believe it's impossible. For her to know that Jedi would be part of the operation, she'd also have to be privy to more information than that. And the *more information* would reveal that her son and her daughter, and my son, were part of the operation. Can you imagine her giving the Corellians information that would oblige them to kill her children and her nephew?"

Niathal spread her hands, palms up—an *I don't know* gesture. "It depends on the strength of her convictions . . . and what those convictions are. You haven't proved that her ideals don't value Corellian independence above family survival."

"Enough," Chief Omas said. "It's out of the question."

"But there is a leak somewhere," Luke conceded. "In the order, here in the seat of government, I'm not sure which. We have to find it and close it."

"Another question," Pellaeon said. "What impression did you have of Admiral Klauskin?"

Luke considered. "Mostly favorable, at least as the operation was coming together. He seemed smart and decisive. When things started to go wrong, though—well, it seems obvious that he chose badly. Improvisation does not appear to be one of his skills."

"That's putting it mildly," Omas said. "But really—that's all you or any of your Jedi could say about him?"

"Well . . . no." Luke suppressed a sigh. Reluctance to speak ill of someone was out of place here. "Except for me, Jedi dealings with him were very limited. I saw him at several briefings. All the team heads except Corran Horn—Jaina, Tahiri, Jacen, and I—were at one briefing, and all the Jedi met him at one dinner. It was after that dinner that one of my Jedi, Tiu Zax, a recently confirmed Jedi Knight, said that she'd had the oddest impression from him."

Niathal asked, "Which was what?"

"That he'd blanked at one point during dinner. That, while I was swapping starfighter pilot stories with Jaina, Klauskin had just . . . gone away, mentally. An absence so strong she felt it through the Force. Just for a few moments."

Niathal's eyes edged forward, a gesture perhaps meant to intimidate. "And you didn't report this?"

"Report what?" Luke shrugged. "The same sort of thing can happen when someone enters a meditative state, or falls into a particularly private memory. Tiu's young enough that she hadn't encountered it before. I have, and didn't think anything of it. Do you believe it could be evidence of a more significant problem?"

"Oh, yes." Niathal nodded, the motion made exaggerated by the size of her head, longer than that of any human. "He has apparently experienced a complete emotional and mental breakdown. Twelve standard hours after the occupation of Tralus, his aide, Colonel Fenn, found him wandering *Dodonna*'s corridors in his robe, looking for his wife. His dead wife. He hasn't responded much to questions or orders since. *Dodonna*'s officers have been told that he collapsed from exhaustion."

"Which brings us to the last subject of significance we need you for, Master Skywalker." Chief Omas rubbed his chin. "The occupation of Tralus and its consequences. Operation Roundabout was supposed to force the Corellians to realize that they can't just rebuild their giant blaster in space. We were to take the giant blaster away and rap their heads with our knuckles. We failed to rap their heads—the arrival of the Corellian fleet prevented that—but we did take their giant blaster away. And had our task force returned to Coruscant from that point, we still would have been ahead, if only slightly ahead, in the game."

"But the occupation of Tralus," Niathal said, "has made them angry. Fighting mad, I believe the expression is."

"Corellia continues to arm herself," Pellaeon said. "Other planets are expressing outrage about the way Roundabout was conducted. Commenor. Fondor. Bespin. Coalitions within the Corporate Sector. More every hour. Some of them are simply playing political games, of course, but others could conceivably join Corellia in a military alliance."

"I know." Luke's voice was rueful. "Maybe those other planets would ease off if we showed them the evidence you've gathered about Corellia's secret assault fleet."

"We can't," Omas said. "Our evidence isn't incontrovertible, and some of those worlds would ally with Corellia even if it were. We'd be tipping our hand for nothing."

"And we still wouldn't know the location of the fleet," Pellaeon said. "But we can still manage this through diplomacy. Prime Minister Saxan has indicated that she would be willing to meet with us in a mission of peace—even travel from Corellia for the meeting. But not here. Not to Coruscant."

"Where, then?" Luke asked.

"Not yet determined," Pellaeon said. "That's not important. It will have to be a system that both sides consider neutral on this issue. Now, Chief of State Omas cannot represent the Galactic Alliance, since his rank is substantially higher than Saxan's—for the leader of hundreds of worlds to travel to meet the leader of five would be too great a sign of weakness."

"Of course," Luke said. He breathed deeply, willing away the sudden stab of nausea he felt. This was the type of politics he hated most—niggling details based on perceptions of relative merit or importance.

"So it will be me," Pellaeon continued. "Each side will have a security detail in place. But Prime Minister Saxan has made an interesting concession. She's willing to stipulate the neutrality of Jedi on this issue, and to have as many Jedi present as you, Luke Skywalker, wish. To defend the diplomatic mission."

Luke nodded. "Give me the details and I'll assemble a team. But I don't understand why she'd do that. The Jedi order is specifically an organization defending the Galactic Alliance. We're not entirely impartial."

Chief Omas said, "I can only give you a guess. A guess based on decades of political dealings. I think Saxan wants peace—not even necessarily for its own sake, but because war will allow Chief Sal-Solo to assume emergency power and control resources she can't regulate or restrain. But she has to find a way to preserve the peace that allows the Corellians to save face. Which means, so do we."

"We could withdraw the units occupying Tralus," Luke said.

Chief Omas nodded. "Correct. But we'll let that be one of Saxan's negotiating points. She'll certainly insist on it, and we'll agree to it."

"We shouldn't." That was Niathal, and, if anything, there seemed to be even more grumble to her voice than before. "We should massively reinforce it now, begin a forced relocation of the civilian population. We'll need it as a jumping-off point if the Corellians don't comply and we have to conquer the system. Not having it available to us could cost us immeasurably."

Chief Omas fixed her with an admonishing look. "We'll agree to it," he continued, and returned his attention to Luke. "It *is* a political, rather than a military, tactic. If we just withdraw now, the Corellians become more belligerent, seeing our action as weakness. If we agree to Saxan's negotiations on that point, we don't look weak, and Saxan's position is strengthened."

"I see."

Pellaeon said, "Please assemble a list of prospects for your Jedi security team. We'll let you know as things develop."

Luke stood. "May the Force be with you, Admiral."

Pellaeon grinned. "Once upon a time, I was certain I'd never hear those words directed toward me."

Luke smiled in return. "Times change." He nodded his respects to the others and swept out of the chamber.

chapter seventeen

CORUSCANT

The airspeeder was big, roomy inside and outside in a way that had not been in fashion for several years. It was sky blue but scarred and dented by a generation's worth of ordinary accidents and mishaps, and it looked as slow as a bantha at naptime.

A human male lounged in the backseat, his feet toward the elevated walkway against which the speeder had docked. He wore dark pants with narrow red stripes running up the outsides of the legs, a tan, long-sleeved shirt, a dark vest, and worn boots. A yellow rag was draped across his face. He looked at first glance as though he was sleeping, the rag keeping sunlight from his face, but something in the way his head was propped up against the side of the seat, orienting his eyes toward the adjacent walkway, something in the way his raised right knee hid his hand and perhaps the presence of a blaster pistol—illegal here but hardly uncommon—kept even the most larcenous passersby from giving too much consideration to stealing the speeder.

Moving briskly, a small woman in a brown traveler's robe, hood up to conceal her face, moved out of the stream of foot traffic and dropped into the passenger seat.

The man in the backseat pulled the rag from his face and rolled forward into the pilot's seat, fast and graceful. He had the speeder backed up thirty meters and was reversing direction, blasting forward into a traffic lane at a rate that seemed remarkable for such an awkward speeder, before other passersby began to register the fact that he was Han Solo.

"What'd you find out?" he asked.

The wind from their movement whipped the hood from Leia's face; it fell against her back. She didn't bother to replace it. Nor did she bother to conceal her unhappiness. "Maybe we ought to get home before we discuss this."

"I've already waited several hours," Han said.

"Maybe you ought to park."

Finally he gave her a close look. "That bad."

"Worse."

"Give it to me."

There was an almost imperceptible pause. Han knew Leia was arranging facts, deciding on order of presentation.

"Some of this I'm guessing, based on things that weren't said and things that were. Some that I'm sure of is based on things I overheard. I guess I'll start with the biggest things and go down from there. The Corellian claims that Centerpoint Station was sabotaged by Jedi are true. The station has been seriously damaged, setting the Corellian scientific corps back several years. And the Jedi who did it . . . were Jacen and Ben."

Han gave her a sharp look. He saw her eyes widen and he glanced back into traffic. In just fractions of a second, the distraction and the tightening of his hands on the controls had caused his speeder to slide partway out of its traffic lane, toward a tiny high-speed model with an elderly dark-skinned human couple in it. He flashed them a *sorry-about-that* smile and returned his attention to Leia, but kept better vigilance on his piloting. "Jacen."

"Yes."

"And Ben."

"Yes."

"Is Luke crazy?"

This time she didn't answer. She continued, "Jedi teams also made attempts to snatch a few critical Corellian politicians out of Coronet. Jaina was on one of those teams."

Han's jaw set and he saw Leia pull back, unconsciously, just a few centimeters. She wasn't afraid, had never had reason to be afraid of his reactions, but he was reminded of something a colleague once told him—when Han Solo got mad, he looked madder than any human in known space.

"He's doing it again," Han said. "He's throwing my children—our children—into dangerous situations they shouldn't be part of. What do I have to do to make him stop?"

"There's more. Are you sure I can't persuade you to pull over?"

"Is there anything you could possibly tell me that would make me lose my skill as a pilot?" Realizing he sounded testy, and not wanting to pour out his anger on Leia, he forced all anger out of his voice. "Just tell me."

"The Corellians had ambushes and traps set up for them. Ambushes and traps meant for Jedi."

They flew along in silence for several long moments. Han held what Leia had told him in his mind like an egg, something too delicate for him to handle roughly.

He noticed, even in his distraction, that the speeder had developed a shudder. Carefully, he experimented with the acceleration, with the controls during turns.

No, the speeder was unchanged. But his arms and hands were shaking so badly that they were affecting performance.

Abruptly he pulled out of traffic, sideslipping with ridiculous, dangerous accuracy into an unoccupied speeder dock at the five-hundred-meter level next to a restaurant-side walkway. The speed of his approach and his rapid, last-second deceleration caused pedestrians on the walkway to shriek and leap out of the way, as though he were going to overshoot and slam through them, but he was at a dead stop centimeters from docking, and let the dock's grappler beam drag him in the final hand span of distance. Automatically, he inserted a credcard in the adjacent slot.

For long moments, he couldn't bring himself to look at his wife. His voice was low and shaky when he finally said, "So *I* did that. I almost got them killed."

"No."

"Yes. I should have figured that our kids would get involved in what was going on with Corellia. And I went there and told the Corellians to line up their gun sights on our boy and our girl."

"Han, you told them your *guesswork*. But you're not listening to me. I said they were prepared for Jedi. What, in everything you told the Corellians, would have alerted them to be prepared for Jedi in exactly the situations where Jedi were used against them?"

Han thought about it. "Nothing."

"That's right, nothing. So?"

"So . . . somebody else told them where and when Jedi would be used."

"That's right. And the whole thing with Centerpoint Station. The Corellians are being kind of disingenuous about it when they say the Jedi came and sabotaged the place. They neglect to point out that they'd restored it to full operating status, or were on the verge of doing so."

Han looked at her, tried to absorb the implications of what she was saying. No politician, he was still a skilled tactician, and the relative military strengths of Corellia with and without the station began clicking like numbers through his mind. They made him uneasy. With the station operable, Corellia could probably have achieved independence quickly, bloodlessly. But the system could only have done so by issuing threats—terrorist threats—against the Galactic Alliance. Suddenly he wasn't sure he could support Corellian independence on those terms, and this lack of conviction made him uneasy. "You're just full of good news," he said, an attempt at humor that, to his own ears, fell flat.

"There's more. And I don't know what this means."

"Go ahead."

"Ben actually did the main bit of work in sabotaging the station. It was quite an achievement. But he's not talking about it. He's reported only to his father, and Luke hasn't released any of that information. Ben's not accepting congratulations very well. And when I went to him to offer mine, he couldn't bring himself to talk to me. He just froze up and sort of nodded, and then made as hasty a retreat as he could. He looked . . . guilty."

"He probably figured out how I'd take the news."

"Maybe."

Han drew a long, deep breath. "Anything else?"

She nodded. "They're still going to try to fix everything by diplomatic means. There's going to be a meeting between Saxan and Pellaeon. Both sides, and the Jedi, will be providing security. Luke asked me to be part of that effort. And he's hoping you will be, too."

"Did you accept?"

"I accepted for me."

He nodded. "Then you accepted for me, too."

Finally, Leia smiled. "I was hoping you'd say that. And we have one last problem to deal with."

"Keep it up, my mind is going to crack. What problem?"

"Admirers."

Han looked up. Just meters away, a crowd of at least twenty people, their attention on Han and Leia, had accumulated on the walkway, slowing foot traffic. When Han looked at them, some waved, some looked away, some stood as transfixed as if they'd been hit by a blaster's stun bolt.

"Han Solo! Princess Leia!" called one, a Devaronian male, his ruddy red skin and white horns somehow out of place in this brightly sunlit spot. "Can we get a holo with you?"

"Our public," Han muttered.

"You love it, you know you do."

He flashed her a smile, stood, and offered her his hand, a gallant gesture, to help her rise. "Sure," he called back.

Then he whispered to his wife, "I hope there are no lip-readers in this crowd."

KUAT SYSTEM, TORYAZ STATION

Five days later, an odd collection of ships converged on a space station in the Kuat star system.

The station itself was of unusual design. At its core was a disc two kilometers across, three hundred meters thick, its edges beveled and smoothed like an ancient, polished credcoin, its surface thick with glowing viewports in every imaginable color, blue predominating. From the edge of the disc, at regularly spaced intervals, radiated a dozen narrow spokes a quarter kilometer in length. At the end of each spoke was a pod a quarter kilometer across, forty meters high at its thickest point; six of the pods were discs, resembling the central core, and six were triangular, affixed to the spokes on one point of the triangle. The discs alternated with the triangles, giving the station symmetry of design.

Toryaz Station was a place of recreation and competition, negotiation and romance, cold-blooded calculation and hot-blooded rage. Its core disc was an environment of hotels and shops, gardens and waterfalls. By dictate of the trade families that ran the station, hotels did not offer single-room accommodations; the lowliest quarters available for rent were lavish suites whose daily rent was equivalent to the yearly earnings of a middle-class family. Here corporations and merchant clans leased or maintained suites, entertained holodrama stars, made business deals that dictated the fates of thousands of occupations and lives.

The twelve pods were somewhat less glamorous, at least on initial inspection. Each would have been a fully self-contained space station but for the spoke, a sturdy, broad traffic conduit, connecting it to the main station—and in fact, in times of crisis, any of the pods could separate from the station's main body, thrust free through use of a slow but serviceable drive unit, and maintain itself in space for days or weeks until rescue arrived.

Each pod, which included hundreds of sets of quarters, conference chambers, exercise and recreation facilities, theaters, kitchens, vehicle hangars, security chambers, cell blocks for rowdy celebrants, and vast atria, could be rented as a single unit for any sort of corporate event. Merchant princes brought in several hundred of their closest friends to celebrate their hundredth birthdays in these pods; Kuat Drive Yards, the single greatest manufacturer in the system, had its trade shows in these pods.

And now one of them, a triangular pod known as Narsacc Habitat, had been hired—at the last minute and for an unspecified duration, displacing a suddenly very unhappy convention of airspeeder and swoop manufacturers from around the galaxy—by the government of the Galactic Alliance. The Narsacc Habitat's crew of stewards, cooks, wait staff, cleaning and maintenance droids, valets, and dressing consultants had been dismissed on full pay for the duration of the GA stay, replaced by carefully screened government employees. The only Toryaz Station employees left were a skeleton crew of security officers, amply reinforced and overseen by GA security specialists.

The first ships to dock with Narsacc Habitat, one large transport each from Coruscant and Corellia, discharged hordes of soldiers and security personnel who immediately began scouring the pod for listening devices, booby traps, and hidden weapons. They found plenty, many of them years or decades old, all apparently left from previous events—the forgotten residue of attempted espionage and treachery in the past. After two days of examination, both sides reported to their respective leaders that there was no sign of ill intent from their opposite number.

Sufficiently reassured that matters could progress, both sides brought in protocol droids and status engineers who examined the habitat's facilities, comparing them with the events of the conference to come, and immediately began negotiating to make sure that their respective sides would have slightly better-than-equal habitat resources. The views from the suites against the outermost hull were best, therefore the delegates must stay there, despite the fact that this increased demands on the security teams; the spinward edge of that bank of suites got to see each view in turn first, and therefore each side demanded them for its own delegation; in-suite breakfasts would be served simultaneously to the Saxan and Pellaeon suites, with no regard to the preferred breakfasting time of the delegates themselves. This went on for another full day.

Wedge Antilles ignored it all. Off-loaded with the first groups of security experts but not truly part of the Corellian force, he found what he thought was the best spot in the habitat—a lush green water garden beneath a top-hull viewport a hundred meters across, showing glorious starfields during the hours when grow-lights were not activated—and spent most of his time there. No other men or women of the security details intruded except for the occasional perimeter search and weapons scan.

On the morning of the fourth day, as he sat in the dark in a lounger that conformed itself to his body with each of his movements, he heard rustling on the far side of the central clearing. He put his hand on his holstered blaster but did not otherwise move. In moments, another human walked into the clearing, oblivious to the surrounding ferns and the artificial waterfall and pool only a dozen meters away. Ramrod-straight, he wore a Galactic Alliance general's uniform, its cap tucked under his arm, and his attention was fixed on the stars above. He was about Wedge's age, with fair hair and a face a little lined by responsibility and old, old sorrow, but not by age. He looked like a prince, with features that could have been coldly aristocratic had the mood ever taken him, but Wedge had never seen him wear an attitude like that.

Wedge grinned and took a deep, silent breath. "Rogue Two!" he snapped. "Break to port!"

Before Wedge was halfway through his shout, the newcomer had dropped, rolled behind a long box planted with glowing woosha plants from Naboo, and then come up-right again, his cap missing. His expression would have been ferocious had he been able to keep himself from grinning. "Wedge! Not nice." He brushed himself off and stepped out from behind the improvised cover.

Wedge rose to take the man's hand and embrace him. "Tycho. I didn't know you were going to be part of this merry mess."

General Tycho Celchu clapped Wedge's back before releasing him. "I knew you were. But there's a little problem with sending you messages these days."

"I know." Wedge gestured to the lounger next to his, then resumed his original seat.

Tycho sat but remained upright, his posture perfect. The humor gradually left his face, leaving behind a combination of curiosity and regret. "I can't believe that we're sitting here wearing different uniforms."

Wedge felt the way Tycho looked. He nodded. "Me, either."

"What is that all about?" Tycho sounded almost angry; certainly, he was upset. "I heard about the kidnapping and your escape. That sent a shock wave through Intelligence, and a lot of idiots were busted down in rank on account of it. Which suits me just fine. But what are you doing in that uniform?" Then he narrowed his eyes and looked around. "Or should we be talking here?"

Wedge nodded, unconcerned. "We can. This place has been screened so often and so well, by your side and my side, that I'd be more surprised to see a listening device than a rancor in a formal gown. But Tycho—we are talking strictly off the record. Correct?"

Tycho nodded.

"Corellia's a coalition government," Wedge said. "Saxan is riding herd on a vast number of ministers and subministers, most of whom want her job or want to decide who's going to have her job next."

"I know that."

"Well, because of various pressures, she's had to appoint Sal-Solo her Minister of War."

"I'd heard that, too." Tycho's face showed his distaste for the longtime politician. "It's sort of like appointing a piranha-beetle your Minister of Meat Supplies. How could the Corellians be so crazy as to let him do anything more important than sweep sidewalks?"

"People redeem their heroes," Wedge said. He heard the weariness in his own voice. "Sal-Solo's a convicted conspirator. Han Solo was a spice smuggler. Luke and Leia are children of the most notorious mass murderer in history." He paused, realizing that he might have gone a step too far in his comparisons—Vader's complicity in the destruction of Tycho's homeworld, Alderaan, was well known—but Tycho didn't twitch. "Anyway, Saxan needs someone to be on hand to interpret Sal-Solo's moves, to give him strategic advice when it's his glands rather than his brains moving units around on the war board, and so on. And to accompany her here and see what I can do to promote the cause of peace. Reunification."

Tycho nodded. "If things go badly, you're aware you could end up being listed as a war criminal."

"I was thinking about that." Wedge stretched and put his hands behind his head to become more comfortable. "It's been a little over forty years since I was a smuggler."

"Oh, don't say it."

"I bet I could get my hands on a good, fast transport. Find some of my old contacts—"

"One or two may still be alive."

Wedge shrugged. "Syal's on her career path, and Myri's going to finish her education pretty soon. Iella and I can wander the spaceways, buy a little here, sell a little there. I could use a good copilot . . ."

Tycho fell silent, considering.

"You're still keeping an eye on Syal for me?" Wedge asked.

"Oh, yes. She's up for a transfer to a test squadron, if she wants it. She doesn't know yet."

"She fired on me at Corellia."

"No."

"Oh, yes. Came close to getting me, too, considering how green she is." Wedge smiled proudly, then sobered. "Tycho, let's get this situation patched up. If it comes to war, with you and Syal where you are, I'll have family on both sides."

"Aww. You're going to make me cry."

Both men smiled. They returned their attention to the stars above and settled into a companionable silence.

chapter eighteen

Later that day, the remaining ships dedicated to the diplomatic mission drew in to land in hangars spaced around the perimeter of Narsacc Habitat. One hangar was larger than all the others, but neither set of status engineers could agree on the envoy from either side arriving there—it would be too great a slight to the diplomats' perceived status—so it went unused. The Galactic Alliance and Corellian envoys landed in hangars of identical size, while the Jedi put in at a hangar slightly smaller than the others.

Then the three groups met in the habitat's largest conference area, roomy enough for two games of zoneball to be played simultaneously. One set of tables had been arranged as a conference area, its seating carefully ordered by the rank of the individual assigned to it. Another set had food laid out upon it, a buffet of dishes from several worlds, including Coruscant and Corellia. A third area was bare of furniture, but a phalanx of musician droids was arrayed against one wall—the area's purpose, as a floor for dancing, was obvious.

Han Solo, technically a consultant with the Jedi party, strode in beside his wife and took a quick look around the broad area. "This isn't a negotiation meeting."

Leia smiled up at him. "No, it isn't."

"It's a party."

She nodded.

"Why are we wasting time with a party when we've got two sides about to go to war?"

Luke, walking two steps ahead beside his wife, grinned over his shoulder at his brother-in-law. "Nobody's going to war while the delegates are here. The only one with any likelihood of wanting to is Thrackan Sal-Solo, because war will give him a better chance to assume control of the entire Corellian system . . . and our Intelligence contacts say he doesn't yet have enough influence over the other four Corellian Chiefs of State to manage that."

"And this gathering projects the idea that things are calm," Leia added. "There are newsgatherers and historians here. They'll see the calm, the unconcern, and they'll report on it to the HoloNet today."

Han grimaced. "I need my blaster," he said.

Jacen, right behind his father with Ben in tow, said, "You feel defenseless without it, Dad?"

"Nothing of the sort. I just want to shoot everyone who decides on these protocols."

Jacen nodded agreeably. "If I ruled the universe, I'd let you do that, as a service to galactic civilization."

Luke's smile lasted for another two steps; then he straightened, looking forward. He stepped to the side of the Jedi formation to let it pass and began looking right and left.

Mara, Han, and Leia stepped out with him, letting the others continue on. Jacen, Ben, Jaina, and Zekk moved toward the center of the room, Ben sparing his father a curious glance. Mara asked, "What is it?"

"He was here," Luke said. "The man who doesn't exist."

Mara began a slow, casual, visual sweep of the room and asked, "How long ago?"

"I'm not sure," Luke admitted. "I just had a flash of him in the Force. But it was clear and distinct . . . and, again, no dream."

"He has to exist, then," Mara said.

Han cleared his throat. "Anybody care to toss a clue to a non-Jedi?"

Leia said, "I'm in the dark, too, Han."

"An enemy," Luke said. "I became aware of him when he didn't yet exist. And now I'm beginning to think he sometimes exists and sometimes doesn't."

"That'll make him hard to track down," Han admitted. "Hard to make him pay up his rent."

Luke shot Han an admonishing glance, then followed the other Jedi.

"He's actually worried," Han said.

Mara nodded. "And getting more worried."

Leia linked her arm through her sister-in-law's. "So tell us about this man who doesn't exist."

The party, Luke had to admit, did serve its main purpose— giving the newsgatherers information that would probably reassure the public at large—and a secondary purpose, that of an icebreaker.

At its start, the attendees stood about in rigid little groups dictated by their function and place of origin—here Corellian politicians, backs to a functionally identical group of Coruscant politicians a meter away, there a cluster of Jedi. At various points around the wall stood pairs and trios of security operatives—here GA, there CorSec, next Toryaz Station experts.

Oddly, it was a pair of aging pilots who began to thaw the hard edges of the groups. Walking together, Wedge Antilles and Tycho Celchu moved from cluster to cluster, shaking hands, clapping backs, telling stories. Their genuine affection for the people they were addressing was obvious, as was their genuine unconcern for the political boundaries of the gathering.

Tycho was first on the dance floor with Prime Minister Saxan; Wedge, with Leia, was next. Soon the noise level in the chamber rose and the boundaries between groups increasingly blurred.

Jaina, dancing with her father, told him, "You can be doing that, too."

Han gave her a puzzled look. "Dancing? I am. If crushing my daughter's toes one by one counts."

"Not what I meant. Did you know, there's someone here that everybody on both sides likes and admires?"

"Sure." Han looked around. "Luke's over there. He's talking to Pellaeon right now."

"No." Jaina shook her head, setting her hair swaying. "I mean you. A hero to the Corellians and the rest of the GA. And you could be walking around, getting to know everyone, and making everybody feel better about being here."

Han gave her a mock grimace. "I hate that sort of thing."

"My father, the hero, won't walk around smiling, even if it keeps war from happening?"

"Not fair. Who taught you to argue?"

"Mom. Besides, you can get up to speed just by staying here on the dance floor. In case you haven't noticed, there are ladies from both sides hovering, waiting for when you find yourself without a dance partner. Like this." The music, a familiar dance number, signaled a twirl, and when Han completed it, Jaina was two meters away, dancing with Zekk and giving her father one last merry smile.

Han pointed at her, an *I'll-get-you-for-this* gesture, then felt a tap on his shoulder. He turned. Before him stood a young woman with short blond hair; she wore the uniform of a junior officer of the GA security team. "General Solo?" she asked. "I'm Lieutenant Elsen Barthis. Could I have this dance?"

"Of course." Han put on a smile he didn't feel and glanced briefly to where Wedge danced with his wife. He'd heard the story of Wedge's escape from Coruscant and knew Barthis to be one of his captors. He decided that discussing her recent demotion wouldn't benefit the cause of détente. "Your accent—you're Corellian?"

"Yes, originally. I'm surprised you can hear an accent. I've worked for several years to get rid of it."

"Oh, some things never fade away completely . . ."

* * *

Four hours after it began, the party ended. A handful of delegates and advisers moved to a much smaller adjoining chamber set up with a long conference table. Prime Minister Aidel Saxan sat at one end, Admiral Gilad Pellaeon at the other, and their respective parties occupied the seats between them.

"So," Pellaeon said. "Rules of order?"

"Let's dispense with them," Saxan said. She looked weary but not ill tempered.

"In that case," Han said, "I'm taking off my boots. Nobody can make good decisions when his feet hurt."

The experienced politicians, except Leia, looked at him in surprise, but Han followed words with action, reaching down under the table to yank his boots free. A security officer knelt to peer under the opposite side of the table, doubtless to make sure Han wasn't securing a hideaway blaster . . . and then the officer had a lot to do as other attendees followed Han's lead and discarded footwear that had been binding and pinching for hours. Pellaeon didn't join in; Han, with a twinge of envy, suspected that the old admiral had enough experience and sense to equip himself with perfectly fitted, comfortable boots.

"Let's get to it," Pellaeon said. "Prime Minister—may I call you Aidel?"

"Please."

"Gilad. I'll stipulate that the arrival of a GA naval task force in the Corellian system was an unfriendly act if you'd be so kind as to make the same admission about the secret reactivation of Centerpoint Station. Let's get that out of the way. Let's neither of us pretend that one side or the other is blameless."

Saxan smiled in mock sweetness. "We can still argue over which is the greater offense."

Pellaeon nodded. "We can. Which is to your advantage."

Saxan looked surprised. "You admit that?"

"Of course. I'm a very old man. Any protracted argument—well, I could die at any moment." The old strategist smiled to put the lie to his words.

Saxan, caught out, smiled despite herself. "All right. Let's prioritize, then. I won't pretend that the only possible outcome of this gathering is Corellian independence. Corellia has, at times, thrived as part of a wider government. She has also thrived as an independent state. But she can't thrive as a disarmed state dependent on GA forces for protection of the system. Corellian pride won't allow for that. Insist on that, impose it, and you transform us into something other than Corellians." She pointed, in turn, to Han and Wedge. "Think how things would be in the GA today if not for Corellians like these. There would be no Galactic Alliance. No New Republic. It would still be the Empire."

A silence fell across the gathering as all present remembered that Pellaeon had been an officer of the Empire at the time of its inception, had served the Empire faithfully—through the years of its wars with the Rebel Alliance and New Republic, through the decades of its existence as a remnant government, to the time in recent years when it and the rest of the galaxy had changed and the Imperial Remnant had become a part of the Galactic Alliance. Those capable of saying anything admiring about the Empire always said that Pellaeon and officers like him represented the best part of it; could have forged it into an ethical and civilized regime had they been in charge from the start.

And Pellaeon, too, was Corellian.

Pellaeon smiled again, this time showing teeth. The obvious reply would have been, *And what's wrong with that?* Instead, he said, "So what you're arguing for, principally, is the preservation of a Corellian space navy above and beyond the Corellian Defense Force."

"Of course."

"That's not necessarily impossible," the admiral said. "But would Corellia still be able to provide resources to the GA military at a rate dictated by its gross system production, as other GA signatories do? That would seem to be a substantial drain on Corellia's economy."

"Well, obviously, our contribution to the GA military would have to be reduced by a value equivalent to our space navy. And that navy would be available to the GA for military activities when called upon."

"Not acceptable. The Galactic Alliance military funding has to come first."

It was at this point that Han's attention wandered. He supposed that the two diplomats must be arguing their agendas with what, in political circles, would be considered blinding speed—otherwise the discussion wouldn't have held his attention even *that* long. But verbiage had reached a toxic level and he could no longer concentrate on it.

Now he looked around the table, from face to face, trying to glean what information his experience as a sabacc player would grant him.

Saxan and Pellaeon were the most interesting studies. Each was alert, energetic, apparently unmovable in argument position. But they had to come to some sort of agreement here, or both sides would lose—war was an unacceptable result. So below the hard surfaces, each had some flexibility to offer. The question was when they would offer it, and in the face of what circumstances.

Leia was intent on the discussions, though Han noticed that each time a provocative statement was offered, she looked not at Saxan or Pellaeon but at the chief adviser of whichever politician was receiving the statement.

Luke was serene, almost in a meditative state. No—Han corrected himself. Luke was calm, but not serene. There was still the faint shadow of anxiety to his manner. This whole situation with the "man who didn't exist" obviously continued to worry him.

It troubled Han, too. Luke could see things Han couldn't. If there were things that Luke couldn't see, it was likely that no living being in the galaxy could see them.

Except . . . Han's attention fell on his son. Jacen was, like

Leia, earnestly following the discussion, but he also occasionally turned away from the talk at hand to stare in some direction that always seemed random. Han supposed that Jacen, with his training in diverse and unusual aspects of the Force, was looking in directions no one else felt the need to.

Perhaps he could see things even Luke couldn't.

Han resolved to talk to his son later.

This first meeting between Pellaeon and Saxan went on for four hours. Eventually, the two diplomats agreed to retire for the evening and resume their talks in the morning, station time.

The delegates and their advisers discovered that they were all quartered on a single passageway of Narsacc Habitat, where the rooms commanded the best view of stars and the moon Ronay. The passageway was named the Kallebarth Way. At each end of its 275-meter run, and at any point a cross-corridor intersected it, a security station had been installed.

The Galactic Alliance delegation was assigned the spinward end of the passageway, having won the right to the slightly more desirable quarters by virtue of the GA having paid for this conference. The Corellian delegation was quartered at the far end. The Jedi accommodations were in the middle. Numerous suites lay unoccupied in the areas between the delegation quarters. The passageways immediately above and below Kallebarth Way were sealed off, all the suites there locked down, in an effort to keep saboteurs from assaulting the delegations from either vertical direction.

Still awake a couple of hours after the breakup of the first meeting, Han sat on a couch facing the Solo suite's largest viewport, a huge expanse of radiation-shielded transparisteel, fifteen meters long and five high. At the moment it was oriented out to space, but the starfield was slightly marred by the presence of the GA frigate *Firethorn*, guaranteeing safety, only a kilometer out. The frigate was not stationary; it paced the occupied edge of Narsacc Habitat and so was, from Han's perspective, fixed in place outside the viewport.

"I think we have the exact center suite," Han commented. "Accident or design?"

"Design," Leia said. She was sitting in a chair two paces closer to the viewport than Han's couch. "Even though Luke's the Master of the order, the two of us are supposed to be the most neutral of all the parties present—except for Toryaz Station Security—because of our, um, unique circumstances. So we're smack in the middle."

Han shrugged. "Still, nice view." He turned his attention to Jacen, seated at the other end of the couch. "So?"

His son looked thoughtful. "I don't like this stuff about a 'man who doesn't exist.' "

"Neither do I," Han said. "Neither does your mother."

"Maybe, but I suspect we don't like it for different reasons." Jacen gave Leia an apologetic look. "Ever since Dad started talking about it, I've been looking. Sensing. Peering into the future and the past, to the extent I can."

Leia nodded. "And?"

"And nothing. I don't see, or feel, any trace of something like that." He frowned. "There's the faintest touch of a female presence that feels antagonistic, malevolent. It has some flavor of the Force with it. But it's so faint that it doesn't have to pertain to the here and now. It could be a leftover from years or decades ago. It could be pre-Imperial."

"Could it be a Force-user who's here now, and using arts to diminish her presence?" Leia asked.

Jacen nodded. "Maybe."

"Then why couldn't it be Luke's 'man who doesn't exist,' using those same arts to impart a different gender feeling, perhaps to throw Luke off?"

Jacen smiled. "Mom, that doesn't make any sense. First, if I could detect the presence Uncle Luke is feeling, then I would probably detect it the same way, at least initially. If it's a man to him, it should be a man to me. Second, and I think this is very important, why hasn't Luke mentioned this female presence I noticed? Did he not detect it all, or has he dismissed it because it's not as strong or as in-your-face as his 'man who doesn't exist'?" He took a deep breath. "Mom, I think Uncle Luke is dismissing a lot of information and premonitions he may be getting, simply because they don't match with what he believes. He didn't think much of my suggestion that the Corellians wouldn't roll over as quickly as the GA said they would, and look what happened. Now he has a pet theory about some shadowy enemy, and nothing else seems to be getting through to him."

"I know he hasn't studied every esoteric Force discipline you have," Leia said, "but that doesn't mean he's wrong. His opinions shouldn't be disregarded."

"Neither should mine." Jacen's tone was sharper than he intended. He softened it for his next words. "I didn't mean to sound angry—"

"You *are* angry," his mother said.

"Maybe. But my point is still worth listening to. Uncle Luke had to carry the burden of the survival of the entire Jedi order all by himself for years. He's faced pressures that no Jedi in history has endured. After forty years of doing this, he may be burning out."

"I doubt it," Leia said. "Jacen, the way he's lived his life, the way he's learned about the Force, that's one path to knowledge. Yours is a different one. Do you really think yours is better?"

"With apologies, Mom—yes, I do. I think Uncle Luke is closed off to some avenues of learning, and it may mean there are things he'll never be able to see."

"All the same," Han said, "keep your eyes open for strangers. Ignoring warnings is a good way to get dead."

Jacen grinned. "We agree on that."

chapter nineteen

Two levels above Kallebarth Way and toward the habitat center, in an auxiliary security command compartment normally occupied only in times of emergency, Captain Siron Tawaler scanned a series of readout boards, looking for trouble.

The leftmost board showed him the station's external tracking sensors, indicating every ship, piece of debris, or asteroid larger than a groundspeeder within several thousand kilometers of the station's position. On the screen, numerous green-for-friendly blips dotted space.

The next board showed a much closer view; only Toryaz Station appeared there. On it, a green blip moved with considerable delicacy among the spokes that connected the station to its satellite habitats.

The third screen on that bank showed an almost identical view, but did not show the green blip. It was this view that command crew on the bridge would be seeing, this view that was being recorded in the station's files.

The rightmost screen showed a diagram of the station's layout, each section colored by alert status. Everything was in the green except for one belt of yellow, Kallebarth Way, the yellow indicating its heightened state of security.

Tawaler felt rather than heard his companion lean over his shoulder, and was for once not startled when she spoke. Her voice was, as ever, quiet and silky: "I am always amazed at the initiative security officers show in ensuring that they can peer through every set of holocam lenses on a ship, pry into every confidential computer file, and access every ship's function . . . even when they're not supposed to."

A comment like that would normally have made Tawaler feel defensive, but here it seemed soothing. Tawaler chanced a glance over his shoulder.

The woman who stood there was a beauty—tall, slender, and aristocratic, her dark eyes intelligent. She wore colorful but cumbersome robes in the latest Kuati style, and she did so with a grace that began with a lack of self-consciousness.

Tawaler shrugged, trying to appear unconcerned. "A security officer has to be able to provide security. Even when commanding officers are killed or subverted. He has to be able to see where everyone is, know what everyone is thinking. Otherwise things aren't safe."

"You're right, of course." There was amusement in the woman's tone, and again Tawaler was surprised that he wasn't even a little offended. The woman's words sounded like condescension. But of course they weren't.

Of *course* they weren't. This woman had come to him with the news that he, Captain Siron Tawaler, was under consideration to be the telbun of a lady—to be the consort chosen to father her child in the ancient tradition of the great ruling merchant houses of Kuat. His intelligence, his personal strength, his determination had brought him to her attention . . . and somehow she had looked past the in-different service reports that had been written about him, had dismissed the petty jealousy and backstabbing competition that had led superior officer after superior officer to label him as "unmotivated" and "adequate." His personal and financial success, and those of his family, were now as-sured, despite the curiously low regard with which the peo-ple of other worlds viewed the role of telbun.

But first, he had to pass a test of loyalty. He had to help this grand lady preserve her house by eliminating the rogue Jedi assigned to kill her.

Why Jedi would want to kill a Kuat mercantile princess

was beyond Tawaler. But that was all right. His specialty was point security, not anticipatory security. Besides, he didn't like the Jedi. They strutted around without any respect for security or authority, they dressed like beggars or hermits when everyone knew they were rich—and the quality of their boots gave them away every time: the poor couldn't afford high-grade footwear—and they lorded it over normal folk with their so-called mystical powers. Unacceptable, unacceptable.

Tawaler again felt a moment of unease. The woman leaning over his shoulder had presented documents proving her identity as a representative of a great house, but at this precise moment he couldn't remember the exact content of those documents—just that he had accepted them without question, had accepted the woman's explanation and mission without hesitation.

Well . . . just more proof that Tawaler *wasn't* unmotivated, was far above adequate. He was decisive and bold, as he was demonstrating now, as he would demonstrate from now on in his new position. His fate was assured.

His eyes were drawn to a constantly updated readout on the first information screen. "Four minutes until dock," he said.

"Good. Let's go meet them."

There were twenty of them, all human, men and a few women uniformed in gleaming black body armor. The chest plates were rigid carapaces, the helmets narrower than pilots' protective gear. Upper arms, legs, and hands were protected by a mesh-like material, heavy but flexible; lower arms and legs were encased in the same heavy material as torsos. They carried gleaming black rifles of types unfamiliar to Tawaler, three different designs, all of them curiously oversized, one of them intended, as the placement of the padding and sights indicated, for shoulder-mount use.

And their faces—Tawaler didn't know what to make of their faces. Slightly obscured as they were behind the amber faceplates of the helmets, they seemed just a little wrong. The analytical portion of his brain went to work on the problem even as the men and women began streaming in through the air lock.

Age range: thirty to sixty, he estimated, older than ordinary recruits, averaging older even than a standard unit of elites. Planets of origin: it was never easy to calculate such a thing, but a certain characteristic leanness of features and the way they made eye contact suggested Corellia. Yet in other ways their mannerisms were strikingly non-Corellian; Tawaler saw none of the good cheer and cockiness that usually characterized the soldiers and citizens of that system.

And there was something *wrong* with them, a hollowness to their cheeks, an odd intensity to their expressions.

"They're dying." The woman whispered the words in Tawaler's ear as if answering his unspoken question. "Each of them, from various wasting diseases that medicine can't arrest. They're all still at something like full strength, with painkillers to keep them that way for a while, and they have no worries about mortality to hold them back. It's delicious, isn't it?"

Tawaler tried to suppress a shudder and did not entirely succeed. "Delicious," he repeated, as if agreeing.

The woman shut the air lock, then held up a datapad and moved to stand at the head of the column of armored soldiers. "I'm transmitting the station plans and the locations of your targets. This information should be appearing in the heads-up displays of your helmet visors."

Tawaler saw dimly glowing green shapes flickering over the visors, and several of the soldiers nodded. None spoke.

The woman's lean features twisted up into a smile. "Good. Get to it."

In two columns, silent except for the faint creaking of their armor, the soldiers passed to either side of the woman and headed down the passageway. The passageway's curve soon took them out of Tawaler's sight. He was glad to see them gone.

"The shuttle that brought them will take you to Kuat," the woman said. "You'd better board."

Tawaler turned and slapped the control board for the air lock. He entered and peered in some confusion through the transparisteel viewport in the door on the opposite side. It showed nothing but stars. "It's gone," he said. "The shuttle."

He heard the air lock door hiss closed behind him. The woman's voice came across the air lock speaker. "No, it's still there. Look harder."

Tawaler felt light-headed. He wanted nothing so much as to sit down and rest for a minute. But he did as told, leaning closer to the viewport.

Oh, yes, he'd been wrong. Through the viewport he could see the docking tube in place, the door into the belly of the shuttle invitingly open.

"You'd better hurry."

Tawaler pressed the control for the air lock door to open. But its speaker made a disagreeable noise and its text screen flashed red. He had to concentrate to read the words appearing on the screen. IT HASN'T RUN ITS DEPRESSURIZATION CYCLE. That was wrong. It didn't need to depressurize. A boarding tube was coupled to the other side. Atmospheric pressure should be approximately equal.

Now his companion sounded exasperated. "Go ahead and depressurize. After all, you have your pressure suit on."

Tawaler glanced down at himself. Yes, he was in his pressure suit. He couldn't remember putting it on, but he was clad head-to-foot in the industrial gray of one of the station's vac suits. He entered the code to pump the air out of the air lock and open the outer door.

In a moment, his ears popped and he felt even more light-headed.

"Don't worry, Tawaler." Her voice grew increasingly faint. "The feeling will pass soon."

*   *   *

The unit of twenty dying killers moved briskly down the corridor from the air lock to a turbolift. They entered, keyed in a command to take them two floors down, and moments later emerged on the same level as Kallebarth Way.

This passageway, which ran at right angles to and intersected with the passageway that was their destination, was dark, faintly illuminated only by emergency glows along the floor. But there was a glow in one direction. The men and women turned that way and began marching. On the space station floor diagram on their helmet visors, a red dot moved to show their location.

Eventually the glow ahead resolved itself into a lighted area situated at the intersection of this passageway and Kallebarth Way. The armored soldiers could make out walls of transparisteel set up as a security station. At the station, a portion of the passageway was given over to a battery of sensors and a small enclosure, just large enough for a desk and two security officers. The rest of the passageway at that point was a lock, a stretch of walkway with a secure door at each end. The barriers separating the sensor area from the lock, and separating both sensor area and lock from original passageway, were made of transparisteel, as were the secure doors themselves, giving the whole station an oddly delicate, crystalline appearance.

Just as the killers came close enough to take in these details, the guidance map on their visors disappeared and the word WAIT appeared. They stopped in place and waited.

In the station sat two officers, human men in the gray-and-white uniform of Toryaz Station Security. At this late hour, with all the members of the delegation parties retired for the evening, they were relaxed, chatting over cups of caf.

Then a datapad sitting on the desk before them erupted in a cloud of white smoke. The smoke completely filled the tiny chamber, looking like a patch of thick fog cut into a square by some supernatural force.

It began to fade. Through it, the twenty intruders could see the two security men slumped over their desks.

Colored lights danced over the control pads of the security station doors, then those doors swung open.

The instruction showing on the helmet visors switched from WAIT to PROCEED, then as abruptly was replaced by the maps to the intruders' destinations.

They marched forward.

Jacen awoke from fitful sleep. The compartment he and Ben had been assigned, one of several chambers arranged around a central living area that offered access to the main passageway, had two beds and its own refresher, quite comfortable by the standards of traveling Jedi. It was dark, the only illumination coming from a dim glow panel above the door to the living room.

Something was—not *wrong*, but different. He glanced around, saw only the inert shape of Ben in his bed, and the rectangular openings into the refresher and the closet.

Jacen sat up into a cross-legged posture and closed his eyes, sinking effortlessly into a contemplative state.

He looked for treachery, hatred, anger. He could feel little twinges of them, but no more than would be expected at any political gathering.

Satisfied, he lay down again.

A handful of meters away, in a chamber on the other side of the same living room, Luke Skywalker also sat up.

Beside him, Mara opened an eye and offered him a lazy smile. "Nerves?"

Luke shook his head. He turned his head back and forth, but his gaze was unfocused. "Something's going on."

Mara stretched and opened the other eye, giving her husband an exasperated look. "You think I couldn't sense an attack or danger?"

"I think that *looking* for an attack or danger is a mistake." Luke slipped out from beneath the blanket and stood, dressed only in briefs and undershirt. "If you look for banthas, you fail to notice hawk-bats."

Mara cast the blanket aside and stood, now suspicious and alert. "I still don't feel any aggression—"

"Not aggression, fatalism. Disease—" Luke threw up his left hand toward the door as if to ward off an attack.

With a *boom* that shook the floor and walls and deafened Mara momentarily, the chamber door blew off its tracks and hurtled toward Luke. Still in midgesture, Luke grimaced and the door instantly reversed direction, slamming back through the portal it had covered and crashing to the floor of the central living chamber beyond.

Luke leapt toward the doorway, gesturing with his other hand. From the nightstand beside the bed, his lightsaber flew into his grasp, and he thumbed it to life, its *snap-hiss* only faintly audible to his concussed ears, before he landed outside the doorway.

Ahead of him was the metal door. It was on the floor, warped to conform roughly to the shape of a large humanoid form—the man who'd triggered the explosion.

The circular room was thick with doors. Three more of them, like his, were off their tracks and smoking. To his left were black-armored figures, two pairs, one pair at each of two destroyed doorways that faced each other. Smoke curled from the barrels of their oversized rifles. To his immediate right was an armored figure within reach, swinging her rifle to bear on him, and farther down, another pair of armored figures stood in front of another ruined doorway. The attackers were moving into the doorways . . .

Ignoring the riflewoman next to him, Luke gestured right and left, and expulsions of Force power swept the armored figures in both directions off their feet, hammered them into doorjambs, caused them to drop their weapons. Simultaneously he twisted, bringing the center of his body out of line of the riflewoman's barrel.

She fired. The shot should have passed harmlessly behind Luke's back, but it was not a blaster shot. Something shining and thread-like expanded from the barrel. It settled across Luke, as unavoidable as a sudden forest fog, and tightened across his head, arms, legs. It was a silvery net, contracting as it touched its target.

He heard it crackle as it wrapped across the blade of his lightsaber, saw it blacken where it touched the green energy blade. In a moment, he knew, he'd be able to use his Force skills to wrench the net off him.

He didn't have a moment. As the net clamped his arms to his sides and drew his legs together in an awkward, unbalanced pose, he saw the riflewoman twist a dial on the rifle's barrel. The interior of the barrel glowed.

Mara's blue lightsaber blade, flashing out from the doorway, cut up through the barrel at an angle and continued across the attacker's neck. The front half of the rifle and the woman's hand fell away, then her head rolled off, smoking at the point of the lightsaber contact, to topple to the floor.

Down the curved wall to Luke's left, armored invaders who'd been preparing to enter the next chamber down turned to fire on him and Mara. One had a weapon like the riflewoman's; another carried a bigger, shoulder-mounted device. Luke could feel their sudden, growing anger, and identical emotions from the invaders down the wall in the other direction.

Luke turned left, rotating on the ball of one foot. He dropped his lightsaber and gestured with the hand that had held it. Ahead of him, the ceiling, a cool-blue, sound-insulating foam over metal, buckled and tore free, slamming down across those invaders. The attackers must have fired; in an instant, the ruined ceiling began to superheat from the blasts, the insulation on the far side bursting into flame and sending sheets of smoke up into the air.

Behind him, Luke heard the hum and crackle of Mara's lightsaber—and a scream from one of the attackers.

Luke flexed both his body and his control of the Force, and the remaining silver netting on him tore away. His lightsaber popped back up into his hand. His Force-senses focused, he walked forward, pushing the glowing metal panel before him, driving it toward his attackers.

*   *   *

Jacen had barely closed his eyes again when his compartment door blasted inward. The shock of the concussion startled him, delaying him a deadly half second . . . but as he rose, as he gestured for his lightsaber, as the long barrel of the first intruder's black rifle entered and swung toward him, the attacker was suddenly bowled off his feet. Jacen felt the pulse in the Force that did it, felt the characteristic traits of Luke's exertion within it. Lightsaber in hand, Jacen snapped it on, took a fraction of a second to wave at Ben's bed and flip it over, sending the boy into the wall and covering him with the bed. Only then did Jacen leap out into the central chamber.

Before him was the attacker who'd just tried to enter his room. To his left was another black-armored figure bringing his weapons to bear on Mara, who advanced toward them clad in black sleepwear. *So we were all caught asleep.*

He trusted Mara to be able to deal with the second attacker. He flicked his lightsaber blade up, slicing through the first intruder's weapon.

Fast as an attacking slashrat, the rifleman stepped back in a crouch, drawing and firing a holstered blaster in a single, practiced move. Jacen tapped the bolt out of the way with a negligent readjustment of his lightsaber blade, then thrust, shoving the blade through the man's armor at the shoulder. Jacen felt it penetrate the armor, burn its way through flesh and bone beneath, and emerge from the armor on the other side. The man screamed and fell, dragging his body off Jacen's weapon.

Jacen glanced left. Mara's foe was falling, a smoking line from shoulder blade to stomach marking the injury that had defeated him. Beyond, Luke was in the midst of four enemies, all of them firing; the oversized bolt from one of their weapons, missing wildly, flashed toward Mara and Jacen, and the two Jedi ducked out of its way. At the end of his spin, Luke stood up, and something fell away from each of his attackers—a rifle barrel, an arm, a severed head. Three of them fell down. The fourth cast his destroyed weapon to the floor, raised his hands . . . then, oddly, followed his companions to the floor, his body limp.

From the door nearest Luke emerged Jaina, wearing a brown sleep shirt, her lightsaber lit. From the destroyed door opposite her emerged Zekk, soot smearing his face, smoke rising from the forward portion of his hair. "They keep trying to blow me up," he complained.

chapter twenty

Han and Leia snuggled together on the couch, sitting in the darkness, wordlessly watching the galaxy rotate outside beyond the viewport. The door to the passageway hissed open behind them, spilling light into the large room. Han and Leia turned to look. Four armored figures marched in, quiet and confident. Apparently not noticing the Solos on the couch, they walked straight to the doorway leading to the main bedchamber. The one with the largest weapon, a shoulder-mounted blaster rig, set up to destroy the door while the other three readied their own weapons.

Han and Leia exchanged a puzzled look. Leia shrugged.

Han drew his blaster. He'd spent frustrating hours not permitted by the various security staffs to carry his favorite weapon, so he had recovered it the instant he'd returned to his own quarters. Now he aimed it at the four intruders, bracing it against the top of the couch. "Hey," he said.

The four turned. One, fastest on the uptake, began to aim more quickly than the others. Han shot him in the throat.

Leia sprang up from the couch, a Force-assisted leap that carried her toward the ceiling of the tall living chamber. She lit her lightsaber on the way up. One of the intruders, the one carrying the shoulder-mounted blaster, aimed at her. Han, not knowing whether her skills and lightsaber could deflect the blast from such a weapon, shot him, too, his blaster bolt burning its way into the side of the man's helmet.

The other two fired at him. The first shot hit the back of the sturdy couch and picked the furniture up, spinning it toward the outer wall. Han and the couch hit the transparisteel of the viewport.

Han felt the viewport shudder under the impact and he wondered, for one eternity-long fraction of a second, if it would give way beneath the blow, buckling free of its housing, sending him into the coldness of space and decompression.

It didn't. It rang metallically as he hit it, pain shot through his shoulder blades, and suddenly he was on the floor, the couch on top of him.

He heard Leia's lightsaber hum and sizzle. He rolled out from under the furniture. In the moment it took him to come upright, blaster in hand, the situation was resolved. One of the two remaining attackers was down with his head off; the other, shaking in pain, was missing both arms at the elbow. Both of Han's targets were down, smoke rising from where the blaster bolts had hit them.

Leia turned her attention to the door, and Han didn't need Jedi powers to know what she was thinking. "Yeah," he said. "You left, me right."

They emerged into Kallebarth Way at a dead run, Han turning toward the chambers of the Corellian delegation, Leia turning toward the delegation from Coruscant.

The first door Han passed slid open and a man leapt out. Han aimed, wrenched his blaster back out of line—the man emerging was his own son. "C'mon, kid," he said and ran past.

Han could see, up ahead, that the double-wide door leading into the Corellian delegation's suite was open. Small-arms blasterfire emerged from the doorway to pockmark the passageway wall opposite. As he watched, a black-armored figure staggered back through the doorway, his chest smoking from what looked like blaster hits, and swung his oversized blaster rifle into line back toward the doorway. The blaster fired. A lance of red light leapt from the weapon, and the interior of the chamber beyond the door was suddenly illuminated in flame colors.

Han fired. His shot hit the attacker's armor just under the armpit, staggering him but not penetrating.

At the same moment, Jacen hurled his lightsaber. It spun in flight, catching the attacker as he was still off-balance from Han's shot, crossing him at knee level, and severing both legs at the joint.

Jacen put on a burst of Force-augmented speed, leaving his father behind, and kept the lightsaber spinning in the air just outside the suite's door. There were more flashes of light from that chamber, more small-arms fire, and he took the last two steps with a sinking feeling.

He snatched the hilt of his spinning lightsaber out of the air and stepped into the doorway.

The room was on fire. No, that wasn't quite right—three members of the Corellian security detail were on fire, their bodies burning briskly, smoke also curling up from their blasters. Oddly, the chamber's fire alert had not activated.

There were three bodies on the ground that weren't smoking; they were black-clad intruders. The burn marks on their heads attested to the accurate fire of the dead CorSec officers.

One of the interior doors was gone, wrenched free, the frame scorched by the power of the intruders' blaster rifles. In the doorway stood Wedge Antilles, dressed in his shorts and ancient Rebel Alliance shirt, a blaster in his hand. He looked Jacen in the eye and shook his head, a sorrowful gesture.

Jacen entered and moved past Wedge. On the floor of the sumptuous bedchamber beyond lay Five World Prime Minister Aidel Saxan, a burned-edge hole the size of a dinner plate passing entirely through her torso, residual charring masking any expression she might have been wearing when she died.

* * *

Leia sped faster as she neared the door to the main Coruscant delegation quarters. Those doors were open, and she could hear blasterfire from beyond them. As she reached the doorway, she dropped the speed burst and stopped with the abruptness of a Toydarian junk merchant flying over a credit.

The chamber beyond, an antechamber providing access to a variety of bedchambers and function rooms, was filled with smoke and bodies. Three of the downed combatants were black-armored intruders. Several were GA security. One, on the far side of the room, sitting half upright, was an elderly man in an admiral's uniform. His head, neck, and the top portion of his chest were missing, the edges of what remained blackened by high energy. A huge hole in the wall above, centered at the two-meter level, showed where the upper reaches of his body had been when the blast had hit.

Nearer, a fourth black-armored intruder was sprawled on the floor, his blaster rifle a meter beyond his reach; he struggled to rise, but another GA-uniformed officer straddled his body, gripping his helmet by the faceplate. As the intruder continued to struggle, the officer brought a small blaster pistol up to the back of his neck and fired down, through the spine. The attacker jerked and lay still.

The officer became aware that someone was standing behind him. He spun and aimed, and as he turned Leia recognized him as Tycho Celchu. The old pilot's friend-or-foe recognition was still incredibly quick—he brought his aim off Leia even as she raised her blade to deflect a possible shot.

Leia looked past him to the body against the wall. "Oh, no," she said. "Not Pellaeon."

Tycho shook his head. "Not Pellaeon."

"My double." The voice came from a shadowy doorway; its door was opened, not destroyed. From it stepped the old admiral, dressed in a dark robe, a blaster rifle in his hands. He looked sorrowful as he gazed at the man who had died in his stead; even his bristly mustache seemed to droop.

Tycho asked, "Is Han—"

"He's fine," Leia said. "Han shot first."

There was no more blasterfire to be heard; the loudest noises were the hum of Leia's lightsaber and the crackling of flames from some of the bodies. Leia switched her weapon off and it was even quieter. "Let's find out how bad the damage is," she said.

"He looked at me," Luke said, "foamed at the mouth, and fell dead."

"The one Jacen crippled did the same thing," Wedge said.

"I saw foam on the lips of several of them," Pellaeon added.

They were crowded into a lounge near the Solo suite— representatives of both diplomatic parties, all the Jedi, and a few of Toryaz Station's security officers.

One of them, Lieutenant Yorvin, a reed-thin woman with hair a rustier red than Mara's, decided to straighten things out. "We need to start taking statements immediately," she said, "as soon as we can set up our truth analyzers. I'll be requesting a judge come up from Kuat to help with the officiating. My lord Solo"—she gestured at Han— "I'll need you to surrender your blaster. You're in the company of the envoys again."

Han gave her a look that was half scowl, half puzzlement. "I'm not sure how to respond to a statement like that," he said. "Except with violence."

Lieutenant Yorvin suddenly discovered herself flanked by Wedge Antilles and Tycho Celchu. "You seem to be asking to suck space," Wedge said.

"I'm sorry?"

"Perhaps the term isn't common in the Kuat flavor of Basic," Tycho said. "What he's asking, Lieutenant, is whether you'd like to patch the station exterior without wearing an enviro-suit."

"I don't—I'm not—"

"Shhh," Wedge said. "Listen. Yes, an investigation is about to happen, but you're not in charge. We are. Here are your orders."

"I—"

"First," Tycho said, "shut up. Second, lock down this entire habitat. Seal off the connection to Toryaz Station, then shut and seal every door, allowing them to be opened only from your security station."

"Speaking of which," Wedge said, "is there an auxiliary security station? Somewhere that can override security controls from the bridge and the main security office?"

"Yes, sir." Lieutenant Yorvin's attention flickered back and forth between the two pilots, and the comprehension dawning on her face suggested that she was beginning to understand what she would and would not be able to do in this situation. "But it's easier to—"

"Do it from there," Tycho said. "And send us your captain, what's-his-name . . ."

"Tawaler," Wedge supplied. "Also, no body, no weapon, no scorch mark, no splash of spilled caf is to be touched."

"Don't touch the security recordings without our say-so," Tycho added. "Just stand by in the security station and be prepared to open doors or provide information whenever I call for it, or General Antilles, or Admiral Pellaeon, or Master Skywalker, or anyone we designate."

Lieutenant Yorvin tried one last time. "But—this isn't the way things are *done*."

Wedge turned back toward Pellaeon. "Admiral, if these people don't do exactly as we say, is Toryaz Station going to be paid for rental of this habitat?"

"No, it's not." Pellaeon, once again in full-dress uniform, settled back in an overstuffed chair.

"If they continue to obstruct this investigation, are they going to be sued?" Tycho asked.

Pellaeon nodded, looking like a kindly old grandfather reluctant to give bad news. "And they'll lose. Oh, how they'll lose."

Wedge looked back at the officer. "Dismissed," he said.

She left. More precisely, she fled, nearly banging her nose on the lounge door as it slid out of her way almost too slowly.

"Since there's only one party here that is plausibly neutral," Wedge said, "I propose we hand coordination of this situation over to Master Skywalker and his Jedi."

"I agree," Pellaeon said. "Which is not to say that I only want Jedi looking into it."

"Don't worry," Luke said. "I'll be happy to draw on everyone's strengths." He frowned. "Allow me the first question here, Admiral. Do you routinely have a double along with you?"

The old officer shook his head. "But then, I don't routinely go on diplomatic missions. The double, and swapping out of the bedchambers we'd been assigned for others that were supposed to be empty, were notions of General Celchu's. And they saved my life."

"Actually," Tycho corrected, "it's something Wedge and I settled on together."

Pellaeon stage-whispered, "This treasonous collaboration has got to stop." His expression suggested he didn't mean it.

Luke turned to Wedge. "But Saxan wasn't protected by the same measures."

Wedge nodded. "I recommended they be implemented, but remember, I'm not—I wasn't—in charge of the Prime Minister's security the way Tycho is in charge of the admiral's. I was overruled by her security chief, fellow named Tommick. He's among the dead."

Han frowned. "Not Harval Tommick?"

Wedge nodded again.

"A member of Thrackan Sal-Solo's political machine," Han continued. "What's someone like that doing in charge of security for a political rival?"

Wedge offered up a humorless smile. "In his secondary capacity as Minister of War, Sal-Solo was able to insist that

Saxan's security be 'augmented' by Tommick's crew. Tommick's crew took over."

"Who's going to take over as Five World Prime Minister?" Luke asked. "Saxan's deputy?"

Wedge nodded. "Fellow named Denjax Teppler. Once married to Saxan, in fact. They parted but remained friendly. He'll hold the post until they can arrange a new election. Months, perhaps."

Han snorted. "You mean, until he gets killed, too."

Luke, seated, finished dressing—he flexed his toes in his boots and then zipped the boots up along the side. Now he was clad head-to-toe in black, somber dress for a somber occasion—and also vaguely menacing dress in a time when he needed politicians and bureaucrats to listen to him very carefully.

"All right," he said, "if I'm in charge of this investigation— a circumstance that can only last until the GA and Corellian delegations receive orders from their respective governments—then I'm going to have to act fast." He rose. "Tycho, Wedge, and the Jedi will spread out to investigate. Admiral, I'd like to ask you to stay here, coordinate data as we obtain it. Han . . ." He frowned, obviously at a loss to make use of Han's skills in this situation.

Leia spoke up. "Han can provide security here. And maybe let the admiral teach him a thing or two about sabacc."

"Teach me," Han repeated.

"Two kindly old Corellians," Leia continued, her expression innocent, "having a harmless game of cards."

Pellaeon fixed Han with a disbelieving stare. "Your lady really does like the sight of blood, doesn't she?"

Han gestured toward the old naval officer, a motion that somehow said, *It's settled.* Luke took one last, quick look around. His attention fell on his son. Ben was paler than usual and unnaturally quiet. Luke saw Mara reach for the boy, probably to give his brow or chin an affectionate stroke, but Ben drew back without looking at her. Luke didn't know whether the boy was shunning contact or simply didn't want to seem to be a coddled child in front of the other Jedi, but he felt a faint pang of hurt from Mara—a pang she quickly, ruthlessly clamped down on.

He felt for her, but had no time to talk to her, to talk to Ben. He rose. "Let's go," he said.

Zekk, beside the door, hit the control panel and it slid open for Luke. His cloak streaming, his fellow Jedi trailing behind him, Luke swept out into the hall and prepared himself for what he knew was going to be a long night of investigating, negotiating, and theorizing.

"Sorry, have I interrupted a veterans' parade?" Jaina asked.

Wedge, in anonymous gray civilian clothes, and Tycho, still in his dress uniform, were walking side by side down an outer-rim corridor; Wedge glanced back at Jaina and Zekk, then he and Tycho exchanged a look.

"Jedi are quiet," Tycho said. "They sneak up on you even when they're supposed to be your friends."

Wedge grinned. "Maybe you're just losing your hearing."

"I was deafened by the sound of your joints creaking."

"That could be it." Wedge returned his attention to the datapad in his hands. It was open, and its small screen displayed a map of this section of Narsacc Habitat. The map background was black, the partitions and bulkheads were narrow yellow lines, and a dotted red line stretched from behind their current position to a point some meters ahead. "Tell her that I'm not sure I should be talking to a traitor."

"General Antilles says—"

"*Traitor?*" Jaina stopped, aghast. "Wait a minute. I'm half Corellian by birth, sure, but I wasn't raised as a citizen. And as Jedi, we're supposed to put the interest of the greater good ahead of planetary concerns—"

"Not what I meant," Wedge said, unruffled.

Tycho nodded. "She's young. She jumps to conclusions."

Wedge adjusted the datapad so that the map scrolled

ahead. It now showed the red dotted line terminating at an air lock. "She also talks too much."

"She has to. The boy who follows her everywhere doesn't say *anything*."

Jaina glanced back and up at Zekk. He nodded, admission that the point was well made.

"No," Wedge said, "what I mean is that anyone as good as you are in a snubfighter, but who gives up the flying life to run around in robes and swing an impractical energy sword, has committed treason to her natural aptitudes."

"I still fly," Jaina said, "and I still fly X-wings, and you're avoiding the subject."

Wedge nodded. "All right. No more avoidance." He drew a deep breath, then let it out in a guilty sigh. "This is *not* a veterans' parade."

"Well done," Tycho said. "Confession does cleanse the spirit, doesn't it?"

"It does," Wedge admitted.

Jaina held up her hands, fingers curled, as if on the verge of reaching for Wedge's neck. "So what have you found?"

Tycho said, "As you know, the head security officer for the habitat is missing."

"We know," Jaina said, ruefully. "That's what Zekk and I have been doing, looking for him. We looked at the holo-cam recordings—"

"Which don't exist for Kallebarth Way for the time period of the attack," Tycho said.

"Correct. We also went through his quarters, tried to get a sense of him . . ." She frowned.

"What is it?" Tycho asked.

Jaina smiled. "Oh, at last *you're* curious. At last I have something *you* want to know."

Tycho rolled his eyes. "Better tell her, Wedge. She's going to get difficult."

Wedge came to a stop so suddenly that Jaina almost bumped into him. They were in front of an air lock; Wedge's datapad indicated that they were at the terminus of the red dotted line. He snapped the device shut. "In the wake of the attack, Tycho and I did the first, most obvious thing—"

"You asked for brandy?" Zekk asked.

"The tree speaks at last." Tycho shook his head. "No, we asked for those selfsame holocam recordings that don't exist."

"So you got nothing," Jaina said.

From a pocket, Wedge pulled a cable. One end went into a jack in the datapad. The other was a standard round wall plug, which he fit into the jack beneath the air lock's control panel. "Running diagnostics," he said. "Seems to be pressurized. No unusual pulses through the internal sensors. No, Jaina, we asked whether Toryaz Station is the sort of place where the engineering department logs all door openings and closings. You know, to measure wear patterns, predict replacement needs, that sort of thing."

"That would never have occurred to me," Jaina admitted.

Wedge smiled. "Me, either. Something my wife taught me. Or, rather, taught my younger daughter while I eavesdropped. I have one daughter going into my line of work, one going into my wife's. Genetically and culturally speaking, isn't that perfect?"

"Perfect," Jaina said, her tone flat. "So? The door openings?"

Wedge rapped the air lock door. "This was open, shortly before the attack, for about a minute at a time when there is no listing of a ship being docked outside. And note that we're on the opposite side of the habitat from its outer rim, meaning that this air lock is out of direct sight of the frigate *Firethorn*—it's the most inconvenient air lock on the habitat, with the most inconvenient approach, suited only to shuttles and smaller craft. Anyway, a minute later it went through a depressurization cycle, outer door opened and closed, and then repressurized."

"So someone arrived here by shuttle, and left here by shuttle," Jaina said.

Tycho shook his head. "That doesn't make sense. You

bring in a crew of assassins, you open the air lock to let them in. You close it, cycle it, reopen it—why? If you're just going to leave, why not leave it open for the sixty or ninety seconds until you leave?"

"Meaning," Wedge said, "ultimately, what we have is a mystery. Add to it the fact that the security door on the tube to the main station opened a couple of minutes later. So a shuttle left here, and then something cycled through the air lock—to throw out some evidence, maybe?—and then someone left the habitat on foot." His datapad chimed, and he opened it up to glance at the screen. "Looks all clear," he said. "Risk it?"

Tycho said, "Put the children up front."

Wedged grinned and typed a series of numbers and letters into the 'pad. The air lock door hissed and slid open. From another pocket, he pulled a pair of thin gloves and donned them. He began prodding at the corners of access panels, running fingers across the tops of glowing WARNING signs, peering into every crack and cranny in the air lock. "Wish Iella were here," he said.

"Or Winter," Tycho added.

"Both our wives are ex-Intelligence," Wedge said, his comment directed at Zekk. "Tycho's wife used to babysit Jaina, in fact. Whatever we've learned, we've picked up mostly through osmosis."

"Normally, we just shoot things," Tycho added.

"We keep trying to retire," Wedge said. "Give up this life of shooting things."

Tycho nodded. "We're really men of peace at heart."

Wedge stepped out from the air lock and shrugged. "Nothing."

Jaina held out her hand. "Give it over."

Wedge looked surprised. "What?"

"I saw you palm something when you were bent over looking at the floor. Hand it over."

Wedge shook his head. "Our lead, our investigation. You and your pole-like shadow can tag along if you want."

"Trade," Zekk said.

Wedge shot him a curious look. "What?"

"Trade. I give you my lead, the one I found on my own."

"You didn't tell me you found a lead," Jaina muttered.

Zekk ignored her. "You give Jaina your lead. An even trade."

Wedge glanced at Tycho. "What do you think?"

Tycho shook his head. "Jedi bluff."

Zekk smiled. "To sweeten the deal, the lead I picked up, if you take it, means you'll have to commandeer a shuttle or a rescue craft and go flying around outside."

Wedge sighed. "It's always the quiet ones. All right, master motivator, you have a deal." From a side pocket he removed a clean orange rag that appeared to be wrapped around something. He held it above Jaina's hand but did not release it. "Your clue?"

"We were looking for Tawaler, too, as Jaina said. His comlink reads as being off-base," Zekk said. "So I dismissed it for a while. But then I remembered. *Off-base*, as a comm term, is normally used on groundside bases. We use the same terms in the order, probably because Master Skywalker is ex-military. Means that the wearer is not on-base, but his comlink is still returning a signal. Right?"

"Right," Wedge said. "Oh."

Jaina caught it just as fast. "So our suspect's comlink is still returning a signal from nearby . . . but we've all been assuming it meant that he'd flown off to some planet somewhere. Give it." She wiggled her fingers.

Wedge dropped the rag into her hand. The object within it had a little weight to it, perhaps half a kilogram.

Jaina turned the rag over and unfolded it, revealing what lay within. "Huh," she said.

chapter twenty-one

Throughout the night when diplomats should have been asleep or planning the next day's negotiations, the Jedi and other investigators scoured pertinent areas of the Narsacc Habitat.

Wedge and Tycho confirmed with the frigate *Firethorn* that a shuttle had departed another habitat at about the same time the assault on the diplomatic envoys was beginning. Hyperdrive-equipped, it had headed away from Kuat and her gravity well at a rate that did not elicit suspicion, and it had entered hyperspace before the first alarms were transmitted from the habitat. After the alarm, Toryaz Station Security had locked the station down, permitting no vehicles or vessels to arrive or depart. The obvious conclusion was that the individual or individuals who'd left via the main spoke to Toryaz Station were still there, or had departed on the shuttle.

Leia and Mara arranged for security operatives familiar with forensics to be brought in to examine the bodies of the attackers. All had been killed either by trauma from blasters or lightsabers, or through the introduction of a powerful alkaloid poison administered by small injectors in their mouths. Preliminary evidence was that each of them had already been dying from incurable illness, as well, and a simple genetics test offered the probability that three-quarters or more of the attackers were Corellian.

Wedge and Tycho, accompanied by Luke, acquired a shuttle and a sophisticated set of comm sensor gear from Lieutenant Yorvin. After an hour's careful flying out from the station, they homed in on the signal being broadcast by Captain Tawaler's comlink. Tawaler, stone-dead, victim of explosive decompression, was still in possession of that comlink. They retrieved his body and brought it back to the station, turning it over to the forensics experts dealing with the attackers' bodies, but those experts could report only that Tawaler had died of hemorrhaging and exposure consistent with explosive decompression. There were no wounds on or chemicals present in his body; there were no signs that he had been bound. To all appearances, he had willingly stepped out into space and died a gruesome, painful death.

Jacen, Ben in tow, wandered throughout the habitat, seeking additional impressions that might point to use of the Force. He found them in the auxiliary security chamber now occupied by Lieutenant Yorvin and in the air lock where Tawaler had died. In each case there was a female aspect to the impressions, but Jacen could get no clear sense of them—the harder he looked, the more they seemed to blur.

Mara and Leia ran a thorough examination of the security auxiliary control room, finding the code modifications that had allowed the shuttle to maneuver into position without being detected by the base sensors. They were able to dig out the true recordings, showing the shuttle's arrival and quick departure.

Admiral Pellaeon kept information flowing from one group of investigators to the next and, when not so occupied, lost hundreds of credits to Han Solo in a sabacc game. Luke and his investigators assembled in the lounge again at about the hour they would have been waking up. No one looked weary; the Jedi sustained themselves through Force techniques, while Han, Wedge, and Tycho relied on caf and stubbornness.

"So what have we learned?" Luke asked. He began

counting off on his fingers. "The killers were mostly Corellians, which doesn't mean anything, since anyone can hire Corellian killers." He noticed Wedge's and Han's stares and amended, "That didn't come out the way I intended it."

"Forget it," Han said.

"This was a sophisticated plan," Luke continued, "at least in its setup. The planner made use of powerful narcotics to subdue the agents on perimeter duty, and a powerful alkaloid to kill assassins who might have otherwise survived. These toxins aren't easy to get. The planner knew exactly where everyone was sleeping—or, rather, was *supposed* to be sleeping, since Admiral Pellaeon and his personnel occupied different chambers without informing the base security detail. Captain Tawaler appears to have been influenced, both into participating in the plan and into killing himself, by means of use of the Force . . . meaning that, regretfully, we have to conclude that a rogue Jedi or equivalent is involved. Supporting that point is the fact that the weapons they carried were designed for use against Jedi."

Wedge interrupted, "Much the way the Corellian response to some recent missions was optimized against Jedi."

Before Luke could reply, Han cut in. "It was Thrackan."

"That's one possibility," Luke admitted. He couldn't state the thought that next occurred to him: that if Saxan were determined to achieve peace, she might put the secret Corellian fleet on the table as a negotiating item. If Chief Sal-Solo were indeed behind the building of that fleet, he would take whatever steps he thought necessary to keep it from being negotiated away.

"Possibility, nothing." Han's voice rose. "Does anybody here not know that it was my boy Jacen and Luke's boy Ben who wrecked Centerpoint Station?"

Silence fell in the wake of those words. Luke noticed that Ben seemed upset by the announcement. A look crossed his features—Luke would have described it as haunted, and again he wondered whether Ben would ever tell the Solos the portion of the story he'd mentioned only during his Jedi debriefing, the details about the droid that had thought it was Anakin Solo.

Finally Wedge said, "I've seen the security recordings from the assault on Centerpoint Station. As the one person present least likely to know otherwise, I'd have to say the answer is no."

"So?" Han asked, his face reddening. "He wants revenge. The damage at Centerpoint throws his plan back years. But if this assault here, last night, had been one hundred percent successful, he'd have avenged himself and cleared the way to take complete control in Corellia. He's the only one who profits from what happened here."

"Not quite," Leia said. "He only profits if he can take control and then achieve peace. The killing of Prime Minister Saxan reduces the likelihood of peace. The Corellians are going to be hopping mad and pushing for war . . . Thrackan's smart enough to realize how ruinous war would be to the Corellian economy. Even if they were to win."

"It's Thrackan," Han said.

"Jacen?" Luke leaned toward his nephew. "While you were running around, chasing Sal-Solo as a distraction for Ben, did you get any sense from him that he'd take your actions more personally than an old conspirator should?"

Jacen thought over the question. In his report, he'd left out the part about him deciding that Thrackan had to die. It appeared that Thrackan had neglected to mention it, too, and now Jacen thought he understood why: by leaving that part of the story out, Thrackan removed a certain amount of motivation that might associate him with this attack. And now Jacen could admit to his attempt on Thrackan's life—a confession that would further damage Luke's already diminished ability to trust in Jacen—or deny it and help obscure Thrackan's association with tonight's misdeeds.

Well, it was enough that he, Jacen, knew. He could make his own calculations based on what he knew of Thrackan's motivations. He shook his head. "No, I really didn't."

Luke leaned back. "We'll investigate the Thrackan angle, of course. Anything else?"

"I've got something," Jaina said. From beneath her outer robe she produced a folded packet of orange cloth a bit larger than her fist. She carefully unfolded it and held it out so that the others could see its contents.

At first Luke couldn't grasp what he was looking at—it seemed to be something organic, the dried, stringy fruit of a mutant tree. It was a pliant thing with a blue-black central core perhaps a dozen centimeters long. From that core sprang twenty or more tubular branches, narrowest where they were attached to the core and at their tips, only slightly thicker in their centers, each about six centimeters long—and each bearing colors, stripes, and other patterns. One, lumpy and knotted, consisted of red and blue stripes in a spiral pattern; another was straight, an eye-hurting yellow with flecks of red and black; a third was a creamy tan with jittery, jagged markings in black.

"We found this in the air lock that Tawaler used when he was going out for fresh air," Jaina said. "I haven't had time to scan it for inorganic toxins, but there's no biological activity going on in it. It just seems to be beadwork."

"Accidentally dropped, or left for us to find?" Luke asked. "Carried by Tawaler, or someone else?"

Jaina shrugged. "No way to tell."

"Excuse me." The words came from overhead and all around—a set of public address speakers. Luke recognized the voice of Lieutenant Yorvin. "I have a priority holo-comm contact coming in for Admiral Pellaeon. He's not in his new quarters. Is there any chance he's still in the lounge?"

"I'm here," Pellaeon said. He heaved himself to his feet, and Tycho stood, too. "That'll be the crack-of-dawn, report-any-changes call, and as soon as I report, this conference is done." He sighed. "I'll be back in a few minutes." He walked stiffly from the room, and the door closed behind him and Tycho.

Wedge consulted his chrono. "The Prime Minister will

be receiving one of those, too. And though she wouldn't be obliged to receive it, I will be. If you'll excuse me?" He rose and departed, as well.

"Leaving only Jedi," Zekk said, "and a Jedi-in-law."

Han scowled at him.

Luke stared at the others over his hands, which he held steepled before him in a meditative pose. "I think we can safely say that our mission at this station has been an utter failure. We've been outmaneuvered, and we have at least one enemy we didn't know about before . . . and we know very little about now. In a few minutes, the delegations will be recalled. It'll be time for Jedi investigations to get under way for real.

"Jacen, Ben, please see what you can find out about Captain Tawaler. We need to find out about the Force-user he apparently had contact with. She can't have left *no* trace. If you can't pick up a trail, continue with the shuttle she apparently escaped on."

Jacen nodded. "Consider it done."

"Jaina, Zekk, I want you to find out whatever you can about that tassel you found. Try to determine whether it was left accidentally or deliberately, where it came from, what it means. When that's done, please return to the task force at Corellia and take command of Hardpoint Squadron until Mara and I get back from our groundside mission, which I'll explain momentarily.

"Leia, Han, I'd like to ask you to continue trying to calm things down between Corellia and the GA. I can't think of anybody better to run confidential messages between the two governments, even as they become more hostile, or to tell the leaders of two governments when they're behaving like bantha bulls in roughhousing season."

Leia exchanged a glance with her husband. "I suspect we can do that."

"Mara and I will travel on to Corellia to see what we can find out about the possible origins of the assault made against us today."

"They're after me, too, aren't they?" That was Ben,

speaking for the first time since the Jedi had reconvened. His expression and voice were somber—not afraid, but far more serious than a thirteen-year-old's should be, and Luke felt a lump begin to form in his throat.

"Yes," he said. "If they're after Jacen because of Centerpoint Station, they're after you, too. Your youth may not mean anything to them. But understand me. Regardless of who they are, or how highly they're placed, I'm not going to tolerate the continued—" He checked himself before he said *existence*. Revenge was not the way of the Jedi, not even when one's own son had been the subject of a murder attempt. "—the continued freedom of people who target children for assassination."

"How delicately expressed," Mara said. "I don't think there's any way they'll refrain from trying to kill us if we confront them, Luke. And when they do . . ."

"It's never a good thing to hope for an opportunity to kill, Mara," Luke said, his voice mild. But he had to admit to himself that the exact emotion was there in his own mind, hovering around his areas of self-control like neks circling a campfire just beyond the reach of its light. "All right. Let's go. Ben, join me and your mother for a few minutes before it's time to leave."

Once the Skywalkers were out the door, Jacen gestured to get his sister's attention, to keep her from following Zekk and the Jedi exodus. "Can I see that thing again?"

"Sure." She held the tassel out to him.

Jacen looked it over. Close up, the mystery object proved to be an unusual example of beadcraft. It seemed to be a set of decorative tassels, each shaped and colored in an entirely different pattern, each attached to the longer central strand. At the top of the central strand was a cord, blue-black like the strand itself but unbeaded; it was three or four centimeters long and ended in a break, the cord material frayed. The object could have been caught on a corner, or grasped by the hand of a dying man and yanked free with relatively little effort, its loss unnoticed by its owner.

Or, Jacen acknowledged, it could have been left deliberately.

One of the tassels continued to draw his eye, the tan one with the jagged black markings. Tiny black threads escaped through its surface, poking out from between the close-set beads. Viewed from the distance of a meter, they made the tassel look as though it needed a shave, but on closer inspection they resembled tiny claws.

The design of this tassel itself—Jacen could almost read the artist's intent. *The smooth tan represents peace,* he told himself. *The jagged black lines, strife. The curled threads are hooks, or claws. The moral: even a peaceful life will know strife, and strife presents hooks to drag you farther into the strife, a trap for the unwary.* There was more to it than that, he knew—or at least felt. There was some sort of story involved in the message, but he couldn't puzzle it out.

Abruptly he felt foolish. He was a Jedi Knight, not an art critic. It was not for him to try to wrest meaning out of patterns found on some bauble that probably cost less than a credit on a backwater planet's street market. But the thing still drew him.

He became aware that Jaina was still speaking, her words lost in his distraction. He smiled at her and shook his head. "Sorry. I was daydreaming."

"That's not like you."

"More like Anakin. Listen, would you like to trade?"

Jaina frowned. "Trade what?"

"Assignments. I'm feeling something from these tassels—can you?"

"No, not really." She stooped to look them over more closely, then shook her head.

"So I should be the one to investigate them. You look into Tawaler, then go and take command of Uncle Luke's squadron."

Jaina briefly considered. "Let's clear it with Uncle Luke first."

"Let's *not.* He's been second-guessing a lot of my instincts lately . . . even though he keeps telling *me* to trust them. Well, I trust this one—I need to be the one to investigate the tassel."

She gave him a long-suffering look. "And when he asks about it—"

"It'll be all my fault."

She nodded. "He'll believe that. You are male, after all."

Luke, Mara, and Ben walked along Varganner Way, one level up from and running precisely parallel to Kallebarth Way. This passageway had been locked down for the brief duration of the GA/Corellia diplomatic mission; now Luke had it opened, temporarily, so he and his family could take a private walk.

They paused at a recess dominated by an outer-hull wall made up entirely of crystal-clear transparisteel. It showed the same view as the viewport in the Solo suite, but even less bounded, and at this moment the Skywalkers could gaze upon a majestic field of stars and the distant sun of Kuat.

Finally Luke said, "Ben, your thoughts are very close to the surface."

"We should all go there together," the boy said. "To Corellia. Us and Jacen and Jaina. And we should hammer on Thrackan Sal-Solo until he admits what he did, and lock him away so he doesn't do it anymore."

"All together as a family, yes?" Luke asked.

Ben nodded, but didn't look at his father. He stubbornly kept his attention on a diamond-shaped nebula far away.

"We're all mad because they attacked," Mara said. "But we can't use our Jedi abilities just because we're mad. We can't attack Thrackan under the *assumption* that he's responsible; we have to have more evidence."

"I know." Ben sounded resigned. "If you're mad, you can't let your instincts guide your actions, 'cause it may not be the Force, it's probably your anger. But we could do it when we're cold inside. Jacen's cold inside a lot."

His parents exchanged a quick look. Luke said, "I think what you're feeling as coldness is really submergence into the Force. His own emotions will go away for a while. That can seem cold."

"Whatever." Ben shrugged. "But we could still do it. We could grab Sal-Solo. And we could stop the Corellians from starting a war."

"That's another issue. What if the Force tells you not to beat them? Or doesn't tell you anything at all about whether they should win?"

Finally Ben did look up at him. "Huh?"

"Ben, can you honestly tell me that the Corellians shouldn't have freedom from the Galactic Alliance if they want it? Think about the Corellians you know—Uncle Han and Wedge Antilles, for instance. If most of the people in their system want to be independent, why shouldn't they be?"

Ben frowned. "That doesn't make any sense. They're part of the Galactic Alliance. They can't just leave."

"Why not?" Mara asked.

"It'll cause unrest. That's what Jacen says."

Mara nodded. "It *will* cause unrest. There is a lot of unrest in life. The Force is created by life, so it has unrest in it. If you open yourself to the Force, how can you not open yourself to a certain amount of unrest?"

Ben gave his parents a suspicious stare. It wasn't a look of mistrust, just the expression of a teenager anxious not to be tricked. "Whose side are you really on?"

Luke snorted. "The Jedi order protects and serves the Galactic Alliance, just as it did the New Republic. Just as the old order protected and served the Old Republic. But we choose to maintain a certain amount of latitude in interpreting our missions, our orders. For the good of everybody. And that means if we're ordered into battle, but we discover we can achieve a victory through negotiation or a bloodless show of force, we do it. If we discover that we can bring peace by obliging the opposing sides to listen to each other, we do it—even if one side is supposed to be in charge of what we do."

Ben returned his attention to the starfield for a moment.

"I hear kids say they hate it when their parents say *Do this because I say so.* Sometimes I think they have it easy."

Mara laughed softly and reached out to brush her hand across her son's fine red hair. "I suspect they do. Of course, they don't get to run all over the galaxy and practice with live lightsabers."

"Yeah, I guess. But thinking is hard. And kind of unfair. There never seems to be a right answer."

Luke felt his lump return, but this time he knew it was caused by pride, not pain. "That's it," he said. "*There never seems to be a right answer* is a right answer."

"Oh."

"Watch out for people who tell you they know the right answer," Mara added. "They may think they do, but often they're wrong. Or they may just know that thinking is so hard, many people don't want to do it. They want a leader they can trust . . . so they don't have to do the hard work of thinking. That's one type of leader you don't want to follow."

Ben opened his mouth as if to ask another question, then closed it again.

"You're right," Luke said. "If you asked whether you should tell Han and Leia about the Anakin Solo droid, we'd just have to say we don't know."

Ben looked up at him. "Sometimes you hate being a Jedi, don't you?"

Luke thought about it, then nodded. "Occasionally."

"Me, too."

Within an hour, all members of the three parties had departed—all but Jaina, Zekk, Jacen, and Ben, who waited behind to begin their investigations from this habitat. They waved at the departing corvettes and transports from the viewport in what had been Han and Leia's suite.

When the last of the departing ships was gone, Jacen turned to the others. "First," he said, "sleep. Then we get under way."

chapter twenty-two

CORONET, CORELLIA

Taking two of the most famous people in the galaxy and smuggling them onto a highly developed, security-conscious world was actually quite simple. Luke knew it would be, at least once, and so didn't bother consulting any of the many Intelligence friends and allies he had—beyond arranging for identicards for himself and Mara.

Now he stood in a crowded line at a crowded security station in the crowded Corellian city of Coronet and stared, smiling, down at the unamused, weathered face of an officer of CorSec, the system police.

The man squinted up at him. "Luke Skywalker," he said.

Luke nodded, his smile broadening.

"I really don't see it."

"Oh, come on." Mara stepped forward, voice raised in Luke's defense. "He looks just like him."

"Too short," the CorSec officer said. "No one would believe in a Luke Skywalker that short."

Luke let a slightly whiny note creep into his voice. "I can do backflips just like him."

"I'm sure you can." The CorSec officer waved Luke's falsified identicard under the needle-like point of a data transmitter. A pinpoint light on the identicard switched from red to green, signifying that the visitor's visa for Emerek Tovall, actor-impersonator from Fondor, was approved. He was now free to enter Coronet and conduct lawful business of all varieties.

"Would you like an autograph?" Luke asked.

"No, thank you. Move along." The disinterested officer took Mara's identicard next.

Three places up in line, a couple who bore a remarkable resemblance to Han Solo and Leia Organa—as they had looked decades before, at the time of the Battle of Yavin, down to Leia's white Senatorial dress and side-bun hairstyle—waited patiently at another station. The CorSec woman there looked skeptically at the screen in front of her and asked, "*Jiyam* Solo?"

"That's right," the Han impersonator said, his voice richer, more theatrical than the real Han's.

"Any relation?"

The impersonator shook his head. "I changed my name for professional reasons."

"Does it help?"

"I get a lot of work. Here, we're doing a bio-holodrama of the Solos, with two endings, depending on whose side he takes in the upcoming conflict . . ."

Just beyond him, the Leia impersonator patted her right-hand bun and spoke to the man in line ahead of her. Over the crowd noise, Luke could barely make out her softer tones: "No, we're not married, but I've worked with him before. Well, yes, maybe. Where are you staying?"

Mara bumped into Luke from behind. "Move along, Shorty. I've cleared customs."

Luke picked up his bag and moved toward the chamber exit, through which other visitors to Corellia were streaming. Inside the bag, its housing replaced by a more innocuous one, its power supply replaced by one far less potent, his lightsaber now resembled nothing so much as a personal glow rod and had passed through customs without raising an eyebrow, as Mara's had. The correct housings and power supplies, shipped separately, would be awaiting them at their respective destinations. "It worked spectacularly," he said.

"It did. Hiring the actors for the various other 'roles' was the clincher, I think. Too bad your Chewbacca couldn't make it."

Luke shrugged. "You can't always get a Wookiee at the last minute. Especially when you'd have to dye his fur and give him a trim. Still . . ." He allowed a false note of hurt creep into his voice. "Still, I think I make a pretty good Luke Skywalker."

"Of course you do," Mara said, her tone soothing, a millimeter short of condescending.

"So before you began impersonating Mara, what was your real hair color?"

"Farmboy, you're asking for a beating . . ."

Outside the customs facility, they posed for a holocam picture with two tourists who were delighted to meet Jedi impersonators. Once the tourists were gone, Luke and Mara kissed, put up the hoods of their travelers' robes, and went their separate ways.

Mara fetched the airspeeder she'd rented under her assumed name and sped off toward a series of meetings where she'd pick up supplies and information she'd need for her mission. Luke, his day's activities as urgent but not as time-critical, waved down a public transportation groundspeeder and directed it to an address in one lightly trafficked area of the government districts of Coronet.

The building that was his destination—actually three buildings down from the address he'd given the driver and where he exited the transport—was simple of design and pleasing to the eye. It was very low, one story only, on its right and left wings, but swept upward toward the middle in a steep curve so that its center was a narrowing spire several stories in height. The entire building was duracrete, tan speckled with black, except for doors and windows of green transparisteel. It was set back from the street some fifty meters, the property decorated with dark green grasses sectioned off by narrow tan duracrete sidewalks, and was entirely surrounded by a fence of blue-black plasteel bars four meters high.

On the fence gate was a printed sign reading, CLOSED DURING PLANETARY EMERGENCY. FOR HELP OR INFORMATION, PLEASE CONTACT CORELLIAN SECURITY. Below that was a communications address. Elsewhere on the sign, hand-lettered, were phrases such as JEDI DIE, GO HOME, and WHO PLACES PHILOSOPHY ABOVE PLANET HAS BETRAYED BOTH. Luke recognized the last quote; it was from a recent speech by Chief Sal-Solo.

There was rubbish on the green lawn, and there were blaster scores on the walls and windows of the building side facing the street. Vandals had been at work. A uniformed CorSec officer walked the sidewalk in front of the fence, keeping her eye on pedestrian and speeder traffic.

Luke walked past the CorSec officer, not making eye contact, the slightest gesture of his hand and exertion of the Force keeping the officer from feeling any curiosity about the robed passerby. Once Luke was well past her, almost to the corner where the fence changed from plasteel to smooth stone and marked the beginning of a city library property, he glanced back.

The CorSec woman was facing away. Another few steps and she'd turn and begin pacing back in Luke's direction. He took a quick look and feel around, detected no one's attention on him, and leapt over the fence.

He came down, rolling to his feet almost silently, and dashed to the cover of the bushes along the side of the small Jedi enclave.

The transparisteel windows along this side of the enclave looked as though they were permanently inset in the walls and could not be opened, but Luke stopped at the third window, looked around again, and brought out his comlink. He changed frequencies to one routinely used by Jedi on field operations, then whistled three notes into it.

The window hissed as it unsealed. Cooler air from inside flowed out. Luke pulled at the window from the bottom—

it remained attached, hinged, at the top—and rolled through it, coming up on his feet in what looked like a small schoolroom beyond. The window sealed itself shut behind him.

The room was darkened but not dark. No glow rods supplied light; the only illumination came from sunlight through the viewport, tinted green by the transparisteel coloration. It revealed chairs and desks, too small for adults, and pictures all over the walls: diagrams showing the angles of attack and defense in lightsaber technique; long-dead Master Yoda, face furrowed in concentration, telekinetically holding an Old Republic gunship weighing many tons over his head; a female Jedi Master—generic and probably fictitious, not a person Luke had ever seen in person or in records—sitting cross-legged in meditation, her eyes closed.

A silver protocol droid, powered down, stood at the head of the room, one arm raised as though to illustrate a point.

The only sound to be heard was the hum of the enclave's air-cooling machinery. Luke shook his head, regretful. A Jedi teaching facility should never be so silent, so empty. But in the wake of the assault on Tralus and Centerpoint Station, the Corellians had declared the Jedi enemies of the state and had made an effort to close down all Jedi facilities and round up Jedi in the planetary system.

That last part hadn't gone so well. Determined not to let the teachings of the order come as close to extinction as they had in the time of Emperor Palpatine, Luke had taught his students what he knew of avoiding hunters. He knew a lot.

He moved to the door. It didn't slide open at his approach. He gripped the edge and gave it a shove; it slid aside on well-lubricated rails.

Just beyond it, a silver lightsaber blade *snap-hissed* into life. The man who carried it said, "You're going to find it hard to loot with both your arms cut off."

Luke grinned. "That's quite a greeting, Corran."

The other Jedi turned his lightsaber off just as quickly as

he'd powered it on. "Luke! Master Skywalker." He stepped forward into the faint light admitted by the doorway.

Corran Horn was about Luke's age and height, but a bit stockier of build, broader in the shoulder. Grandson of a famous Corellian Jedi of the Old Republic era, he'd come into recognition and training of his Jedi powers even later than Luke had—careers as a CorSec officer and Rebel Alliance fighter pilot had come first. As conflicted as he might have been in early days about aptitudes, duties, and careers, he was now a Jedi Master, whose graying hair and beard gave visual support to his reputation as an elder statesman of the order.

He wasn't dressed as a Jedi now. He wore anonymous blue-and-white pin-striped coveralls, spattered with grease and hydraulic fluids, and a set of welder's goggles pushed up on his forehead. As he held out his hand for Luke, he looked like a pit mechanic ready to explain just how much his hyperdrive repairs were going to cost.

Luke took his hand, an embrace of brothers in arms. "How's your family?"

"Good." Corran's voice suggested he wasn't entirely happy. "Mirax is under house arrest. Quite a flap over that, too. Some in the government want her expertise in smuggling critical materials into the system. Others don't trust her because she's married to a Jedi. So she waits at home, under arrest, every need being catered to by government personnel, enjoying a vacation." He snorted. "As for Valin and Jysella . . . well, I suspect you'd know better than I would what they're up to."

Luke nodded. Corran and Mirax's children were both Jedi, raised as much by the teachers of the Jedi academy as by their biological parents, off doing the business of the order.

Corran's face softened. "Thanks for not using them on the Corellian missions."

"That was an easy decision," Luke said. He moved forward, Corran stepping aside so he could enter the hall, and slid the door shut. Now they were in deeper darkness, illuminated only by dim emergency glowstrips at the base-boards of this hallway. "I didn't want any Jedi to be considered traitors by their homeworlds. For most, it's nice to be able to return home from time to time."

Corran didn't comment. Luke knew that he, Luke, was an exception to that generalization. His own homeworld of Tatooine held no lure for him—hadn't in all the decades since he'd left it to find a new home elsewhere.

Corran gestured down the hallway toward the rear of the enclave. "I've set up one of the bolt-holes as a staging area. Your lightsaber components are there. Also clothes, supplies, credits—"

"Thanks." Together they walked down the hallway and then down a spiral flight of stairs. "So," Luke said.

"So."

"So, what's the attitude of the Corellian Jedi? What do I need to know?"

They emerged from the staircase into another corridor that was lit only by emergency glowstrips. Corran took three steps from the entry into the hall, then raised a hand, holding it against one wall almost at ceiling height. "It's here," he said. "A simple bolt and counterweight. Just give it a tug."

Luke reached out with the Force, felt past Corran's hand, past the wall, to the machinery beyond. A weight suspended from a metal cable; a hole in the center of the weight; a crossbar that passed through the hole. Delicately, he drew the crossbar out of the hole and pulled down on the weight.

A section of the wall rose smoothly into the ceiling. Light spilled out into the corridor. Beyond the wall section was a medium-sized chamber, tables laden with lit computer screens, wall lockers, four cots. They entered and Luke released his hold on the weight; the wall section slid smoothly into place behind them.

"How do you do it?" Luke asked. One of Corran's few weaknesses as a Jedi was his lack of ability with telekinetic disciplines; Corran couldn't, under most circumstances, operate the crossbar and pull-weight machinery.

"A backup system. Say *Halcyon Endures*. That'll trigger the door. It uses battery power, though. I have a hand-crank device to keep the battery charged." Corran shrugged. He sat at a chair in front of one of the computer tables and gestured at the items in front of the other chair—the housing and power supply for Luke's lightsaber.

"So," Luke said again. He sat, brought his false glow rod from his bag, and got to work reassembling his weapon.

"So you know my position. You accept the role and duties of a Jedi, you put the order, and the general good, ahead of planetary interests. Even family interests. Doesn't mean you cut yourself off from your family or world . . . just that you recognize that putting personal interests above the greater good basically constitutes maintaining attachments."

Luke slid the main lightsaber machinery out of the glow rod housing and set the housing, and the feeble battery that belonged to it, aside. In moments, he had his lightsaber reassembled. He turned it on experimentally, felt the heat from its green blade, and turned it off again. "What about the younger Jedi here?"

"The ones who aren't Corellian are fine. Standing by. The Corellians, on the other hand, are . . . distressed. Distressed at having to remain in hiding, distressed at the fact that the government is trying to recruit them for anti-GA activities, distressed at being considered potential spies and saboteurs. But they're holding to the Jedi bylaws."

"For now."

"For now. Let me ask you a favor. Transfer them out of Corellia. Get them out of this environment. Let them do their duty to the order without having to choose between the order and their homes, their families."

Luke nodded, not an answer but simply an acknowledgment that he'd heard Corran's words and recognized their gravity. "And the children?"

"I . . . don't know." Corran's face was impassive, but his

voice sounded pained. "Taking them offworld would put them even farther from their families. Leaving them here would keep them in a potential danger zone, keep them looking between teachers and family members who represent divided loyalties. What's the right answer?"

Luke held out his hands, palms up, a *your-guess-is-as-good-as-mine* gesture. "I think I'll arrange to get them offworld. Continue their education someplace more neutral. Minimizing the degree of influence their attachments have on them. I'll make those arrangements today. How many young students do you have?"

"Only five."

"That's not too bad. And speaking of attachments, Mara's going to be very unhappy if I don't have all my facts straight and errands completed before her mission gets under way. If she has to leave in a hurry and I'm not ready to go . . ." Luke rose. "I'll see myself out."

"May the Force be with you, Master."

"And also with you."

Mara decided that Thrackan Sal-Solo's surroundings quite expressively reflected his mentality. He had a bunker mentality; he lived in a bunker. Perhaps he'd had more aesthetic sense and a prettier dwelling in the past, but if so, he had purged that weakness in his personality in recent years.

Thrackan's estate, as unlovely as any Mara had ever seen in the possession of a major political figure, was a flat sheet of land a kilometer west of Coronet's government precincts. A blue clover-like plant grew on the grounds, and nothing else—no trees, no flower beds, no exotic carnivorous plants.

Toward the center of the estate was its one building, a four-story monstrosity of blue-green painted duracrete. Had the arc of its exterior been more perfect, it would have been a proper dome, but it looked flattened, like a half-buried ball of immense size that had been sat on by a giant and partially compressed.

There were several doors at ground level, all sideways-sliding slabs of blue-green durasteel, two of them large enough to accommodate speeders, but there were no visible windows. It was said that instead of windows Thrackan had had the exterior riddled with holocams, and each interior room had screens on the walls that would display window-like views from those sensors.

The estate was ringed by a high, gray duracrete wall—not too high for a Jedi Master to jump, but certainly high enough to silhouette a leaping intruder quite nicely.

Mara knew, from Intelligence reports, that there were pressure and movement sensors installed at random intervals under the ground cover, that the exterior holocams fed into monitors in Thrackan's security chamber as well as the decorative wall displays of the rooms, that the complex had its own generators should city power lines be cut, that its water and waste processors were set up so that nothing above the size of a Kowakian monkey-lizard could fit through the pipes and enter from underground.

Mara had set up on the roof of a building across a broad but lightly traveled avenue from Thrackan's estate. Ironically, the building, a flat two-story affair whose simple, unmemorable architecture was still far more pleasing than that of Thrackan's home, was a local precinct house of Corellian Security. It had taken her very little time to scale the exterior and disable the sensors on the roof; now it made an ideal position from which to spy on the estate opposite.

Team Tauntaun, the Jedi strike team that had invaded Thrackan's home at the same time Team Purella was attempting to kidnap Prime Minister Saxan, had faced the same difficult task: get inside without being seen. Galactic Alliance Intelligence observers had provided information on the times and routes taken by Thrackan when traveling from the government buildings to his home. Setting up in a drainage culvert on a blind curve on one stretch of that route, the three Jedi—Tahiri Veila, Doran Tainer, and Tiu Zax—had leapt up against the undersides of the ground-speeders in Thrackan's caravans, tucking themselves between the repulsorlift generators and hanging on by virtue of powerful magnets, and were conveyed into the bunker by Thrackan himself—or so they thought. It swiftly developed that, as with the assault on Prime Minister Saxan's home, the speeders were loaded with combat droids, the security staffs of the building alerted to the high probability of a Jedi attack.

Two of the Jedi had fled. The third, Tiu, now waited for nightfall in Thrackan's home as Mara waited here.

While the shadows thickened, Mara stretched out not too uncomfortably on the roof's edge and listened to the conversations of CorSec agents as their words floated out from the windows below her.

". . . say we just take everything we have to Tralus and blow them right out of their beachhead . . ." ". . . acceptable losses . . ." ". . . not a very popular position, but we don't really *need* a full-sized navy . . ." ". . . saw Tarania Lona's new holosquirmer. She has the most . . ." ". . . continue to refuse to cooperate, we're going to have to . . ." ". . . if they were *true* Corellians, they'd never have let themselves be taken alive . . ."

Full darkness fell, and a tiny green dot appeared halfway up the squashed dome of Thrackan's home. It remained there for half a minute and then disappeared.

Mara checked to make sure her lightsaber and other equipment were in place. Then she rolled over the lip of the roof and fell two stories to the sidewalk, landing as lightly as a leaf fluttering to the ground.

She held herself in a crouch, her dark robes making her all but invisible, and waited until there was no speeder cross-traffic to be seen. She came up out of her crouch like a sprinter and was across the avenue and up against the base of the featureless duracrete wall a moment later. A quick flex of the legs and boost of the Force and she was atop that wall—

Not quite. She did not allow herself to come down on the walltop. It, too, was said to have pressure sensors on its walkway and would reveal her presence if she did so. Instead, she caught herself with the Force, creating a bubble between her and the top of the wall, and drifted just over that surface until she was above the blue clover on the far side.

It was time to be a Jedi instead of a spy. As a spy, she'd probably have fixed a line thrower to the top of the CorSec building, launched a driller projectile, trailing a nearly invisible cable, to affix itself to the top of Thrackan's dome, and used a powered or hand-cranked winch to carry her the quarter kilometer from rooftop to rooftop . . . and even so, her chances of detection would have been very high. Instead, she carried almost no equipment, and her chances of detection would be determined by her own concentration.

She allowed herself to float down to stand just above the blue clover. The bubble of Force energy that kept her aloft was easier to maintain when she was mere centimeters above the surface—merely having the mental image, the paradigm, of it as a sort of air-filled balloon improved her ability to perceive it, to maintain it. She'd need to employ all the concentration tricks she knew, because what she was about to do was very tricky.

At the base of the wall, she stood a moment, eyes closed, and focused on the other things she'd have to do to cross two hundred meters of sensor-filled open space.

Air. She could not keep air from moving, of course. As she moved, she would displace it. But she added motion to the air she displaced, so that it moved out in a single stream, losing neither speed nor coherence for dozens of meters ahead of her. To a sensor, it would read not as the movement of a person across the lawn, but as a breeze.

Heat. That would be the trickiest part. If she radiated heat, infrared sensors would inevitably pick it up. She surrounded herself with another bubble, this one of containment . . . and immediately felt her temperature begin to rise as the heat she expended stayed within centimeters of her skin. She could even control herself to the point that she did not sweat, and would need to do so here—but that, too, would increase her internal temperature.

She couldn't sustain the effect of heat entrapment for

long; she would end up collapsing. But she should be able to sustain it long enough to cross the open space between wall and bunker . . . and in that time, infrared detectors would not see her.

Probably.

She stepped forward, concentrating on the act of walking, reminding herself that the movement of her legs was only a comforting paradigm—levitating in some other pose would require more of her attention. Each step felt a bit wobbly, as though she were moving across a flexible playground surface, but she fell into a regular pace and let her muscle memory do the work for her.

Yes, any Jedi Knight might know one of these three techniques—most commonly, the technique of levitation. But only a Jedi Master was likely to know all three or be able to sustain them simultaneously across such a broad distance.

Mara bumped her nose into something hard and stopped. Immediately ahead of her was uniform grayness.

She looked up along the curved surface of the bunker wall. *And only a Jedi Master is likely to become so focused that she walks into a wall,* she told herself.

She swayed where she stood, suddenly dizzy from the heat. *Come on, Tiu,* she thought. *You should have detected me by now—*

A cord, millimeters thick, transparent and almost invisible in the darkness, fell across her face. Hurriedly, she grasped at it, wrapped it around her waist three times, and gave it a tug.

It hauled at her and she walked up the wall, her arms trembling and legs increasingly faltering as the heat threatened to overwhelm her. An eternity later, she was ten meters up the wall and a wedge-shaped slit in the duracrete surface beckoned her. She stepped into darkness, dropped a meter to a hard floor, and landed badly, collapsing to the floor as her legs failed.

She released the heat entrapment and felt the built-up energy flow away from her. With her last bit of strength, she held her control over the surrounding air long enough to send much of that heat streaming out through the slit in the wall, even as the slit slid closed. And then she burst into a sweat, a sudden head-to-toe sheen that felt like heavy motor oil against her skin.

In the darkness, a female voice said, "Goodness. You smell like a rancor after a footrace."

Mara smiled weakly. "That's no way to greet a Master. And you've never smelled a rancor after a footrace."

"Yes, I have."

There was a click, and brilliant light from overhead blinded Mara; she raised an arm over her eyes.

As her vision settled, she could see she was in a tight chamber, narrower against the bunker exterior wall but long. It was dominated by a neutral-blue flying craft, a tubular vehicle like a starfighter but with abbreviated fins instead of maneuvering wings; its canopy, which opened at the rear instead of forward, was up.

At the far end of the chamber, beside a circular hatch a meter in diameter, stood Tiu Zax, with her hand on a control panel mounted on the wall. Short of stature—she stood a centimeter shorter than Leia, and was lean like most of her kind—she had pale blue skin, hair so pale that it seemed translucent, and delicate features dominated by eyes that seemed oversized. She wore the black pants and tunic of her Jedi outfit; her boots, belt, and cloak were not in evidence.

Mara struggled to a sitting position. Though tired and still flushed with heat, she felt much better already. "What is this place?"

"A secret escape chamber." Tiu came forward and reached up into the vehicle's cockpit, pressing dashboard controls without looking. A side panel on the craft popped open; inside, Mara could see bundled clothing, packaged field rations, items she couldn't make out. Tiu reached for one of them and came forward to hand it to Mara; it was a transparisteel canteen. "I think there are four of them in this building, but I haven't gotten at all of them. The entry is concealed on the other side. This and the other one I found both had two-person escape vehicles in them."

"That's very Thrackan-ish." Mara took the canteen, unscrewed the cap, and took a long drink of its contents—water, tasting slightly of its storage in a metal container. "So, first: Master Skywalker says 'Good work' on your staying here like this."

Tiu beamed.

"Second—your report?"

Tiu sat down, cross-legged. "The short form? I've been here several days, have figured out how to patch a datapad into their internal holocam system and beep my comlink whenever the area I'm in is about to fall under active observation. I've dived under more tables recently than you can possibly imagine."

Mara grinned and took another drink.

"Sal-Solo isn't spending much time here," Tiu continued. "Which has given me several opportunities to enter his personal quarters. I've found equipment there I think is a master control set for this building's security and communications computers, but they're too well defended for me. They apparently require Sal-Solo's biometric identification, which I didn't think to bring."

"I did." Mara patted one of the pouches beneath her robes. "What else?"

Tiu shrugged. "I've mapped out as much of this building as I've been able to visit, but I've concentrated more on not being discovered. Which is tricky, as Sal-Solo seems to be very paranoid, and has security agents with mentalities to match his. I don't think I've been that effective."

"You've been very effective. But I think we've asked all we can of you here. You'll be leaving with me."

Tiu smiled again and mimed a sigh of relief.

"All right," Mara said. "I'm going to rest for a while—until whatever time you think is best for a visit to Thrackan's quarters. That's when we go to work."

chapter twenty-three

Two YVH combat droids led Han and Leia along the curved hallway. Only a third of the glow rods in the ceiling were activated, and the shadows in the hallway were deep. Most of the doors from the hall were on the right wall; an occasional door or side passage led away to the left.

Marching in lockstep unison, the droids came to a halt before one of the right-hand doors. One of them gestured at it, doubtless transmitting a security code, and it slid up.

The droids waited. Leia and Han exchanged a look. Han shrugged, and they entered.

The chamber beyond was spacious and airy. The far wall was mostly transparisteel, looking down on a larger chamber; from the doorway, Han and Leia could see the far wall but not the floor of that chamber. That chamber seemed to be circular and ringed by viewing chambers like this one; it was dimly lit like the hallway.

The chamber they stood in was completely unlit; its only illumination came in through the transparisteel wall and the door, and the latter source of light vanished as the door slid closed behind them.

There were chairs and couches scattered throughout the chamber, including a line of high-backed swivel chairs set against the transparisteel wall, and one of them now rotated so that its occupant faced Han and Leia. It was a male human. The dimness made it difficult to make out the man's features, but he seemed to be dark-haired, with handsome but rather bland features; he wore garments that were similar to Han's in cut and style, but all in red and brown hues and topped by a long-sleeved military-style tunic, unfastened along the front seam for its wearer's comfort.

He rose. "Captain Solo. Princess Organa. I'm glad to meet you at last."

Han and Leia approached and shook hands with him in turn.

"Prime Minister Teppler," Leia said. "Thank you for seeing us. And allow us to offer our condolences on your loss."

"Losses, actually," Teppler corrected. "My brother died defending Aidel."

Han looked at the man more closely. There was something familiar about the Five World Prime Minister pro tem, and even in the dimness Han could now make out what it was—Denjax Teppler was the slightly older, slightly softer-edged image of the CorSec guard who had been with Aidel Saxan during their first meeting with her.

"I apologize," Leia said. "We didn't know."

"I shouldn't have mentioned it," Teppler said. "I'm too used to a role as a minister dispensing information, not used to being a Prime Minister keeping it all bottled up. Please, sit." He gestured to chairs opposite his, and resumed his seat.

His visitors settled into chairs. Leia said, "We were surprised to receive your coded communication."

"Surprised that Aidel had shared her secrets with me, as we were no longer husband and wife?"

She nodded.

"Well, she didn't, not exactly." Even in the poor light, Teppler seemed to lose his focus, his intensity, and Leia felt the man was staring back through time. "After she died, I received an *in-case-of-my-death* package from her. Her dealings with you were part of that package. Also part of it was an apology for getting me killed."

Han frowned. "She hasn't, has she?"

"Not yet. And I'm likely to remain alive as long as certain parties see me as an asset rather than a liability." Teppler shrugged. "I'd like to remain alive. I'd prefer that even to coordinating Corellian government. But most of all I want to keep Corellia from being ruined. Devastated by war, her economy depleted by a lengthy struggle against the Galactic Alliance, or—perhaps worst of all—her economy and critical faculties drained away by years of rule under the wrong regime."

The Solos nodded. Teppler was obviously speaking of Chief Sal-Solo and his political allies.

"And that's why I've asked you here," Teppler continued. "To defend my people, my world, I'm going to commit an act of high treason. I've smuggled you in here, into the most secure portions of our war department facilities, so you can be a witness to a meeting I'm forbidden to attend."

"Forbidden?" Leia arched a brow. "How can they forbid you?"

"By having more pressing matters scheduled for me during this meeting." Teppler looked increasingly glum. "With my brother dead, and never having gone through the process of building myself a reliable, loyal society of conspirator-allies, I haven't had anyone I can trust with me since Aidel's death. Which my political opponents know all too well. I'm the perfect front man—hapless and helpless. And then Aidel's message about you two comes to me, and I discover that perhaps the most incorruptible Corellian of all is visiting us on the sly, and willing to risk his home, his relationship with his own government, in the interest of keeping people alive and keeping his homeworld intact . . ."

Han felt shock creep across his face. "Incorruptible? When did I become incorruptible?"

Leia grinned at him. "It's your stubborn pride, dear. It keeps you from accepting the wrong kind of bribe."

"Hello? *Smuggler?*"

"Ex-smuggler." Leia returned her attention to Teppler and sobered. "You actually want us to spy on this meeting."

"Yes. A top-secret military meeting. It's supposed to deal with throwing the GA forces off Tralus."

Leia frowned at him. "And why do you think I'd refrain from telling the GA military about the plans we listen to?"

The Prime Minister gave her a sad stare. "Because you know as well as I do that there can't be a peace initiative until the GA is off Tralus. The GA can't negotiate their departure because that's already been tried and failed. The GA can't just leave because it would be too great a loss of face—even greater than being driven off, because it suggests they were wrong in the first place. And the Corellians won't even start thinking about peaceful solutions while there's an occupying force on Tralus."

His expression graduated from sad to positively miserable. "There can't be peace until an act of war drives the GA out of this system, and you know it. And if you were to tell the GA government our plans, we couldn't succeed at driving them out. It's as simple as that."

Leia was silent for a long moment. Finally she said, "I've underestimated you, Prime Minister. You're more calculating than I thought."

"Aren't I, though?" He offered her a self-deprecating smile. "At this rate, I wonder whether, when assassins or war-trial executioners come for me, I'll welcome what they have to offer." He shrugged. "As for now, the only forces I know are loyal to me are four YVH droids my brother programmed for my security. I'm hoping that, after you've witnessed this meeting, you can tell me if there are any others. Or at least confirm the disloyalty of others I suspect. It would be helpful."

"We'll consider it," Han said. "I think we'll watch your little meeting and then decide what to do."

"That's about as much as I could ask for." Teppler rose, and the Solos did, as well. "My droids will be back for you when it's safe to smuggle you out of here. In the meantime, the polarizing tint on the viewport here, and the darkness of this chamber, will prevent anyone below from seeing you."

"Meaning we shouldn't turn on the lights," Han said, deadpan.

Teppler stared at him a long moment, then managed a slight smile. "Meaning exactly that."

Once she was set up before the computer console in Thrackan's quarters, it took Mara just short of three minutes to crack his security.

First was the medical portion of the identification process. She used a dropper tube to place a single drop of Thrackan's blood onto a sensor needle resting in a depression on the console surface. The blood, taken during one of his visits to a doctor, had been more recently purchased, surreptitiously and at an extravagant price, by Galactic Alliance Intelligence. Then there were his fingerprints. The transparent, almost undetectable glove Mara wore bore his prints and was sufficient for most security purposes.

Third, there was visual confirmation. Just before the computer got to that portion of its security sequence, Mara activated a small holoprojector-scanner unit that detected her face, mapped it, and projected a three-dimensional representation of Thrackan's features over her own. No living creature would be fooled by the device—Thrackan's face *glowed,* and the effect was made worse in the dimness of his chambers. But the computer scanner accepted the image.

After that, it was a matter of entering the correct password. Mara got it on the third try.

Tiu, now leaning over her shoulder, asked, "What was it?"

"The name of one of his mistresses." Mara shook her head over the obviousness of that choice. "Now let's go prowling."

And prowl she did, downloading everything she looked at into her own datapad. Not that it amounted to much.

"He apparently forwards all his files and records to a system in the government halls," she complained. "He's very tidy. Not good for us."

"So this was all for nothing?" Tiu's serene Jedi mask cracked for just a moment. "All those days of terrible, spicy Corellian food?"

Mara grinned. "Maybe not for nothing. We just need to look farther afield."

She found security procedures and passwords that would make subsequent departures from and entries into this building much easier—until they were changed, that is. She found poorly hidden personal files kept on the building's computer system by its security operatives, many of them constituting blackmail evidence against fellow agents, private citizens, and low-level government officials.

And then she found what she was looking for: an incoming message from several days earlier.

" 'To Thrackan Sal-Solo, Chief of State, Corellia, all greetings and respects,' " she read. " 'Let me begin this communication by offering you a gift, the gift of knowledge: The impending meeting between representatives of the Corellian and Galactic Alliance governments will take place on Toryaz Station, Kuat System.' Well, he or she was right about that."

"Who sent it?" Tiu asked.

" 'But, sadly, this gift is incomplete by itself, as security at the station will be formidable. Fortunately, I have information on that matter, too—I can provide exact details on the locations of all delegates at all times, as well as the security measures guarding them, for the duration of their stay here.' "

"*Here,*" Tiu repeated. "So whoever wrote him was already on Toryaz Station."

"Not necessarily. The word choice could be deliberate, to convince Thrackan of just that detail. 'Should this information be of interest to you, please contact me on the HoloNet frequency indicated below, at the times shown. Standard encryption, using the contents of my next mes-

sage as the encryption key.' Then there's the time and frequency information."

"No name?"

"No name." Mara scanned the file listing for follow-up
messages with the same characteristics as this one. "I'm not
seeing any sign of the message with the encryption key. It
was probably delivered by other means."

"I'm not feeling any animosity toward the sender of that
message."

"You're not?" Mara looked up at Tiu, surprised.

"No. So it's all right for me to kill him, correct?"

Mara grinned. "Self-deception is always a bad idea,
Tiu."

"Except when it amuses a Jedi Master."

"Well . . . true."

Tiu sobered. "But the fact that Thrackan received this
message doesn't mean that he paid for that information.
He isn't necessarily the one responsible for the attack."

"Yes, he is. Regardless of whether he received the second
information and dispatched the killers. Not reporting it to
CorSec and Prime Minister Saxan constitutes treason, betrayal. Whether he arranged for assassins or just sat on information, he's at least partly to blame for Saxan's death
and the mess we're in."

"Oh." Tiu brightened. "Well, then, I'm not feeling animosity toward him, either. Can I—"

"No." Mara glanced up as though she could see through
intervening floors into the chamber by which she'd entered
the bunker. "That escape craft . . . is it hyperdrive-equipped?"

"It is."

"But I assume that if we were to board it and blast out of
here, we'd have CorSec fighters on our tail in a few moments."

"I wondered about that, too. And I had no way to confirm or disprove that as a theory . . . but I doubt it."

"Explain."

"It's for Thrackan to escape in. One of the things he
might want to escape from is a vengeful pursuit by new

government forces that have chased him out of office, and those government forces could put CorSec on his tail. So my bet is that he's given it transponder codes that will be registered as good and valid, no matter what, until all traces of Thrackan are scoured out of the computers."

Mara nodded approvingly. "Which could take awhile, particularly if I pump some malicious code into this machine and wait long enough for associated computers to sample it, too. What say we steal Thrackan's escape vehicle? If we don't accumulate any pursuit, we can pick up my husband and go home. If we do, we can dump it over there in the ocean and leave Corellia by the route we'd planned originally."

"I like this plan."

Half an hour after Prime Minister Teppler's departure, politicians and military officers began entering the room beneath Teppler's viewing chamber. They traveled in groups, one important dignitary backed by three to five members of support staff, with the dignitary and one aide seating themselves at the large, triangular table dominating the room, the others exiled to secondary tables or far corners, there to remain until summoned.

As these people spoke in their small groups, Han and Leia could occasionally make out their words, whenever they were projected across the table or the room. Soon enough, Han realized that they were being augmented by a set of speakers in the wall beneath the long viewport.

Eventually, the highest-ranking officer so far, Admiral Vara Karathas, chief of staff for the Ministry of War and operational leader of the Corellian military, entered with her retinue. All the other officers straightened, looking busier and more efficient, and the big chamber's upper lights came on in full strength.

"What's keeping them?" Han frowned down at the military officers below. "They're still not starting. We were more prompt back in the Rebel Alliance days."

"You weren't, you specifically."

"No, but *we* were. When you didn't wait for me."

Even from the altitude of the viewport-side chairs in Prime Minister Teppler's box, Admiral Karathas looked years older than the last time Han had laid eyes on her, a holonews spot broadcast the day of their first meeting with Aidel Saxan. There were no more lines to Karathas's face, no more gray to her hair, but the ramrod-straight military rigidity that always seemed to characterize her had apparently fled. Her posture now was that of a tired woman, and her face seemed softer, no longer stretched into taut planes and sharp angles by unyielding muscles.

She didn't look beaten. But she did look beatable. Han grimaced, not appreciating the change.

Standing at one truncated point of the triangular table, Karathas pointedly drew a chrono out of a jacket pocket and consulted it. As she did so, several of the other officers glanced in the direction of Teppler's box—beneath it, actually, and a trifle to the left—and exchanged eye contact and words with one another, reacting to some new arrival and indicating that, at last, things might proceed.

From the direction they had been looking, Wedge Antilles, again in Corellian uniform, walked into the room, without retinue.

Admiral Karathas gave Wedge a wan smile. "Cutting it rather close, aren't you, Antilles?" She projected her voice sufficiently that it was clearly audible in Teppler's box—that, and perhaps the microphones that fed Teppler's speakers were oriented more toward the main table than other portions of the chamber.

Wedge nodded and moved up to the table beside Karathas. "Admiral, if I had a credit for every time someone told me that . . ."

"Yes, you could probably buy our way out of this situation." Karathas looked up, in a direction disconcertingly close to where Han and Leia sat, but her eyes seemed to be focused on a point to their left, beyond the wall that separated them from the next room. "Are we all ready? Yes?

Then let's begin. Please sit." She did as she suggested, and there was a momentary delay as some officers fled the main table and others trotted up to it, seating themselves.

"All right," Karathas said. "We find ourselves in the unenviable—unacceptable, but unavoidable—position of having to wage a battle against enemy forces occupying the center of one of our own cities. We cannot do this without a gruesome toll in the lives of our own people, which could very well swing public opinion against us . . . which would be increasingly harmful to our defense of the Corellian system. Nor can we just ignore the enemy beachhead, as leaving it intact will allow them to reinforce it, expand it, and begin bringing more and more potent offenses against our insystem positions. Their command post in Rellidir on Tralus has to be obliterated . . . and so Operation Noble Savage has been designed to obliterate it. And to turn what would be a public opinion disaster into an asset." Her voice did not convey military confidence. If anything, it carried more than a hint of regret, and even resentment.

Han saw Leia shiver. He gave her a questioning look.

"She didn't say anything about minimizing expected civilian deaths," she said.

Han leaned forward to give Karathas a closer look. "Maybe she's getting to that."

"Maybe."

Below, Karathas gestured to someone out in the shadows along the big room's walls. A hologram sprang into existence above the center of the table—a view of the center of the city of Rellidir, inverted so that those at the table, looking up, were actually looking down into the monolithic block of spacescrapers as if from a great height. Some wavered at the unsettling perspective, but most were or had been pilots—amateur, professional, or military—and had no problem with the view.

The disc-shaped hologram began a slow rotation, and then a large region at the center of it—a massive, circular white building with eight narrowing points around its rim, giving it the appearance of a royal crown—began blinking, red–white–red–white. The building was easy to make out among all the spacescrapers, as it was surrounded by a broad belt of green occasionally decorated with narrow gray lines—a large city park with foot trails tracing through it. Small wire-frame objects in blinking red were scattered around the building, arrayed in rows and columns, but they were too small for Han to make out; a few larger wire frames in the same color scheme appeared to be troop transports and corvettes.

"This," Karathas continued, "is their command post; they have occupied the Navos Center for the Performing Arts. This was a very good choice, speaking from a military point of view. It's commodious, has an extensive underground storage area not accessible through any of the city's normal underground infrastructure, and commands a good view of the surrounding airspace. Shield generators have been set up inside, powering a two-level shield defensive system." On cue, a hologram wire grid of defensive energy shields appeared, blinking on and off in orange, just outside the green park areas surrounding the command post, and another wire grid, this one in red, began blinking several blocks out in all directions, a greater dome enclosing the smaller dome.

"It's also sound strategically because the center is right in the heart of one of the most densely occupied portions of central Rellidir," the admiral continued. "Any standard action waged there will result in thousands of civilian casualties. One concussion missile missing its target could bring down an entire superhabitat building . . . and inevitably there *will* be missiles missing their targets. Many of them. Our grim task has been to turn that terrible but inevitable consequence of war to our advantage." Karathas's voice was raspy and faint on those last words.

"However, despite their good choices, the GA has made some poor ones, too. Situating several starfighter squadrons and some planet-landable fighting vessels around their command post as a show of strength gives us more things to destroy—explosively, catastrophically, and most important, recordably—when we do hit that site."

"This is bad, bad, bad," Han said. He couldn't keep an edge of anger out of his voice.

The wire-grid shield indicators began blinking more erratically. "In the first part of our operation," the admiral continued, "teams of commandos will be infiltrated into Rellidir. They will attempt to reach the shield generators and destroy them with high explosives. Success on their part is to be considered a bonus to our plan, but the plan does not rely on it."

"Who came up with this plan?" Han didn't speak loudly enough to be heard down on the floor or in adjacent observation chambers, but his voice was rising. "See-Threepio could have done better. This is exactly what the GA is going to be expecting."

He could see Leia tense. It couldn't be in response to his anger; she was used to that. She had to be growing unhappier because she suspected the plan was going to get even worse.

On the upside-down view of Rellidir, half a dozen green dots appeared at various points along the view's rim and sped toward the enemy command post, each followed by a stream of red dots.

"In the second part of the operation," the admiral continued, "Corellian YT-Fifty-one-hundred *Shriek*-class bombers will assault the shielded region from all sides, closely pursued by Galactic Alliance starfighters and warships. They will bombard the shields, if any survive, and then continue their bombardment of the command post until it is destroyed."

The admiral mopped her brow with her sleeve. Her voice turned pained. "The *Shriek*-class bombers have been chosen because they are distinctly, uniquely, unmistakably Corellian. Designed by the Corellian Engineering Corporation, they have not entered full production yet—only ten late-model prototypes and a few earlier prototypes are in existence." The city view abruptly winked out of existence and was replaced by a slowly spinning view of a sleek gray saucer shape with forward-projecting mandible, like a streamlined *Millennium Falcon* without the side-mounted cockpit projection.

"The pursuing spacecraft," Karathas continued, "though bearing the colors and insignia of vehicles and vessels of the Galactic Alliance fleet, will actually be units of the Corellian Defense Force. Instead of shooting down the Shrieks, other than hitting them with a few reduced-strength laser blasts for cosmetic effect, their mission will be to reinforce the firepower of those bombers . . . and to reassign blame for civilian deaths to the Galactic Alliance."

Silence fell in the wake of the admiral's words. Leia put her face into her hands—not an expression of grief, but a way to keep her composure. Han took a long, deep breath. It *had* gotten worse.

Wedge turned a brilliant, bitter smile on the admiral. "It would seem," he said, "that the plan would actually benefit if we *maximized* civilian casualties."

Leia lifted her head, her eyes wide.

Admiral Karathas's face relaxed into a nonexpression, as though she'd just been hit by a blaster set to stun. "General Antilles, that might be the most callous thing I've ever heard you say."

Wedge looked scornful and made a dismissive gesture. "Admiral, let's call a skifter a skifter. Operation Noble Savage is, as you yourself said, designed to take what is inevitably going to be a public relations nightmare—the deaths of *thousands* of civilians from friendly fire—and turn it to the advantage of the Corellian independence cause. It will take outrage that would have been directed against us and turn it against our opponents. That outrage will stiffen Corellian resistance against the GA, allowing us to hit harder, more ferociously. By an inevitable progression of logic, the more horrible the offense we can blame on the GA forces, the greater that outrage. Correct?"

Karathas blinked. Finally, her face resumed the hard angles and planes that had characterized it for most of her adulthood. "General, I'm within seconds of ordering you to shut up and leave this council."

"That would be a mistake," Wedge said. His voice was as hard as Karathas's had become. "If you did that, you'd prevent me from showing you how to achieve your military objectives without wantonly killing fellow Corellians. And let me point out that Operation Noble Savage, though it would probably divert the population's outrage from our military to the GA, drastically increases the odds that we will go to war—our population wouldn't easily back away from further confrontations if all those lives on Tralus remained unavenged, would it?"

Karathas paused. The respect with which most Corellian military officers held Antilles, and the admiral's own evident discontent with the plan just outlined, obviously kept in check any outrage she might have felt at being addressed in that fashion. Leia felt only so much sympathy for the woman, however. Karathas had bought into a plan that was ghastly. Leia would have had far more respect for her had some other officer, Karathas's replacement, been explaining this mission—meaning that Karathas had been replaced for her opposition to Noble Savage.

A square of light fell across the table as another of the observation rooms was illuminated from within; its occupant had obviously turned on its interior light so as to be seen from below. Han and Leia looked around the bank of observation booths, but none they could see was now illuminated, meaning that the one they were looking for had to be close to theirs.

Then a voice, electronically amplified, boomed from the room just to their left. "General, am I to understand that the operation I helped design, that I approved and am ready to set into motion, is *wanton*?"

Leia winced, and Han felt like drawing his blaster. That cutting voice was distinctive, instantly recognizable. It was Thrackan Sal-Solo. Han also felt a little foolish. Of *course* the Corellian Chief of State would have a viewing chamber

near the Five World Prime Minister's; of *course* Thrackan
would be here to observe this meeting.

Han glanced to the left, toward the source of Thrackan's
voice. On the other side of a thin wall was a man who'd
given him grief across decades. He whispered, "It's sort of
like being a kid again. Hiding in your bed because there's a
monster in the closet."

Despite herself, Leia grinned.

Han mimed drawing his blaster and aiming it at the wall
to his left. He wondered how many shots it would take for
him to hit Thrackan under these circumstances, and whether
he and Leia could get out of the building afterward.

It was probably not wise to try. Not this time. He sighed
and mimed reholstering his weapon.

Wedge turned to face Sal-Solo's viewport, meaning he
was staring almost directly up into Han and Leia's, as well.
"No, sir," he said. "As I'm sure your protocol droid is now
telling you, my use of the word *wanton* referred to the unnecessary deaths of so many of our kinfolk and fellow citizens. And there's the additional factor that, while this
group might be able to maintain for years the terrible secret
that we were responsible for those deaths, we wouldn't be
able to keep it forever. Secrets, like hydraulic fluids, have a
nasty habit of seeping out into the open just when it's worst
for everybody."

Sal-Solo's voice boomed again: "Was that a threat, Antilles?"

Wedge made a dismissive gesture Han knew would have
to outrage Sal-Solo. "No, it was a realistic appraisal. And
my realistic appraisal of Operation Noble Savage suggests
to me that it would be effective, in that it would probably
succeed . . . but that it would not be *efficient*. To be efficient, it would have to accomplish our goals with minimal
loss of civilian life, and with a chance to reduce, instead of
increase, our chance to enter a full-scale shooting war."

"And can *you* do all that, General? And put a shine on
your reputation while you're at it?"

"I can. And put a shine on *your* reputation. Since you're

the military commander in chief approving an operation that might not rid the system of scores of thousands of loyal Corellians."

Han saw Leia holding her breath. Wedge was playing a tricky game here—appealing to Sal-Solo's political instincts of self-preservation, but still batting the man's words back into his teeth. Perhaps Wedge was getting too tired to keep his politics soft-spoken and pleasing. Perhaps, like Han, he hated Sal-Solo so much that he simply couldn't bear to accommodate the man.

"Let's hear it," Sal-Solo said. "If I like what I hear, you might not find yourself begging on a street corner come morning."

Wedge turned his back on the man's booth. From a breast pocket he removed a datapad. Looking around, he apparently spotted the room's hologram input sensor; he pointed the datapad at it, and abruptly the hologram image overhead changed.

Once again it was the center of Rellidir, but a less realistic plotting of it; the spacescrapers were all simple gray rectangles, their windows, balconies, and decorations not represented. A moment after the hologram resolved into crisp detail, dome-like translucences in pink appeared to show the two sets of shields maintained by the Galactic Alliance occupiers.

"Same problem, different solution," Wedge said. On the hologram, two flights of green blips—six blips per flight, two half squadrons—appeared at the edges of the displayed region, the first from one angle, and the second from an angle ninety degrees to that of the first. The first flight overflew the shield-protected region; a moment later, the second flight followed suit. Now red dots appeared on the display, in numbers rapidly swelling from twenty to a hundred, and formed up to follow the green dots. Both the pursued and the pursuers exited the scene within moments.

"Stage One," Wedge continued, "is a diversionary bombing run on the shields, standard operational procedure to overload shields and bring them down. Given that the GA occupiers have not only installed military power generators at the site but also commandeered city power generators and can feed them straight into their shields, the shields possess a lot of power. This run will fail, and the bombers will make a quick bounce up to orbit, drawing off a certain amount of pursuit."

Wedge tapped another button on his datapad. Just barely within the outer perimeter of the shields, a massive gray building began to blink in color, alternating between green and yellow. "This is the Terkury Housing Complex, currently under construction, being built on the site of an old complex that had to be deconstructed for safety reasons. The new complex will be somewhat more upscale than many of the surrounding housing units, providing modern amenities and a broad underground hangar area for private skimmers, shuttles, and the like."

Sal-Solo's voice was richly mocking. "You almost make me want to live there."

"At the moment, sir, it's not a very good investment. Stage Two of this operation involves taking a couple of those *Shriek*-class bombers and flying them clean through the Terkury Housing Complex, then continuing on to the arts center and initiating its destruction."

Sal-Solo cleared his throat, the electronically augmented sound echoing off the chamber's walls. "Surely, given your reputation for military strategy, you've noticed that the housing complex you propose to fly through is *enclosed within their shields*."

"Yes, sir."

"And you don't see this as a problem."

"No, sir."

"And correct me if I'm wrong, but I'm familiar with the payload that a Shriek bomber can carry, and it seems to me that two of them would not be able to carry enough ordnance to punch through two rings of shields and then destroy the shield generators themselves."

"That's correct, sir. I've compensated for that factor by

planning for the Shrieks to be carrying almost no ordnance at all."

There was a long pause before Sal-Solo replied, and Han could imagine the man standing there, his expression pained, no words emerging. Finally Sal-Solo said, "You're right on the verge of that street corner I was mentioning, Antilles."

Wedge glanced over his shoulder up at Sal-Solo, an amused expression that all but said, *You shouldn't interrupt when grown-ups are talking.* He raised his datapad and thumbed another button. The angle of the schematic changed, dropping the point of view until it was oriented mere meters over a broad thoroughfare; at the far end of the thoroughfare was the blinking green-and-yellow building.

"I mentioned," Wedge said, "the housing complex's broad underground hangar." The hologram's point of view went into motion, traveling toward the blinking building at a high rate of speed. "Here you can see a simulation of the Shriek bombers' approach toward the housing complex. When they get to the distance of a few blocks, they release some of their ordnance—" Blue dotted lines leapt forward toward the blinking building, but dropped at the last moment to strike the thoroughfare just ahead of it. "—and blow a broad hole in the avenue, straight down into the hangar area. They fly through the hangar, blowing out an exit ahead of them, and emerge through that hole on the far side, then continue on to their target.

"As they approach their target, they release their payload of targeter droids, rather crude droids used by our armed forces to teach sharpshooting and ballistics. Those droids use laser range finders and other sensors to paint their target, defining not just the command center but a precise point on its shielding."

"And then?" Finally, Sal-Solo sounded interested rather than mocking.

"And then the hundreds of missiles fired in the wake of the two Shrieks, following the telemetry sent by those targeter droids, come pouring out of the hangar bay, hit that point on the shields, overload them until they fail, and continue on to hit the command post, plus the vehicles and vessels on the ground, surgically eradicating them."

"They could still overfly their target," Admiral Karathas said.

Wedge nodded. "As surgical as we'd like for this operation to be, we can't eliminate all risk of friendly-fire fatalities. Believe me, I'd love to. But one thing we can do is have the targeter droids make their target the *summit* of the enemy shields, then the summit of the command post building. We can program our missiles to go as high as possible once they exit the hangar, then dive on their target from above. The likelihood of them shooting past a target and hitting the side of an occupied building is thereby reduced."

"Let me make sure I understand," Sal-Solo said. "Your two Shriek bombers—they'll be sustaining fire from any GA defenses not drawn off by our diversion."

"Correct," Wedge said.

"That means gunships, starfighters, antispacecraft gun emplacements, and who knows what else."

"Correct."

"How do they do this?"

"Well," Wedge said, "first, the performance characteristics of the Shrieks are known to the GA government, but since the bombers aren't in production yet, that information hasn't been widely distributed. It's not likely to be in the databases of the GA forces around Tralus. This means the defenders won't know exactly what to expect from these machines. Second, the fact that the assault force seems inadequate to the task means the forces arrayed against the Shrieks will probably not be overwhelming. And third, I plan to choose—assuming I'm selected to implement this plan, otherwise I'll just recommend—pilots who are especially well suited to this sort of mission. I don't mean the pilots who've been testing the Shrieks, good men and women though they are. I mean canny old veterans who have decades of experience with YT-series spacecraft. Pilots familiar with

terrain-following assaults and other seemingly suicidal flying techniques."

Han leaned farther forward, almost pressing his forehead
against the transparisteel, his attention fixed on Wedge. He
heard Leia whisper, "Oh, no."

Thrackan, sounding cheerful, boomed, "Admiral Karathas, I think this plan deserves close scrutiny . . ."

chapter twenty-four

KUAT SYSTEM, TORYAZ STATION

Jacen sat in the rolling chair with his feet up on the desk before him. He knew that the image he was holocasting would show his boot soles up close, the rest of his seated body at a slightly greater distance, and then Ben, solemnly standing behind his chair. "A what?" he asked.

The three-dimensional image of an old Twi'lek male, his skin a wrinkled desert tan, his head-tails wrapped artistically around his neck, was less than a meter tall and situated atop the center of the desk. It was large enough for Jacen to make out the Twi'lek's expression, one of merry amusement. "It's a thought," the Twi'lek said. "An idea."

Jacen held the grouping of tassels up before him and studied it. "All of it?"

The Twi'lek's head-tails twitched, then he apparently realized that he wasn't speaking to another of his own kind and indulged in a cruder, broader gesture—a shrug. "I don't know," he admitted. "I can only speak for the one at the very bottom."

Jacen examined that tassel in greater detail. It was composed of six separate braids of tan and red beads, each one knotted intricately. "How is it a thought?"

"It's like writing," the Twi'lek said. "A pattern of knots so individualized, so specific that they can carry thoughts the way writing does. I actually had to take the highest-detail holocam scan you sent me of it and run it through a sculpture interpreter, generating a three-dimensional replica in a flexible material, before I could interpret it. It must be held, manipulated by touch, in order for its meaning to become clear."

"And its meaning is what?"

"As close as I can translate it into Basic, it means, 'He will strengthen himself through pain.' "

Jacen gave the Twi'lek a close look.

"You look startled, Master Solo."

Jacen shook his head. "I'm not a Master, just a Jedi Knight, For'ali. I apologize if I've led you to believe that you're speaking with a social equal."

"I do not think in such segregated terms, Jedi Solo."

"As for my startlement—that phrase has echoes of an old Jedi saying, 'There is no pain where strength lies.' Could it actually be translated that way?"

For'ali shook his head, the gesture deliberate and artificial. "No. It is closest to 'He will strengthen himself through pain.' "

"And you can't read any of the others?"

"No. They are not Twi'lek. In fact, the one I can comprehend isn't *universally* Twi'lek. It is a remnant of the Tahu'ip culture of Ryloth, an ancient subset of our modern culture. We are not one homogeneous people any more than humans are."

"Of course. How long has it been since a recording technique like this was used?"

"Perhaps five hundred standard years? Now the technique is known only to a few scholars. I do not elevate myself too much by claiming to be one of three individuals with sufficient knowledge to have translated that item through a reproduction."

Jacen considered. "So these other tassels, if they are not of Twi'lek make—"

"Of Twi'lek cultural origin, at any rate."

"Yes, that's what I meant. Could they still be the same sort of item? A form of writing?"

"Yes. Or, I think, several. They are distinct in the ways they were made, each fabricated through a different technique; I suspect it means that, if they all convey messages, each does so through a different method of communication. Perhaps from a different world or culture altogether."

Jacen gave him a smile. "I know that this is going to sound lazy—"

"But is there a central source of knowledge that might be able to decode *all* of them?"

"You're very good at mind reading, For'ali. Are you Force-sensitive?"

"No, I am merely well acquainted with academic laziness." The Twi'lek considered. "I would recommend the world of Lorrd. It is a repository of academic knowledge, and its people, like my own, have developed a greater facility with nonverbal communication than most. Perhaps it would improve the odds that they have concentrated knowledge in this field. But you must take the item there. I can't guarantee that experts in other fields of communication could interpret the meaning of one of those tassels from a replica."

Jacen nodded. "Just what I wanted to know. My compliments to you, For'ali."

"Thank you for bringing me a task suited to my interests. Perhaps, when all is done, you could send me the original item to study." For'ali smiled. "Replicas are never quite as good."

"I'll see what I can do. Thank you, and good-bye."

"Farewell."

Jacen leaned forward to punch the disconnect button, and the hologram of the Twi'lek faded from view. Jacen relaxed back into his chair and sat for long moments studying the bottom tassel.

"It bothers you, doesn't it?" Ben asked.

Jacen nodded, absently, and gestured for the boy to sit in the next chair.

Ben sat. "Because those words are kind of like a Jedi saying?"

"Partly that. It's like the old mantra, but less, I don't know, *wholesome*. The other thing that bothers me is that the statement could have been made about *me*—at least, the way I was during the war with the Yuuzhan Vong. The way I was treated when I was a captive . . . well, pain is all they know."

"So we're going to Lorrd?"

"We're going to Lorrd. Go pack."

CORONET, CORELLIA

The war conference room was almost empty. Wedge Antilles shook hands with Admiral Karathas and her aides, then watched them depart the chamber. He began fiddling with his datapad, doubtless organizing the innumerable files he'd been beamed by various officers once his plan for the liberation of Tralus had been given tentative approval.

"We do need to wait for the YVH droids to come back for us," Leia said.

"I know that," Han protested. "I wasn't planning on popping out into the corridor while Thrackan's security team waits out there."

"Well, you looked impatient."

"Ah." Han tried to force himself to look less impatient.

He couldn't. Wedge's plan occupied almost all his brain's processing power.

Nor was he fooling her. "Don't volunteer," Leia said.

"Huh? For what?"

"For Wedge's plan."

"I—" The part of Han's mind that could convincingly spin excuses and arguments didn't have enough resources available to it. He resorted to the truth. "I have to, Leia. That mission was made for me."

"You don't think Thrackan will find out who the pilots are? You could survive the mission only to be blown up by remote control when returning to Corellia."

"I'm sure Wedge can—"

"General Antilles." It was Thrackan's voice again, still booming from the next observation room.

Below, Wedge glanced up again. "Sir."

"I have a favor to ask of you. As Minister of War. Something that's distinctly in your patriotic duty to do. Something you really should have done by now." Thrackan's tone was pleasant, not at all urgent.

Wedge returned his attention to his datapad. "Let's hear it."

"You have a daughter serving with the Galactic Alliance armed forces under the name of Lysa Dunter. She's assigned to the force occupying Tralus."

Even from this distance, and even seeing as little of Wedge's face as his current orientation afforded her, Han and Leia could see the man's sudden stillness.

Han could imagine what Wedge was feeling. He had a sudden urge to ask Leia to cut a hole in the wall separating the two chambers so he could take a few shots.

Wedge closed his datapad and tucked it into a pocket, then casually turned in his chair to face up at Thrackan. "Yes, she's in the GA armed forces. As a lot of Corellians are. Though I'm not sure where she is right now."

"I'm going to send her a message," Thrackan said. "I'd appreciate it if you'd include a note asking her to cooperate with what I suggest."

"And what are you going to suggest?"

"That's not really your concern."

Wedge didn't even attempt a pretense at unconcern or amusement. "Of course it is. I'm supposed to endorse whatever you suggest to her, regardless of what it is?"

"Yes. It's your duty. I have to insist."

"Go ahead."

Now Thrackan's voice sounded confused. "What?"

"Go ahead, insist. I'm interested in hearing this "

"All right. General Antilles, acting as Chief of State and Minister of War for Corellia, I hereby order you to communicate with your daughter Syal and do your genuine best to persuade her to follow whatever course of action I recommend to her. Is that clear enough?"

"Absolutely."

"And?"

"Go to hell."

"Thrackan's trying to get himself killed," Leia whispered.

Han nodded. "Let's go next door and wish him luck."

"Shush."

Thrackan said, "Antilles, you've refused a direct order given during a military crisis, and I have it on record. Should I choose to, I can have security agents haul you away right now. I can conduct your trial within the hour and have you executed by morning."

"Of course you can." Wedge stood and stretched, extending his arms over his head and flexing his back, a gesture of supreme unconcern. Leia could almost hear the popping from his vertebrae and joints. Then Wedge relaxed into a more normal standing position. "You could also have me assassinated in a time of peace for having nicer hair than you. If I worried about that sort of thing, I'd never get any sleep. And now I'm going to explain to you why it would be a bad, bad mistake for you to do this."

"Go ahead."

"If I refuse, which I have, and you have me murdered, you've traded a senior officer for whatever opportunities at sabotage and information gathering a very junior officer could provide you. It's not a smart trade. I'm no Garm Bel Iblis, but I'm the best strategist you have available. I also have friends in positions of power and influence all over the galaxy, and if I'm executed, I can't use them to your advantage—can't issue recommendations that they use their own influence to swing their planetary governments to the Corellian viewpoint, for instance."

"What's the difference between your doing that and your doing what I just recommended?"

"Ordered, Minister, not recommended. The difference is that asking, say, Wes Janson to put in a good word about

our cause to the military or government of his world of
Taanab is honorable. Asking my daughter to violate the
oaths she took when she became an officer and to participate
in treachery is not. Have I communicated the difference sufficiently?"

"Don't condescend to me, Antilles."

"Leave my family out of things, Sal-Solo."

"I'm going to communicate with your daughter. I'll convince her to do what I say."

"Go ahead." Wedge shrugged.

"You're not worried that I'll succeed?"

"You might succeed. But I won't be party to it."

There was no reply. A few seconds later, the light from
Thrackan's chamber, still spilling in a distorted rectangle
across the main table below, switched off.

Wedge walked toward the exit and disappeared out of
sight below Thrackan's chamber.

"Wedge just got himself killed," Leia said.

Han nodded. "He's too smart not to know that. It won't
be soon, though. Thrackan needs Wedge for now."

"But as soon as he gets angry enough to overcome his
self-interest—"

"Yeah."

RELLIDIR, TRALUS

"I am not happy," Jaina said.

She stood under sunny blue skies on a flat green lawn.
Gentle breezes stirred her hair and cooled her. Beside her
stood Zekk, offering silent support . . . and occasional
twinges of amusement as her mood whipped from one position to another.

In the distance ahead was the white Navos Center for the
Performing Arts with its eight beautifully fluted towers.
Closer at hand, on a patch of grass unmarked by duracrete
walking trails, were the nine X-wings of Luke's Hardpoint
Squadron.

Undefended.

Well, not entirely. In the astromech slot of Luke's own X-wing sat R2-D2, and the little droid offered a plaintive trill in counterpoint to Jaina's statement.

"Where are the pilots, Artoo?" Jaina asked.

R2-D2's top dome swiveled, bringing his main eye cam to bear on the distant performing arts building.

"And the security detail for these snubfighters?" she asked.

The astromech turned his main eye on her and issued a series of rapid beeps and tones.

"Reassigned." Jaina shook her head, exasperated.

"Want me to do this one?" Zekk asked.

"Please."

Zekk smiled and brought a comlink out from a pouch at his belt. "Artoo, would you give me the squadron frequency?"

The astromech beeped his compliance.

"Thanks." Zekk activated the comlink. "Zekk to Hardpoint Squadron. Your new squadron commander is on-site and wishes to see you immediately at your X-wings. Immediately means ninety seconds from the end of my transmission. No one will be punished for arriving in dirty robes, formal gowns, or bubbles and bathwater, but no one wants to arrive late. That is all. Out." He pocketed the comlink.

"Nicely done," Jaina said. "Effective, but with a potential for humor."

Zekk bowed, then straightened. "Your orders?"

"We need to find a place to house these snubfighters securely, and I don't care if they've been put out here to demonstrate our overwhelming military might and contempt for the Corellian forces. And we ought to do some drills so I can feel out the pilots' skills." Jaina caught sight of some motion in the direction of the center. A tall, dark-skinned human male, clad only in a white towel, which he held around his waist with both hands, was running in their direction. "It's going to be an interesting set of exercises."

BATTLE CARRIER **DODONNA**,
ORBITING TRALUS

Ensign "Lysa Dunton" and her Quarren wingman rose toward the field holding the atmosphere within *Dodonna*'s main belly hangar. With casual ease, they reduced velocity as they neared the glowing opening, popped up through the field to allow the air resistance to slow them down another crucial few kilometers per hour, and floated on repulsorlifts to their designated landing zone. Moments later, they raised their cockpits. Crew members, rushing forward, hung ladders in place, allowing them to exit their vehicles. Mechanics arrived, plugging in diagnostic units, beginning refueling.

Her Quarren wingman pulled off his helmet and issued a slurping sigh of relief. His facial tentacles wiggled in the cold artificial breeze blowing through the hangars. "Bath," he said. "I need to submerge. I'd kill to submerge." He turned and began a brisk march toward the doors out of the hangar.

Syal grinned after him. Long patrols were hard on the Quarren and their kindred, the Mon Calamari; they dehydrated faster than humans. She pulled off her own helmet and decided that her wingman's decision was the best one, though—a thorough cleansing, after hours of fruitless touring around the edges of the Corellia system, would be great for morale.

"Ensign Dunton?" The chief mechanic, a lean man with dark eyes, approached her with his diagnostic datapad in hand. "Can I speak to you for a moment?"

"Of course." She shook her hair out. Short as it was, it didn't give her too much grief on long missions, and at least this time she'd donned her helmet so that her bangs didn't cause her additional trouble. "You usually work with the X-wing units, don't you?"

"Yes, Ensign. But everybody's being shifted around to cross-train while we have some downtime. I put in a request to work with the Eta-Fives today."

Syal eyed his datapad. "Is there a problem with my interceptor?"

"Not exactly." He moved close and lowered his voice so the rest of the crew couldn't make out his words. "Actually, I just wanted to bring you some greetings from home."

She gave him a sharp look. "Greetings from Ralltiir?"

"Greetings," he said, "from Corellia. Perhaps we should talk somewhere private."

An hour later, VibroSword Leader, a tall human with graying hair and features suggesting that he was an actor hired to play a squadron leader, leaned over the interrogation table toward Syal and asked, "So you shot him."

Beside him sat a human woman, dark-skinned, with big eyes that looked bright and uncritical enough to belong to someone much younger; Syal had never seen her before. She wore civilian clothes all in blacks and light blues. Her face was expressionless, though her eyes were on Syal, awaiting her response.

Syal nodded. Her face felt tight, especially around her eyes, from the brief bit of crying she'd done when no one was looking, and her bangs, now lank with perspiration, flopped into her eyes. She wished that VibroSword Leader would just take his chair and stay in it. All his standing up, doubtless to appear to be more intimidating, was getting on her nerves. Plus, she could use a friend right now, and it sure wasn't him.

"I still don't understand," the woman said. "Why did you shoot him?"

"He lunged for my blaster pistol," Syal said.

"Why did you have a blaster pistol?" Leader asked.

"So I could take him into custody."

"No," the woman said. "You took it out to take him into custody. Why did you have it in the first place?"

"I always do," Syal explained. "When I got old enough to begin dating, my father insisted that I carry one." That was a small lie. Her father had insisted that she carry two.

But she'd made do with one most of the time since leaving home.

"And you drew on him because he was trying to suborn you," the woman continued.

Syal nodded. " 'Do a few things for us,' he said, meaning the Corellians."

The woman looked skeptical. "Ensign Dunton, you're a very low-ranking officer in a carrier full of people who could do the GA more harm than you if they were turned. Why you? What makes you so vulnerable to this sort of attempt?"

"Your leg," Leader said.

"What?" Syal turned an uncomprehending expression on him.

"Your leg," he repeated.

Syal looked down. Her right leg was vibrating again. She glared at it and it stopped.

"Answer the question, please," the woman said.

"I'm . . ." Syal looked at her, then turned apologetic eyes toward Leader. "I'm Corellian."

He glanced toward his datapad. "Right. Born on Corellia. Raised on Ralltiir."

"No. Born on Corellia . . . *raised* on Corellia. The recruiting officer assumed, and put down, that I was raised on Ralltiir because I have Ralltiir citizenship. But I didn't get it the usual way. I bought it."

The woman said, "What else in your record is incorrect?"

"Nothing. But Lysa Dunton, well, that isn't the name I was born with."

Leader scowled at her and sat again. "You achieved an officer's rank on a falsified name. We're deep into court-martial territory here."

"No, Lysa Dunton *is* my real name. I changed it, legally, at a court on Ralltiir that is known for being horribly disorganized. I knew it would take years for the records to reach the GA military. I changed it to avoid comparisons with my father, so I could achieve a reputation of my own."

"What's your real—" The woman checked herself. "Your original name?"

"Syal Antilles."

Both the woman and Leader blinked. The woman reacted first. "Corellian. Antilles. You aren't by chance—"

"He's my father."

"And Iella Antilles your mother."

"I'm surprised you know that name."

The woman nodded. "So the mechanic tries to persuade you to perform unspecified actions for the Corellian government."

Syal nodded. "And he threatened to do things to my family if I didn't comply."

Leader gave Syal a hard stare. "So you've just gotten your family killed. You refused; that agent's superiors will now begin the purge. Good going."

Syal settled back in her chair, putting a precious few more centimeters' distance between herself and her squadron leader. "I hope not."

"The smart thing to do," Leader said, "would have been to go along with whatever he said and bring Intelligence in later."

Syal shook her head. "I'm no good at that sort of thing. Don't you think I know what I'm capable of? My mother was in Intelligence. My sister got those genes, I guess. I wouldn't be able to pull it off, and in the meantime, that man would have been free on *this* ship, maybe sabotaging the starfighters of *my* friends. No, that's not smarter." Syal heard her voice rise in indignation.

"I'll tell you what," Leader said. "We'll look into this. If you're lying, you get a dishonorable discharge and whatever criminal punishment you deserve. If you're telling the truth, things are much better. You get an honorable discharge and can go home to Corellia and fly with your daddy's squadrons . . . and give us a crack at you. Either way, this is the last day you'll wear the Galactic Alliance uniform. Dismissed."

Syal tightened the muscles of her face, struggling to hold back new tears that wanted to stream forth, and started to rise.

"Sit," the woman said. She turned to Leader. "You. Be a good boy and go away."

Leader gaped at her. "You—"

The woman smiled at him, showing teeth. "The correct response is *Yes, ma'am.* Now go."

Leader evaluated her expression, then hurriedly rose. "Yes, ma'am."

The woman waited until he was out of the interrogation room. She returned her attention to Syal. "Yes, we'll verify the details of your story. If they check out, you'll be returned to active service. But I doubt you'll be returned to VibroSword Squadron. I suspect that it can be considered a hostile environment for you now."

"I think you're right."

"Your leg is going again." The woman turned her attention to the datapad in front of her. "It says here that you were offered the chance to join a new squadron handling the first deployment of the *Aleph*-class fighters. Is that correct?"

Syal nodded. "I didn't want to, though. I've played around with Aleph simulators. They've got plenty of speed, but they maneuver like big plugs of duracrete."

"And if your only options are to fly Alephs or work as a communications officer aboard a sensor ship?"

"Alephs sound great, ma'am."

"Spoken like a true Antilles." The woman closed her datapad.

"You're from Intelligence, aren't you? I would have thought that my own squadron leader would have been the sympathetic one and you would have been a plasteel nek about the whole thing."

The woman nodded. "Never can tell how the past is going to affect things, can you?" She rose. "I don't know what your squadron leader's problem is. Jealousy, or maybe he needs to be in complete control, and the fact that you didn't divulge about your famous father constitutes a betrayal. As for me . . ." She offered Syal a slight smile. "Once upon a time, not long after the New Republic won Coruscant that first time, I flew with your father for a few months. I've known some of his pilots considerably longer. I know what sort of children he'll have raised. If you're really Syal Antilles, I suspect you're in the clear."

On her way out the door, she added, "And you might as well legally change your name back. Your secret's out."

chapter twenty-five

LORRD CITY, LORRD

She was willowy-tall, with long black hair in a flowing ponytail. Ben saw her first from the cockpit of Jacen's shuttle as the vehicle drifted down on repulsorlifts. The woman was neither distinct nor interesting at that time, merely a shadowy figure leaning, arms crossed, against the hangar pit wall.

But once they were grounded, cleared to emerge, and descending the shuttle's boarding ramp, she strode forward out of the shadows, and Ben suddenly found her very interesting indeed. Her robes—a green and tan-yellow combination not commonly seen on Jedi—were tailored to her, flattering her figure, and her widemouthed smile was a celebration that invited all who saw it to join in.

Sadly, Ben's sudden interest was one-sided. She walked quickly to the ramp's base, her attention fixed on Jacen, her hand extended toward the adult Jedi. "Jacen!" she said. "It's good to see you."

Jacen reached the bottom of the ramp and took her hand, but did not draw her into an embrace, not even the cordial embrace of old friends—though her body language, even to Ben's inexperienced eye, suggested that this was what she expected. "Nelani," Jacen said. "When I heard that you were the Jedi assigned to the Lorrd station, that you'd be the one meeting us, I was glad—"

"Really?"

"Glad to realize that you'd passed your trials and were fully vested as a Jedi Knight," he continued. "Congratulations."

Her smile faltered slightly. "Thank you." She released her grip on his hand, and her attention finally turned to Ben. "And this must be Ben Skywalker."

Ben stood silent. It wasn't that he didn't want to say anything. It was just that his entire vocabulary, including some choice swear words in Rodian and Huttese he'd gone to great pains to memorize, had just vanished. He wondered where it was.

Nelani cast a worried glance at Jacen. "Does he talk?"

Ben's vocabulary suddenly returned. "You're being condescending," he said.

Absently she ruffled his hair. "Certainly not. You just had me puzzled for a moment." She returned her attention to Jacen. "So what did you want to do first? Get settled in your quarters at the station?" She gestured toward the exit from the hangar pit, then led them in that direction.

"Have you researched the matter I commed you about?" Jacen asked.

Ben fell into line behind them, furiously smoothing his hair.

"Yes, and I've found a contact who seems to know something about your tassels, a Doctor Heilan Rotham. Tactile writing and recording methods are her specialty . . ."

Dr. Rotham's offices—also her quarters—were on the ground floor of a university building built of duracrete bricks and falsewoods, then comfortably aged for a couple of centuries. The walls of the corridors and chambers were dark—either soothing or shadowy and threatening, depending on one's attitude toward such things—and so somber that it seemed to Ben that they could swallow all humor.

Not that, in the office chambers, the walls were all that easy to see. Shelves lined the room, displaying books, scrolls, figurines of strangely misshapen males and females of many species, coils of irregularly knotted rope, and small wooden boxes with hinged lids.

He looked over to the table where Dr. Rotham sat with Jacen and Nelani. Dr. Rotham was a human woman, tiny and ancient. Her hair was white and wispy; her skin was pale, traced with blue veins, and almost transparent. She wore a heavy maroon robe, even though Ben found the temperature in these chambers to be on the warm side, and her eyes were a piercing blue unclouded by age. She sat on a self-propelled chair, a wheeled thing with a bulky undercarriage that suggested it was equipped with short-range repulsorlifts. She held Jacen's mass of tassels up before her eyes, scrutinizing them from a distance of only four or five centimeters.

"You have a lot of stuff here," Ben said.

Without looking at him, Dr. Rotham said, "I do, don't I? And what's remarkable is that every datum that can be derived from those objects has been recorded into my office memory for my datapads, into Lorrd's computer system, and into the computers of any person who has ever asked for them."

Ben took another look around the room's extensive banks of shelving. "But if it's all recorded, why do you keep the original things? They take up a lot of room."

"A reasonable question from a Jedi, who must travel often and lightly. But you must remember that there is a tremendous difference between a thing and the *knowledge* of a thing. For instance, think about your best friend. Would you prefer to have your best friend, or a datapad stuffed full of knowledge about him?"

Ben considered. He didn't want to give her the obvious, "correct" answer—it seemed like a defeat. Instead, he said, "That's a good question." It was an answer he had heard adults offer many times, one he suspected they used whenever they couldn't think of anything better to say.

Jacen chuckled and Dr. Rotham did not follow up on her question. Ben concluded that he had held his own.

"This one," Dr. Rotham said, "is definitely Bith, a recording method of an isolated island race, the Aalagar, that concocted the knotting style as a means of recording genealogies—'strings of ancestors.' Later the technique was expanded to permit the recording of thoughts and statements. Roughly translated, it means, 'He will ruin those who deny justice.' "

Nelani frowned. "That's . . . curiously ominous."

"Why?" Jacen asked.

"Yeah," Ben said. "Jedi do that all the time. Ruin those who deny justice."

Nelani shook her head. "Ruination is sometimes a result of what we do. But it's not usually the *goal*. Ruination as a goal sounds like vengefulness. Not a trait suited to a Jedi."

Ben caught Jacen's eye, silently requesting confirmation of Nelani's assertion. Jacen shrugged unhelpfully.

"I'm certain I can translate many of the others," Dr. Rotham continued. "Though, since they all appear to be separated from their cultural contexts, how *accurate* those translations will be is somewhat up in the air. Perhaps they provide a context for one another. If so, that will be helpful."

Jacen nodded. "I'd appreciate whatever you could tell us."

As he spoke, Nelani beeped—or, rather, something on her person did. She hurriedly fit a small hands-free comlink to the back of her right ear; she pulled part of the device loose and it swung out, a little black ball, to bob and sway gently at the corner of her mouth, suspended by a black wire so fine as to be almost invisible. "Nelani Dinn," she said.

After a few moments of listening, Nelani frowned. "Did he say why a Jedi?" She paused, cocking her head to one side. "And you think it's credible . . . Yes, I'll be right there . . . about ten minutes. Out." She tucked the bobbing microphone back up under her ear and rose. "I apologize for ducking out, but I have to go."

"Emergency?" Jacen asked.

"Yes. Some sort of lunatic in a starfighter threatening to launch missiles if he's not allowed to talk to a Jedi."

"I get the impression that it will take Doctor Rotham some time to complete any more translations." Jacen glanced at the elderly woman for confirmation, and at her nod he rose. "I'll come with you."

"You'd be welcome," Nelani said.

It was an odd situation at the Lorrd City Spaceport. A Y-wing starfighter, so battle-scarred and patched that it had probably been ancient at the time of the Battle of Yavin, had set down fifty meters from the approved landing zone. Nor had it landed on a flat surface; its ion jet drive pods rested on a repulsorlift taxiing strip, at right angles to the normal direction of traffic, and its nose was up on a meters-high duracrete traffic barrier, leaving the starfighter at a thirty-degree upward angle.

"He's short an astromech," Ben said. Indeed, there was nothing in the circular gap immediately behind the cockpit. "And it's modded for concussion missiles instead of proton torpedoes."

"He also has a nice firing angle on the most populous area of the city," said Lieutenant Neav Samran of the Lorrd Security Force. A heavyset human man with brown hair and mustache grown just a bit longer than regulations probably permitted, he had his forces deployed all around the Y-wing at distances of fifty to two hundred meters, and snipers were conspicuous on hangar rooftops. Samran's command post, where the three Jedi had joined him, was at the corner of the corrugated durasteel-sided hangar a hundred meters from the starfighter. Ben stood behind Jacen, but to one side, where he could keep an eye on the Y-wing and the faintly visible figure in the cockpit.

Ben found he could actually *feel* the pilot there, as a hard knot of pain and confusion that faded and swelled, moving in and out of the boy's perceptions.

"Do you have any indication of whether he actually has

live concussion missiles and how he got them?" Jacen asked.

Samran nodded. "He sent us the telemetry from his weapons board—a one-way feed, blast it, else we'd have been able to slice into his controls and solve this without calling you in. He has a full brace of missiles aimed at the student housing districts—precisely where, we can't be sure. As for how he got them—he doesn't have a credit left in what had been a decent-sized savings and investments account. With all the weapons smuggling going on these days, it's no surprise that an old pilot with lots of connections could get his hands on ordnance like that."

"What can you tell us about him?" Nelani asked.

Samran opened his datapad and consulted it. "Ordith Huarr, age eighty-one standard years. Human male originally from Lorrd. Back in the Old Republic and Empire days, he was a shuttle pilot. At the height of the Rebel Alliance, he joined them and spent the war as a Y-wing pilot, during which time he scored one-half of a kill. His record as a Rebel pilot was undistinguished."

Nelani shot Samran an admonishing look. "He was no less brave than pilots with better kill records."

Samran held her stare, unruffled. "The comment about his record was offered as a possible key to his mental state. In my experience, people with mediocre skills and unremarkable records are more likely to come unhinged. They experience more frustration, less appreciation. Or do you disagree?"

Nelani's expression relented a bit, to one of milder disapproval, and she turned away to stare at the old starfighter again.

"Anyway," Samran continued, "he became a flight instructor after the Empire fell, and eventually retired and returned to Lorrd. He came out of retirement a few years back to shuttle Yuuzhan Vong war refugees around, and the records suggest that being kicked around from planet to planet unwilling to accept refugees did something bad to his outlook. After the Yuuzhan Vong war, he came back again, bought some rural property with his wife, and spent the next several years living off his pension and shooting blasters at intruders."

"Any children?" Nelani asked.

"No children," Samran said. "And his wife died about two years ago."

"Two years," Jacen said. "What happened *recently* that put him behind a missile board, threatening students?"

Samran shook his head.

"I guess I'd better talk to him," Nelani said. She turned back to Jacen. "Unless you'd like to? You're senior."

Jacen shook his head. "No, I have another tactic I'll explore."

She nodded, made sure her robes were suitably straight and that the lightsaber hanging at her belt was clearly visible, then marched across the plascrete parking area toward the Y-wing.

When she was fifty meters from the starfighter, the pilot's voice, broadcast over an external speaker system, boomed at her. "That's close enough." The voice was thin, raspy.

Nelani cupped her hands around her mouth to shout her reply. "Whatever you say. Huarr, you didn't have to endanger all those students to talk to me. My station office can be reached by planetary net or comlink."

Ben felt the pilot's pain and confusion surge, stronger than he'd experienced it previously.

"You wouldn't have taken me seriously," the old man said. "You only understand force. Force and *the* Force." He laughed, a bitter noise, as if briefly entertained by his own play on words.

"Not true, but we don't need to argue the point," Nelani shouted. "I'm here now. Why did you want to talk to me?"

"What is a Force ghost?" Huarr asked.

Nelani was silent for a long moment. "It's a survival, a sending from someone who has died but still exists in a certain way."

"My wife is a Force ghost," Huarr said. "She talks to me. But she can't, can she?"

Nelani took another step forward. Even distorted by shouting, her voice sounded dubious. "Was she a Jedi? Or did she ever do things that suggested she might see things, feel things that normal people don't?"

"No."

Caught up as he was in the dialogue between Nelani and Huarr, Ben had lost track of Jacen. Now he became aware that his mentor was concentrating, channeling the Force.

Jacen reached out and pulled a handful of air toward him. Simultaneously the Y-wing's ion jet pods skidded backward across the duracrete, sending up showers of sparks, just until the starfighter's nose slid off the barrier and crashed to the ground, facing directly into the duracrete.

Then he added a twisting motion, and the Y-wing rotated along its long axis, crashing onto the taxiing strip upside down.

"There," Jacen told Samran. "Problem solved. He can't lift off with repulsors or thrusters, and he can't fire his missiles at the city."

Samran looked at him in surprise, then choked up in laughter. Unable to speak, he waved the men and women of his security force toward the starfighter. They emerged from their protected positions and advanced. Ben could hear some of them laughing, too.

"What are you doing?" That was Nelani, returning at a quick trot. "I had the situation under control!"

Jacen turned a dubious look on her. "No, you didn't. You were executing a decent negotiation. But to be 'in control' you would have had to be able to prevent him from firing at any moment. Could you?"

Nelani reached Jacen and stood there, her features flushed, her expression confrontational. "No, but he wouldn't have fired while we were talking."

"Tell that to the families of all the students who would have died if he had somehow fired without your detecting it—or if he had his missiles set up on a timer, which you *wouldn't* have been able to feel. And don't tell me he wouldn't have. You had no control over his actions, and every moment you negotiated with him, you risked the lives of those students."

"You think I wasn't aware of his emotional state? His feelings were lit up like a landing circle!"

While the two Jedi argued, Ben watched the spaceport security team approach the helpless starfighter. Then he felt a surge of despair from its pilot, despair and determination—

"Get back!" Ben astonished himself with the volume of his scream, with the fact that he was screaming without meaning to, with the fact that he was running forward with no voluntary control of his legs. "Run! Run!"

The security agents froze at his first cry and looked back at him. Apparently the force of will he was projecting and his proximity to Lieutenant Samran were enough for them. They turned away from the Y-wing and began running.

There was a hum from the starfighter, and Ben saw ignition within its missile tubes. There was a sudden expulsion of flame, missiles punching out of their tubes and into the duracrete just in front of the starfighter—

And then the Y-wing exploded, propelled into metallic confetti by a hemispherical wall of flame and concussive force.

As if in slow motion, Ben saw the wall of energy swell out toward him. He dropped to the permacrete-covered ground, wrapped his robe tightly around him, and focused his mind on the blast he could still visualize. He saw the point where it would hit him. He pressed against that spot, willing it to weaken, to slow—

It hit him. He felt himself pushed as if by a giant hand, a hand radiating ferocious heat. He rolled and skidded backward, then came to a stop.

There was no sound. His ears felt as battered as if a wampa had boxed them. But he felt oddly peaceful, as though he had been exercising all morning and was ready for a rest.

Languidly, he threw his robe off his face and stood up.

The Y-wing was gone. Where it had been was a crater,

and the duracrete barrier that had stood before it was interrupted by a rough-edged gap many meters long.

The buildings nearest the explosion were still standing, but they leaned away from the source of the blast, their metal skeletons bent, the exterior walls facing the blast dented in or missing entirely.

Everywhere there were bodies, some of them licked by flame, and Ben thought for one cold moment that his effort had been too late. But one of the burning men suddenly began to roll on the ground, smothering the flames rising from his back and shoulders, and a woman a few meters from him stood up on shaky legs.

Ben saw Jacen racing toward him, but then Jacen, seeing that his cousin was not badly hurt, veered off toward victims who were still unmoving.

Ben chose a nearby group of security personnel and moved toward them, his steps unsteady at first, then gaining in balance and sureness as he ran.

An hour later, Ben sat in a hangar. A brightly painted but antiquated shuttle dominated the center of the building. Ben had his back against a corrugated durasteel wall, which flexed slightly as he leaned against it. Other rescue workers sat against the same wall, drinking cups of caf some of their number had provided, exchanging gruesome stories of explosion disasters of the past. Mostly they left Ben alone, but they had brought him caf and told him he'd done well. And now the crisis was over, and the medics and firefighters were resting and replenishing themselves for a few minutes before returning to their respective bases.

Jacen and Nelani reentered the hangar through the main sliding door. They spotted Ben and headed his way. Jacen sat beside his cousin while Nelani remained standing.

"Guess what?" Jacen asked.

Ben could hear him clearly enough now, a very faint ringing in his ears the only remnant of the effects of the explosion. "What?"

"No dead."

Ben looked at him, startled. "None of them died?"

"Not one. Well, not counting the crazy man in the Y-wing. But it seems that every one of the security men and women will make it. Not one seems to be in critical condition, thanks in part to their body armor, but mostly to you."

"Lubed," Ben said.

Nelani said, "While Jacen and I were arguing about procedure, you were doing what a Jedi should—being mindful of the Force."

"So we get to take note of *your* example today, instead of the other way around," Jacen continued. "I also thought you should have a reward."

"What reward?" Ben asked.

"The rest of the day is yours. Nelani and I are returning to Doctor Rotham's now. You can accompany us, you can go sightseeing, you can check out a groundspeeder and improve your piloting skills, whatever you like. You have enough credits to get by, and you know how to get to Doctor Rotham's, I believe."

Ben nodded. He didn't let it show on his face, but his mind was spinning—the rest of his day left to his own devices, *unsupervised*! That was indeed a reward. And, he was dimly aware, it was also a sign of trust. "Thanks," he said.

Jacen rose. He and Nelani headed back out the way they'd come, heads bowed together as though they were renewing their argument, leaving Ben to figure out what he wanted to do with himself.

Though he didn't know it, Ben was right: the two Jedi Knights began quarreling again as soon as they reached the exit from the hangar, though they handled their disagreement more civilly than before. "I really wish," Nelani said, "that you'd given me another minute or two with Huarr. I'm really curious about this 'Force ghost' business of his."

"Students," Jacen said, in a tone that suggested his one-word argument should settle the whole matter.

"Yes, yes, the students in their quarters were in danger, I'm not disputing that. But couldn't you have surreptitiously squeezed the ends of his missile launching tubes closed? That way, if he'd fired, same result, but until then, I'd have been able to talk to him. Maybe I could have gotten to the root of his craziness."

They reached the anonymous gray speeder that had brought them to the spaceport. They hopped in, Nelani behind the controls.

"I suppose I could have," Jacen admitted. "It didn't occur to me, and it does beg the question of whether someone who threatens the lives of thousands of innocents deserves any consideration whatsoever."

"Maybe he deserved consideration for being a war hero." Nelani activated the repulsors and sent the speeder skyward.

Jacen made a dismissive gesture. "My father is a war hero, too. I don't recall him ever doing what Huarr did."

"And Huarr never smuggled spice for Hutt crimelords, either."

Jacen shook his head. "Sometimes it's a disadvantage having a father so famous they make holodramas about him."

Nelani grinned. "With you, I have to exploit any conversational advantage I can get my hands on."

"You're definitely not the late-blooming Force-sensitive I taught lightsaber technique to."

"I'm glad you noticed."

Jacen ignored that remark, as well as the rather personal tone with which it had been communicated. "It's time we turned our attention back to Doctor Rotham and those tassels."

"Not just yet. I've been trying to turn your attention to *me*."

He grinned. "You really have gotten bolder."

She nodded. "Learning how to, and having the *ability* to, cut gundarks in half went a long way toward overcoming my shyness problem. And being a Jedi, the only Jedi assigned to this world, means I have very little time of my own, so I tend to get to the point rather quickly. Does that bother you?"

Jacen shook his head, but kept his attention on the terrain—long banks of warehouses graduating to blocks of low-rent businesses—speeding by beneath their vehicle. "No, but there's someone . . ."

"Someone occupying that particular place in your life?"

"Yes."

She made a chiding noise. "Well, then, let's just spend a little time together. Which, incidentally, I wanted very badly to suggest seven years ago, when you were teaching me lightsaber technique, but I was too self-conscious."

Jacen smiled and offered no further explanation.

Nelani shook her head, a gesture of mild regret, and fell silent.

chapter twenty-six

CORUSCANT

It was like a replay of their first conference from days earlier, with Cal Omas, Admiral Pellaeon, and Admiral Niathal occupying the same seats at the conference table when Luke was escorted into the chamber. They and their aides looked up as the Jedi Master entered, and even before he seated himself, Omas said, "So it appears you have good news for us."

Luke looked startled. "What makes you think that? If I may ask."

"Your expression," Omas said. "You were smiling. In these times, a smile from a Jedi is a hopeful sign."

"Oh." Luke let his expression fall into more serious lines. "I'm sorry. I didn't mean to mislead you. I just had some good news about my boy, Ben. He managed to save a number of lives on Lorrd just a few hours ago."

Niathal nodded, her protruding eyes surprisingly adept at projecting cool displeasure. "Admirable. I'm sure he'll grow up into a fine Jedi Knight . . . years and years from now, when this new Corellian crisis is behind us. For now, though—"

"For now," Pellaeon interrupted, "we could use some more *universal* hopeful signs from the Jedi."

"I'm not sure about hopeful," Luke said. "Useful, perhaps. As you probably saw in the report I forwarded, there's little doubt that Thrackan Sal-Solo sabotaged the Toryaz Station conference—or, at least, through his inaction permitted it to be sabotaged."

Omas's mouth turned downward. "Unfortunately, the difference between those two behaviors is the difference between the most serious sort of crime and a noncrime."

"Noncrime." Luke looked appalled. "You're joking."

"No." Omas, for this moment, looked like a man impervious to humor—certainly not a generator of amusement. "Assuming that he did not pay for the information offered in the message he received, can you prove that he took the message seriously? That it was credible to him? Because he can always claim that he did not consider it a credible offer, that it was a communication from a crank, and therefore did not need to be acted on in any capacity."

Luke shook his head, unhappy to be thwarted by so negligible an obstacle. "Still, if a strike team were able to capture him and bring him to Coruscant, a criminal trial based on the assumption that he did buy the information could drag on for months. Or longer. Keeping Sal-Solo out of commission during all that time. And that would be a boon to the peace process."

The others exchanged glances. "That," Niathal said, "is a far more pragmatic suggestion than I expected from a Jedi. I like it."

Luke leaned back. "Jedi are among the most pragmatic beings in the galaxy. We tend to operate under the assumption that it's better to get things done than to observe all the niceties—we consider justice to be of more consequence than law, for instance. Even justice is often overrated. Sometimes the imposition of justice prevents redemption."

"We'll consider that recommendation," Omas said. "But we have to consider it against the precedent it sets. If we kidnap a planetary ruler, even a subruler who theoretically still belongs to our own government structure, despite our evident right to bring a suspected criminal into custody for trial, it opens a *pragmatic* precedent for the kidnapping of rulers within the Galactic Alliance. I might, in effect, be setting the stage for my own eventual kidnapping."

"We might have the blessing—even the unofficial blessing—of Sal-Solo's chief rival on this," Luke said. "My sister reports a surreptitious meeting with Prime Minister Denjax Teppler, and a subtext of the meeting was apparently Teppler's concern that he'll survive, both politically and as a living being, only so long as Sal-Solo views him as an asset."

Pellaeon snorted, his expression amused but derisive. "That's what I love about politics," he said. "We and a Corellian puppet ruler might have to conspire to remove a politician who's an impediment to us both before we can make headway in the peace process. How much sense does that make?"

Luke spread his hands, palms up. "I can't always make sense at the tables of politics. Let's see . . . I've finished bringing the underaged Jedi trainees off Corellia, removing them as potential targets for retaliation. Mara came away from Coronet with information about Corellian midlevel government officers that you might be able to use as leverage on them—a matter for Intelligence. My report included evaluations from many of the Jedi elsewhere in the galaxy, all pointing to a rise in support of Corellia's position in specific planetary systems. And that's most of what I had to report."

Pellaeon nodded, his manner brisk. "Were you planning to remain on Coruscant, or return to Corellia and resume control of your squadron?"

"I was planning to return to Tralus."

"We would appreciate it if you would stay here for a few days more, until we have a better sense of how the Jedi would best be posted during this crisis."

Luke nodded. "As you wish."

"And I'm sorry about your boy."

Luke's eyebrows rose. "Sorry?"

"I don't mean about his accomplishment. I mean about his involvement." Pellaeon gave Luke a wry smile. "The young go through wars and think that the experience is enough to teach them to fear such conflicts. And then, years later, their children go to war, and suddenly the parents learn what fear really means."

"True enough," Luke said, and, taking Pellaeon's words as the beginning of a dismissal, rose. "And I'm glad that you're still able to comprehend that fear."

CORELLIAN SYSTEM, ABOVE TRALUS

"He's on our tail! He's on our tail!"

Syal Antilles didn't reply to the Sullustan gunner's musical, trilling shout. She simply slapped the control yoke to the left.

The *Aleph*-class starfighter didn't bank to port. Instead, there was a kick to the starfighter's side as thruster ports all along the starboard hull vented energy. The starfighter slipped to port, its orientation and forward speed not noticeably changing. Syal slapped down on the yoke's top and the Aleph lurched again, this time dropping with stomach-jolting suddenness several meters as ports on the top of the hull vented.

Laserfire from behind raked through empty space to the starboard side of the Aleph, then traversed to port but missed the starfighter again as it dropped.

Zueb Zan, the Sullustan in the cockpit's right-hand seat, finally got the Aleph's starboard-side turret spun around and facing aft. A graphic image of the X-wing pursuing the Aleph jittered briefly in Zueb's targeting brackets. The Sullustan fired, and red wire-image versions of laser blasts converged on the X-wing. In the monitor showing Syal and Zueb a holocam view of the Aleph's stern, they could see a live feed of the real laser beams hitting the real X-wing, but the beams were pallid, far below combat strength, and the snubfighter's shields soaked them up without difficulty.

"That's a confirmed kill," the X-wing pilot reported. "Good job, Antilles. Zan."

"Thank you, sir," Syal responded, mechanically. She

began a quick check of her diagnostics boards, all but ignored during the mock battle, and saw no impairment to the Aleph's fighting abilities other than a slight energy drain from shield and laser usage.

The X-wing accelerated in a way the Aleph never could, causing Syal to bite her lip in envy, and pulled up to the Aleph's starboard side. "Opinions?" the pilot transmitted.

"I'm still not used to the lateral thrusters," Syal said. She worked hard to keep a tone of complaint from creeping into her voice, though complaining was precisely what she wanted to do. "It's just not the same as high-speed jinking."

"Maybe not," the X-wing pilot said, "but you're handling them very well. You made me miss you. Zan?"

The Sullustan considered. "Starboard turret sticks," he said. "If it keeps doing that, we're going to get our butts shot off."

"Well, talk to your chief mechanic."

The Sullustan's lips twisted, an expression of dissatisfaction. "Wanted to know if turrets on the other Alephs were sticking. If so, bad sign."

"I'll ask. All right, this run is done. Bring her in." The X-wing abruptly veered away, banking back toward Tralus and the vessels orbiting her, including the Mon Cal carrier *Blue Diver*, Syal's new home.

Jealous, Syal watched the nimbler snubfighter maneuver. She slowly began to turn in its wake. Her Aleph starfighter was capable of getting up to tremendous speeds—Eta-5 interceptor speeds—in atmosphere, but was so much more massive than the sort of craft she used to fly that simple banking maneuvers took much longer. The lateral thrusters with which she'd been dodging incoming fire just weren't the same as native nimbleness. She clicked her comm board over to receive only and said, "I still hate it."

"Me, too." Zueb nodded vigorously, causing the fleshy folds of his face to wobble.

"It's like flying a freight speeder. Which I've done."

"On Corellia?"

Syal nodded. "Just a job. To save up credits for my education."

"Your father is a famous retired general and you have to pay for your own education?"

"Not exactly. Every credit I put into my education fund, he matched with four. But I had to earn. That's the Antilles way: no easy path." Oriented on a course to intercept *Blue Diver*'s orbit, she switched control over to the black-and-yellow R2 astromech situated in the well between and behind the pilot and gunner's seats. "By the way, thanks."

"For?"

"Not making a deal of my being Corellian. Or being a famous general's daughter."

Zueb waved her remarks away. "I'm taking long view. You're not Corellian daughter of famous general. *He's* father of famous Twee test pilot. Just wait."

Syal grinned. "I like your attitude."

Test pilot. Her father had done some of that, too, over the years, but probably hadn't done so in a vehicle like the Aleph. By comparison with the X-wings that her father so loved, the *Aleph*-class starfighters were flying tanks. Heavily armored two-crew craft with overbuilt generators, the Alephs had been designed in the last months of the Yuuzhan Vong war, more than a decade before, as a one-to-one match for the Yuuzhan Vong coralskipper, a massive single-pilot organic starfighter protected by thick shells and by voids, mobile singularities that could slide in front of incoming lasers or missiles and swallow them completely.

The Alephs didn't have any defenses that esoteric. Instead, they relied on their thick hulls and on shields powered by those overbuilt generators. Weapons included two turrets, one on either side of the ball-shaped cockpit, each equipped with quad-linked lasers—lasers that could be unlinked, permitting an unpredictable spray fire pattern, an option to confound those coralskipper voids. Forward were the explosives tubes, one for concussion missiles and one for proton torpedoes. All in all, the Alephs packed a heavy punch—*heavy* being the operative word for much of the vehicle's performance.

But—and Syal winced—it was a shame the Alephs looked so blasted stupid. With their ball-shaped cockpits, reminiscent of TIE cockpits but larger, and the circular transparisteel viewports before both the pilot's and gunner's seats, with the smooth ball cockpit lines graduating to two trailing thruster pods narrowing the farther they were from the cockpit, and with the turrets to either side of the cockpit, the Aleph looked like nothing so much as the head of a gigantic Twi'lek, trailing its head-tails behind and wearing clumsy earmuffs. It was no wonder the Aleph test pilots and just about everyone else who saw them referred to the craft as Twees.

Still, flying them was better than flying garbage scows, rescue shuttles, or tugs.

Test pilot. Syal considered that. Much as she'd come to dislike the Twees in the few days she'd been flying them, she realized that it wouldn't be fair to this class of starfighters if she didn't demonstrate every one of their positive traits for their GA evaluators. It also wouldn't be fair to the Antilles family name. Now that she'd reclaimed her name, she owed it to her family to put a bit more polish on it. She needed to be able to run this craft through maneuvers so exacting that onlooking pilots would have no idea how she did it.

She switched her comm board back on to broadcast. "Gray One, this is Four. Over."

"Go ahead, Four. Over."

"Would it be all right if I dropped down into Tralus's atmosphere before I return to the *Diver*? I'd like to run this unit through some paces. Atmospheric speed and heat tests, some aerobatics. Over."

"That's showing some initiative, Four. You're authorized. Over."

"Thanks, and out." Syal returned the comm board to its previous status.

Zueb gave her a sorrowful look. "Going to fly me dizzy, aren't you?"

Syal nodded, her expression sympathetic. "Only till you throw up."

"All right."

LORRD CITY, LORRD

Ben returned to Dr. Rotham's offices just as the elderly scholar was commencing her initial evaluation. He walked in, seeing the real tassels set out on the main table and a hologram of them floating above, each tassel labeled.

Rotham was speaking: "—top to bottom, as that seems, from internal evidence, to be the order in which they're to be read. Hello, Ben."

"Hello." Ben moved forward to stand behind Jacen's chair. He stared up at the hologram.

"So," Dr. Rotham continued, "number one, at the top, is from Firrere, a dead world, its population scattered; the knotting technique was originally for recording and, in some superstitious cultures, magically influencing names. Its message, 'He will remake himself'—or perhaps 'rename himself,' the two concepts being identical in this context.

"Next is the one I translated for you earlier, from the Bith species, Aalagar race: 'He will ruin those who deny justice.'

"The scarlet-and-black one was easy, as it was the second of the tactile writing systems I learned—a recording technique used by the prisoners on Kessel. 'He will choose the fate of the weak.'"

Though Jacen didn't move, Ben felt a jolt of emotion from him. Nelani must have felt it, too; she gave Jacen a curious look, but he did not acknowledge it, keeping his attention on Dr. Rotham. The scholar seemed to be oblivious to the exchange.

"I can't determine the meaning of the next one in sequence, the poisonous-looking yellow-and-green one. After that comes a very tricky one. The red, yellow, and pale green tassel is actually a representation of a flower arrangement, from the old Alderaanian language of flowers—imagine it as a bouquet in a vase, the red and yellow splotches constituting the petals and the green the stems, and you get a sense of it. Its meaning is 'He will choose how he will be loved.' Actually, instead of 'he' it should be 'I,' but I'm taking the liberty of assuming that the third person is to be used here, as it is everywhere else."

"Speaking of which," Nelani interrupted, "is it definitely 'he,' or could it also be read as 'she' throughout?"

Dr. Rotham shook her head. "It isn't defined in all the tassels, but everywhere it is, it's distinctly 'he.' Where was I? Oh, yes. After that, a very simple one. The gray-and-brown one is from a still-extant Coruscanti subculture of indigents, transients who pride themselves on being jobless, living by theft and begging. They leave messages for others of their kind, symbols on the walls of shops to say, for instance, that a restaurateur is an easy touch. This three-dimensional representation of their language states, 'He will win and break his chains.' "

She continued. Ben, increasingly bored, began to lose focus, taking only distracted note of her translations: " 'He will shed his skin and choose a new skin,' 'He will strengthen himself through sacrifice,' 'He will crawl through his cloak,' 'He will know brotherhood,' 'He will make a pet'—by which I don't mean he will tame some creature, but that he will somehow *fabricate* a pet . . ."

Mostly Ben kept his attention on Jacen, for on one or two other occasions the revelation of a tassel's meaning again caused his emotions to spike to the point where Ben could detect them.

Finally Dr. Rotham's translations reached the end. "This one you already knew. Ryloth, Tahu'ip culture: 'He will strengthen himself through pain.' To be honest, I don't know whether the order of presentation is significant. It could be random, or it could add up to a specific thought. I just have no way of knowing."

Jacen nodded. "That's all very helpful, Doctor. Um, you

skipped one." He stood and reached out to the hologram, his fingertips touching a tan tassel featuring jagged black lines.

"Yes . . . I could not translate that one. Though I've seen the recording method before, the zigzag patterns, the arrays of protruding claws and teeth." Dr. Rotham looked uncertain. "In statuary and figurines from the world of Ziost."

This time it was Nelani who looked startled.

Jacen accepted the information with a simple nod. "It means something like 'He will be drawn from peace into conflict,' or maybe 'His life will be balanced between peace and conflict.' "

The scholar gave him a curious look. "How do you know?"

"Believe it or not, I just feel it. The tassel's meaning is imbued within it in a fashion that only a Force-wielder can read."

"I can't read it," Nelani said.

Jacen shrugged. "Maybe when you've broadened your range of Force-related learning a bit."

"What's Ziost?" Ben asked.

"One of the worlds central to the origins of the Sith," Nelani said, her tone low, as if she wanted to avoid being overheard.

"There's actually a substantial Sith influence to this collection of statements." Jacen gestured at the hologram. "Several of them seem to be paraphrases of portions of the Sith creed. The one about victory and chains, for instance. What we have here is an item fabricated by someone who is at least as familiar with Sith matters as a Jedi historian would be."

"I hope it is only a historian," Dr. Rotham said. "One last thing I can tell you is this: I brought in a beadcrafter to look at these items, and he's certain that they were crafted by different hands. So you're not dealing with a single individual who is expert in all these recording techniques. You're dealing with someone who has collected them, arranged for their assembly, rather than someone who has fabricated them all. Which is a considerable relief to me, because the alternative would be that I have an academic rival I've been unaware of all these decades." She drew a hand over her brow, miming a gesture of relief.

Jacen gave her a smile. "Doctor, your help has been invaluable. And we've asked you to do far too much work in far too short an amount of time. I do appreciate it."

She beamed up at him. "I consider it my chance, so late in life, to offer some thanks to the Jedi for all they've done."

"We'll leave you now. But if anything does occur to you about any of the tassels, any of the translations, don't hesitate to get a message to us." Jacen wrapped the collection of tassels in a cloth and returned it to his belt pouch.

"Good luck with your investigation, Jedi Solo."

Once the Jedi were in the corridor outside Dr. Rotham's quarters and headed toward Nelani's speeder, Jacen asked, "So how was the rest of your day, Ben?"

"Oh, pretty good, I guess." Ben struggled to look, and feel, nonchalant. "I found the shuttle."

Jacen smiled. "Well, that couldn't have been too difficult. You started out at the spaceport."

"Not *your* shuttle."

Jacen frowned. "Whose?"

"The shuttle that escaped Toryaz Station."

Jacen almost stumbled, and Ben suppressed the urge to laugh. Jacen said, "Wait. Are you sure?"

Ben nodded. "The transponder code is a match, and so is the design. It's a *Sentinel*-class lander with the weapon systems stripped out." *Sentinel*-class shuttles, slightly scaled-up and more heavily armored cousins of the *Lambda*-class shuttle that Jacen piloted, were familiar sights along the galactic space routes.

"How did you find it?" Nelani asked. She'd been impressed by Ben's efforts during and after Huarr's spectacular suicide, and sounded impressed again. Ben had to work hard not to preen.

Ben grimaced. This was going to be difficult to explain, to put into words. On the other hand, Nelani *was* a Jedi. "I waited around for a while, trying to figure out what I wanted to do. I guess I wasn't thinking. More like feeling. And I kept noticing when shuttles landed. They kind of drew my attention, even when transports and cargo ships didn't. Which seemed weird at the time."

Nelani nodded. "The Force was guiding you. You were open to it."

"I guess. And then I remembered something my mother says a lot. She says that any detail, no matter now small, could turn out to be important. And I remembered about the shuttle from Toryaz Station. Mom's a spy, you know."

Nelani grinned. "I know."

"So I went through my datapad, all Jacen's notes on details we haven't had time to go through, and I decided to see if the spaceport records showed anything about that shuttle. And there it was, parked half a kilometer from where the Y-wing blew up."

"Who's it registered to?" Jacen asked.

Ben pulled out his datapad and opened it. He'd left all that information on the screen. "A human woman named Brisha Syo. She's from Commenor. She wasn't at the shuttle; she'd just paid for a week's worth of hangar space. She left no contact information. The spaceport authority thought she was staying aboard, but the ship's systems were all shut down. I told Lieutenant Samran. He's got somebody watching it now."

"Very good," Jacen said. "But what if this Brisha Syo sneaks aboard and takes off when Samran's guard is snoozing?"

"Then the transmitter we stuck on the top of the hull will tell us where she goes." Ben shrugged as if the matter were of no consequence.

Jacen laughed. "Good work. And what did you do with the *rest* of your time?"

Ben scowled at him. "Now you're making fun of me."

Jacen nodded. "You're getting so good at what you do, if we don't make fun of you, you'll have a colossal, Lando Calrissian–sized ego."

"That would be fun." Ben modulated his voice to something like the smooth, insinuating tones of the old Solo family friend. He turned toward Nelani. "Hello. I'm Ben Skywalker."

"Oh, that's ghastly," she said.

"And I'm trying to figure out whether I'm more suave or more debonair. Maybe you can help."

"Stop it," she said.

"I'll pour the wine, and you tell me what you like best about me."

"Jacen, now he talks too *much* . . ."

chapter twenty-seven

CORELLIA

Roaring at tremendous speeds along the avenue, tall buildings flashing by to either side so fast that he couldn't register details of their color, much less their design, Han kept his attention focused on the vehicle just ahead of his own. It was a black disc with three fiery apertures, thruster tubes, pointed back at him—the tail end of a Corellian YT-5100 *Shriek*-class bomber just like his own. It galled him that Wedge's bomber was in the lead—it was an unnatural state of affairs, and he planned to correct it as soon as possible.

Laserfire flashed over his cockpit from ahead, and the monitor screen showing data on his shield status flashed red in his peripheral vision, signs that his Shriek had been hit—but there had been no shudder, so the impact had to have been glancing. He saw Wedge's Shriek waver and sideslip just a little, a successful bid to reduce the amount of laserfire converging on him from ahead. That, Han realized, was his key to getting in front.

He saw another series of red flashes from ahead, more concentrated laserfire, and gauged that the thickest stream of fire was moving in toward the Shrieks from the port side. He did not swerve, but hit his thrusters.

Wedge did swerve, sideslipping again to avoid the worst

of the fire, and Han's perfectly timed acceleration brought him alongside Wedge's bomber, then just ahead of it. Han ran into the thickest of the laserfire and his shield monitor flashed alarmingly bright—but he was ahead.

And ahead of him, too close, was the artificial gray mountain of the Terkury Housing Complex, the building he was supposed to fly beneath in less than a second—

He pulled the trigger on his first concussion missile load, knowing that it was too late for the missiles to hit the street and the debris to clear. He thought about breaking off, going skyward—a suicidal tactic, considering all the laser emplacements and pursuing Galactic Alliance vessels that would be able to fire on him, but not as suicidal as plowing into the side of that building—but there was a flash of yellow to his starboard side as Wedge's missiles, already launched, shot ahead and plowed into the correct spot on the avenue. The street was suddenly replaced by an expanding cloud of debris, dust, and flame.

Han dived toward a spot just beneath the center of the cloud. He'd be flying blind for a second or two, but he knew the distances, the ranges, the depths. He waited a fraction of a second, until his gut told him that he had to be beneath the level of the street; then he leveled off and fired his second brace of missiles.

He cleared the first cloud. All around him were duracrete support pillars and the broad expanses of empty subterranean hangars; unlit, these features were presented in shades of blue by the heads-up display on the viewport before him. Then his missiles hit, and the wall directly ahead detonated into a second cloud. He plunged into it and climbed, trusting his instincts and timing—

And there above him was the sky, tinted by the presence of military shields. "Dropping starting load," he said, and hit the buttons that would propel the dozens of targeting droids out of his bomb bay.

There was an odd echo to his words, and he realized that the echo was in Wedge's voice. Wedge had dropped his own ordnance load and announced the fact at the exact moment Han had.

The viewport went black. The Shriek's vibration and sense of motion ceased. The cockpit was lit for a moment only by the glows from the various displays Han hadn't looked at once during the mission; then brighter light from behind him illuminated the space as the simulator's access hatch opened.

Han sighed and used the metal rungs overhead to clamber backward out of the simulator and into a dimly lit corridor. There was another access hatch, identical to his, a few meters to his right, and two more to his left; Wedge Antilles stood beside one of them, dressed, like Han, in the stylish green-and-black flight suit and helmet of a Shriek pilot, and was already closing his hatch.

Wedge's features were entirely obscured by the tinting of his helmet's full-coverage blast visor, but he popped that up to glare at Han. "You don't have to be in front, you know," he said. "The mission doesn't depend on it."

Han rotated his helmet a quarter turn and pulled it up and off. He offered Wedge his most insufferable grin, the one that, from time to time, came closest to driving Leia to violence. "Sure, I do."

Wedge's expression was unrelenting. "Did you notice the part where jockeying for position caused you to miss your missile launch window? Remember that?"

"You covered for me pretty well," Han said. "You show a lot of promise as a pilot. You ought to consider a career in the military."

Despite himself, Wedge grinned briefly. "You need to consider working as a team player." He pulled his own helmet free.

"I'm a team player," Han protested. "As long as the rest of the team stays behind me."

"Your flying tactics alarm me—"

"Ooh, General Antilles is alarmed—"

"Because if you end up as a thin red film on the surface

of Tralus, Leia will haunt me to the end of my days, which might be only one or two if she's mad enough."

Han nodded. "That's actually a good point. I recommend you keep me alive."

"Antilles!" That was a new voice, raised in a shout from the far side of the simulator chamber . . . and the voice was distressingly like Han's. "Where are you?" The voice was moving closer; the speaker was just around the corner.

Wedge's eyes opened wide, and Han knew his own expression matched. That was the voice of Thrackan Sal-Solo, who did not know that Han was part of this mission—or that Han and Leia were even on Corellia.

Han looked frantically back and forth, but the corridor with the Shriek simulators was a dead end.

Wedge mimed putting on his helmet. Han did so and slapped the visor shut. A moment later, Sal-Solo turned the corner to face them. Behind him, trotting to catch up, were four CorSec guards. A moment later, the last elements of the retinue, two YVH combat droids, rounded the corner.

Sal-Solo put his hands on his hips, a gesture of aggressive impatience. "Well?"

Wedge gave him an unconcerned look. "Well, what?"

"How goes the mission training?"

"It goes very well. We just completed the third of three consecutive successful simulations at the anticipated difficulty level. Tomorrow, we'll begin cranking up the difficulty level to unreasonable extremes."

"Good, good. That's what I thought. I was just watching the simulators' visual feeds up in the control room." Sal-Solo looked at Han. "Who's this?"

"Minister of War Thrackan Sal-Solo, allow me to present you my mission partner, Aalos Noorg. Aalos spent most of his career in the Corporate Sector, flying corporate mercenary missions, until the crisis here convinced him to come home. Aalos, take your helmet off."

Han put his hands on his helmet and tried to rotate it in its locking collar, but did not actually exert any strength.

Naturally, it didn't budge. He tried again, and then, miming desperation, he went through the motions of trying to open his helmet visor. It, too, remained obstinately closed.

"Prototype helmets," Wedge said. "Obviously they need to work some of the bugs out of the system."

"Obviously," Sal-Solo echoed.

Han turned and banged his helmet several times against the side of the simulator, then began again. Still the helmet and visor remained in place.

"Never mind, never mind." Sal-Solo stepped forward and extended his hand. "It's good to meet a patriot."

Han shook his hand. Speaking in a low voice and mumbling so his words would not emerge distinctly, he said, "I want to thank the powers that be that my helmet is stuck, because it keeps your stink out of my nostrils."

Sal-Solo shot Wedge a confused glance. "What did he say?"

"He wants to thank you and his luck, because he never dreamed he'd land this assignment."

"Ah. You're welcome."

Han added, "And I'd like to chain you to a bantha and drag you across fifty kilometers of dart flowers and meat-eating plants until you're just a stain."

Wedge cleared his throat. "Aalos, try not to be so effusive with your praise. The Chief of State will think you're trying to flatter him."

"What he says doesn't matter." Sal-Solo clapped Han on the shoulder. "What matters is a successful mission. Keep up the good work." He turned and strode away as quickly as he'd come, his escort hurrying to keep up.

When a distant *whoosh* and the cessation of footsteps signaled that Sal-Solo and his entourage had left the chamber, Han pulled his helmet off again.

"That," Wedge said, "was close."

"Too close."

"To celebrate our narrow escape, let's get a drink."

"Two drinks."

LORRD CITY, LORRD

Ben was awakened by someone shaking his foot. Resentful, he opened one eye to see Jacen standing at the end of his cot. "Time to get up," Jacen said.

"M'wake."

"Get dressed, get your gear."

Ben managed to get his other eye open. He sat up. "Did Doctor Rotham translate more tassels?" he asked.

"No. We have another situation where they've asked for Jedi help."

"Oh." Ben concentrated on getting his brain working correctly. "I hope I don't blow up this time."

"I'm going to blow up again, aren't I?" Ben said.

Jacen nodded absently. "Probably."

They stood just outside the edges of the milling, uncertain crowd at the perimeter of a broad plaza. The duracrete of the plaza surface was inlaid with river-smoothed pebbles, making the surface aesthetically pleasing and artificially natural, and even out at this distance it was darkened by water.

At the far side of the plaza, just in front of the Lorrd Academy for Aquatic Studies, was a huge transparisteel aquarium. It had been preciously designed to look exactly like the sort of aquarium found in the living chamber of any set of quarters, or in the bedroom of any curious child, but it was the size of a three-story private residence; a Quarren or Mon Calamari family could have been happy there, if its members had an exhibitionist streak. Stairs and a small open-air lift were affixed to the narrower south wall, and stretched across its top was a mighty durasteel beam supporting the weight of a housing for the water-conditioning and -monitoring equipment.

The water had been drained from the giant container— hence the liquid darkening the plaza for a considerable distance around it. At the bottom of the aquarium, inside, was the skyline of downtown Lorrd City, including the most prominent university's administration building, styled as a white tower, and the broad, welcoming student assembly building. They were reproduced in miniature and in gaudier colors than the original buildings enjoyed. Huddled among these buildings, stumbling across the colored stones, gravel, and dying aquatic life-forms that littered the aquarium bottom, were representatives of many species— Ben saw humans, Bothans, Mon Calamari, and Verpines among them. All of them paid close, fearful attention to the being that now stood at the aquarium's southeast corner.

He was a human, huge, two meters tall and at least 150 kilos, of which a significant portion was muscle. He had dark hair, mustache, and beard, cut close but styled rakishly, as if he viewed himself as a space pirate from a children's holoseries. He wore severe black garments. In his left hand was a blaster pistol and in his right, some smaller object the Jedi could not make out.

He also wore a human man. Strapped to his back by a series of bands of binder tape was a middle-aged, dark-skinned man of average height. He was strapped to the larger man back-to-back, so that they faced in opposite directions.

"This man," Nelani said, "is obviously crazy."

According to witnesses, a few hours earlier the aquarium had been full of water and of aquatic life-forms going about their usual business of idly swimming or eating one another. Then a crew of workers or thugs had arrived, led by the big man. While some of them opened emergency vents on the aquarium, spilling its water out across the plaza, others had rounded up visitors to the museum portion of the academy, led them here, and forced them to climb the stairs and jump down into the water before too much of it was drained. There they had bobbed, frightened and unhappy, while the thugs had strapped one last hostage to the leader's back, then fled. Once the Lorrd Se curity Forces had begun arriving, the captor had leapt in and bobbed along with the others until the water had reached floor level in the aquarium.

"What do we know about *this* one?" Nelani asked.

Lieutenant Samran, a couple of meters away, directing the activities of his security officers via comlink, glanced at her and shook his head. "We don't know who he is. When you talk to him, do us the favor of finding that out . . . We do know that he gave his comlink frequency to one of our officers." He held out a little scrap of flimsi, which Ben took. Ben began tuning his comlink to the frequency written there. Samran continued, "Also that he claims there are explosives packed in between his back and his hostage's. The thing in his right hand is supposed to be a triggering device. Oh, and he wants to talk to Lorrd's pet Jedi." He gave Nelani an apologetic look. "His words, my lady, not mine."

"Of course."

"Have you had any luck tracking down his men?" Jacen asked.

Samran shook his head. "They were all garbed in simple dark clothes and stretchcloth masks. When they fled, they could have mingled with crowds in the streets or in any of several dozen public buildings. They could be anywhere." He gestured to the near edge of the crowd.

"I think," Jacen told Nelani, "that this time I will exercise my prerogatives of seniority, and speak to the man first."

"Just remember that this time you can't blow him up without taking an innocent life," she said.

"Let's go." Jacen led the other Jedi on the long walk across the empty plaza. As they walked, Ben took Jacen's comlink and adjusted it, too, to the kidnapper's frequency.

They were only twenty meters from the imposing transparisteel wall of the aquarium when they saw the captor's lips move. Jacen's and Ben's comlinks carried his words: "Hello, Jedi."

Jacen stopped, and the other two drew to a halt behind him. "I would say *Good morning*," Jacen said, "except that you've kept it from being a good morning for several people. Myself included; I was looking forward to sleeping late."

The captor swung around to look at his captives. He did so apparently without even noticing the weight of the man strapped to his back. The Jedi had a glimpse of this captive, a balding man with fear on his face, before the captor swung back to look at them. "They were bored," the captor said. "Else why would they be here? Now they're not bored. They'll be able to talk about this day for the rest of their lives. I'm doing them a favor, allowing them to tan themselves in the glare of my transitory importance."

"Literary critic," Nelani said.

The captor's eyebrows shot up. "Actually, my education *was* in literary issues—literary syncretization, the process by which the popular story cycles of different worlds merge, their archetypal characters becoming unified, as the individual worlds enter the galactic community. So literary criticism is part of my profession, yes."

"You look more like a professional wrestler," Ben said.

The captor looked delighted. "I probably should have been. I would have derived more pleasure from my life."

"What's your name?" Jacen asked.

"I am Doctor Movac Arisster. Of Lorrd City, tenured with the University of Pangalactic Cultural Studies."

"I'm Jacen. This is Nelani, and this is Ben. You indicated that you wanted to speak with Jedi. Was this because someone suggested it to you?"

"Yes." Arisster seemed unconcerned that Jacen had divined his secret. "The most remarkable part was who it was. Have you ever heard of Aayla Secura?"

Jacen nodded; he'd run across the name on several occasions—in his early studies at the Jedi Academy, and subsequently in his travels to worlds he had visited.

But apparently Ben and Nelani were unfamiliar with it. Arisster turned more toward them. "She was a Jedi Master at the end of the Old Republic. Alleged to have been shot down by clone troopers like so many of your order at that time. A blue Twi'lek, and surviving holos of her show her to be beautiful of face and form. Well, in her career, she benefited the people of many worlds, and entered the folk-loric cycles of several primitive cultures, where she often was merged with local historical figures or goddess-characters." Arisster lost focus for a moment, staring into the distance. "Even today, educated immigrants from those cultures will write fictive cycles about her, some of them amazingly prurient."

He returned his attention to the Jedi. "Tell me, Jacen, do people do the same about you? Write stories about you and pair you off with unlikely romantic partners?"

Jacen ignored the question. "Aayla Secura told you to do this?"

"No." Arisster shook his head so vehemently that it rocked the body of the man strapped to him. "I chose to do this. Then Aayla Secura—or, rather, someone in her form—came to me and suggested that I bring the Jedi in to talk."

Jacen gave him a puzzled frown. "For what purpose?"

"To enter your story cycle, of course. I'm a nobody, and I'm dying. In six months, incurable cancers of the lungs and other organs, probably caused by a radiation leak I experienced on a trip many years ago, will kill me. No one will ever have heard of me. Except now I'll have a little trace of literary immortality as a man, a normal human man with no combat skills or Force abilities, who beat a Jedi."

Arisster leaned in closer to the transparisteel, staring intently at Jacen. "I want to thank you for being here. I'm sure that Nelani is a competent and loyal Jedi Knight, but she's not *famous*. Jacen Solo's cycle will be a much better one to be affixed to."

"Beat me, how?"

"By denying you a happy ending." Arisster went from merry to almost apologetic. "This apparatus in my right hand is the trigger for the bomb strapped to my back. By which I do not mean Haxan, here, but an actual explosive layered between our bodies. If I release the trigger, it blows up. And if you should be considering using your Jedi powers to grip my hand, well, too *much* pressure and it blows up. Other things will set it off. Keywords I might speak. Too long a silence between keywords I'm supposed to speak. A key press on a datapad, or a laser relay from allies who are watching these events."

"Being famous won't do you any good if you're dead," Ben said.

"True. But it's something I always wanted, and I'll die knowing I've achieved it. I'll talk with you until you're convinced that I can't be stopped. You'll use Jedi mind tricks, to which I already know I'm immune, or other techniques, which won't work. Then I'll throw myself into the midst of this crowd of wet, frightened, smelling-of-fish tourists, and detonate myself."

"That's selfish," Nelani said. "Destructively, cruelly selfish."

Arisster snorted, amused. "All decisions are selfish. Your becoming a Jedi? Probably based on your desire to 'improve the galaxy,' which is just another way of saying 'imposing your view of what's good upon people who don't agree with you.' "

"What if I promised to make you famous?" Jacen said. "If I gave you my word. I'd take you along with me as a sidekick and put you in dangerous situation after dangerous situation. Believe me, you wouldn't last six months in that sort of circumstance, and you might actually do some good before you died."

Arisster blinked at him, obviously taken aback. "I hadn't considered that. But . . . no."

"Why not?"

"Well, you might be lying. Jedi lie. Also, the disease might kill me early, before I saw any action. And third, as a sidekick, I'd merely be a footnote, and I could be forgotten trivially. This way, I'll be firmly attached to any account of your career."

"I see." Jacen fell silent, pondering.

Ben could feel a sorrow, a solemnity growing within Jacen. His mentor was not doing anything to conceal it, and it flowed from him through the Force. It made Ben jittery, and he crossed his arms as if against a cold wind.

"Oh, please." Arisster stared a rebuke at Jacen. "You can't have given up already. You haven't tried any tricks, unless that sidekick offer was a trick, and you haven't begged."

"I haven't given up," Jacen said. There was a faint sadness in his voice. "Can I speak to your captive, please?"

"Of course." Obligingly, Arisster swung around, whirling the other man to face the Jedi. The man was pale and looked as though he was on the verge of throwing up.

"Your name is Haxan?" Jacen asked.

"Yes, Serom Haxan."

"I'm very sorry, Serom." Jacen began backing away from the aquarium.

Ben and Nelani backed up, too, keeping pace with Jacen. "What are you doing?" Nelani asked.

"What I have to."

They'd taken half a dozen steps before Arisster noticed. Arisster swung around to face them. "What are you doing?" he asked.

"Getting to what I hope is a safe distance," Jacen said.

Arisster stood there, transfixed, for a long moment, long enough for the Jedi to take another half a dozen steps backward. Then he turned as if to charge toward the other captives.

Jacen reached out with his open hand and squeezed it into a fist.

Arisster and Haxan disappeared, engulfed in a misshapen ball of fire.

Fire and smoke filled the aquarium, and the crack of the explosion rolled across the plaza—but, confined as it was by the transparisteel walls of the aquarium, it hurt Ben's ears far less than the detonation at the spaceport had.

And the transparisteel *held*. The near wall buckled outward slightly under the force of the explosion, but the other three merely distorted for a moment before returning to their proper shapes, and most of the force of the explosion was channeled upward.

Immediately the Jedi charged forward again, up to the transparent wall, and tried to peer through the smoke obscuring the tank's contents. But the smoke was already thinning, rising, and they could see men and women beginning to emerge from behind the scorched ruins of the reproduction of Lorrd's downtown. None of them seemed badly injured—Ben saw smoke on faces, some blood from gravel shrapnel.

"Emergency crews!" Nelani shouted, waving toward Samran and his agents. "Get up here!"

The emergency crews used a portable winch to lower medics into the tank and begin extracting Arisster's hostages from its floor. None ventured near the gruesome blood slick that represented the largest portion of what was left of Arrister and Haxan.

Meanwhile, meters away, Ben listened to Nelani and Jacen argue again.

"Are you insane?" Nelani asked. "We didn't explore a single option other than your *I'll-make-you-my-sidekick* offer."

"There were no options," Jacen said. "He was right. He had won. The only thing we could do was limit the scope of his victory. That meant limiting him to one life instead of several."

"You don't know. We didn't try—"

"You could feel his determination, his strength." Jacen's tone chided her. "He had decided to die today. When someone decides to die, it's hard to dissuade him."

"Haxan hadn't decided to die."

"True. But he was going to, no matter what we did."

"No—"

"What was the blaster pistol for, Nelani?"

That brought her up short. "What?"

"The blaster pistol he held. What was it for?"

"To compel obedience?"

Jacen shook his head. "He had his bomb for that. The bomb was all he needed, and he knew it. So what was the blaster for?"

"What do *you* think it was for?"

"To shoot hostages, one by one, as the afternoon wore on. To shoot them, and to mock us for our helplessness."

She considered that. "Maybe."

"Definitely. And with the first one he shot, our loss, our failure, would have been already equal to the one we eventually did face—one innocent life. With two shot, we'd have been worse off than we are now. And so on."

She stared at him for a long moment, and Ben could see in her expression a tragic mask of disappointment, disillusionment. "Jacen, you have a good argument for everything you do. But my gut tells me that you're doing wrong."

"Your gut, or the Force?"

"My gut."

"What does the Force tell you?"

"Nothing. The Force tells me nothing about what just happened."

"Then it wasn't the wrong choice." Jacen turned away to head back to the Jedi speeder.

chapter twenty-eight

With the meaning of the tassels offering the Jedi clues but no clear path to follow, and with the Toryaz Station shuttle and the mystery of the Jedi-related terrorist encounters lingering in Lorrd City, Jacen put off his departure from Lorrd.

And it was only a day later that the mystery encounters continued.

First, in the morning, the Lorrd Security Forces received an anonymous communication that the kidnapped daughter of a prominent businesswoman was being held in steam tunnels beneath the School of Conceptual Design. The security operatives, after scanning plans of the tunnels, found no access that would give them an approach to the child's prison chamber without getting the girl killed. So the Jedi were called.

Examining the same plans, Jacen noted that the diameter of one of the steam pipes, while insufficient for a full-grown man or woman to slither through, would provide a tight access for an average-sized adolescent. So the security forces had the steam cut off to that pipe, and after it cooled, Ben crawled through, cutting his way out of the pipe at an appropriate point, dropping into the kidnapped girl's chamber, and defending it against all comers for the three minutes it then took for Jacen, Nelani, and the security forces to storm and secure the hideout.

The kidnapping's mastermind, a frustrated radical who wanted to replace the Lorrd planetary government with something ruled by logical, pitiless legal-analyst droids, died during the attack, but his surviving allies said that the girl had appeared to him in his dreams and recommended the kidnapping in the first place.

Later that day, a man dressed in Jedi-style robes and carrying a nonfunctional, pre-Clone-Wars–era lightsaber he'd stolen from a museum, climbed to the summit of the main university's administration building and perched there, threatening to leap to his death unless he was admitted to the Jedi order. Jacen, Nelani, and Ben went to deal with the situation. Jacen climbed to the summit to talk to the man while the other two remained at ground level.

As it turned out, the desperate Jedi applicant had no Force sensitivity whatsoever, and could not bring himself to believe that Force sensitivity could not be taught. Mindful of Nelani's desire that he talk things out more with the desperate people who provoked such encounters, Jacen argued politely but fruitlessly with the man for over an hour.

"Tell me," the man finally said, "how to do your Jedi tricks—*one* Jedi trick—or I'll step off this roof."

"I'm tired of talking, and I don't have the energy to lie convincingly right now," Jacen said. "Go ahead and jump."

The man did.

Nelani, assisted by Ben, caught him, slowing his descent with the Force, and the worst he sustained from his twenty-story plummet was a broken ankle. Security agents bundled him off for medical evaluation, and still he shouted that the Jedi had betrayed him.

But Nelani hugged Jacen, when he reached ground level again, for doing his best to argue the man out of a bad decision.

As they stood there, security agents keeping the crowd and the press at bay, a comlink beeped. Jacen and Nelani sighed and reached for their respective communications devices . . . but it was Ben's that had sounded. He pulled it out of his pouch. "Ben Skywalker here . . . Really? Did she put up a fight? All right, we'll be there in half an hour or so." He sought Jacen's face for confirmation, got a nod, and concluded, "Out."

"You know," Jacen said, "the more like a Jedi Knight you act, the more likely your father is to send you off to put down a planetary insurrection or delve into the mystery of a Sith Holocron."

Ben flushed. "This was stuff I'd been communicating with him about."

"Him?"

"Lieutenant Samran. That woman showed up. Brisha Syo."

"The shuttle pilot?"

"Yeah. She's in custody."

"Let's go." Jacen led the dash for the speeder.

The human woman sitting alone in the security interrogation room did not look like a criminal, at least on the surface. Clad in a purple jumpsuit that suggested both money and a preference for simplicity, she was about the same age as Ben's parents, at the height of vigorous middle age. She was lean, with well-defined muscles suggesting an active life, and had dark hair, slightly curled, cut short in an easy-to-maintain hairdo.

Her features were fine, and she was attractive. Her beauty was very approachable; she looked like the sort of woman who had been a greeter in a shop or hotel in her youth, and still carried the mannerisms of that profession. Alone in the interrogation room, she did not look bored, but seemed to be impatiently awaiting the moment she could begin interacting with others again.

The chamber she waited in featured a one-way reflective panel that showed her a mirrored surface, while the Jedi, on the other side, could look through it like a viewport. Ben had the unsettling feeling that she was restraining herself from looking at the Jedi—that any moment she would look up and lock eyes with one of them, despite the physical impossibility of her seeing them. Ben knew better than to assume that her good looks and apparent friendliness meant she was a good person. His upbringing had grounded him in principles of both logic and the Force, and both disciplines knew that an attractive appearance could conceal malevolence. Still, he detected none in her.

"Perhaps she just isn't feeling wicked right now," Jacen said.

Ben looked up at him. "Huh?"

"Your thoughts are very much at the surface. Still, they're good thoughts. You're keeping sharp." He shrugged. "Let's go in."

A Lorrd Security guard led them into the interrogation chamber. Jacen waited until the guard had exited, then sat and gestured for Nelani and Ben to do likewise. They took the chairs on the opposite side of the table from the woman.

"Hello," she said, her voice warm. "Jedi Solo, Jedi Dinn, young Skywalker."

"You know us," Jacen said.

"Of course. I've been meddling in your business for some time."

"You admit it."

"I admit to that, yes."

"You admit to inciting people to acts of violence and terrorism."

"Certainly not."

"Then you're denying that you had anything to do with the actions of Ordith Huarr, Movac Arisster, the Lorrd Logistician Liberation League, and . . ." Jacen frowned, trying to remember.

"Borth Pazz, Jedi candidate," Ben said.

"No, I admit that. Certainly."

Jacen gave her an exasperated look. "Your confession and your denial are mutually exclusive."

The woman's mood began to alter from cheerful to irritated. "Of course they aren't. Involvement is not the same as guilt. Who taught you to think, boy? Certainly not your mother. She's brighter than that."

"Leave my mother out of this." Then he gave in to curiosity. "You know her?"

"We've met."

"So what's your story? A story that magically involves you in all the tragedies I've mentioned, yet leaves you blameless."

"I'm a Force-sensitive."

"I'm shocked."

Finally the woman's demeanor became chilly, hostile. "Sarcasm is inappropriate. That's bad manners. If you'd like me to continue, you will apologize for your rudeness."

"You're out of your mind."

"Then you can go to hell." She fell silent.

Jacen let the silence grow between them. Finally he said, "I'll refrain from interrupting for purposes of scoring conversational points."

"Good for you." She fell silent again and waited.

Jacen sighed. "I apologize for my manner. Please continue."

"I'm a Force-sensitive, and in my dreams I hear people planning evil deeds. 'I will kill that woman.' 'I will make them understand, and if they don't, I'll wipe them all out.' But they're *dreams*. I know they're grounded in reality, but when I awaken, not all the details are available to me. So in my dreams, I've been telling them, 'Bring in the Jedi. Your victory will be greater if you defeat the Jedi. You'll never be famous if you can't outwit the Jedi.' That sort of thing."

Ben watched as Jacen fell silent, considering the woman's words for a long moment. Ben knew that each Jedi experienced the Force, including the possible future events the Force had to show them, in different ways; he supposed that someone could experience them as dreams.

"What was your involvement with the events at Toryaz Station?" Jacen asked.

"I was there to observe you. I used my arts to stay out of the sight of the Jedi and the station's security forces, and I spied on you. Then, when everything went wrong, I decided that I needed to get out of the way until that mess was settled for the time being. I left something to lead you to me—"

"The tassels."

"Yes, of course."

"You were pretty confident that they would lead me to you."

She nodded. "I knew one would speak to you and you alone. And from my own researches I already knew that this collection of tassels would inevitably point to Dr. Rotham on Lorrd for decipherment; any other so-called experts in the field would eventually refer you to her. So you'd be here, sooner or later."

"You killed the security captain, Tawaler."

She shook her head. "I saw him killed, from a distance. A hooded figure spaced him through an air lock. Knowing that the Jedi investigations would lead to that air lock, I chose to leave the tassels there. Then I walked out of the Narsacc Habitat before security measures closed off the corridor to the main station."

"And you coincidentally ended up in the same shuttle by which the soldiers arrived at the station."

"No coincidence. I used my own resources to track it down. Not tricky at all, since I assumed it would go to the Corellia system; and there it was, hangared at the main Coronet City spaceport. I confronted its pilot, but he attacked me rather than answer questions, and I was forced to kill him. Which left me in possession of the shuttle. When I ran its identification numbers, I found that it had been stolen on Commenor a few months ago, and the title had been vested in its insurers after they'd paid off its value to the company it had been stolen from. I bought it from them, clean and legal."

"How did you kill the pilot?" Jacen asked.

"Bare hands. And I buried him. No sense in involving the authorities on Corellia . . . when the authorities on Corellia were the ones who sent those killers to wreck the Toryaz Station meeting in the first place."

"You're assuming."

"I'm concluding, based on evidence."

"And then you came here, because you knew that the tassels would lead the Jedi who found them here to Lorrd."

She shook her head. "Not *the Jedi who found them*. You."

"You almost ended up with my sister running down their origin."

"I don't think so. In all the galaxy, only you, Jacen Solo, would be sufficiently intrigued to follow them all the way here and beyond."

"Why me?"

"Because only you could read and understand one of the tassels. Only you could detect its significance. And so you'd demand to be the one who investigated it."

Ben studied Jacen's face. His mentor gave nothing away with his expression. But Ben remembered that there was one tassel Jacen had been able to translate when even Dr. Rotham hadn't—the one from the Sith world. He felt a little chill of unease.

"All right," Jacen said, "let's put all this into some sort of context. Let's have your story from the start."

"From the start? From when I was a little girl?"

"Sure."

"No, not here. I'll tell you at my home."

"On Commenor?"

"No; my true home, on a planetoid in a star system close to Bimmiel. Not far from here, as galactic distances go. We could take your shuttle or mine."

"No, thanks."

"Then you're not getting any more answers."

"And you'll rot in custody here for quite a while."

Brisha Syo offered him a cool smile. "I don't think so. What charge would I be held on? The best you could do would be suspicion of complicity in the Toryaz Station incident. There's enough evidence there to begin assembling a case . . . but not enough to deny me my freedom while the machinery of the justice system grinds along. I'll spend a day in jail, then be freed, ordered to stay on Lorrd while things are investigated. Having the run of this lovely educational planet is not exactly what I call rotting. And in the meantime, you get no more information."

"I could just decide that you're guilty of conspiracy to commit murder, and then kill you."

The woman's smile did not falter. "No, you couldn't."

"What makes you think that?"

"First, the Force is not telling you that I'm guilty. I know this because I'm not. I doubt you'd murder when not even the Force is defining me as evil, or a threat. Second, to kill me you'd first have to kill Nelani here. Wouldn't you?"

Jacen and Nelani exchanged a look. Jacen's face was as free of emotion as it had been for most of the interview. Nelani's expression, hard to read, had elements of determination and sadness to it. Ben could feel her emotions, though, naked and unconcealed—a hope that Jacen would make "the right choice," a grim determination to face him if he did not, an underlying attraction to Jacen that was increasingly sad.

Ben backed away from that surge of feelings. They were too complicated, too intermixed. They unsettled him.

Jacen stood. "Let's talk outside," he told Nelani and Ben, and left. They followed.

Once in the corridor, he said, "I'm going to visit her home."

Nelani shook her head, not taking her eyes from Jacen's. "Why?"

"I have to know how she spoke to me through the tassel," he said. "Does she know something about me I don't myself know? Or is it a method she could use on other Jedi, perhaps to lure them into traps? I can't just ignore this, or assume that imprisoning her would eliminate the risk she may represent."

"But it's a trap," Ben protested.

Jacen gave him a dismissive look. "A trap to do what?"

"Well . . . kill you, I guess."

"Ben, she was able to lure me to several different scenes of violence over the last few days, and she knows a lot about

Jedi and the Force. If she were going to kill me, wouldn't one of those situations have been enough? Pack enough explosives into the aquarium and we'd all be dead. Find a sniper combat droid to shoot me from half a kilometer—I wouldn't feel any emotional intent; there's a good chance such a plan would succeed. Why lure me out to some planetoid?"

"I don't know." Something about Jacen's assuredness suddenly annoyed Ben. "And neither do you. Just because you can't figure out what she's up to, doesn't mean it isn't bad."

"Ben's right," Nelani said. "The woman's story is too weird and complicated, so there have to be important lies, or at least omissions, in it. Going to where she's the master of the environment is just a bad idea."

"Nevertheless, I'm doing just that."

Nelani looked even unhappier. "Then I'm going with you."

Jacen shook his head. "That's outside your jurisdiction."

"I don't have a jurisdiction. I'm just assigned to live on Lorrd. It's fine for me to investigate something as near as Bimmiel. Especially when it involves the safety of another Jedi, and a mystery that involves the Sith world of Ziost. Do you think Master Skywalker would object to my going? I suspect he'd insist on it."

"All right." Jacen shrugged. "I just think it's a bad idea for you to go."

"Is that the Force talking to you, or your gut?"

Finally, he smiled. "My gut."

CORELLIAN SYSTEM, ABOVE TRALUS

Leia, led to the bridge of *Dodonna,* marveled as she always did at the extravagant open spaces of a Star Destroyer–style command area. Though the *Galactic* class battle carriers had been designed after the decline of the Empire—after the fall of the New Republic, in fact—they preserved the basic design of the Imperial-era Star Destroyer bridges, with the main walkway stretching from the main entrance to the gigantic forward viewports, with the officer and data stations on a lower level to the right and left of the elevated walkway.

Admiral Tarla Limpan, flanked by the ubiquitous aides and advisers any top-ranking naval officer warranted, stepped forward energetically as Leia moved onto the bridge walkway. A female of the Duros species, she had pale gray-green skin and facial features that looked like a cartoonish simplification of a human's—large red eyes without visible iris or pupil, an almost featureless mouth, and a broad empty space where a nose should have been between them. She smiled and extended her long arms to seize Leia's hand between her own, shaking it enthusiastically.

"Madame Organa Solo," she said. "How should I address you? Princess, Senator, Head of State? It must wear you down, carrying around so many titles and honors."

Leia smiled, disarmed by the admiral's informal manner and energy. "Well, all those titles should begin with *former*. Now I'm just a Jedi Knight and sometimes diplomatic consultant. Call me Leia."

"I am Tarla. Except for those rare moments when I must be Admiral. I was informed you were in the Corellian system, keeping lines of communication open with the new Prime Minister. And a good thing it is." She belatedly released Leia's hand. "To what do I owe the pleasure of this meeting? And I must add a certain sadness at seeing you arrive alone, by shuttle; someday you might grace me by introducing me to your husband and his famous transport?"

"Of course. But Han, at the moment, is out visiting old smuggler haunts, trying to get a sense of black-market traffic and what it means to the current crisis." That was a blatant lie, but one that anyone from either side would find difficult to disprove—no one knew which contacts Han might or might not be consulting, and never would, as insular and secretive as the informal society of smugglers tended to be. "I'm here just to visit, in whatever minutes would be at your convenience, and perhaps to get a tour of your vessel. I haven't seen one of the new battle carriers up close."

It was another lie. She was here in the hope that by being in the right place at the right time she might, however slightly, be able to improve the chances that her husband would survive the next few hours.

"I shall be glad to oblige. Allow me to introduce you to my aide. I will volunteer him for the tour, and then you and I can chat . . ."

CORONET, CORELLIA

"Circuit trace routes?" The female voice sounded equally strong in both of Han's ears, and was pure, true of tone. Han shook his head. It must be nice to own a vehicle where every component was brand new and flawless, like the YT-5100 *Shriek*-class bomber whose cockpit he occupied.

On the other hand, something that new and shining lacked spirit. *Millennium Falcon* had spirit in abundance, memories ground into every surface. By comparison, this Shriek was a . . . machine.

"Circuit trace routes?" the voice said again.

Its persistence jolted Han out of his reverie. He scanned the control boards ahead of him. "Ninety-nine point seven three two," he said.

"Energy output?"

"One hundred two point three percent of class standard, ninety-four point eight percent of record, ninety-nine point nine percent of individual standard." Checklists. How long had it been since he'd had to do a checklist for a military authority?

"Droid tactical assist?"

"Three artificial intelligence nodes functioning optimally, but they're all speaking Dosh."

"You're joking."

Han winced. "Sorry. I thought I was talking to a droid."

"I get that a lot. Atmospheric pressure?"

"Corellia sea-level standard one point zero zero zero

three, and zero variance from the pressure reading when we started the checklist."

"Complete. You are ready to launch. Reenabling comm lines to Panther One."

There was the faintest of clicks, and then Han heard Wedge's voice: "I hear you're finally ready to join the operation."

"Blasted checklists take forever. In a real vehicle, you can *feel* what's right and what's wrong."

"Don't feel guilty. You gave me time for a nap."

"I suspect you needed it."

"Ready to launch?"

"Ready." In truth, Han didn't feel entirely ready. He was, at last, beginning to question his role in this operation. Leia had questioned it days ago, become resigned to it, supported Han in his decision ever since. Now her doubts had finally wandered into his brain—was it the best idea for him to join this mission, having to train for it in secrecy?

On the other hand, when had he ever decided against something just because it was a bad idea? Not in forty years or so, and seldom before then. Doing things even though they were bad ideas had gotten him a decades-long friendship with a noble Wookiee, had landed him a wife no other woman in the galaxy could compare to . . .

. . . had gotten him beat up a lot . . .

"Launch," Wedge said.

Han kicked the thrusters and put the Shriek into as steep an ascent as possible, going to a true vertical climb within two seconds. Through his forward viewport, the blue skies of Corellia gave way within a startlingly brief time to black space decorated with untwinkling stars.

He glanced at his sensor board. Wedge's Shriek was just alongside. It was impossible to say which of them was ahead—at an altitude of four hundred kilometers above the ground, measuring the difference of one meter or less was slightly problematic.

As gravity became microgravity, Han called up the first

leg of his trip and sent that course to his nav computer. Not waiting for Wedge's confirmation, he ran through the Shriek's pre-hyperspace checklist and, as soon as he was far enough from Corellia, launched.

Wedge's Shriek dropped into hyperspace at the same moment.

Han twisted his mouth into a disapproving grimace. Wedge was *so* competitive. This mission was going to be complicated by Wedge's trying to stay out in front, Wedge trying to be the one to shoot straightest, Wedge trying to plot the most efficient route.

Well, Han would just have to show him who was best.

chapter twenty-nine

STAR SYSTEM MZX32905, NEAR BIMMIEL

On the viewscreen at maximum magnification, Brisha's home was a hemispherical, light gray bump, a blemish on an irregular dark gray surface. When Jacen stepped the viewscreen down to a medium magnification, he could see the entirety of the asteroid as a dark shadow in the midst of a sea of stars, and, beyond it, the tiny, dirty-orange glow of this star system's sun, not far from the Bimmiel system, whose fifth planet was notorious for its slashrat population and for being the site of an early Yuuzhan Vong surveying expedition.

Nelani, hovering over Jacen's shoulder, stared at Brisha's asteroid and said, "Lovely." She turned back to Brisha, who lounged in the seat behind the copilot's position; Ben was copilot on this flight. "I can imagine you enjoying day after day here, sitting by the shores of the lake, watching the glorious sunrises and sunsets . . ."

Brisha's face was reflected in the transparisteel of the forward viewport, and Jacen saw her offer Nelani a smile that was just one step short of condescending. "It's private," she said. "I like privacy."

Jacen ignored them, and ignored the sensor readouts before him. Instead, he concentrated on sensing the Force.

On that planetoid, there was something active within the Force, something strong and vibrant . . . but not alive. Jacen had once had a sense of something like that when, in a restful hour on a visit to a dead coral bed, he'd tried to sense it in the Force and had succeeded. The bed had held dim feelings, like faint, blurry memories, of the accretion of lives that had made it. What was before him now was stronger, more complicated, with more personality . . . and there was a lot of dark side energy in its vigor.

"It's a big iron asteroid," Ben announced. "It's got a little gravity, but not enough for an atmosphere. We're going to be floating around a lot."

Brisha shook her head. "The habitat has artificial gravity. The generators will start up once your shuttle is docked."

"Aww." Ben's was a noise of exasperation. Jacen grinned. He imagined that the boy had been looking forward to a low-gravity environment.

The docking bay was large enough to hold four shuttles, or the *Millennium Falcon* and one or two smaller craft. Entry to it was at the base of the ten-story-high habitat. Inside, the bay was lofty, the outside wall curved, the inner walls angled, making a near-trapezoid shape. The walls were riveted metal painted a soothing sky blue, and everything was remarkably clean.

As Jacen's shuttle settled into place in the berth nearest the doors into the habitat proper, the big bay doors slid into place laterally behind them. Jacen felt himself settle deeper into his seat as the habitat's artificial gravity dialed up. Without being asked, Ben dialed the shuttle's own gravity down correspondingly, an exercise, and did a fair job of keeping the gravity close to Coruscant standard. Jacen gave him an approving nod.

But Jacen's mind was elsewhere, part of him still seeking the source of the Force energy he felt.

He saw Brisha smile at him in the viewport reflection. "All the answers you're looking for are inside," she said.

Jacen nodded. "Which is not the same as saying every-thing we *want* is inside . . . or that we're safe inside."

"Correct," Brisha said. She rose.

A flexible air lock corridor attached itself to their exterior hatch. Inside, the air was cold, but little eddies of warmth moved through it, evidence of the habitat's heaters begin-ning their business.

The hallway, off-white and featureless on the inside, led them to a cross-corridor in the same sky blue as the bay in-terior. Jacen suspected from the corridor's curvature that it was a complete circle around the habitat, providing access to the chambers up against the exterior wall.

Ben looked around, blinking. "It's really clean. I thought this was a mining station."

Brisha shook her head. "No, it was the administration habitat for the mining company. The administrators and their families lived here, as did the families of several of the more important company officers. And when representa-tives of the owning company came to visit, there were big chambers where they could have lavish dinners and enter-tainments. This place was more like a hotel than a mining camp."

"In terms of design, it's like an early-model Sienar Mo-bile Command Post," Jacen said, "but older. Maybe cen-turies older." At Brisha's slight nod, he continued, "It would have been assembled in space, near where it was to be set up originally. Tugs would have placed it on founda-tion columns built at its landing zone. But it was a valuable piece of equipment. When the operation was done, its foundation clamps would have released, and it would have been towed off to its next station. Not left here."

Brisha gave him an encouraging smile, then turned and led the way along the corridor. "Very true. No, the last ad-ministrator here arranged for the habitat to be left behind when the mining operation left this asteroid field. To be left behind—and forgotten." At the first side corridor, she turned left, toward the habitat's center, and the others followed. The blue walls continued, interrupted by doors suitable to private chambers or small offices. The doors were curved at the top, an antiquated design element.

Jacen quickened his pace to catch up to Brisha. "That's a lot of arranging. This would have been lot of money for a company just to forget about."

"Yes, it is." Brisha looked agreeable. "But the administrator who arranged it was capable of coming up with the bribes and persuading people to look away. He was, after all, a Sith."

Brisha brushed off further questions until they'd reached a turbolift near the habitat's center and ridden it up four floors. It opened onto a circular chamber twenty meters across. The ceiling was fifteen meters above, a curved surface made of a thick layer of transparisteel; scratched so much over the centuries by minor meteorite impacts that it seemed frosted in places, it was still clear enough to show a glorious starfield beyond.

The chamber itself could have been an extension of Dr. Rotham's quarters. Its walls were lined with shelving, and there were narrow catwalks along the shelving at three-meter height intervals, with black metal staircases providing access between the catwalks. The shelves were thick with books, rolls of flimsi, flickering holograms, statuettes, kinetic art, and even, Jacen saw, the bottled head of a Rodian, its funnel-like snout pointed straight at the turbolift doors through which they'd entered. There was furniture at floor level, mostly long, dark sofas. They looked hard and uninviting, but Jacen recognized them as a modern brand whose surfaces inflated and deflated according to the movements and postures of those who sat upon them.

The room fairly reeked of Force energy—dark side energy. But as strong as it was, this was not the source of all the power, all the dark influence Jacen had been detecting since their arrival. That lay below them, a long way down.

Why does dark side power always seem drawn to the depths? he wondered. *Is there something intrinsic that as-*

sociates it with the deep places, the gorges, the cracks?
Even after decades of study, he'd never figured that out.

As Jacen stood in the turbolift doorway, taking in the
sensations of Force power like a hungry man sampling
scents in a restaurant, Nelani moved into the room's center,
her hand on the hilt of the lightsaber at her belt. She spoke,
her voice artificially, mockingly light: "So you're some sort
of Sith."

Brisha shook her head and moved to stretch out on the
nearest sofa, her back supported by one end. The sofa
puffed up a little under her weight. She leaned back, her
posture negligent, and stretched her arms above her head.
"No. If you pay attention to what you're feeling, you can
detect the light side here, as well as the dark side. In these
relics, and in me."

Jacen couldn't be sure if the last statement was true.
Brisha hadn't manifested any sort of Force energy beyond
the energy with which any living being—other than the
Yuuzhan Vong—resonated. But he could detect little waves
of light-side energy here, intermixed with the dark side.

"So how do you define yourself?" he asked. He moved
forward, torn between curiosity—part of him wanted to
race among the shelves, looking at each item in turn—and
caution.

"A student," Brisha said. "A student of the Force in all
its aspects. And yes, I've concentrated on knowledge of the
Sith . . . on utilizing their techniques without greed, without self-interest, to make things better, the same way the
best Jedi use the light-side techniques."

"Then you've been corrupted," Nelani said.

Brisha gave her a pitying look. "You're so young. Nelani,
wielders of the Force *all* face possible corruption, and many
of them give in. It's just the form that the corruption takes
from dark side to light side that differs. The corrupt light-
siders become hidebound, so governed by regulation and
custom that they can no longer think, no longer feel, no
longer adapt—it's what destroyed the Jedi at the end of the
Old Republic."

"There's something to that," Jacen admitted. "You're not the first person I've heard suggest a sort of light-side ossification. But that doesn't prove that prolonged use of the dark side doesn't inevitably lead to corruption."

Brisha sighed, exasperated, and crossed her arms before her. "What is corruption, Jacen? A hard-line light-sider will say that any use of the Force for personal gain is 'corrupt.' But someone who mixes altruism with self-interest in very human measures, across a span of decades, isn't corrupt; he or she is just behaving according to the nature of the species."

Now she, rather than the items on the shelves, had Jacen's attention. He moved over to stand before her. "Explain that."

"I'd love to. But first, some context."

Jacen heard Ben sigh. Jacen grinned, and Brisha's smile matched his. Ben was as well behaved as anyone could expect, but his impatience with adult concerns such as providing context for a complicated issue matched that of any adolescent.

"This planetoid," Brisha said, "was populated long before the miners came. A species of creature settled here. Desiccated bodies I've found in the deep places, and signs I've seen through the Force, indicate that they were akin to mynocks—silicon-based, invertebrate, subsisting on stellar radiation and silicate materials. The ones here evolved or mutated into a sapient species, over how many millennia I can't speculate, and developed a society involving cultural hierarchies, stratification as we see in human cultures."

Jacen nodded. "And the remnant Force energies I'm feeling originated with them?"

"Yes. Their records—for they invented a form of record keeping, a sort of information-imbued sculpture, some forms of which I've learned to translate—"

"One of the tassels?"

"Yes, one your expert probably couldn't read. These creatures' records indicate that at one point a ruling class exiled a whole subsociety, sealing them within caves and caverns of this asteroid, cutting them off from the stellar energies that sustained them. They lived there, slowly dying of starvation, sustaining themselves poorly off the mineral content of the stones within the asteroid. And it was there that one of their number learned to detect, and then manipulate, the Force. That one eventually became leader of the other exiles, then led them to break out of the asteroid interior and conquer the others."

"So why aren't all mynocks now Force-wielding star travelers ruling the galaxy?" Nelani asked.

Brisha shrugged. "I can only guess. In their writing, there's a reference for the Home, this asteroid, plus mentions of the Return, suggesting that they could not spawn— or divide, as the mynocks do—anywhere but here. If that's true, then they couldn't spread too far through the galaxy, and a fatal contagion or similar disaster here could wipe out the entire species within a matter of years. The point, though, is that for quite a while they were a species led by a caste of Force-users, who eventually became a caste of dark side Force-users. They learned techniques related to their mynock natures, such as the ability to leach energy from living beings, including their own kind, at great distances, and associated skills with communicating instantaneously at those distances, a phenomenon the Jedi sometimes experience. They wielded tremendous amounts of dark side energy, and a lot of that energy was eventually radiated into the cavern system that had been their home during the exile, and which had subsequently become a sacred place to them.

"So they died out," she continued, "and centuries or millennia later, an operation settled here to mine this asteroid belt. And it wouldn't have begun mining underneath the directors' habitat, except someone discovered the caverns and all the metal-bearing ore lodes that had been denuded by the mynocks eating all the silicon-based stone out from around them."

"I can guess some of the rest," Jacen said.

"Go ahead."

"Prolonged exposure of the miners to a well of dark side energy led to weird incidents. People seeing things, Force-sensitives manifesting odd abilities. Perhaps channeling your mynocks, behaving like them, and being considered insane."

"Very good." Brisha nodded. "The director of that time hushed up the reports, closed down that mine—the rest of the operation in these asteroids was unaffected—and kept things tightly under wraps. He, too, was a Force-sensitive and had been experiencing things, experimenting, acquiring and testing new powers. When this asteroid belt eventually became less profitable as a mining operation, he closed it down, carefully mismanaged things so that the habitat would be left here and forgotten . . . and then, leaving it behind, he went out into the galaxy, finding the Sith, apprenticing himself, eventually becoming the Sith Master Darth Vectivus."

"Never heard of him," Jacen said.

Brisha's expression showed a little impatience. "That's because he did no evil. He didn't attempt to conquer the galaxy, try to wipe out the population of a star system, or start an all-out war with the Jedi. He just existed, learned. Died of old age, surrounded by family and friends."

Nelani gave her a skeptical look. "A patron of the arts, supporter of charitable causes, and inventor of the cyclonic highball, favorite alcoholic drink of island tourists everywhere."

"You mock," Brisha said, "which is fine, but you mock out of ignorance, which is not. You don't know anything about Darth Vectivus."

Nelani gave her a frosty smile. "Including whether he ever existed, or whether he was the jolly nice man you describe."

"And you can only find out the truth by learning."

"How did he keep from being ruled, and ruined, by greed?" Jacen asked.

"Ah. That's easy. He developed a strong ethical code before he ever felt any pull from the dark side. He was an adult, a hardheaded businessman with a keenly balanced sense of both profit and fairness, and when temptation whispered in his ear he could ignore it as easily as he could ignore the importunings of equally destructive softheartedness." She glanced at Nelani as she spoke those last few words, then returned her attention to Jacen. "The Sith who were famous for being bad, Jacen, were the way they were because they were badly damaged men or women to start with. Not because they were Sith. Usually, they were weak, or deluded, or greedy to begin with. Like your grandfather. I knew him, you know."

Jacen shook his head. "How could I know? I don't know anything about you."

"Conceded. I haven't been using my true name. It's inconvenient."

"So you're saying that you didn't lure us here to kill us."

"Correct."

"And it wasn't because you're lonely, or just wanted to show the place off."

Brisha's smile turned genuine again. "No."

"Then why?"

"Because, down in the caverns, where the dark side power is greatest, there is a Sith Lord, and I didn't think I should face him alone."

CORELLIAN SPACE, ABOVE TRALUS

Leia sat in the officers' mess with Admiral Limpan, steaming cups of caf on the gleaming white table between them. "The GA tends to fall into the old trap of thinking of the Corellians as naughty children," she said. "They're not. They're people who have never lost the pioneering spirit, even though their system has been well settled for millennia. Pioneering spirit, pioneering contempt for authority, pioneering disdain for complication or overanalysis. Think of them as children and you inevitably forget how dangerous they can be."

Limpan said, "That's surprisingly candid for one who is married to a Corellian."

"Han is one of the most dangerous people in the galaxy." Leia did not look at all abashed by this admission. "And I've been proud for more than thirty years of the ways he uses his dangerousness—"

A shrill alarm cut off her words. Uniformed officers at the surrounding tables stood, as did Limpan and Leia. "Intrusion alert," the admiral said. "I'm needed—"

"I'll stay with you, if I may," Leia said.

The bridge was only a few dozen meters away, and when Limpan and Leia charged through the blast doors onto the elevated walkway, it was buzzing with activity. Officers shouted reports to one another, and a hologram of nearby space hung above the walkway. It showed the curved orbital line of distantly spaced Galactic Alliance ships and a formation of incoming craft in three groups, the fuzziness and blob-like nature of the formation informing Leia that its exact composition had not yet been determined by the sensors.

"All vessels and ground control, go to battle stations, launch all ready squadrons," Limpan shouted. "Scramble all squadrons. Recall all scouting vehicles that can arrive here before or within three minutes after the arrival of that formation. All other scouts, initiate fishnet scout patterns on a slow traverse back toward Tralus. Navigation, what's their course?"

A male officer, also a Duros, in one of the pits below, called up, "Sixty–forty probability Rellidir or *Blue Diver*."

"Starfighter control, route one squadron in four down toward Rellidir, two in four toward *Blue Diver,* one in four remains with each launching ship." The admiral's head whipped around as she studied each station below the walkway.

"Admiral," Leia said, "I have some experience with starfighter coordination, if I can be of any help . . ."

Limpan nodded absently. "Back through the blast doors we came in, immediate right—that is, to ship's port—first door, tell Colonel Moyan to confirm your involvement with my aide. And thanks."

"You're welcome." Leia turned to rush back toward the bridge exit. Her words caught a little in her throat. The admiral had just thanked her for volunteering to commit what might end up being an act of treason—for if Leia could help Han survive the battle to come, she would do so, even if she had to act directly against the interests of the Galactic Alliance.

Syal cursed as her Twee cleared the exit doors of *Blue Diver* hangar and slowly began to accelerate. It still seemed so slow . . . She and her squadmates, five of them, lined up in a V-formation; her commander, who had been the pilot of the X-wing that bedeviled her during test runs, at point.

Gray One turned to lead the rest of the squadron down into the atmosphere. Syal checked her navigation board, saw that their destination was a point due south of the city of Rellidir. She nodded. The Corellians were coming to take their city back. She didn't know whether, in her heart, to wish them luck or not.

Panther Flight—Han and Wedge—stayed well toward the rear of the Corellian formation.

Han chafed. It was wrong to be at the rear of any formation. When you were at the rear, spiteful enemy gunners concentrated their fire on you and you got your butt shot off. When you were at the rear, your placement marked you as a slow or indifferent pilot. Even the missile-launching craft were ahead of them; they had to be in place in the skies east of Rellidir before Han and Wedge made their approach.

To make things more irritating, Han still hadn't heard from Leia. Admittedly, communication between them was going to be tricky and occasional. He glanced at the comm-equipped datapad that he had carefully glued to the Shriek control board once he'd been sealed into the vehicle—its lit screen remained aggravatingly blank.

Worse still, Wedge seemed to be reading his mind. "Don't get impatient," he said, his voice so clear in Han's ears that he could have been sitting in the now empty copilot's seat. "We'll get there soon enough."

"Impatient?" Han added an edge of disbelief to his voice. "Sonny, I'm just sitting here playing sabacc with the droid brains."

"Good. Getting skinned will make you mean."

Han grinned. He put on a little thrust, bringing him up slightly ahead of Wedge's Shriek. "And getting your hatches blown off will make *you* mean."

Wedge's voice became less cordial, more military. "Forward starfighter edges now encountering enemy units."

"Lucky them," Han said.

RELLIDIR, TRALUS

This time, Jaina spoke each word with brilliant, individual clarity, making it impossible to misunderstand her. "I. Said. Drop. The. Shields. Over."

"Negative on that, negative." The groundside officer's voice sounded young and a little panicky. "The enemy is less than three minutes away and descending rapidly."

"Goodness," Jaina said. "At two seconds to drop the shields and two to raise them again after we're outside, that gives you, what? More than two and a half minutes to dither and still be safe? *Drop the karking shields and let us out!*" She pounded a portion of her control boards, unoccupied by buttons or readouts, with her fist.

Her squadron circled above downtown Rellidir, confined by the energy shields defending that portion of the city. Other starfighters were buzzing beneath her, but none of the other squadrons seemed as anxious to leave the shielded area.

"Orders are for all squadrons to stay close at hand and defend the center," the anonymous officer said. "So you're to stay put."

"This is Hardpoint Squadron, the Jedi unit." Jaina's

voice was a hiss of anger. "We're not part of your immediate command structure. Let us out and we'll do a much better job of defending you."

"That's a negative, Hardpoint. My orders are specific, and I'm not going to bother the commander right now with your request. Out."

"Cringing, whimpering, mewling idiot," Jaina said. "I've seen mouse droids with more guts and thud bugs with more brains."

"I doubt he can hear you, One." That was Zekk's voice.

"I know." Jaina sighed. "I guess we're stuck here. Hardpoints, maintain your flight patterns and call out when the opportunities start raining down on us."

She received a chorus of affirmatives but was too discouraged to pay much attention to them.

STAR SYSTEM MZX32905, NEAR BIMMIEL

The three Jedi and Brisha rode the turbolift back down to the bottom level of the habitat.

"That's something you could have mentioned from the beginning," Nelani said. "*There's a Sith in the basement.* Any other home in the galaxy, that'd be the first thing out of someone's mouth."

"What's his name?" Ben asked.

Brisha shrugged. "He hasn't revealed himself to me, and so certainly hasn't told me his name." Then she grinned, suddenly playful. "*Darth* something, I expect."

"There haven't been any Sith in the galaxy since—what? The death of the last clone of the Emperor?" Jacen asked.

"True and not true," Brisha said. "In terms of the classic Master-and-apprentice Sith structure, 'there can be only two,' you're correct. I'm not sure I even count the Emperor's clones as Sith. After all, they didn't earn their Sith knowledge, didn't acquire it through sweat and sacrifice; they inherited it like a package of downloaded computer programming. I think that the last Sith were gone when the Emperor and your grandfather died on the same day.

"But," she continued, "plenty of Sith legacy survived. Individuals who were candidates to become Sith and failed for some reason to achieve full apprenticeship. They knew enough to survive, knew enough to continue learning. One may have learned enough to become a Master."

The turbolift thudded to a halt at the habitat's bottom level, the level by which they'd originally entered the structure. Brisha led them from there through a side door into a hexagonal room dominated by a tube. Tilted at a forty-five-degree angle, it was a cylinder of transparisteel marked by a pair of metal rails. The tube was just under two meters in diameter, and suspended above it on a metal brace was a sort of metal-wheeled cart. The cart had six seats up front, a copious cargo area in the middle, and a backward-facing set of six seats at the very end. Its nose was partly within the cylinder, pointed downward, the front set of wheels on the rails.

Ben peered at the tube. It led down past the floor into darkness, but as he watched, the interior surface of the tube began to glow. Meters below, he could see the rocky surface of the asteroid, and the tube continuing into the ground. "This is going to be fun," he said matter-of-factly.

"The boy shouldn't go," Brisha said. "He's not yet strong enough to face a Sith."

Ben felt a flash of resentment but kept it from his face. "Tell you what, I'll just resist all temptation," he said.

Brisha gave him a severe stare. "The last time I met your father, our parting was not pleasant. He may have had time to forgive . . . but he certainly wouldn't forgive me a second time if I managed to get his only child killed."

"Then I won't do that, either."

Jacen climbed the skeletal metal stairs up to the mine car and hopped into the front seat. "He comes with us. That way no one can assault him while he remains behind."

"If you say so." Brisha followed and settled into the seat beside him.

In moments Nelani and Ben were in the rear seat.

Brisha flipped a button. Gauges and controls suddenly lit

up on the mine car's control panel. "Atmospheric pressure in the caverns is at point nine five of habitat standard," she said. "Your ears may pop." She hit a button. The railcar rolled into the tube, picked up speed, and plunged toward the asteroid surface.

And through it, into blackness.

chapter thirty

CORELLIAN SYSTEM, ABOVE TRALUS

The leading edges of the Corellian fighter squadrons hit the defensive screen of Galactic Alliance starfighters and engaged. Subsequent waves of Corellians plowed into rapidly arriving squadrons of GA fighters.

Panther Flight, Han and Wedge, accompanied by two squadrons of Corellian attack fighters, simply went around the engagement zone and screamed down into the atmosphere.

"Ride's too smooth," Han said.

"Are you out of your mind?" Wedge asked. "The ride's too *smooth*?"

"Right. There should be some vibration, some dangerous-looking heat warnings to indicate that you're punching through into the atmosphere. These Shrieks, they don't offer the atmosphere any *respect*."

"What you're saying is, unless a transport is leaving a thin stream of pieces behind, like a trail of bread crumbs, during atmospheric entry, it doesn't match up to the *Millennium Falcon* standard."

"Well . . . right."

"You could fire a few blaster shots into your own control panel and deal with the resulting malfunctions if you just wanted to feel at home."

"Oh, yeah? Well, I could get drunk on leave and cause a massive interplanetary incident, then call on you to straighten it out, since you're my commanding officer."

"You could do that. Or I could have the mechanics sabotage your hyperdrive so when it conked out you could tell everyone it's not your fault."

"Owww. I could arrange for you to receive orders to conquer Coruscant, but your only resources would be twelve drunken Ewoks, four malfunctioning speeders, and forty kilos of beach sand."

"That'll take at least two weeks, sir."

Han grinned.

RELLIDIR, TRALUS

"Incoming fighters," Gray One called out. "Coming in from orbit, north-northwest."

Syal could see them on her sensors, big fuzzy blips resolving into two or three squadrons of starfighters and at least two larger targets.

"We'll do this as a simple strafe," Gray One continued. "Wait until they commit to a course, and then follow me in. Punch a big hole through everything you see."

On Syal's sensor board, orange lines, extrapolations of the intruders' course transmitted by Gray One, appeared, pointing east of the city—well clear of the layered shields that protected the GA beachhead. As soon as the transmission came, Gray One rolled into a vertical descent, a course that paralleled that of the Corellian squadrons but was well in advance of it. The other Alephs followed.

STAR SYSTEM MZX32905, NEAR BIMMIEL

The railcar plunged through blackness and Ben felt his stomach rise into his throat, then break free and float, like a ghost, away from his body. He almost sent his lunch after it as an escort, but managed, through force of will, to keep himself from that embarrassment. A mere vertical drop wasn't enough to make him queasy; the railcar must also have left the region of artificial gravity.

In the first moments there was almost no wind in his face, then suddenly the air currents increased and became cold. He guessed that they were now out of the tube and hurtling down through the caverns Brisha had spoken of.

The clattering of the metal wheels on the rails became louder, more echoing, a sign that they were moving through a narrow gap, and suddenly they were in light again—a broad cavern lit at intervals by glow rods affixed to the ceiling and wall surfaces.

Not that it was particularly well or effectively lit. The cavern, in the brief glimpse Ben had of it, was huge, its walls uneven and pitted, and through the vast empty space stretched curious columns of red-brown material. They seemed as ponderous and massive as stone, yet flowing and elongated like rivers of rusty water suddenly frozen into stillness. The glow rods illuminating the landscape were situated at intervals, sometimes on the surface of stone, sometimes within the pits of the walls, sometimes behind the columns of flowing material to silhouette them; the effect was more artistic than it was helpful.

As if sensing his question, Brisha pointed toward one of the columns, which flowed laterally in a curving wave, and called out, "Ferrous ore. Denuded by the mynocks eating around it."

Then the railcar, continuing its descent, dropped toward another narrow, dark crevasse and plunged into darkness again.

Now Ben could feel the concentrated dark side energy that waited below. It didn't feel so much malicious as merely ominous—less an enemy threatening death than a somber realist reminding him that death was what he ultimately faced.

The rail noises, suddenly close and echoing, then distant and quieter, told Ben that they'd passed through a narrow region and emerged into another cavern, this one unlit.

He was grabbed by the collar from behind and yanked up out of his seat. He found himself floating, drifting through the darkness, perhaps hurtling at dangerous speeds toward sharp rock formations, and was so startled by the sudden transition that he didn't even cry out.

RELLIDIR, TRALUS

"Incoming starfighters." The voice of the leader of one of the two squadrons now escorting the Shriek bombers crackled in Han's ears. "You two stay put, we'll handle them."

One of the fighter squadrons broke away from the formation. The other stayed in array around the Shriek bombers.

Han didn't reply. His comm board was fixed to broadcast on a frequency and encryption code that would allow only Wedge and the mission controllers to hear him—it wouldn't do for someone to recognize his all-too-distinctive voice. But Wedge said what Han was thinking, his tone ironic: "Thanks, sonny. I was mighty scared until you spoke up."

On the sensor board, Han could see the dozen attack fighters head out southeastward against the incoming flight of half a dozen starfighters, unknown type.

Unknown type. Han frowned over that. He liked surprises, but only when he was springing them on someone else.

The outbound attack fighter formation neared the enemy formation and their lines blurred for a moment, then suddenly there were nine fighters instead of twelve, frantically turning in the wake of the unknown enemy. The enemy still numbered six.

"Not good," Han said.

"Lasers to power," Wedge answered.

Han checked his weapons board. The lasers in his top-side turret were charged and ready to go.

Half the remaining attack fighter escort broke away from the Shrieks and turned toward the incoming fighters, forming a defensive screen. Red laser flashes, missed shots by the incoming enemy, flashed by laterally ahead of Han's viewport.

Suddenly the six attack fighters that had just turned away became four on the sensors, and Han's targeting alarm shrieked with the news that one of the enemy had a weapons lock on him. Han kicked his thruster, then fired repulsors, tactics to vary his speed and throw off the aim of his enemies. He spun so that his Shriek was presented edge-on to the enemy, dropped his own targeting brackets over the foremost enemy, and fired. The too-informative sensor board responded with an almost comical *ding* indicating he'd hit his target.

Six enemy starfighters, oversized silver balls trailing narrowing twin thruster pods, flashed by from right to left, pursued by a flight of Corellian attack fighters. In the distance to the left, the enemy craft began a slow turn back toward the fight.

Han blinked. "What the fierfek are those?"

"Sienar *Aleph*-class starfighters," Wedge said. "Originally nicknamed Pondskippers because they were to be countermeasures to coralskippers. The current nickname is Twees. They're out of prototype and in limited production."

"Great. I hit mine with a good quad-linked punch and it didn't even shudder."

"Yeah, they're supposed to be like shooting solid metal ball bearings." Wedge switched over to the squadron frequency. "Nebula Flight, Panthers are making our break. Good luck."

"Panther One, this is Nebula Leader. Blow something up for us."

Han anticipated Wedge and broke first from formation,

a dive that took him down, still eastward, toward the start of their approach to Rellidir's downtown district. Wedge slipped neatly into his wake.

BATTLE CARRIER DODONNA,
ABOVE TRALUS

The starfighter control chamber was an exercise in controlled chaos—a sight familiar to Leia, who'd helped coordinate many starfighter skirmishes, starting with the Battle of Yavin.

Aboard *Dodonna,* they had bells and whistles she'd never enjoyed in the control room at Yavin. The entire battle was being reproduced via holograms over their heads, the skirmishes not exactly to scale but with each individual starfighter or vessel shown in a wire-frame form color-coded to whichever side the fighting vehicle represented. The GA forces were blue; Corellian forces, red; unknowns—including several vehicles, probably civilian, above Rellidir and heading away from that endangered city—in yellow. As they moved around, firing, sustaining damage, disappearing, the disconcerting combination of colorful icons and event noises made the whole display seem like an oversized console game experiencing delirium tremens.

Equipped with a specialized datapad handed to her by the chamber's coordinator, a black-furred Bothan colonel by the name of Moyan, Leia could gather all sorts of data about the various forces. By pointing the datapad at any vessel or vehicle and tagging it with a beam of light from the device, she could display information about the target on the datapad screen.

For example, the fighter that had just winked out in the fight above Rellidir was designated Nebula Eleven, its pilot Gorvan Peel. The Corellian vessels were equipped with ejectors, and a moment after the fighter vanished, Leia's screen was updated: EJECT SUCCESS, LIFE SIGNS OPTIMAL, QUEUE RESCUE #37.

As several of the coordinators in the chamber were doing, she pointed at one of the "mystery bombers" descending on Rellidir and sampled its information:

F/F: ENEMY
CLASS: CEC YT-VARIANT (UNKNOWN), EST.
   BOMBER
PILOT: UNKNOWN

Information on the other Shriek was identical.

Leia spoke quietly into her datapad, allowing its speech-to-text translator to add a notation to the data on the bomber: "Believed damaged, as it is turning away from GA targets. Recommend concentration on fighter escort." She tapped the screen to send that datum to *Dodonna*'s database.

A flash of guilt washed across her. She was pretending to be helping the GA forces, and instead she was protecting her husband as he bombed them. She shook her head, trying to force the emotion away from her. No matter what she did during this fight, she'd be coping with guilt, and not keeping an eye on Han's back would be worst of all . . . especially if he was hurt.

She turned her attention to the Alephs skirmishing with Han's fighter escort.

CORUSCANT

His head filled with a baffling mix of emotions and images, Luke sat up in bed. He spared Mara a glance, saw that she was still asleep, and rose.

So pounded was he by sensations reaching him through the Force that it was actually difficult to think. Cautious, he opened himself to them, trying to sort them out.

betraying trust, to act is to betray, not to act is to betray

A mynock, its eyes glittering with unusual intelligence, stared at him from the distance of centuries.

the Sith are not what you think

Leia, her features smoothed by grief so great it could not be expressed, fell forward, folding over as she did.

dark dark I will not be afraid of the dark

Han, regret on his face, a vibroblade in his hand, lunged forward and slammed the blade between the ribs of a pretty young woman with dark hair.

I loved you in my own way, I would have repaired the harm I did you

Instinctively, Luke reached out through the Force to offer support and strength to Leia. The others he wasn't sure about, whether they were really the individuals the visions represented, but he could feel the true Leia within the vision of her. He just wasn't sure whether he was extending his gesture to the Leia of here and now, the Leia of some future time, or the Leia of a future that would actually never occur.

His attention was drawn back to Mara. Now her eyes were open, staring sightlessly upward, her body cut and butchered, the edges still black and steaming, by a lightsaber blade.

Luke shook his head and exerted himself through the Force, willing the visions, the voices away. They faded, leaving him in the dark with his wife asleep and unharmed.

He took his lightsaber from the nightstand and moved out into the hallway. He didn't want his perturbation to awaken Mara.

Something was happening; events at distant points of the galaxy and even of time were focusing toward him and those he loved. The confusion, the turbulence of those thoughts and emotions pressed down on him, soured his stomach.

On the cold stone floor outside his chambers, he sat crosslegged and tried to sink into a meditative state—a state to give him real knowledge, a state to grant him peace.

STAR SYSTEM MZX32905, NEAR BIMMIEL

Ben took his lightsaber into his hands and thumbed it on. Its *snap-hiss* was less welcome than the blue light it emitted—suddenly he could see all around him, even if dimly.

He floated through open space, but ahead of him, thirty or forty meters, was a broken stone wall, and he floated toward it at a rate of several meters a second. He was also losing altitude, slowly—though gravity was weak here, it wasn't entirely absent.

"Two-handed form," Nelani said, behind him, "makes it rather hard to hold on to stone walls."

Ben twisted to look behind him. Nelani floated there, following his aerial path, at least as comfortable in the minimal gravity as Ben was.

He turned back to face the onrushing wall. "Did you pull me out of the railcar?"

"Don't be stupid."

"I'm not stupid. Don't be snide."

"Sorry, I'm upset." Her tone changed. "Nelani to Jacen, come in."

As the stone wall came nearer, Ben spotted a feature on it he thought he could grab, a rocky projection that narrowed to a needle-like point. He held his lightsaber back and to one side with his right hand, extended his left, and as he reached the projection he grabbed it, swinging his feet ahead of him to sustain the minimal shock of impact.

A moment later Nelani hit a few meters down, her fingers slipping into a crack in the stone, her hips and shoulders taking the impact.

"So who did it?" Ben persisted. "The Sith?"

"We have company."

Ben looked down at her, then around, then up.

Above him, ten meters up, a pair of eyes stared down at him. They glowed blue in the reflected light of his lightsaber blade. They were not human eyes, but slitted and triangular.

Beyond them were more, hundreds of pairs of eyes, cool and unblinking.

Ben shook his head. He'd had that portion of stone wall in sight as he'd approached the wall. There had been no creatures there at the time. He reached out for them within the Force, and could feel them there, hundreds of them, strong in dark side energy. "Not good," he said.

"Drop," Nelani said.

"Yeah." Ben released his hold on the projection and drifted downward. He gave the rock surface a little shove to open up a few more centimeters' room between himself and the stony surface.

Above, the eyes began to descend, staying at their respective distance from the gleam of his lightsaber, but definitely following.

The railcar slowed to a halt, curving around in a circle. Brisha and Jacen were in a well-lit chamber, large enough to house a good-sized transport, but the only thing present was the end of the rail line. The track here curved around in a teardrop shape and rejoined itself on the way up, allowing the railcar to head back up the track it had just descended.

Jacen didn't bother with the scenery. He stared at Brisha. "Why did you do that?" he asked.

She gave him an innocent stare. "Do what?"

"Shove Ben and Nelani out of the car. Did you think I couldn't feel your pulse of Force energy?"

"I suspected you could." She stood and stepped out of the car. She floated for a moment beside it, then slowly drifted down to the stony surface of the floor. "I separated them from us for their own good. What they'll face will be dangerous, but not as dangerous as what we're going to encounter—if they accompanied us here, they'd probably die."

"Your Sith." Jacen pushed off from his seat and drifted upward a dozen meters. From this altitude he could see all corners of this chamber, with its natural stone walls and glow rods all over them. There were no menaces, no strange beings to confront them. "What can you tell me about him?"

"His knowledge is of the lineage of Palpatine, but is

broader than the Emperor's. He's young. He was not yet born when the Emperor died."

"How was the Sith knowledge transmitted to him?" Jacen began to float back down toward the railcar. "Through a Sith Holocron? Through loyal retainers?"

"Through disloyal retainers. Through Sith trainees who could never achieve Mastery themselves . . . and who rejected Palpatine and his teachings as too selfish, too controlling, too destructive."

Jacen gave her a curious look. "You make them sound benign. If they're benign, isn't he?"

She shrugged. She kept one hand on the railcar so that casual motions would not propel her across the chamber. "All the same, he must be found and mastered. Ah." She turned toward a shadowy corner of the chamber, a place where a huge, rounded outcropping came within meters of the curved section of rail.

From around that outcropping walked a man. He was tall, slender, garbed in a traveler's robe of black and dark gold; it was styled like a Jedi's but made of expensive silks. A lightsaber, its hilt also in black and gold, swung at his belt. His hands were gloved, and his face was in the deep shadow cast by the hood of his cloak, though his eyes—a liquid, luminous orange-gold—glowed from within that darkness.

He came to a stop just at the edge of that outcropping, several meters from Jacen and Brisha.

"So you're the Sith," Jacen said.

The dark figure bowed.

Jacen gave him a scornful look. "How am I supposed to take you seriously? You're not even here."

The hooded man's voice came back as a whisper. "What do you mean?"

"I mean, you *walked*. As if we were in Coruscant-standard gravity instead of a tiny fraction of it. You're an illusion."

"Yes, I'm an illusion. But I'm also here. Right here."

"Care to explain that?"

"No."

"Ah." Jacen thumbed his lightsaber into life. "Well, I suppose I should be cutting you in half now."

"I am a Master. You are a Jedi Knight. Do you know what that means?"

"That I can't win?" Jacen punctuated his question with a mocking laugh.

"No. That you must go through my subordinates to get to me. Allowing me to test you, to evaluate you. That's tradition, you know."

"If you say so."

The reflection of the Sith's gold-orange eyes disappeared— and then the Sith himself vanished, ghost-like.

But there was a sound from beyond where he had stood, a slight scrape, and another figure moved forward into view. This one walked, as the Sith had, in a fashion appropriate for a standard-gravity environment, and stepped out to stand where the Sith had stood.

He was not tall, but he was well muscled and agile. He wore black pants, tunic, boots, and gloves, and held an unlit lightsaber.

His features were those of Luke Skywalker, but rakishly bearded and twisted into a grin that was all malice and scorn.

"Not nice," Jacen said.

Nelani reached the bottom of the cavern first, taking the minor shock of impact on bent legs and being propelled a few meters back up into the air. On his way down, Ben passed her on her upward bounce, but he had eyes only for the creatures clustered on the stone wall above. He hit stony floor, bounced upward a few meters, passed Nelani again as she descended. Soon enough, both had their feet none too firmly on the surface beneath.

Now Ben could hear rustling, hissing that sounded like muffled, sibilant speech, from above—from hundreds of sources above.

"They're going to swarm us," Nelani said. She sounded rattled.

As if her words were a cue, a form of permission, the eyes above suddenly descended en masse, pouring downward as if carried by a waterfall. Nelani's lightsaber snapped into life, adding a yellow-white glow to the proceedings. Ben raised his own blade in a high defensive stance.

The first wave of descending creatures broke before it reached the Jedi, splitting into two streams, each headed a different direction parallel to the stone face. But two of the creatures did not veer away. One came at Ben, one at Nelani.

Ben darted to one side—or tried; despite having some experience in low-gravity environments, he wasn't accustomed enough to them for appropriate movements and tactics to be instinctive. He pushed off but floated mostly upward, straight toward his attacker.

No matter. The creature—revealed in the light of Ben's lightsaber to be a fleshy stretched wing with eyes at one end, a tail at the other, and a wet mouth toward the center of its underside, something like a mynock—flew straight at him. Ben swung, felt his blade cut into skin and meat, and was propelled back down by the impact as the two halves of the beast hurtled lifelessly past him, one to either side.

The soles of his feet hit stone again. He absorbed as much of the impact as he could with his knees and did not bounce up very far this time.

The two mynock halves were partly embedded in the stone, and as he glanced at them, they slipped beneath the stone's surface like two halves of a boat sinking. They left nothing behind—no blood, nothing.

"They're not real," Ben said.

"Projections of the Force," Nelani answered from behind.

"So they can't really hurt us, right?"

"Wrong." Her tone chided him. "You know better than that. It's like saying *A laser beam can't hurt me—it's only light, right?*"

"I was just hoping."

"Oof." Nelani sounded as though she'd taken a shot to the gut, and her lightsaber winked out instantly.

Heedless of the swarms of mynocks overhead, Ben spun, the motion bouncing him a couple of meters up.

Nelani was gone. In her place stood Mara Skywalker. Her eyes glittered with anger and her body language suggested punishment to come. Her lightsaber, in her hand, was unlit.

Ben floated back to the ground. "You're not my mother," he said.

"Good," she said. "Then it won't be a family crime to cut you down." She ignited the lightsaber, and its blade glowed red.

RELLIDIR, TRALUS

Han and Wedge lined up on the boulevard that would carry them straight to the Terkury Housing Complex. Far ahead, Han could see the tiny, indistinct shapes of bombers flying over the dome-shield above the beachhead, dropping their explosives charges. Other ships engaged in dogfights with the better, newer starfighters of the Galactic Alliance.

Han, in the lead by a handful of meters, brought his Shriek down almost to the deck—he left just enough clearance for speeders flying at legal altitudes to be clear beneath him and ignored the fact that many Corellians, like himself, disregarded what was legal when blasting around in their personal vehicles.

Han's sensor board blipped at him uncertainly a few times, telling him that he was being tagged for fractions of a second at a time by someone's targeting radar. He paid no attention to it. Only when the signal strengthened and became constant would it constitute—

It strengthened, became constant. Up ahead, a pair of starfighters crested a row of skyscrapers and began a plummet toward street level, turning toward the Shrieks. Though they were tiny dots in the distance, Han guessed from the way they were moving that they were E-wings. Tough, fast, fixed-wing spacecraft with a nose similar to the X-wing, the E-wings had only three linked lasers but carried a tremendous load of sixteen proton torpedoes, any one of which could cripple or kill a capital ship under the right circumstances.

Worse yet, a new warble in the sensor alarm indicated the presence of an enemy or enemies coming up from behind. Han glanced at the board again. The new opponent was one of the Alephs, flying, like the Shrieks, at almost street level and roaring up in their wakes.

Han brought his turret lasers to bear on the E-wings. A good laser hit would damage or eliminate them, while a concussion missile could cause wreckage from surrounding buildings to fall into the path of the Shrieks. His targeting brackets chittered around the foremost E-wing, and he fired. The shot missed; kilometers in the distance, the green laser shot hit the face of a building adjacent to the Terkury complex. Incoming laserfire, red streaks, flashed by beneath Han's bow.

Then the datapad glued to his control board beeped. Han bit back a curse at the timing of this distraction and glanced at the screen.

ALEPH PURSUER IS WEDGE'S DAUGHTER

A cold current seemed to cut through Han's stomach as he read the words.

They had no way to communicate with the girl, to warn her off. Well, maybe Wedge did—but did he have enough time to dig it out, power it up, and reach her before they were upon their target? Han didn't think so.

Han didn't want to kill Wedge's daughter, even to fire upon her. But it would be worse if Wedge did. Worse still if she killed Wedge, worse for Corellia and their mission.

Almost as soon as he registered Leia's words, Han kicked in his repulsors, bouncing his Shriek several meters higher, and hit reverse thrusters. Wedge's Shriek flashed by beneath him and was suddenly in front. "You have more experience with itty-bitty starfighters," Han said. "You deal with them. I'll take the tugboat on our tail."

"Thanks, Grandpa."

Han's sensor board howled as the pursuer's weapons locked on to him. He added a little wobble to his flight path, and the incoming lasers missed, firing off harmlessly into the air above the skyscrapers ahead.

Han brought his turret lasers around and returned fire. As he squeezed the trigger, the ungainly-looking Aleph jerked to port, avoiding his beams, and crept closer, dropped lower, making Han's next shot even harder.

Blast it. She *would* have to be a good pilot.

chapter thirty-one

CORUSCANT

Luke felt a presence, the arrival of someone strong in the Force. He opened his eyes.

Hovering over the floor in front of him, meters from him, was his nephew and onetime prize pupil, Jacen, lightsaber lit in his hand. Except it was not truly Jacen; whoever it was reeked of dark side energy, and his stare promised only malevolence. "Not nice," the false Jacen said.

Luke rose. "Who are you, really?"

The not-Jacen snorted. "You barely exist. You don't need to know." He took an odd, gliding step forward—it was only the slightest of exertions, but he floated meters toward Luke.

Luke lit his lightsaber.

The not-Jacen struck, a fast, powerful lateral blow that Luke met with little effort, without conscious thought. Not-Jacen's blade was immediately in guard position for an anticipated counterstrike, but Luke held back. Oddly, the force of the impact sent his opponent floating backward. Not-Jacen drifted until he hit the corridor wall, which checked his motion, and he floated gently to the floor.

Then Luke heard the humming and chattering of lightsabers in conflict. The muffled noise was coming from his own quarters.

Mara rose, throwing her covers off in a move designed to whirl them over attackers and give her a moment to collect herself. As she came up on her feet, she reached out and pulled through the Force, and was rewarded with the comforting weight of her lightsaber hilt thumping into her hand.

The room was lit in hues of red by the lightsaber blade hovering in the middle of the room. It was held by a small, misshapen form whose feet were well off the ground. The figure was faced away from her as she rose, but now, boosted by a little push in the Force that Mara could detect, it turned in midair and presented glittering red eyes to her.

It was a boy, maybe thirteen years of age. Its features resembled Ben's but were twisted in anger, an anger that looked like it had years of abuse, jealousy, and rage behind it. The boy's hair, unlike Ben's, was blond, styled in a sort of bowl cut with bangs, and Mara realized with a shock that it was the hairstyle of Luke Skywalker in his youth—she'd seen the holos of him in his adolescence. Worse, for she'd seen those holos as well, it was the hairstyle of the juvenile Anakin Skywalker.

The boy drifted gently down to the floor. "You're not my mother," he said. His voice was a serpentine hiss, full of loathing.

"Good," Mara answered. "Then it won't be a family crime to cut you down." She lit her lightsaber, and its blue glow clashed with the red already suffusing the chamber.

The blond boy leapt at her, lightsaber extended in a spearlike thrust, but as he came within range he spun the blade around and low in a sweeping cut.

Mara danced back and to one side, out of range of the attack, and negligently waved a hand at the boy. His eyes widened as her wash of Force energy caught him and threw him against a wall.

Against—and *through*. He disappeared and the glow of his lightsaber vanished with him.

Mara could still feel his presence, his proximity, even if she could no longer say in which direction he was to be found. She brought her lightsaber up in a defensive posture and waited.

Then she heard the clash of lightsaber blades from outside her quarters, in the corridor.

STAR SYSTEM MZX32905, NEAR BIMMIEL

Nelani reached up and struck, her yellow-white blade cutting through dense muscle and other tissues. There was a squeal of pain and her captor, a mynock—but one with grasping, supple hands at the ends of its wings—released her and drifted in two different directions, its halves severed by her blow.

All around her, more mynocks flew; they darted in at her, reaching with those too-wrong hands, lashing with their tail-like appendages. She lashed out at whatever came near her, cutting limbs away, using the Force to turn her around in the air.

She was dropping, too, but the rocky cavern floor was well out of sight beneath her. That was a quandary. Gravity was not strong here, but if she began dropping at a great enough altitude, she could still pick up considerable speed, deadly speed, by the time she hit the stone below.

Why hadn't Ben reacted when she was grabbed and whisked away from him? Why hadn't he responded to her sudden shriek?

The part of her brain still working on problems and logistics arrived at an answer to the problem of falling. A factor that endangered her would also be her salvation.

The next time a mynock drifted in and tried to snap at her with its claws, she grabbed its fleshy wrist and tugged, allowing her to roll up onto the creature's back. It banked, trying to dislodge her, but she sprang away from it, sending her away from the floor once more.

Now she could move where she chose. She bounced up toward a mynock, eluded its nasty central mouth, and kicked off from its underside, hurtling almost horizontally. The next one she encountered she used to send her downward, onto the back of one dozens of meters below. Each tried to grab her, tail-whip her, or snap at her as she approached, but she was always nimbler.

On one of her descents she saw the stone floor of the cavern. She calculated that her speed was not too great for a safe impact. Instead of bouncing off the next mynock in line, she rolled across its back and allowed herself to fall. She came down on the floor on her feet, sinking into a low crouch to absorb the impact, bouncing up half a dozen meters just from the flexion of her muscles. But she drifted down again, and now the mynocks whirled by overhead, not attacking.

"Well done." That was a smooth male voice from behind her.

She spun, the move carrying her up a meter into the air.

Behind her stood a human man, dignified of bearing, his dark beard cut close in an elegant style. He was tall and a trifle overweight, but his loose-fitting black garments suggested that he was carrying around some muscle as well as fat. A silver lightsaber hilt, inlaid with polished black stones shaped like diamonds, hung from his belt.

Nelani drifted to the floor again and kept her own lit blade between them. "Who are you?"

He shrugged. "I doubt you'd know my birth name, but the other you may recognize. I am Darth Vectivus."

Nelani waved a hand at the caverns around them and gave him a smirk. "The Master of all this."

"Once, maybe. Now I'm merely a ghost. Or perhaps less."

"What would be less?"

"A remnant. A sliver of a ghost." He looked just a bit unsettled. "Even as I speak, I am unaware of myself. Of thinking, of decision making. Could I, in fact, be nothing?"

"No, I can feel you. Gleaming in the Force. Shining with the dark side."

He shook his head. "That's not me. That's whomever I am connected to."

"Connected to?"

Now it was his turn to wave around. "Every phantom you see here, every one you encounter, is connected to something that is distinctly real, distinctly alive—though possibly far, far away. Every time you struck a mynock, a living being somewhere suffered the pain and injury you inflicted."

With his statement, a knot of sickness formed in Nelani's stomach. "You're lying."

"No, I'm not. You struck, and somewhere, some creature, perhaps a baby bantha, squealed in pain and was severed, killed before the disbelieving eyes of its mother—"

"Stop it."

"Why? It's the truth. Baby banthas are quite cute, you know. A terrible shame to see one cut in half."

"You're sick."

"But perhaps it wasn't cute little baby banthas. Perhaps it was piranha beetles. You wouldn't mind cutting piranha-beetles in half, would you? Or perhaps Kowakian monkey-lizards." He shook his head. "They say that every creature is cute when it is a baby. A mechanism of nature to help creatures reach the age of reproduction. But it's not true of every species. Have you seen immature monkey-lizards? Ugliest little larvae in the galaxy." He shuddered.

"What do I have to do to shut you up?"

"Oh, that's simple. Kill me." He took a bounding, gliding step forward. "Sweep your lightsaber blade across my neck, topple my head from my shoulders. The mynocks will go away, and you'll be able to find your way back to your friends." He landed only two meters from her and knelt before her. "Go ahead."

"You can't be that anxious to die."

"I died centuries ago." Darth Vectivus bowed his head. "So I won't feel anything. Go ahead and strike."

"And what about the life you say you're connected to?"

Vectivus looked up again and grinned at her. "He or she will become a free-floating head, I'm afraid, rather to the surprise of everyone in the vicinity. 'Why, look, Father, Mother's performing a new trick. Mummy? Mummy?' "

Nelani glared down at him. "Is this taunting necessary?"

"Yes, it is. To goad you into the action you need to perform." Vectivus bared his neck for her again. "By killing one—whoever it is I'm attached to at the moment—you'll save scores. Hundreds. Thousands. What you think of as the evil of my dark side teachings will not spread so far. So kill me."

"No."

"Would it help if I took on a more hateful form? A piranha-beetle in human guise?" Vectivus's clothes shimmered and flowed. Suddenly he was in a full-coverage cloak and hood, his face in deep shadow. He reached up with suddenly white, suddenly wrinkled hands to pull back the hood and reveal the pallid, almost reptilian features of Emperor Palpatine, Darth Sidious, dead now for more than thirty-five years.

His voice, too, was Palpatine's, insidious and cloying. "How about this? Could you strike this down?"

"Not while you're connected to an innocent life."

Palpatine rose and, shimmering as he did so, was Vectivus again by the time he was on his feet. His expression was sympathetic, but a bit pitying. "Jedi girl, you're not strong enough to save lives. You're not strong enough to sacrifice one to save many."

"I could sacrifice myself to save many."

"Yes. But then you wouldn't have to face the accusing eyes of the survivors of those you sacrificed. You don't have that kind of strength."

"That's ruthlessness. Not strength."

Vectivus laughed at her. "Strength that is never touched by ruthlessness is touchingly irresponsible. Perhaps you will be fortunate and never have to decide the fate of an innocent life." He gestured at Nelani—no, beyond her, and she felt a pulse of Force energy in the distance behind her.

She moved, a floating bounce that allowed her to turn but keep Vectivus in the periphery of her vision. In the distance, where Vectivus gestured, the rails that had borne Brisha's car to these depths were briefly illuminated. Even when the light faded, she could still feel them, could mark their presence in the Force as though they were living things.

"Go there," Vectivus said. "And climb those rails to safety. Wait for the others to join you once they have made their decisions about their own fates." His voice took on a kindly tone. "I don't want you to die unnecessarily . . . and as weak as you are, if you meddle in the affairs of others, that's precisely what will happen to you."

"Go to hell," Nelani said.

Vectivus shrugged. "Perhaps I did. I wouldn't know." Then he faded from sight, and as he disappeared, the susurrating noise of the mynocks wheeling overhead also vanished.

Nelani spared a look upward. They were gone, leaving not even a trace in the Force.

Anxiety welled within her, a fear concerning the fate of her friends, and she began bounding toward the distant, unseen spot where the rails reached the floor of this cavern. They were her path to the surface, true, but also her path into the lower reaches where Jacen and Brisha awaited.

RELLIDIR, TRALUS

Han winced as his pursuer's lasers hammered at his stern. He'd diverted extra power from his bow shields to reinforce the stern, a dangerous gambit—if laserfire from the oncoming F-wings missed Wedge, it could accidentally smack into Han's bow and ruin his day. Ruin the rest of his life, in fact.

But Wedge had managed to vape one of the E-wings with laserfire of his own, and the other had peeled off. It was

now circling around to drop in behind the Aleph and reinforce it.

Not that the Aleph needed much reinforcing. Wedge's little girl was good at her job. She'd dropped so low and come
in so close behind the Shriek that Han's turret lasers couldn't
depress enough to attack her, and meanwhile she could
chew up his thrusters with impunity. If only he had a stern-
mounted weapon—

Wait a minute, he *did*. He had a bomb bay full of spotter
droids.

His fingers flew over his weapons console, punching in a
set of unusual commands. He hit the EXECUTE button. Two
of his spotter droids would now be sliding into the bomb
drop slots . . .

"Control reports missiles launched," Wedge said. "They'll
be showing up on our sensors any second."

"Good," Han said. He gritted his teeth to keep from
continuing, *I hope your baby daughter, whom I've
bounced on my knee, doesn't shoot my tail off before I see
them. I hope she makes a run for it when she sees them. I
hope I don't have to kill her.*

The READY light glowed green on his weapons console. He hit the temporary-command button he'd just programmed.

"Got him, got him, got him," Zueb called, gloating, as his
lasers continued to chew the tail end of the mystery bomber
to pieces.

"Something's going on with the underside," Syal said.
She wanted to drop another meter, but suspected she'd bottom out on the street. Even so, she could already see something changing on the bomber's underside, panels sliding
aside, something moving into position there on either side
of the bomber's centerline. "That looks like—does that
look like *feet* to you?"

Zueb ducked his oversized Sullustan head as far as he
could. "Yes. Feet. Silvery feet. One pair on either side."

"What the blazes—"

Those feet, and the humanoid bodies they were attached to, suddenly plummeted from the bomber. Syal had a glimpse of two flailing bodies, like dull-silver protocol droids with oddly shaped rifles, as they dropped into her path and hurtled toward her bow.

Syal couldn't help it—her hand twitched on the control yoke, an instinctive attempt to avoid the collision. Then came the impact, one droid hitting each of the Aleph's forward viewports.

The one hitting the starboard viewport shattered. In her peripheral vision, Syal had a momentary impression of arms and legs flying in all directions.

The one hitting the port viewport, directly in front of her, didn't shatter. It held on, its face right there in the center of the transparisteel, and it offered Syal what seemed to her like a reproachful expression. In that moment she recognized it as a type of standard spotter droid.

Then Syal's involuntary sideslip carried the Aleph far enough that its starboard laser turret began scraping along the building fronts there, tearing marquees and signs off edifices. She jerked the yoke to port, trying to free herself from that deadly friction before it spun her right into a building, and felt the shuddering end as she broke free.

No time to think, now she was traversing toward the buildings to port, and the droid was still looking at her. Gently she corrected her course, noting absently that the bomber had gained scores of meters on her.

"Great flying, Gray Four." The voice was male, unknown to her, the accent Coruscanti.

Syal couldn't risk taking her attention from the avenue ahead long enough to consult her comm board. "Who's that?"

"You've got Ax Three as your wing."

"Ax, you tear him up while I get my life in order here."

"Will do. Be advised, I'm picking up a huge pursuit squadron on our tail, and it's not ours."

Zueb unbuckled and leaned forward. With his fist, he pounded on the inside of Syal's viewport. The droid outside turned its head to look at him, and this change in its aerodynamics was apparently enough—the Aleph lurched and the droid was suddenly gone, whipped away by the altered air flow across its surface.

"Thanks," Syal said.

"No problem." The Sullustan eased back into his gunner's seat and rebuckled. "Right turret is jammed. Ax Three correct, huge cloud of incoming vehicles on our tail."

Syal gave the control yoke a tentative adjustment. The Aleph moved back to the center of the avenue, responding correctly. Only then did she check her sensor board.

It showed the E-wing high overhead, and in her peripheral vision she could see red lasers from the fast-moving starfighter hammering the bomber ahead of her. Far behind was an immense cloud of vessels moving up at tremendous speed—it would be on her in thirty seconds or less, and the sensor board still couldn't tell her what the individual vehicles in it were.

And up ahead, beyond the first of the bombers but too close, was the end of the avenue, a huge, newly constructed housing building.

Syal looked up and her eyes widened. If she pulled up into a climb right now she might—*might*—be able to clear the tops of the surrounding buildings. But the foremost bomber was so close to the building there was no way it could avoid a collision—

She saw that bomber fire missiles ahead and downward. The street just before the big building erupted in smoke and dust. And in the split second before it was swallowed by the dust cloud, she would have sworn she saw the bomber dive toward the street.

The second bomber, the one she'd been harassing, lost altitude. Its pilot had no distractions—Ax Three was now climbing away from the engagement, ascending to safety.

Syal became aware that Zueb was screaming at her, something about climbing, about continuing to live. She ignored him and glanced at her sensors. The zone where the missiles had hit was still only partly realized on the screen, but it was a big hole, and the first bomber was gone. It wasn't hitting the building, wasn't veering right or left in a futile attempt to get free of the surrounding construction—it was just gone.

Into the hole.

Syal aimed her Aleph along the second bomber's wake.

Zueb was shouting something about insanity and destruction. She ignored him. She took the control yoke in both hands.

The second bomber disappeared into the smoke cloud. On the sensor board, it dropped into the hole in the street.

As Syal reached that point, she slammed downward on the yoke, compressing it for a fraction of a second. Her top-mounted vents fired, jolting the Aleph downward.

It didn't hit anything. Through the viewports there was only smoke and darkness. On the sensor screen was the tail end of that chewed-up bomber blasting forward between banks of heavy-looking columns. There was debris, heavy dust and particulate matter, ahead of it. It rose toward the debris.

As her Aleph reached the point where the bomber began its rise, she jerked upward on her yoke and the bottom-mounted vents fired. She added some repulsorlift kick. The Aleph jolted upward, compressing her backbone and cutting off Zueb's shrieks, and suddenly they were in sunlight again.

Green parklands and the shimmering dome of a military energy shield lay ahead. The first bomber was circling to port around the shield, the second bomber to starboard. Both were dropping their bomb loads—spotter droids floating to the ground, their descents slowed by the sort of short-use repulsorlift plates used by airdrop commando troops. Above circled squadrons of X-wings, Eta-5 interceptors, E-wings—the complete ground complement of the Rellidir garrison.

Zueb was shrieking something about great flying and having children and holodramas. Syal ignored him. Something was adding up in her head, cold numbers and facts.

She slammed on the reverse thrusters to slow the Aleph, jerking Zueb forward in his seat, and switched her comm board over to the general fleet frequency. "This is Gray Four to all GA forces," she said. She felt curiously emotionless, but she knew that she had merely contained her emotion, not eliminated it. "Incoming enemy squadrons traveling east to west toward Rellidir central are missiles, and they have an unobstructed path to the interior shield. Be ready." She switched back to squadron frequency. As the front end of the Aleph swung around and the building they'd just flown beneath was framed by their viewports, she brought the Aleph to a dead halt in the air. "Zueb, fire missiles. Bring that building down. Hit the base first."

"What?"

"That's an order. Bring that building down, from ground level up."

Zueb's hands reached for his weapons controls.

CORUSCANT

The Not-Jacen came at Luke again and again, making prodigious leaps, bounding from wall to wall, from ceiling to floor, as if immune to gravity. With each pass he hurled one, two, three lightsaber blows at Luke, striking again and again until, thrown back by the impacts, he was too far away to engage.

Luke countered every blow and pitched attacks of his own. He felt the skin of his left forearm pucker a little from the heat of a near hit, saw the Not-Jacen's robes catch fire just under the right armpit from an especially close thrust of Luke's . . . but Not-Jacen patted the flames out and merely grinned at him.

Not-Jacen seized a ceiling glow rod fixture and hung there as though his weight were nothing. "You're just about as good as my *true* Master," Not-Jacen said.

Luke gave him a quizzical look. "And who is that?"

"*You* know," Not-Jacen said. "By the way, you'd look good with a beard."

"You think so?" Luke ran his free hand over his clean-shaven chin. "Well, I'm not sure what our disagreement is, but perhaps it could be settled by talking."

"I try not to negotiate with phantoms, with things that don't exist. Better to just cut them in half and watch them disappear." Not-Jacen kicked off from the wall and flew forward again.

STAR SYSTEM MZX32905, NEAR BIMMIEL

As the Sith Mara's Force attack swept him away from her, Ben switched his lightsaber off. Whirling within the power of her attack, instead of fighting against it, he added some Force energy of his own—shoving him laterally across the direction of her attack, and suddenly he was being swept at almost right angles to the direction she'd sent him. For half the duration of each spin he was making, he could see her, illuminated by her lightsaber, and now she was looking in the wrong direction; his maneuver had worked.

He slammed into a wall of stone, managed to keep from grunting in pain. He rebounded off the surface and began to drop toward the floor below; he calculated it as only ten meters down, an easy drop in this gravity. When he hit the ground, he did so with a silence that would probably please his real mother.

In the distance, the Sith Mara stood ready, her head turning this way and that, seeking for him with her Force-senses as well as with her eyes. Ben tried to blank out his mind, to erase his thoughts, to give her nothing to look for. And he wasn't using the Force; that would help.

But he was the only person within hundreds of meters of the Sith Mara. That should make it child's play to find him . . . yet somehow it didn't, and she kept looking.

Ben made one long lateral bound, circling the Sith Mara's position. In that time, Sith Mara stopped moving; she stood stock-still, her lightsaber down at an angle suited to bringing it up in a blow or an umbrella-style defensive posture, and Ben suspected that her eyes were closed.

Silently, he launched himself forward. He brought his unlit lightsaber back at a ready-to-strike angle and kept his thumb on the power stud.

His jump was accurate; he didn't need to correct it with little Force adjustments. He flew directly toward her, closing the gap between them as fast as a thrown zoneball.

Then he was near enough to see her face, her features. She was at rest, her eyes closed.

At peace. This wasn't his mother, but it was his mother's face, and there was no evil in it, no Sith malevolence.

He couldn't thumb on his lightsaber and kill her. He just couldn't.

She turned toward him and her eyes opened, red-glowing as before. She continued her turn into a spin. A chill of fear cut through his middle and he knew that her lightsaber blade would follow where the chill had been.

But it was her foot that came up, snapping into his gut with the power of a combat droid's pistoning arm.

In slow motion, he felt the wind leaving his lungs, felt himself folding over her foot, felt his internal organs compress and bruise. Then he was flying away, blackness washing across his eyes where the image of his mother had been.

chapter thirty-two

Jacen seized a rock outcropping and held it, keeping him from dropping once more toward the man with the face of Luke Skywalker. "You're just about as good as my *true* Master," Jacen said. And it was true—the phantom he fought had the speed and moves of a Jedi Master. He'd be a fair match for Luke.

The bearded man gave him a mocking look. "And who is that?"

"*You* know," Jacen said. "By the way, you look good with a beard."

"You think so?" His opponent stroked his facial hair. "Well, I'm not sure what our disagreement is, but perhaps it could be settled by talking."

Jacen considered that. This combat was not just pointless, being carried out at someone else's wish for someone else's ends, but also dangerous—the false Luke was potentially good enough to kill Jacen.

Still, the false Luke reeked of the dark side of the Force. There could be no enduring benefit in cooperating with him. Could there? For a moment Jacen was confused, weighing the preponderance of Jedi history and claims about dark-siders against his own limited experience.

But he decided in favor of history and tradition. "I try not to negotiate with phantoms, with things that don't exist. Better to just cut them in half and watch them disappear." Jacen kicked off from the wall and flew forward again.

He knew that this solidly planted, gravitationally advantaged Luke had adapted to Jacen's low-gravity tactics, so he altered them—the instant he touched down before the false Luke, he planted his feet and used the Force to brace him there, then threw a flurry of hard blows.

It was no use. The false Luke adapted instantly to his change in tactics, reverting to a softer, defensive style, turning away each of Jacen's all-out attacks. And he did so grinning, silently mocking.

The false Luke, instead of countering Jacen's fifth blow in sequence, sidestepped it, luring Jacen forward and off-balance. Luke's counterstrike whipped around and down toward Jacen's unprotected back—

"Enough," Brisha said, and the false Luke vanished. Jacen, straightening, still felt a tremor of pain from the area where the blow would have landed, and looked down to see a portion of his robe, a long black mark, on fire. He patted it out and looked up at Brisha. "Who was that, really?"

She shrugged. "A combination of the real Luke Skywalker and the dark side energy of this place. A combination that would have beaten you, since you weren't utilizing the same energy, the resources available to you." She still held on to one of the rails—sagged against it, actually. She was perspiring.

"You've been using a lot of energy yourself," Jacen said. He switched his lightsaber off.

She nodded. "Coordinating the actions of several Force phantoms at once? Very tiring. Try it sometime."

"So you admit that you're behind this assault on me."

"Oh, it was no assault. Just a test. If it had been an assault, I would have let the Luke phantom kill you. Don't you think?"

Jacen frowned. Her words had the ring of truth to them. "I think it's time for you to tell me your whole story."

"Of course." She pushed off from the rail and floated

toward the stone outcropping where the false Luke had originally arrived. She bounced lightly past Jacen and beckoned for him to follow. "All the answers are this way."

He followed.

RELLIDIR, TRALUS

Han grinned as he completed his circuit around the shield-protected Center for the Performing Arts. His spotter droids were raining down on the ground, sustaining but ignoring small-arms fire from GA ground crews and infantry, and already his board was lighting up with the data the droids were feeding to the Corellian operations HQ. On the wire-frame representation of the local area, the top of the shield was a hot spot where numerous droids had their laser sighting rifles trained. Above, many of the starfighters trapped within the outer range of shields were also being targeted.

Han's and Wedge's Shrieks were on the spotter droids' matrix, as well—as nontargets. Missiles that detected and turned toward the Shrieks were supposed to move away to find new targets. Missiles that came in too fast to divert their flight paths were supposed to detonate prematurely. In theory, the Shrieks were safe from the missile barrage.

In theory.

Han didn't rely much on theory. He'd prefer to have some buildings between him and the incoming missiles—

There was something wrong. Ahead, as he completed his circuit, was an Aleph where no Aleph should be. This one was battle-scarred, its fuselage scraped, its forward viewports scratched and dented.

Han's eyebrows shot up. This had to be the Aleph that had pursued them on the approach boulevard, Syal Antilles's craft. Inexplicably, it had managed to follow them in. And now it was slowing, turning toward the Terkury building.

Alarm bells went off in Han's head. If he were in Syal's

position, he would know that missiles were roaring up behind. He would be figuring out how to stop them before they got here. And that meant dropping a rackful of missiles into the Terkury building, collapsing it so the missiles would hit the falling debris, never making it past the outer shield zone.

That's what Syal was doing, and he had to stop her. He switched his weapons board over to missile fire and dropped his targeting brackets over the Aleph.

And hesitated.

This was Wedge's little girl. He couldn't kill her.

If he didn't, the mission would be a failure, and the GA wouldn't leave, and war might break out.

He heard a howling, and realized, as if his mind were functioning at a distance, that it was no cockpit alarm, but his own voice, an inarticulate roar of anger and frustration, filling his ears.

There was no time to find the perfect solution. His thumb settled on the firing button.

No *perfect* solution—but the fraction of a second's delay let him find a *possible* answer. He pushed the weapons control forward. The targeting brackets clicked off the Aleph and dropped to the ground several meters beneath the hovering starfighter. The brackets skittered around, trying to identify anything on the ground that might constitute a target.

Han fired. His concussion missile flashed forward to hit the duracrete beneath the Aleph.

Syal watched impassively as Zueb targeted the building just above the huge hole in the ground that the Aleph and the two bombers had emerged through. He seemed to be moving in slow motion. Everything seemed to be in slow motion.

The astromech beeped an alarm—a targeting lock on the Aleph. Syal frowned. She kept her hands steady on the controls. A sideways jerk might cause Zueb to miss his target, and she couldn't afford for that to happen. Besides, the incoming fire was probably a laser barrage by an opportunistic X-wing pilot, and she could survive a few seconds of that—

The world exploded around her. The Aleph was kicked as if by a rancor the size of a skyscraper. She felt her backbone compress, like one of the Aleph's vent-based upward jumps but worse, like ejecting from a doomed starfighter but worse. Redness filled her vision and she clearly saw the control yoke of her starfighter. Her hand was not on it. She tried to reach for it but couldn't seem to make her body move.

Outside the viewports, banks of buildings spun, sometimes above, sometimes below, intermixed with enemy starfighters and the sky and the ground.

The Aleph disappeared in the dust-and-debris cloud of Han's concussion missile, and for a moment Han thought the starfighter had gone to confetti from the force of the blast. But the Aleph leapt up out of the cloud, spinning, out of control, on a ballistic arc that would carry it within seconds back to the ground and its final destruction.

Han's curved flight path carried him past the dust cloud. His Shriek and Wedge's crossed each other, heading in opposite directions. He could hear Wedge's voice, chiding: "Han, you *missed*." The words weren't making sense; he ignored them.

All his attention was on the tumbling Aleph. *Fly, blast it, fly,* he told it, reaching out for it and its pilot as though he had Force powers, as if he could help Syal—

He couldn't, of course. He watched the doomed Aleph reach the top of its arc and begin descending toward the ground.

Its tumbling roll—was it changing? As it spun, did it seem to linger for a moment with its nose pointed to the sky?

On its next spin he was sure. The pilot was attempting to regain control. The thrusters, as they began to be pointed toward the ground, fired and continued firing until they were horizontal. They cut off again. But the spinning was slowed, and the next time the thrusters oriented downward they fired again and held, propelling the Aleph upward. The explosion-blackened starfighter wobbled as it resumed powered flight, but it was under control.

And turning back toward the Terkury building, its mission not yet accomplished.

Han stared in disbelief. Was he going to have to blow her up again?

No. A cloud of what looked like flaming insects roiled up from the crater at the foot of the Terkury building—missiles, in their hundreds.

Most headed skyward. Their flight plan would have them turn just under the dome of the outer shield and dive toward the inner, hitting two or three spots, overwhelming them with explosive power, allowing the subsequent missiles to rain down on the Center for the Performing Arts. Others would target the starfighters overhead, and the larger ships still on the ground.

Han saw two turn toward the Aleph. The Aleph, in response, banked straight toward Han's Shriek, flying underneath and past it. As soon as the Aleph and Shriek were so close to each other that their signals would be mixed on the missiles' sensors, the missiles turned away, hunting new targets. The Aleph dropped to ground level and skidded to a stop among several parked speeders, making it an unlikely target for continued missile targeting.

Han grinned. The girl was in good enough shape to try to kill him again—her tactic, leading pursuit missiles across his path, would have worked had he not already been designated a nontarget by the droids. All was right with the world. He could have cheered.

At least, all was right until his datapad beeped again at him. Its screen read,

TRANSPONDER TRAGOF1103 ON FREQ 22NF07 IS JAINA

The majority of missiles reached the summit of their arcs and turned back toward the ground.

Some didn't. A few hit targets in the air—starfighters circling above the Galactic Alliance beachhead, pilots waiting to get into the fight, pilots who weren't fast enough to elude missile fire or eject in anticipation of the impact.

The other missiles completed their turns and roared downward, concentrating into three streams.

The leading missiles of those streams hit the glowing dome of the GA shield, matching their explosive energy against its coherent force.

The first several lost that match; the shields were too strong. But the missiles kept coming, each one adding new explosive power to the equation.

The shields shivered. Complicated energy matrices began to lose their coherence. Within the Center for the Performing Arts, alert, failure, and overload lights began to flare on shield generator machinery; operators began to look at one another uncertainly, and the more fearful of them glanced around for a place to take shelter, for a direction to run.

Then, in one thousandth of a second, it happened: the complex fabric of the shield unraveled at one point, and the next missile entered the empty space where it had been. It did not detonate. The computer at the heart of its guidance system relayed its new position, meters beyond what had been designated the shield limits, to the other missiles in the flight, and those that could still maneuver to position themselves along its path began to do so.

That missile was halfway down to the crown-like top of the Center for the Performing Arts when the next spot atop the curved surface of the shield gave way. More missiles flashed through the widening gap.

The foremost missiles roared down toward the roof below, calculating at each minute fraction of a second their current position, estimated range to target, estimated fuel reserves—

*   *   *

Observers weren't aware of what happened in thousandths of a second, of course.

When the first missiles struck the shield, onlookers saw a glow begin there, accompanying the distant *whumpf* of the missiles' detonation. The glow grew larger and brighter; the noise from the detonations became louder.

Then a lance of fire shot down from the position of the shields and hit the roof of the Center for the Performing Arts.

The center seemed to swell, its walls bulging outward with flame behind them. Then the whole immense building erupted like a cake of solid fuel. Ironically, though the shield projectors were in the act of melting, disintegrating, the shields they created had not had enough time to fail utterly, and the leading edges of the explosion hit them, were contained by them.

Then the shields gave way, and the flame and debris behind them spilled out in all directions.

Missiles continued to rain down, many of them pouring into the increasingly cavernous hole that the center had been. Others hurtled onto the hulls of the small capital ships that had landed around the center. Their shields were up; their shields went down, collapsing under the relentless explosive barrage, and those fighting ships began erupting with explosions of their own.

CORUSCANT

"I was fighting a simulacrum of Jacen," Luke said. He paced through his bedchamber, looking in the closet and then under the bed, as if more enemies were likely to be found there.

"Mine was a twisted form of Ben," Mara said. "Rather cruel of an enemy to try to kill you in the image of your own son."

Luke, on his knees by the bed, looked up at her. "Why didn't they send a Ben against each of us? Wouldn't that improve the odds that one of us would hesitate, at least in theory?"

Mara shrugged. "What did this?"

Luke rose. "A dark side Force-user of some sort. Or a group of them. Something new? I don't know." He moved back to the closet and pulled out his off-white pants and tunic. "Something's happening out there, where Leia is, maybe where Jacen and Ben are. I'm going to get on the comm and see what I can find out."

"Give me my robe. I'll join you." Mara tried to push aside her sense of unease. It had gripped her the moment she'd kicked the mutated image of her son, and it hadn't left her.

STAR SYSTEM MZX32905, NEAR BIMMIEL

Around the rock outcropping, Jacen came face-to-face with another rock—a boulder of black stone, its surface shiny and smooth. It was unlike any other surface he'd seen while in these caverns.

And it reeked of dark side energy.

"A door," he said.

Beside him, Brisha nodded.

Jacen reached out to explore the barrier with his Force-attuned senses. The stone seemed to be resting on a pivot of pure energy. The slightest exertion would swing it to one side . . . but the exertion had to be made through the Force. Through the dark side of the Force. Perhaps a light-side exertion would swing it open as well, but he sensed that such an exertion would have to be much greater.

He shrugged, gestured, exerted himself minimally along dark paths. The boulder swung obediently to one side. There was darkness beyond.

Brisha moved into the darkness and Jacen followed her. Just past the boulder entrance, on the similarly smooth stone to the left, a set of sturdy metal levers and controls was revealed, and she flipped several of those switches from the bottom to the top position.

In the distance a light came on—bright, golden light, cheerful and warm in hue, revealing that Jacen and Brisha stood in an irregular stone corridor, triangular, wide at the base, coming to a point a couple of meters above their heads. The corridor widened a few meters before them, and the cavern beyond was being illuminated by the new light.

Gravity, too, was asserting itself. Jacen's second step was half the floating, bouncing distance of the first, and the next was almost correct for Coruscant-standard gravity. After that, he felt that he could have been on Coruscant, except for the coldness of the air.

"The heaters are now on," Brisha said, as though reading his mind. "But it takes awhile to warm a space as large as this."

"Of course," Jacen said.

They moved out from the corridor and into the open cavern, and Jacen blinked at what he saw.

The cavern was open, its walls slightly irregular but still of the same dark, smooth material as the boulder-door. The cavern ceiling was perhaps 50 meters up at its lowest point, 60 at its highest, and the space was longer than it was high, some 200 meters in length in one dimension, 150 in another.

But none of that registered at first. Jacen's eye was drawn to the building that occupied the cavern's center.

It was a mansion, five stories of stony construction, and it did not seem in the least ominous. The building's outer surfaces were rock, but dressed white and green marble slabs rather than the ponderous dark stone of this asteroid. Its windows were wide, unshuttered, inviting.

At each corner of the building was a tower, the chamber at its summit roofed but open to the sides, and figures moved there and in various windows of the building. In one tower window, a figure painted; in another, one played an oversized harp, and distant notes, soft and true, reached Jacen's ears; in one of the lower windows, a figure juggled three glowing yellow balls. At the center of the fifth floor a huge mechanism, all gigantic gears and levers, operated, its whole purpose apparently being to drive a single dial on the face of the building; it turned at a rate of two or three times a minute, carefully watched by a figure who stood on the fifth-floor ledge in front of it.

The moving figures were all protocol droids, and gaily painted, one red, one forest green, one gold. The machine tender was a pastel blue.

And it was all suffused with dark side energy.

"This," Jacen said, "is insane."

"Not really." Brisha walked toward the building with him. "Darth Vectivus enjoyed the architecture of Naboo and incorporated some of its building materials into his home away from home. Other architectural elements are from other worlds."

"But it's not very Sithly. The Sith citadel at Ziost—"

"I've been there. Very gloomy place. Unnecessarily so." They reached the steps up to the main doors, and, as they began climbing, those doors swung open for them. Beyond was a marble-lined hallway; waist-high columns along its walls supported busts of men and women, mostly human, some of other species.

"All right," Jacen said, "no more delays. The truth." He reached the top of the stairs and moved into the hallway. He felt a little off-balance—the dissonance between the energies he felt and the cheerful surroundings bothered him.

"The truth is, I trained to be a Sith. I was trained by your grandfather, Darth Vader." She did not seem in the least ashamed by this revelation.

Jacen drew to a stop at the first of the busts. It showed a serene-looking woman, her hair in a layered style that reached high. "But you don't talk like a galaxy-conquering psychopath."

"Vader wasn't a galaxy-conquering psychopath. He was a sad man whose one love in life had died, and whose one anchor to the world of the living was, yes, a galaxy-conquering madman. Palpatine. The bust, by the way, is of Vectivus's mother. She wasn't Sith, she wasn't Jedi."

Jacen shot Brisha an irritable look and gestured for her to keep going.

"All right. My true name is Shira Brie."

Jacen blinked at her. "But you're better known as Lumiya." In his mind he called up holographic images he'd been shown of the famous monster, the woman whose lower face was always concealed behind a tight-fitting veil, who always wore a triangular headdress, who carried a unique weapon—a lightwhip, as destructive as a lightsaber but pliant and with a greater reach. There was no place for this woman to carry one in the jumpsuit she now wore, but he did not deceive himself that she was unarmed.

"Yes."

"Under which name you tried to kill several members of my family."

"Decades ago. Yes." Now she did look abashed, regretful. "Don't judge me too soon, Jacen. My history is very much like your aunt Mara's . . . except she received some lucky breaks I didn't. I took longer to straighten out my life."

"Tell me about it."

"I was raised on Coruscant, tapped for Imperial service, and, when Luke Skywalker became a hero of the Rebels, I joined them."

"To kill him."

"No, to do worse—to discredit him. A ruined hero is much more devastating than a dead one." Her gaze slid off to one side, and Jacen sensed that she was reliving events that had transpired before he was born. "I actually developed quite an attachment for your uncle. Once he was ruined as a Rebel, I planned to draw him over to the Imperial side. But during a starfighter battle, he relied on the Force instead of transponder data to differentiate friend from foe, and shot me down."

"I'd heard that."

"I lived, but it cost me. Cost me more than half of my body, in fact. My limbs, some of my organs . . ." She looked down at herself. "Cybernetic replacements." When

Jacen didn't answer, she continued, "And that's when Darth Vader took special interest in me. Perhaps because of our similarities. He could feel the Force potential in me, and it didn't take a master psychologist to pick up on my desire for revenge."

"Which you did attempt."

"Again and again, after my Sith training on Ziost. Yes."

"You seem singularly unapologetic."

"I don't have anything to apologize to *you* for. Bring me into the presence of Luke Skywalker or Leia Organa, and, well, things will be different. Would you like to see the rest of the house?"

"Is there anything to it but bright cheerful colors, bedrooms, refreshers, and so on?"

"Not anymore. There were lots of artifacts in his library, but I removed them to the library you saw in the habitat. There are all the gaily painted protocol droids."

Jacen shuddered. "So far, the one irrefutable sign that Vectivus was evil . . . No, we can do the house tour after your explanation, after I retrieve Ben and Nelani. So— Palpatine and Vader both die, and you have no chance to be educated enough to become the Mistress of the Sith."

"Oh, there you're wrong, Jacen." Lumiya shook her head as if chiding him for his ignorance. "I never had *any* chance to become Mistress of the Sith. No matter how much I learned."

Jacen moved to the next bust in line. This was a Bothan face, alert and intelligent. "Why not?"

"The Force is the energy of the living. You interact with it, its eddies and flows, with your own living body. It's all right to have a mechanical part or two—an implant, a replacement foot. But for true Mastery in the Force, light side or dark side, you have to be mostly organic. I'm not, and so the greatest, the most significant powers, I can never learn."

Jacen frowned. "Wait. That means that Darth Vader could never have become the Lord of the Sith . . . a true Master."

"That's correct. I'm not sure he ever understood that. He might not have cared. He was numbed by tragedy. The Bothan you're looking at, by the way, was an old family friend of Darth Vectivus. Taught Vectivus basic principles of negotiation."

"Are you saying that none of these busts is a Sith?"

"That's right. This isn't a museum for Sith matters. It's a celebration of Vectivus's youth and life. His *life,* Jacen. His joys and triumphs."

Jacen propped his elbow up on the Bothan's head. "So that's what the trap is."

"Eh?" Lumiya looked surprised.

"You didn't lure me here to kill me. You lured me here to persuade me to take up the path of the Sith."

"Yes."

"Because I have all my body parts."

She grinned at him. "Not exactly. Because it's *you*. All the portents, all the convergences flowing into the future say so, particularly since you've already received quite a lot of Sith training."

"Explain that."

"In a minute. What was I saying? Oh, yes. I'm not trying to turn you into a Palpatine. He was, as you say, a psychopath. Destructive, uncaring, manipulative. He chose the dark side to achieve his ends, but was weak and confused enough to be twisted by the dark side. Unlike your uncle Luke, you haven't been twisted by the *light* side, so I'm certain you can resist the temptations of the dark."

"I've heard enough." The voice was Nelani's, and there she was, striding in through the front doors, her unlit lightsaber in her hand. "As I'm sure you have, Jacen."

"Where's Ben?" Jacen asked.

Nelani shook her head. "We were separated."

"You were never together," Lumiya said. "When you were talking to Ben and he to you, you were actually hundreds of meters apart, talking to Force phantoms of each other. A trivial thing to arrange in this place, where there's so much energy to manipulate." She returned her attention to Jacen. "Energy *you* could use, in the name of improving people's lives, if you chose to."

"Quiet," Nelani said.

Jacen turned to Lumiya. "Where's Ben?" he repeated.

"Unconscious. Not hurt. He'll wake up a little sore." Lumiya shrugged. "If I were the monster you thought I was, he'd be dead, Jacen. The son of the man who shot me down and destroyed my body? Think about it."

"Think about this," Jacen said. "Brisha—Shira—Lumiya—whatever you choose to call yourself, there are still outstanding charges against you for crimes committed back when you were an Imperial. Whatever you are now, you have to face those."

"Perhaps." Lumiya suddenly looked tired, dispirited. "I just wish you weren't taking me into custody from your own fear. That's sad."

"Fear?" Jacen frowned at her. "I have nothing to fear."

"You're afraid that my words might be true," Lumiya said. "That the dark side doesn't corrupt in and of itself. That you're destined to become the next Sith Lord—the first Sith Lord to be active in decades, the first one in centuries with the strength to use the Sith techniques to help others. Because if it is true, you have to make a decision, choosing between your life as it is—comfortable, but almost purposeless—and life as you know it should be."

Nelani's lightsaber *snap-hissed* into life. "I think you need to shut up," she said.

"There's no need for that," Jacen said. There was a sting to Lumiya's words—the jibe about his life being purposeless was too close to the mark to be entirely ignored. Luke would have said that obedience to the guidance of the Force would give him direction and purpose, but since the end of the Yuuzhan Vong war, except for those times when he faced foes whose behavior lit up the Force like a KILL ME SOON sign, the life of the Jedi hadn't given him the sense of purpose it seemed to have provided his uncle. "No need unless she resists."

Lumiya smiled. "There's no worry. Nelani would never

attack me *unless* I resisted. She's a very good girl. A sweet, doctrinal Jedi."

"This sweet, doctrinal Jedi is about to kick your teeth in," Nelani said. "Jacen, I can feel you wavering."

"I'm not wavering. I'm just curious about her arguments. There is merit to some of them."

"Like any dark-sider, she mixes truth with lies until you can't separate them."

Jacen ignored her. He waved at the busts and walls around him. "Lumiya, you present me this house as though it constitutes proof that Darth Vectivus was a nice man despite his dark side training. Well, that doesn't wash. Anyone can commission the building of a pretty house. Palpatine was a patron of the arts. As for Vectivus himself, you not only can't prove that he was uncorrupted—you haven't offered any proof that he actually *existed*." He fixed her with a look he intended as amused condescension. "The dark side corrupts. The Sith are inevitably drawn to evil."

"I can give you proof of one who wasn't," Lumiya said.

Nelani glared at Jacen. "Don't listen."

Jacen shrugged. "Go ahead."

Lumiya looked dispirited. "Should I? Why bother? With sweet Nelani whispering in your ear, you're certain to automatically disbelieve every word I say." Then the forlorn look left her face, replaced by a slight smile. "After all, everything I tell you is a lie."

Jacen stared at Lumiya, but she did not continue. Nelani looked between them, confused, sensing that something had changed in the conversation, something she had missed.

Jacen cleared his throat. "An interesting turn of phrase," he said.

"Not an accidental one." Lumiya turned to look at Nelani. "Turn that thing off, dear. You'll run the battery down."

Nelani didn't budge. Her blade remained lit and glowing. "Jacen, something's wrong. What is she saying?"

"She's saying nothing."

"Then I'll give you a name," Lumiya said. "Vergere. She

said that, didn't she? When she was training you to be a Sith?"

"She was training me to *survive*," Jacen said. He thought of his onetime mentor, the diminutive bird-like alien who'd been born in this galaxy but had lived for years among the Yuuzhan Vong, accompanying them back when they swept into the galaxy on their mission of conquest and destruction.

"Yes," Lumiya said. "To survive. Survival is a Sith trait. Jedi train themselves for self-sacrifice, for union with the Force, and they can afford to be suicidal, because there are so many of them. Sith train to survive."

"Now you're making things up," Jacen said. "Nelani, keep her here while I go find Ben."

Lumiya shook her head. "You don't want Ben to be here. Someone's about to die. It might be you, it might be Nelani, and it might be me. Bring Ben here, and it might be him. Death is here among us, and it will be a very distressing one."

Frowning, Jacen cast out his senses like a net, sampling the present and the future. Pathways led in all directions, but in each of them one of the three people present fell dying. Jacen, head severed by a pliant whip of light. Lumiya, Nelani's lightsaber cutting her in half—lengthwise, so there was no chance of missing the organic parts. Nelani, her heart speared by Jacen's lightsaber. Jacen, stabbed from behind by Ben, the boy's uncomprehending features making it clear that he was seeing something very different from the reality before him. Lumiya, swept into a marble wall by Jacen's control of the Force, her skull shattered—

Jacen shut his eyes against the parade of tragedy. He opened them to view reality. "You're right. I can't see a path that doesn't lead to death. Let's revise our circumstances and see if any more options open to us in a minute or two."

"Good," Lumiya said. "Now. Vergere. A Jedi, but one who was quietly resentful of the hidebound ways of the old Jedi Council, its resistance to any learning outside the rote procedures that had been part of the order for so long. She was a rogue student of the Force, of techniques and pathways that are not all part of the Jedi school. You agree?"

Jacen nodded.

"In her investigations, she studies Count Dooku, and his trail leads her to Darth Sidious, who has just taken Dooku as apprentice. Darth Sidious, who, the galaxy learns decades later, is Palpatine. Sidious accepts her as a student and candidate. There can be only two Sith at any time, the Master and the apprentice, but there can be many candidates, and she is one."

"Proof," Jacen said.

"You'll find the proof in your feelings." Lumiya spared a look for Nelani. "Assuming the good Jedi girl doesn't kill me for saying things she doesn't like."

"She won't," Jacen said.

"Vergere learns from Palpatine . . . and she learns *about* him. She observes. She sees his weakness, his greed, his compulsion to rule and manipulate. She realizes that he could be the most destructive living force in the galaxy. And she decides to kill him."

Jacen didn't answer. It troubled him that there was nothing in Lumiya's words inconsistent with the Vergere he knew. Had Vergere been a student of the Force in that time period, which he knew she was, he was certain that she would have studied every facet of the Force she could find. And if she became certain that her teacher was a force for destruction, she would have tried to find some way to doom him.

"But Vergere strikes too soon," Lumiya continued. "Palpatine survives, and puts killers on her trail. She uses Jedi order resources to keep her a step ahead of her pursuers, and soon accepts a Jedi mission that may get her clear of her enemies. It takes her to the world of Zonama Sekot, and from there she chooses to leave with the mission that eventually reaches the galaxy of the Yuuzhan Vong."

"That doesn't make her Sith," Jacen said. He kept his voice even, but he could feel the doubt growing within him.

Lumiya's words made so much sense, casting Vergere within a context that finally made her comprehensible to him . . .

. . . but only if Lumiya's claims about the nondestructive, noncorruptive basis to the Sith were actually true.

Lumiya's tone turned chiding. "Think about it, Jacen. She cared for you, cared for the fate of the galaxy, cared for everyone. She gave Mara Jade the healing treatment that allowed her to carry that boy. *She was a Sith, and yet she helped give Luke Skywalker a son.* She could be cruelly ruthless, couldn't she? And yet each act of ruthlessness improved matters. Improved her surroundings. Improved you."

Nelani gave Jacen one more look, and in her glance there was worry and anguish. "That's it," she said.

She struck at Lumiya.

chapter thirty-three

Nelani's lightsaber blow was lightning-quick, but by the time it landed the older woman had twirled to one side, positioning herself behind a bust. The glowing blade sliced off the marble top of the head of some long-dead Rodian scholar.

Nelani advanced. Lumiya retreated, slapping her thigh—digging her fingers through the cloth and *into* her thigh. She yanked, and suddenly in her hands was a whip. She flicked it back, preparatory to striking with it; its tendrils, for there were several instead of just one, spread out into something that moved like a weaponized cloud, some of them shining iron-like and jagged, some of them glowing like a lightsaber's blade. Lumiya cracked the weapon forward; Nelani, her body language suggesting confusion as she faced this unusual weapon, twisted to one side, but one of the lashes, a metal one, grazed her face, drawing blood all along her left cheek. Nelani took a step back, shaking her head.

"I don't just talk, Jedi girl," Lumiya said. "And, you'll notice, unlike *you,* I don't strike at a target who doesn't have a weapon in hand."

"Let Lumiya talk," Jacen said.

"Can't you feel yourself wavering?" There was a shrill tone of desperation in Nelani's voice. "She's bending your mind, bending your will."

Jacen shook his head. "No, she's not. If I'm wavering, it's before a presentation of fact, not mind tricks. Come on, Nelani. If mind tricks were involved, don't you think you'd feel them?"

"Here's the truth about the difference between Jedi and Sith," Lumiya said.

"Shut up." Nelani lunged forward again, spinning her lightsaber into a defensive shield.

Lumiya's lightwhip flicked around the edges of the shield. Ends of several tendrils rapped into Nelani's chest and right bicep, creating small blood and burn spots. Nelani cried out and danced back again, baffled by the older woman's superior technique.

"Both Jedi and Sith gravitate toward rule," Lumiya continued. "But the Jedi believe it's contrary to their nature, so they create guidelines that are only supposed to govern their own actions . . . until the inevitable day when the secular governments fall so short of Jedi ideals that they feel they have to impose their own rules on the others, to save them. That's what happened at the end of the Old Republic. But the rules they put together are strange, ascetic, not designed for ordinary people, and they can't be sustained as a form of government.

"The Sith recognize from the start that they can choose to impose their rule on others . . . or not. If society is functioning well, a Sith doesn't have to act. Vectivus didn't. If it's not, he should act. And since he knows that fixing a broken government is his mission, he can design a system of government that works, that is fair, orderly."

Nelani gestured with her free hand. The bust of Darth Vectivus's mother flew forward, hurtling toward Lumiya like a marble missile. Lumiya flicked her lightwhip toward it, and nine or ten tendrils converged on it. The bust exploded into countless marble shards, raining down on the floor.

"The galaxy is dissolving into chaos," Lumiya said. "Its leadership can't save it; they're the leftovers of what failed fifteen years ago during the Yuuzhan Vong war. The Jedi can't step in and fix things—you know their methods, the way they think. What has Luke Skywalker told you? Have his tactics, his recommendations fixed anything? No. As good a man as he is, he and his order are just tools of the Galactic Alliance."

Nelani tried again, this time with the bust of the Bothan. It reached a halfway point between her and Lumiya, but the older woman reached out with her own free hand and the bust stopped in midair. Now it strained forward toward her; a moment later, it crept back through the air toward Nelani. It was a piece in a game of push-of-war between the women, and neither was winning.

The strain showed in Lumiya's voice, causing it to hoarsen. "Vergere sacrificed herself so you could assume the Sith mantle she wanted for you. That's the kind of self-sacrifice no Jedi would admit is possible for the Sith, but it's the truth. Take what I have to teach you, Jacen. Take this place and the dark side power it contains. Take the knowledge that rests in its tombs on the world of Ziost. And use them against the forces that are trying to tear this galaxy apart. Restore order. Give your cousin, give the children in your family and your life the chance to grow up in a galaxy without war."

"You're still withholding the truth," Jacen said. His voice was hard now, his manner uncompromising, unconfused. "You killed the security chief on Toryaz Station, didn't you?"

"Yes," she said. "Of course. I caught up to him too late to prevent the attack on you—it was already under way. But I could force from him an admission of who he was working for, and avenge the dead."

"Who was he working for?"

"Thrackan Sal-Solo. Who else?"

"And all those situations on Lorrd—you didn't 'dream' about them, did you? You had direct access to the perpetrators."

Lumiya cast a sideways glance at the bust hovering between her and Nelani. It was beginning to creep back toward her, and the strain of keeping it at bay was showing on her face. "Yes. My visions were waking visions. I could have interfered directly with their plans—probably with exactly the same results you experienced."

"Why didn't you?"

"I used them as a test for you." Lumiya closed her eyes and strained, but the bust still moved toward her. "Sith, like Jedi, have to determine the fates of others. Unlike Jedi, they know that sometimes this means sacrificing one so that twenty may live. I had to find out whether you understood that. *And you do.*"

"How about your confederate?" Jacen asked. "The man Master Skywalker keeps glimpsing but can't quite see? The man he says doesn't exist?"

Lumiya managed a laugh that was half-exhausted gasp. "Jacen, that's *you,* visions of you. The Sith you will become. Luke can't make out his features because he's not willing to accept what he sees through the Force—your face where the next Lord of the Sith stands." Her last words were little more than a gasp, and her control slipped at that point. The bust of the Bothan hurtled toward her. She cracked her whip at it, a foreshortened stroke that might have missed in any case, but the bust's trajectory changed, sending the statuary beneath the tendrils. Instead of striking Lumiya's head or chest, the bust cracked into her right hand, sending the whip spinning from her grip; its tendrils twisted across the floor like living things, scarring it with their passage.

Nelani leapt forward, slashing at her enemy. Her blade came down—

On Jacen's. His blade held hers, his eyes held her eyes. "I'm not through here," he said.

There was despair in Nelani's voice. "I don't know how, but she's turning you. Can't you see it?"

"Stop listening with just your ears," Jacen said. "Look into the Force. Do you really see any flow from her to me, from me to her, something that could alter my mind or my perceptions?"

Nelani held his gaze for a moment more, then closed her eyes.

For that moment, she was vulnerable to a counterattack. But Jacen merely kept his blade before hers. Lumiya did not attack, did not even summon her whip back to her; she merely held her forearm and hand where the bust had hit them. Finally Nelani's eyes opened again and she seemed calmer. "No," she admitted. "Lumiya isn't using any Force techniques against you. You're not being influenced by the dark side energies here. I don't understand what's happening."

"Turn off your lightsaber," Jacen said.

She did.

He turned his own off. Now the only sound of menace came from Lumiya's lightwhip. The older woman looked at the weapon and the glowing tendrils faded to darkness, to almost invisible threads.

"There," Jacen said. "Now we can work things out."

"Yes." Nelani turned toward Lumiya. "Shira Brie, I arrest you in the name of the Galactic Alliance. You will be tried for—"

"No," Jacen said. "I've decided to learn what she has to teach me. That means she needs to remain free. To remain here."

Nelani looked at him, disbelieving. "Jacen, the law—"

"The law is what we make of it." He shrugged. "She has said she's Lumiya, Nelani, but she hasn't proven it. All we have to do is not believe her, to leave that claim out of our reports, and we've followed the letter of the law."

Nelani moved slightly, stepping back, bringing the hilt of her lightsaber a few centimeters up. "I am arresting her."

Lumiya interrupted. "I'll consent to be arrested."

Both of the Jedi looked at her. "You will?" Jacen asked.

"Of course." Lumiya looked sober, unhappy. "I know my fate is no longer my own. I want to see the Sith rise with you at the head of the order, Jacen, and for that reason I swear myself to your service." She knelt as she spoke, lowering her head—an invitation for a blessing, or for a killing stroke. "But whichever one of you is in charge here will choose my fate, my future."

Her voice low, Nelani said, "Put your hands behind your back." As Lumiya obeyed, Nelani pulled a pair of stun cuffs from her belt pouch.

Jacen frowned. There was something wrong about this situation, and for a moment he suspected treachery on Lumiya's part, but a glimpse into the likely immediate future dispelled that notion. He saw Lumiya obedient, unresisting, being led back to the shuttle.

His mind flickered forward through the likely time streams. The future, as Yoda had said so frequently and famously that the quotation littered the Jedi archives, was always in motion, and many potential futures led from this event.

But they began congregating in certain areas. Nelani testifying against Shira Brie, also known as Lumiya, also known as Lumiya Syo. Lumiya convicted, being executed, being locked up in solitude, being locked up in a mass prison and assassinated by someone whose father she had killed decades ago. All she knew vanishing, dying with her.

Along all these paths, the galaxy continued to come unhinged, rebellion sparking in all corners, the Galactic Alliance crumbling, like a cancer-racked body, eating itself from the insides out, whole populations dying.

Detonators destroying this place, blowing the asteroid into millions of pieces, scattering the knowledge hidden here. An ancient Star Destroyer raining turbolaser destruction down on the surface of Ziost, purging it of knowledge lingering there.

Scores of time lines congregated on Jacen Solo and Luke Skywalker, bringing them together. The two of them faced each other, their surroundings changing every second as the scene slipped from time line to time line, yet their poses and the lightsabers lit in their hands remained the same, as did the anger and tragic loss twisting both their faces.

They spun, they struck, the impacts of their lightsabers causing flares of light to cast the walls and floors behind them into greater darkness. On and on they fought, their loss giving them strength, until—

Jacen cut Luke down. Sometimes it was a blow across the shoulder, down into the chest. Sometimes it was a slash, too fast to see, across the throat that sent the older man's head from his shoulders. Sometimes it was a thrust to the stomach, followed by minutes of agony, Luke writhing in a futile struggle for life while Jacen, tears running down his cheeks, knelt nearby.

Luke died.

Luke died.

"No," Jacen whispered. He summoned himself back to the here and now.

Nelani and Lumiya were walking away. The younger woman held the older by the shoulder, guiding her.

Jacen lit his lightsaber and struck. Nelani jumped away, but the glowing blade merely parted the cuffs that held Lumiya's hands together behind her back.

Both women looked at him.

"She remains free," Jacen told Nelani. "If you take her . . ." He could not say the rest of the words. *Luke dies. And I kill him.*

There was more to it than that. For a moment, he was drawn back into the streams of probability that led him into the future.

Nelani could leave without her prisoner. She would return home to Lorrd and tell all to her superiors. To Luke.

Jacen cut Luke down. Luke died.

Nelani could be persuaded not to tell. She would rethink her promise later and break it, telling all to Luke.

Jacen cut Luke down. Luke died.

Only in the time streams where Nelani fell, never to rise, did Luke remain on his feet, in command, alive. Other tragedies, shadowy and indistinct, swirled around him, but he lived.

Jacen returned again to the present. The truth of what he had just experienced through the Force numbed him.

But it was the truth, and he had to be strong enough to face it.

Lumiya knew it, or had some sense of it. There were tears on her cheeks to match the ones he felt on his own. "There is this about being Sith," she told him. "We strengthen ourselves through sacrifice."

Jacen nodded, grudging acceptance of that fact. "Yes."

Nelani looked at him, and beyond him, into his intent. With a noise that was half moan, she turned and fled.

Jacen raced after her.

RELLIDIR, TRALUS

More missiles poured into the downtown area that had surrounded the Center for the Performing Arts. The spotter droids on the ground didn't direct them to the crater that had been the Galactic Alliance beachhead. Instead, they sent the missiles toward enemies in the skies—the starfighters of the Galactic Alliance.

Han rose toward one of them, the X-wing whose transponder signaled TRAGOF1103, Tralus Ground Occupation Forces Number 1103, on frequency 22NF07.

His progress was not easy, fast, or safe. The skies were still cluttered with Galactic Alliance starfighters, and a surprising number of them seemed intent on shooting him down. They dived at him and rose toward him, firing lasers; a vengeful interceptor pilot even tried to ram him, a tactic that would have constituted suicide had Han not side-slipped and allowed the tiny, high-speed fighter to roar through the space he had just occupied.

Han's intent was simple: get close enough to his daughter that missiles chasing her would abort, would turn away to find new targets.

In the few moments he had to watch her, moments when he wasn't ducking incoming laserfire, he saw that she was doing pretty well on her own. Her X-wing, moving higher and higher in the sky, dipped and fluttered, firing its own lasers at Corellian attack fighters and Vigilance Interceptors. Those starfighters tended to veer away, smoking, or detonate, leaving oddly peaceful and colorful clouds in the sky.

Missiles roared toward her from the front; she sideslipped and they missed, or fired her lasers and they detonated, eliminating the missiles around them in an explosive act of fratricide. Missiles roared toward her from the side, the back; she eluded them, now rising, now dipping, an indestructible leaf caught in a speed-of-sound wind, and the missiles shot past.

Sometimes another X-wing rode at her wing, supporting her tactics with movements that were eerie in their instantaneous adjustment, in their perfect complementarities.

Once a trio of missiles roaring toward her from the starboard side detonated two hundred meters from her X-wing for no reason Han could see. Had they hit shrapnel? Had Jaina destroyed them with a flip of her hand and a Force technique? Han didn't know.

He did realize two things. The first was that as fast as he climbed, as fast as he could afford to climb while being pestered by enemy pilots, she was rising faster. The second was a more painful realization, which settled on him like a weighted net wrapping itself around a tired swimmer:

She didn't need him.

She was a brilliant pilot with a brilliant wingman. She was older than Han had been when he'd pitted the *Millennium Falcon* against pilots from the first Death Star, and was more experienced. Part Han, part Leia, and all herself, she dominated the air around her.

Mixed in his heart were pride and pain in the discovery that she had outgrown him.

Green laserfire flashed from the vicinity of his starboard hull and an incoming Howlrunner exploded. Snapped back to the here and now, Han looked to starboard and port, realized that he was flanked by two attack fighters on either side, and almost jumped out of his seat.

But they were green on his sensor board—friendlies.

Wedge's voice was in his ears and Han realized it had been there for some time. "What was that, uh, One?"

"We have escorts out of the combat zone," Wedge said. "You should be picking yours up now."

"They're here."

"We have to leave the zone, Two. The enemy still has numerical superiority, and we're not in fighters. Also, I think the really nimble X-wing up top is your daughter. It would be a karking shame to be shot down by your own daughter, wouldn't it?"

Han laughed. It was a brittle noise. "It sure would. All right, lead me out of here. Speaking of daughters, I need to talk to you."

"Go ahead."

"Later, back at base."

"Whatever you say."

Across long minutes, the battle over Rellidir moved farther and farther away from downtown. The incoming missiles were spent against the Center for the Performing Arts, against starfighters too slow or luckless to elude them, against each other when a random detonation would claim an entire flight of them.

Syal kept her attention on the skies beyond her viewport. She ached all over and could taste blood in her mouth. "How's it look?" she asked.

Zueb, kneeling in his chair, facing backward, pulled his hands and face out of the mess of dislodged circuits and wiring he'd been working with. He gave her a noncommittal look. "Not good."

"Will we make orbit?"

"Orbit, yes." The Sullustan shrugged. "But no hull integrity. Blow up a balloon and let it go to fly around, venting air? That's us."

"Plug our suits in for direct atmosphere and power for heating. We'll put up with a few minutes of cold."

"Yes, boss." Zueb fiddled around behind their seats, plugging both their flights into power and air suppliers, then turned around and settled into his chair. He uttered a bark of pain. "Oww. Think I have no spine left."

"You had one to begin with?"

"Not nice." Zueb strapped in.

Syal brought the engines up. They whined, unnaturally loud, the noise strained and wrong, but the diagnostics board indicated that they were supplying power to the thrusters. Gently, slowly, Syal lifted off, pointed the Aleph's battered nose away from the portions of the sky where combat was still thick, and accelerated.

"We lost this one," she said.

"You did great."

"I'm a great loser."

"I fly with great loser any day. Also, Lieutenant Baradis thinks you're really good looking."

"What?"

"Said so in mess yesterday."

"You're trying to take my mind off all this."

"Yes. Am doing a good job?"

"No." She frowned. "Baradis, huh?"

"Don't see it myself. Human heads too tiny to be good looking."

She grinned. "Shut up."

STAR SYSTEM MZX32905, NEAR BIMMIEL

Nelani ran with the speed of a trained athlete, but as soon as she passed beyond the cavern where Darth Vectivus's house stood and where the artificial gravity generator operated, her gait became inefficient, her leaps too long—she didn't have Jacen's experience with low gravity.

He began to catch up to her.

She bounded up along the rails, toward the surface habitat, her lightsaber giving her enough light to see the cross-rungs where she needed to place her feet.

Jacen saw spots of blood on some of those rungs, evidence of the injury Lumiya's whip had inflicted on her.

The rails rose through a gap in the cavern ceiling, and

beyond that point Jacen could no longer see Nelani. He left his own lightsaber on but closed his eyes, seeking her with his Force-senses—

And there she was, hurtling toward him in the leg-forward posture of a vicious side kick.

Not looking in her direction, he twisted aside and swatted at her with his lightsaber. He put no strength behind his blow; he didn't need to. The blade caught her on the inner thigh, slicing through cloth and skin and muscle. She shrieked, flew past him, hit the stony surface of this cavern floor, and rolled, in the curious way that low gravity mandated, to a halt.

He bounced toward her, slow, sure, and predatory.

When he reached her, she was sitting, unable to stand, her now lit lightsaber in her right hand, her right leg, now useless, beneath her. He could see part of the wound, black with cauterized flesh and blood. She looked up, the pain on her face made more stark by the glaring brightness of both their blades.

"Jacen, don't do this," she said.

"You don't understand what's at stake."

"I'm not concerned with living or dying," she told him. "I surrendered my fate to the Force when I joined the order. It's *you*. If you do this, you'll become something bad. Something destructive."

"A Sith."

"No. Call it whatever you want to. What do you call someone who kills without needing to? Someone who joins sides with evil because of a well-reasoned argument?"

He stood there and looked at her, and was battered by emotions—his, hers, lingering dark side energies from thousands of years before. Her health and beauty, which had been marred and which he would mar further. Her despair and disillusionment, which were almost palpable energies, scarring his nerves like sanding surfaces.

A deep sorrow settled across him, sorrow at the tragedy being perpetrated. In Nelani's myriad futures he could dimly glimpse good and kind acts, love, perhaps family and children. He was about to cut through the connective tissues between Nelani and those futures, and he could feel the pain of that cut. In a way, the sensation was almost comforting, reminding him that he was still possessed of human emotion, of human values.

"Nelani," he said, "I'm sorry. You're . . . a deflector that would send the future spinning into tragedy. And you're too young, too weak to understand it, to correct it."

"Jacen—"

He struck, a slash that turned into a twirl binding her blade. The maneuver disarmed her, leaving her arm untouched but spinning her lightsaber off into the darkness.

He struck again, a surgical thrust that entered the precise center of her breastbone, emerged from her spine.

Jacen pulled the lightsaber free. Nelani slumped to the side, and he felt her begin to vanish into the Force.

Until she finished her slow fall and her head lolled against the stone, her eyes did not leave his.

chapter thirty-four

CORELLIAN SPACE, ABOVE TRALUS

Leia watched the status boards as they provided updates on the situation at Rellidir.

Headquarters shields down. Headquarters destroyed. Tralus citizens spilling into the streets, sniping on GA ground occupation forces with hand blasters, hunting blasters.

Corellian capital ships and hyperdrive-equipped starfighters dropping out of hyperspace on the far side of Tralus, joining the furball in the skies above Rellidir, swelling its numbers even as the GA retaliated with more and more starfighter squadron launches.

Covert messages from Han relayed in tight-burst data packets; they arrived from his datapad through a sophisticated comlink currently glued to the bottom of a mouse droid scurrying around somewhere in the vicinity of the bridge. Those messages reported Han alive, Jaina alive, Wedge alive, the Antilles girl alive.

Withdrawal command from *Dodonna*. The GA squadrons obeyed, disengaging where and when they could, some of them staying behind for last-minute exchanges with the gloating Corellians.

Leia was called back to the bridge, where she rejoined Admiral Limpan on the walkway. Together they watched

Dodonna's complement of surviving starfighters line up for landings in the ship's hangar bays.

"We could have held on here," Admiral Limpan said. "By throwing more and more forces into the mix. And yet that would have been counterproductive. Making peace harder to achieve. We didn't, we won't . . . but that makes this conclusion a scripted one. The men and women who died, young and brave, did so for a predestined conclusion."

Leia nodded in silent agreement.

"It feels not like a victory, or even like a loss. It feels like dancing to someone else's tune."

"The GA isn't playing it," Leia said.

"Nor the Corellians." The admiral shrugged. "Perhaps it's random chance. I believe in randomness; I see it often. But one can never think of it as friendly. It never has our best interests at heart." She turned her attention to Leia. "Colonel Moyan says your tactical recommendations were very well reasoned, very helpful. Though he was surprised to find them a bit conservative, considering your reputation."

Leia shrugged. "We get older, perhaps we get more protective of those we lead. If I'm more conservative, that's why."

"Of course. Will you be returning to Coruscant or Corellia?"

"Corellia, for now. Where I can conservatively argue for peace while the warmakers are strutting around, crowing about their victory."

"I'll arrange for a starfighter escort for your shuttle."

Leia shook her head. "No one's going to fire upon an unarmed shuttle. This isn't like the Yuuzhan Vong war, fought in mindless savagery. Both sides . . . are us."

"For now." Even on the admiral's Duros features, considered expressionless by human standards, Leia could detect sorrow, pessimism. "In my experience, it doesn't take long for 'us' to become 'them.' And when that happens, every savagery becomes possible."

"True."

The admiral returned her attention to the viewports. "May the Force be with you, Princess."

"And also with you, Admiral."

On the shuttle flight back to Corellia, Leia sat wrapped in something like sorrow, and for the first few minutes of the flight she could not understand where it came from, what it meant. Her family had survived.

Then the answer came to her. Her family had survived—but she hadn't, in a sense. She'd turned into something else for a while. In protecting her husband and daughter, she'd lied and deceived, not even as any politician must, but as a conscienceless manipulator of others. Anyone finding out the truth about her activities could use them as leverage against her, weakening her, perhaps disillusioning others about her.

She tried to think of what she wouldn't have done to protect Han and Jaina. If she'd had access to a self-destruct code that would annihilate any pilot getting too close to them, would she have used it? If she'd been able to swap transponder codes so that friends seemed like enemies, causing the GA forces to shoot one another out of the skies wholesale, sacrificing a hundred or a thousand lives for one she loved, would she have done so? Would she sacrifice the peace they were so desperately seeking, would she send whole populations to war with one another, to keep her loved ones safe?

She didn't know, for the answer was mixed within her, and she wasn't exactly the same person she'd been half an hour before. But there was enough *yes* to it that it worried her, caused her to imagine what she would become if all her answers were in the affirmative.

That was what attachment was, she decided, the kind of attachment the Jedi had traditionally worked to avoid. It was sacrificing lives that were not hers to preserve her own happiness.

In the future, she would willingly give up her life to preserve that of Han, or her children, or Luke and his family . . . but she would not give up a life she did not have the right to sacrifice.

She could not keep Han alive forever, nor herself. Someday he would die, or she would. That was life. She would do whatever she could to keep it from happening—whatever she could short of evil.

Making that decision was like plunging a blade of transparisteel into her heart, breaking it off so the tip remained within her.

But it was the right choice.

When the pilot finally announced "Entering Corellia atmosphere" over the shuttle's speakers, Leia was at peace. She was not happy—she could almost feel her heart's blood dripping from her wherever she walked, pooling beneath her wherever she sat—but she was serene.

STAR SYSTEM MZX32905, NEAR BIMMIEL

"You'll give her appropriate rites?" Jacen asked.

Lumiya nodded. "She was a noble warrior. I will treat her as such."

They stood together in the large air lock adjacent to the hangar bay where Jacen's shuttle waited. The docking tube was pressurized and coupled to the shuttle's side. Ben, unconscious, was aboard, strapped onto a seat with his lightsaber once again hooked to his belt.

"I know this was hurtful," Lumiya said. "But you have been strengthened by it already."

Jacen, pained, looked at her. "Words, Lumiya. *He will strengthen himself through pain.* They don't diminish the tragedy of what just happened, not at all."

"It's not a cliché, Jacen. It's a necessary component of the ethical assumption of our powers." She gestured out past the shuttle and the hangar doors, to the unseen stars. "The Jedi find their balance through the abandonment of attachment. The Sith celebrate attachment . . . but find our balance in the deliberate, agonizing sacrifice of some of the things we love most. Only by that means can we retain our appreciation for loss, pain, mortality—those things that ordinary people experience."

Jacen considered. Her words made sense. Such a philosophy would allow the Sith to retain their passion . . . but pain would keep those passions in check. Sith like Palpatine had not followed this principle, had followed philosophies of gain without loss, and their greed had doomed them and everyone around them.

Including Jacen's grandfather, Darth Vader.

"You will be the man your grandfather couldn't," Lumiya said. "Go home, do what you can to stop the war, and to free up time to study. Eventually you will need to find yourself an apprentice. Ben may be worthy, but I think he is already too steeped in the Jedi ways of softness and serenity, so look elsewhere, as well as at him. You'll need to train to open your mind to facets of the Force you've been instructed to ignore or despise. And your greatest attainment of knowledge and power will come at the same time as your greatest act of sacrifice, when you give up something that is as dear to you as life—making your love immortal through its sacrifice."

"We'll see," he said.

"Come back and I will help you see."

She stood watching through the air lock's transparisteel wall as he boarded, sealed his shuttle, uncoupled the boarding tube. The shuttle rose on its repulsors, gently turned toward the opening doors, and departed.

Tired, drained, jubilant, Lumiya returned to the living chamber at the top of her habitat. She lay on a couch there and stared up through the scratched transparisteel dome at the stars. "I've won," she said.

Jacen—dark-garbed, a gold-and-black lightsaber hilt at his belt, the pupils of his eyes golden-orange—moved out from a shadowy nook and turned to face her. His mouth did not move, but his words carried to Lumiya's mind: *And so I must go. Become nothingness.*

"You always were nothingness. You're a projection—

dark side energy from the caverns, shaped by my imagination and Jacen Solo's form. But you'll be back. Bit by bit, Jacen Solo will become you."

And at last I'll have a name. A Sith name.

"Yes."

The phantom Sith moved forward to stand over her. *He will learn that the attack at Toryaz Station was your doing. That good men were ruined by the phantoms from your mind, phantoms taking the forms of those they loved. That this war to come could have been prevented but for your interference.*

"Yes, someday, perhaps. In the meantime, his anger, the anger of his family, will be directed at Thrackan Sal-Solo, who's more to blame than I am for that attack—since he did what he did out of self-interest. And by the time Jacen discovers the full truth, he will understand how important he is, how he could not come to *be* without those events occurring, and he will forgive me."

I feel his emotions. He will hate you for these events.

"But he will love me for them, too."

Yes.

Lumiya smiled. "Then I know balance. The balance of the Sith."

The false Jacen nodded, then slowly, and without evident distress, faded to nothingness.

Bleary-eyed, gently rubbing his stomach, Ben moved into the shuttle's cockpit and dropped into the copilot's seat. "How long was I unconscious?"

"Hours," Jacen said.

"Where's Nelani?"

Jacen paused, looking for the right words. But the gentle ones would, in the long run, do more damage than the cold, short, truthful ones. "Ben, she's dead."

Ben sat up straight. The expression he turned on Jacen was pained, disbelieving. "How? The Sith?"

"Yes and no." Jacen considered his answer, considered

the mix of truth and lies he would someday have to un-
ravel. "There was a person in the lower caverns who called
himself a Sith. But he wasn't. He was just a dark side Force-
user who'd learned to tap into the powers imbued in the
place. They made him very strong . . . but only there, on
that asteroid. He sent deadly illusions against us."

"I remember. I fought Mom. She kicked the stuffing out
of me."

"Just as she would in real life. Nelani fought the phantoms of her own inadequacy, phantoms I thought I'd
helped her deal with when she was just an apprentice, and
she was too weak for them. They killed her."

"Oh . . . Sith spawn." Ben slumped. "What about . . .
about . . . Bisha? Birsha?" The boy looked confused.

"Brisha," Jacen supplied. He well knew why Ben looked
confused, why he faltered over Brisha's name. Jacen had interfered with Ben's memories while the boy slept, brushing
away Ben's recollections of the woman he knew as Brisha
almost as artfully as a painter might restore a classic por-
trait. Doubtless Ben was confused by his sudden inability
to remember her features. Jacen would attribute it to the
many knocks and blows Ben had sustained. "She died, too.
Succumbed to her injuries." He heaved a false sigh. "I've
ordered a tremendous quantity of explosives to blow the
asteroid up." It was true that anyone following the coordinates now in the shuttle's memory to the listed location of
her habitat would find only boulder-size chunks of stone.
Jacen had falsified details in the shuttle's memory, charting
a route from Lorrd to a different uninhabited star system,
another asteroid field. Lumiya was safe from discovery, for
now.

"Good." Ben sat, not speaking, for a few minutes, drum-
ming his fingers restlessly on the arm of the copilot's chair.
"It's not fair. That they died."

"No, it's not. But that happens. It's life. We just have to
find a way . . . to make ourselves stronger because of it."

Ben nodded. "I guess you're right."

CORUSCANT

"He exists." Luke looked up from his terminal. On its screen scrolled updated reports of the engagement at Tralus, but Mara could feel that the worry on his face was caused by something else. "He finally exists, for real."

"Your phantom enemy."

"Yes." Luke rose. "That must have been why we were attacked tonight—the false Jacen, the false Ben. They occupied our emotions so thoroughly that we missed the creation of—whatever he is, wherever he is. Maybe it happened close by, or there would have been no reason to divert us." He looked in all directions, as though the smooth stone walls of the enclave interior chamber would become transparent and reveal the enemy, but they remained stubbornly opaque.

"We'll find him," Mara said. "And we'll beat him." Her attention returned to her own terminal and a smile crossed her features. "Message from Jacen and Ben. They're coming home."

IN HIS IMAGE

Karen Traviss

It is natural for him to want to destroy me. It is not crude mundane ambition, as it would be in an ordinary man; it is part of his growth. And of course it does not offend me—it is why I chose him. But he needs to grow still further.

—Emperor Palpatine, on his apprentice, Darth Vader

IMPERIAL PALACE, CORUSCANT

The trooper was a stranger.

Vader had now served long enough beside the remnant of what had been the Republic's Grand Army to know *exactly* how tall a cloned soldier would stand in relation to him. The crowns of their white helmets were consistently level with the mouthpiece of his mask, every single one of them, *always,* without variance.

But this one barely reached his jaw.

"Take off your helmet," said Vader.

"Sir!" the trooper responded automatically and popped the seal. He eased off the helmet, an equally unfamiliar thing with its new design of flared mouth guard, and tucked it under one arm in a practiced motion.

He was far from the reassuringly standard Fett clone. The wide pupils of his pale blue eyes were the only indication of his anxiety at being scrutinized as the potential template for a new batch of dutiful warriors.

Vader estimated that he was ten centimeters too short and ten kilos too light.

He circled the soldier a few times with slow, heavy paces that echoed around the polished gray-green walls. At first Vader had been forced by his prosthetic limbs and armor to take such deliberate strides; he was now comfortably one with the suit, but he retained the gait.

It made people wary. It *announced* him. It served his purpose.

He paused in front of the trooper, chest plate almost close enough to touch him, and looked down into his eyes again until they began to water and the man finally blinked. Vader didn't even have to test him with the Force. He only needed to stand too close. It fascinated him.

He won't hold his ground. He's loyal and he's competent, but he has his limits. And there's too much at stake to be rushed into making an inferior choice.

"Dismissed," said Vader.

The almost-adequate trooper brought his helmet around to his chest in a choreographed move with one hand, and placed it back on his head two-handed with equal precision. Then he saluted, pivoted 180 on his heel, and marched out.

Vader watched him disappear through the great double doors, and waited for the man he knew was watching from behind to show himself.

"He comes highly recommended, but I trust your judgment," said Emperor Palpatine, stepping out of the shadow of the archway. "I sense your disappointment."

"No, with respect, you don't, my Master," said Vader. They walked now, side by side, Vader shortening his stride to match Palpatine's. "I'm not disappointed. Merely refining my search. A good man, but not good enough."

"We have time. There are already clones in production. You know this."

"Forgive me, but I prefer to oversee a project from inception. The Empire might appear settled, but we need the ability to project power in these early years. And that means maintaining quality as well as restoring numbers."

"We have sufficient of both to allow you some leeway."

Vader slowed still further and looked down at Palpatine, almost a caricature of old age whom he neither hated nor feared nor loved. The absence of passion was almost a state of bliss in itself. "I thought you trusted my judgment. Perhaps it's *me* you don't trust, Master."

"I trust you to do what I *know* you will do."

Vader was still wary when they teetered on the brink of what appeared to be a mutual test. He chose not to react. "Peaceful order rests on a strong, well-equipped, satisfied army. I've just defined loyalty for you. The ideology doesn't concern them."

"Then you must look further." Palpatine pulled back his hood a little. "And I'm interested that you care about their *contentment*."

"I care that none of them are malcontents, and that isn't the same thing," said Vader. It wasn't entirely true: he had more time for the lower ranks than he did for the Moffs and some of the other officers. "And it's more efficient to inspire respect than to rule by terror."

Palpatine paused at the doors as if he had been exhausted by the walk across the chamber. His voice was almost a whisper. "I don't think I understood you correctly. You sound as if you wish to be . . . *liked*."

Vader heard the subtext. *Are you weakening so soon?* He was purged of anger now, but what would have been an insult between ordinary men still had to be addressed. "Harsh enforcement takes effort. I prefer to avoid the need in the first place. That doesn't mean that I won't do whatever is necessary. You know me by now."

Palpatine paused, a single heartbeat. "A pity we can't yet clone from other clones."

"We have a galaxy of potential templates, Master."

"Then widen your search." The Emperor managed a pleasant and rare smile. "Let us arrange a trip."

Vader gave him a deferential nod—a gesture, nothing more—and strode down the hall. A dozen or so stormtroopers were standing at intervals down its length, and they snapped from *at ease* to *attention* at precisely the same moment. They saluted.

All of them were exactly the same height, the same build.

There were, Vader was *almost* happy to note, some things you could still count on.

One day I'll have only myself to rely upon.

He was comfortable with that idea. A year ago, a few months ago, it would have made him unbearably sad.

For once he returned the stormtroopers' salute. They were almost as dependent on their armor and confined by it as he was. He felt a brief moment of purely professional kinship. Vader had passed beyond the rule of his emotions.

And he knew what it was to be shaped in someone else's image.

There had been many Emperor's Hands—under less Imperial titles and even no titles at all—during Palpatine's time in office, and none of them seemed content with that necessity. It was the nature of assassins, Palpatine decided. They were not team players.

He let the doors close behind him and settled into a carved apocia chair against one wall of his throne room. His current Hand, Sa Cuis, was waiting for him, jaw muscles twitching ever so slightly, clearly impatient even if he thought he was presenting his Emperor with a façade of calm. Palpatine wondered why the assassin bothered to disguise his feelings in front of someone with Force mastery; but it was habit, he imagined, and he allowed him his ingrained need for deception.

Cuis had a totally benign face and a drab charcoal tunic that made him look like a harmless but well-built accountant. It was another elegant camouflage. Palpatine respected a man so secure in his own strength that he needed no external displays of menace.

"My lord, I don't fully understand this mission, and you know that I need to if I'm to complete it."

It wasn't an unreasonable question, even for a Dark Jedi. "There's nothing complex in it. Follow Lord Vader to the Parmel sector and, with colleagues of your choosing, kill him."

"There are so many questions I must—"

"Kill him. He needs this."

"He's your *apprentice*. You invested so much in him." Cuis had very dark eyes, almost perfectly black, and for a moment Palpatine wondered if he had more than human blood in him. He had stopped blinking and now focused slightly to one side of the Emperor. An idea had apparently occurred to him; he seemed relieved.

"You mean give him a test, my lord? A run for his credits, sharpen him up—"

"No, I mean *kill* him. I mean *no quarter*. Not a feint. A genuine assassination."

Yes, Cuis *had* gotten the idea. Palpatine needed none of his Force skills to see that. The assassin was now swallowing frequently. "What if I don't succeed?"

"I doubt you will succeed. And he'll kill you—probably."

Not a pause, not a flicker. *A good man, Cuis.* "A team would—"

"You *will* need a team, trust me. Lord Vader is not as strong as I had hoped he might be at this stage, but he remains a formidable opponent."

Cuis took out a lightsaber and held the hilt in both hands. "I know. I have acquired a more suitable weapon." With one snap he separated the hilt into two sections; energy streamed straight and vivid from each, one blade red, the other white. He swept slow, careful arcs with both weapons, shafts almost touching, and then shut them down and pressed the hilts back into one again. "This might be enough."

Palpatine probed discreetly at the Dark Jedi's mood. *Yes, worried, but determined. Professional pride and a little healthy, welcome fear.* Death was an occupational hazard for his kind. "I hope not."

"But what if Lord Vader finds that you're behind this?" asked Cuis, concern for his own chances of survival apparently set aside.

"He will," said Palpatine. Oh yes, he would, and that was what Vader needed. "I hope he does."

A Sith could pass beyond hatred and anger too quickly.

Vader needed to become stronger, and fast. Betrayal would not surprise his apprentice, but there was a world of therapeutic difference between waiting for it and experiencing it.

If Palpatine had still been able to experience regret, it would have pained him at that moment.

PARMEL SECTOR, THE OUTER RIM

Vohai sprawled beneath the *Lambda*-class shuttle, a quilt of grim industrial sites interspersed with parkland and incongruously attractive residential towers. From the view port, Vader watched a single gleaming carriage zip along the unirail that hung two kilometers above the planet's surface, reflected sunlight forming a burning pinpoint.

"We'll dock very soon, Lord Vader," said his aide-decamp, clearly interpreting his head movements as impatience. "My apologies for the delay."

Delay? Vader hadn't noticed. He was simply testing his focus again. It was interesting how much he could intimidate without even intending to now. This, he learned, was the value of sheer *presence:* the art of illusion. And to think he had once resented this grim black suit and longed for his whole body again.

"I expect our clonemaster at Arkanian Micro *not* to be late, though, Lekauf."

The officer twitched. He made as if to put his hand to his chest—a self-comforting gesture—and appeared to think better of it. "He's waiting, my lord. He's at the facility, ready to run the demonstration."

So easy: Vader was comfortable with himself now. *Entirely* comfortable.

The ship docked in a cool, cavernous hangar that smelled as if oiled machinery had recently passed through it. A small group of technicians and managers—he noted their variations in clothing—moved forward to greet their customer.

Vader's sensor-enhanced olfactory system detected mineral components, the rasping metallic sharpness of swarf from milled parts, even Quara and human sweat: the mundane events of the last hour here replayed themselves for him. Equipment had arrived, probably, and had been moved by maintenance staff.

And there was something beyond the immediate physical impressions of the facility. Vader could feel anxiety, the tension just before conflict.

Someone *else* was waiting for him. Several people.

He scanned the length of the blue durasteel ribs that formed the structure of the hangar's walls and roof, looking for a door, a gantry, *any* access point for the threat. It was above him. Someone was *coming* for him.

Two doors were set into the upper walls with just a ladder beneath. Access hatches. *Corridors behind.*

They're moving around up there. Five, six . . . seven of them.

The barely perceptible ripples in the Force also let Vader taste something else at a very great distance: his Master.

It's inevitable. You knew he would do this, didn't you?

Vader reached carefully into his black robe and slid his gloved hand down the hilt of his lightsaber. He tightened his grip. He had no sense anymore that the mechanical hand was any less his own than the flesh-and-blood one had been. The lightsaber felt a continuation of his own arm again, natural and complete.

"Lekauf," he said quietly to his aide. "Lekauf, withdraw. *Now.*"

"What's wrong, my lord?" Lekauf was looking up at the stark walls, too, following Vader's lead. He reached for his blaster and held it two-handed, eyes darting. "I can't see—"

The managers and technicians stood rooted, shoulders slightly hunched and looking around frantically to spot what they imagined Vader could see. They ducked. They couldn't have seen anything. They were reacting to him.

"Lord Vader—"

"*Get clear.* I can deal with this."

Vader felt he would need Lekauf one day, but not now. He thumbed the hilt and a shaft of brilliant red energy seared the air, sending the facility technicians suddenly scattering for nonexistent cover. The staccato *thud-thud-thud* of boots running on durasteel flooring echoed suddenly above and to both sides of the hangar and Vader spun around, lightsaber raised in both hands.

He faced the hangar doors.

Rappelling ropes paid out with a loud slap and the opening was instantly blocked from outside by a line of four hooded men with Thunderbolt repeating blasters. Vader felt the Force ripple with the presence of three more about to enter through the doors at his back.

Lekauf stepped in front of him to block their shots, blaster raised. Vader struck him aside with one armored blow, sending him to the floor and to safety as the stream of bolts flew at his chest plate in a concentrated V of blue light. Then he whirled his lightsaber in a neat circle at arm's length, two-handed, blocking the shots in one economical blur of energy.

The assassins paused for a frantic reload.

"Lord Vader—" said Lekauf, but he was pinned flat by the Force, arms flailing.

"Stay down," snapped Vader. *I'll need you one day.* The other three hit men were still at his back, hidden behind the door. He could sense it. He backed toward it, beckoning one-handed to the four strung in a ragged line now across the entrance, taunting them, buying time. They tracked their blasters and tried to settle on a clear shot that would beat the slowly sweeping lightsaber. They didn't seem able to find one.

"Come to me." *They're behind me. I feel them. Oh, a little right, a little more to the right . . .* "I'm not in the mood to chase today."

They knew where their comrades were, he was sure of it. And so did he.

It was just a matter of timing to bring this to a quick end.

"Now!" yelled one man.

Vader dropped and spun as the doors behind him snapped open. From his crouched position he saw legs run at him and he swung left, right, left again, slicing through bone and tendon and screams. He carried the arc through to bring the ruby blade up as he turned and rose simultaneously to face the four other assailants now right upon him. It felt like minutes even though he knew it was two seconds, no more.

A Thunderbolt repeater was *not* a close-quarters weapon. But a lightsaber was.

One man dropped instantly without his intervention. Vader lunged forward and sliced through two more, left–right. The fourth lost his arm and blaster in the same slicing movement and dropped to his knees, utterly silent, mouth open wide in frozen agony as he stared at the seared stump.

Vader brought the lightsaber down across his neck. The hangar was silent now except for the sound of his own breath. He looked down at the back of the one man he hadn't killed. The black tunic was still smoking a little.

"Fine shot, Lekauf," said Vader. He released his Force pressure. "I told you to stay down."

Lekauf got to his knees and holstered his blaster. "I never rose, my lord. I *can* fire from a prone position, though, and you made no mention of that."

Lekauf stood up and went to him as if to check him for injury. It suddenly struck Vader that he was solid and a good height. And he was loyal enough to step in the line of fire, and then—*defy* him to cover his back.

Good man. At least one possible template, then.

Vader took one step back in case Lekauf actually intended to minister to him, then looked to see where the facility staff had gone. They were huddled by the bodies near the door, silent in the way of people who were afraid they might say the wrong thing at the wrong time. More staff were edging in cautiously through both doors in the ringing silence that followed the blasterfire.

"Who's your most senior executive?" Vader asked.

"Tef Shabiak," said one of the technicians hoarsely.

Vader turned to Lekauf and tilted his head slightly. When your eyes weren't visible, a gesture was necessary.

Lekauf understood perfectly. "What would you like me to do with him, Lord Vader?"

"Remove his head, please," said Vader. "This is very poor customer service. And now I'll see his deputy."

Sometimes people gasped, and sometimes they didn't. The range of reaction to horror was fascinating. Compliance was proving to be a common reaction. Lekauf walked briskly at Vader's side but a fraction behind him as they followed a visibly agitated manager through the corridors into the heart of the cloning complex.

"If you think the company was involved in this attempt, I should—"

Vader cut him short. "I know who's behind this, and it certainly isn't the company."

Lekauf's next question hung in his silence. There was only the creak of his boots as he kept pace with his Sith Lord.

Vader answered anyway. "I need to encourage better security, or we invite an open season from now on."

"Understood, my lord," said Lekauf, sounding and feeling genuinely satisfied to Vader.

But more than encouraging security, executing the top executive was another eloquent statement of intent that took little effort but spoke loudly across the Empire: there would be consequences for any act that didn't meet with Vader's approval.

Power was as much a matter of presentation as using the dark side, Vader had learned.

In his throne room, Palpatine paused while flicking through the screens of his datapad. The Force sighed slightly: he felt it. Vader had reacted.

He had survived whatever Cuis had thrown at him. Palpatine thought he actually felt his apprentice's sense of betrayal. He concentrated harder, searching for some hint of anger or hatred, but there was nothing, and he wondered if Vader had not yet discovered the obvious.

Palpatine drew on his reserves of patience and settled

back into the chair, adjusting the cushion behind his back. He let the datapad absorb his attention again.

Vader had to take the next step. If he didn't, Palpatine's long search for another worthy apprentice would be a very long one indeed.

Vader stared at the tanks full of liquid.

As he passed down the rows, the tanks acted like lenses, distorting the figure of the suddenly promoted chief executive of Arkanian Microtechnologies standing behind them.

"I take it you favor Arkanian cloning technology, then," said Vader.

"As good as the Kaminoans', sir." He was nervous; he would have been stupid if he hadn't been. "And a full year's lead time to adult, as well—we don't rush the process. We guarantee a stable product."

"Are you prepared to attempt recloning our existing Fett template?"

"If you want us to, yes. It's not a genotype we've worked with before, so there might be uncertainties. And there's a higher failure rate with secondary cloning, but we would certainly put all our expertise into it."

"I would appreciate it if you'd try. They've proved excellent troops, especially in terms of discipline."

Vader ran the fingertip of his glove down the permaglass of one vat and stared at the adult soldier forming within it. The Kaminoans decanted their clones as juveniles and matured them naturally: he wondered what made more difference in the long run, the quality of the template or the training. He didn't care for shortcuts, not with an entire division's efficiency hanging on a single selection. But he wasn't a scientist, and this was one area where he would have to rely on his uniquely motivational leadership to get the job done.

As he concentrated on the form floating in the liquid, trailing a web of fine tubes, Vader saw himself for a moment: burned, barely alive, mutilated, rescued, rebuilt. He wondered whether beyond the external appearance of a

Sith droid there might be more that was shaping him in another's image. And he could still feel two things in the Force above all others: Palpatine's saber at his back, and the less distinctive shape of a threat that was physically much, much nearer.

"So we spread the risk," he said, and shook his equally divided attention away from both vat and threat for a moment. "Reclone a Fett template, and continue with this batch. And we'll ask Lieutenant Lekauf if he'd be so kind as to provide a tissue sample of his own for you to work upon."

Lekauf, standing with one hand on his unclipped holster, inclined his head deferentially. "Thank you, Lord Vader. It's an honor indeed." His pride and pleasure were tangible. And at Vader's side, he stood almost exactly as tall as a Fett clone. He would do.

"Would you care for some hospitality, Lord Vader?" said the new and nervous head of Arkanian Micro. As soon as the words were out of his mouth, his face fell and his gaze fixed for a few awkward moments on Vader's mouth grille. Then he looked from mouth to eyepiece, clearly thinking that his promotion would be exceptionally short-lived.

People were so transparent.

"I regret that I have other business to attend to," said Vader. A moment of graciousness contrasted exquisitely with summary execution, light and dark, combining to achieve a balanced outcome. Arkanian Micro would never present the Empire with any production problems now. "I'm looking for someone." Lekauf took a step forward as if to accompany him, but Vader held up a gloved finger. "You have a sample to contribute, Lieutenant. I can handle this on my own."

He could. He didn't even need a map of the city: he would find the man he was looking for because the man was also looking for him.

The last assassin stalking him had a distinctive effect on the Force. Vader tested, probing carefully, letting the impression wash through him.

It was a Dark Jedi. It was what he should have expected of his Master. This one would at least test him. And in his heart of hearts, Vader felt that he wanted to pass the test for his own sake, not Palpatine's.

Your hatred will make you strong.

Vader slipped along the passageway that connected Arkanian Micro's management suite to the large courtyard at the center of the facility. It was a square of perfectly manicured lawn fringed with identical trees whose crowns were clipped into precise cube shapes. A fountain formed of a single spout of water bubbling over a pyramid of smooth stones provided soothing ambient sound.

The last thing Vader wanted was to be soothed. He sought his hatred again. Palpatine had sent men to kill him. However inevitable that was, however much the malice was intricately bound up with and inseparable from his Master's wish to see him succeed, he had to focus on the motivating strength of pure loathing.

He paused and activated his lightsaber, listening.

He sensed the Dark Jedi coming long before he heard him.

Vader felt a presence slipping through doors and drawing closer. A sensation of melting ice shivered down what remained of his back, and he seized it: a little precious sliver of fear to be picked up and used. No—*caution.* His armor was not indestructible, and he was facing a Jedi this time. And he was still less than he had been when he was wholly flesh and blood.

Vader stepped out onto the lawn, clear of the trees, and waited like bait.

He didn't have to wait long. He knew the man was there, watching him, for nearly a minute before he moved from a doorway out into the sunlight. Suddenly, to Vader's right, another door opened and two women came out chatting with flimsi cups in their hands. They both looked at Vader, and then at his lightsaber, and rushed back inside, slamming the door after them.

That second was enough. The Dark Jedi took his light-saber hilt in both hands and jerked his arms apart, releasing two beams, a red one in his left hand and a white one in the other. Vader had a brief thought that it was a marvelous piece of theatrics until the man came at him whirling the sabers slowly like a juggler preparing to perform with clubs. And the white blade whisked so close to his helmet that he had his own lightsaber raised and blocking it before he even had time to think.

"Cuis, Lord Vader," said the man. "Nothing personal, believe me."

Vader matched him step for step in the standoff as they circled each other. *Nothing personal.* Perhaps Cuis thought that an ice-cold act would intimidate him. But it was anger and all the other brutal emotions that would win the fight. Vader lunged.

My Master wants me dead.

He brought his saber down hard in a straight arc and Cuis blocked it with both of his, rasping them straight down its length as if sharpening a metal blade. Vader withdrew and sliced upward, then feinted to the left, wrong-footing the Jedi, who leapt back against the trunk of one of the trees. Vader made a double lunge on his right leg, dipping under the swirling twin beams.

He needed to force Cuis into a confined space to deny him the advantage of two lightsabers. There had once been a boy called Anakin who could have done that with sheer technique, but he was forgotten, and the transformed man that was Vader opted for sheer power and began a fast, furious slashing assault, slicing through a tree trunk as Cuis dodged behind it.

My Master forced me to live and now he wants me dead.

The trunk creaked and toppled and Cuis deflected the weight of branches with the Force. It bought Vader a second. He used it to send Cuis's white beam spinning into the fountain, clattering down the wet stones. As Cuis's remaining lightsaber flew from his left to his right hand, Vader intercepted it, jerking it high into the air and using the Force to throw it to the other side of the courtyard, out of reach.

Cuis leapt high and saved his legs form a savage low sweep, but his opponent had him backed up almost into the angle of the walls. Vader couldn't match Cuis's agility, so instead he reached out with his left hand: the Force seized Cuis's throat.

It gave Vader a familiar and painful jolt of recognition. He shut out what he knew was a memory. Instead he concentrated on using a wholly unexpected surge of rage and hatred to flood the gap it left and overwhelm it. Cuis staggered back against the wall, struggling against Vader's remote, crushing grip with his own Force power. Then he sank to his knees, shaking with the effort. Vader forced him lower, and lower.

He could have killed him in that instant.

He relaxed his grip enough to let Cuis suck in a rattling gasp of air and held him there, suddenly aware of faces that appeared at a window and then bobbed down again— harmless, shocked, terrified women's faces. *Office workers.* Hatred worked for him now, telling him he needed not to think about—not recall—the look on their faces.

"Go on," said Cuis. He was barely audible. "Finish it."

"Who sent you?" *I know. But I want to hear.* "Tell me."

"Kill me."

"Join me." Vader squeezed, still a meter away. "And you can live."

Cuis stared back at him with unnaturally black eyes, panting, contemptuous. He had no fear, none at all.

"That's not how I work. I have my code."

"Name him."

Cuis simply looked back at him.

Vader throttled him to the point of unconsciousness and loosened his grip again. "Last chance."

"No."

"Name him, and join me."

There was no answer this time. Cuis simply stared. He wouldn't be broken. Vader clamped and relaxed, clamped and relaxed, taking Cuis to the point of death each time, but he got nowhere.

Good man.

He let go completely and Cuis pitched forward, taking huge gulps of air with the sucking wheeze of a dying old man.

A door opposite him flew open. "Lord Vader!" Lekauf came running out, blaster drawn, but Vader held up his hand and stopped him a little more insistently than perhaps he should have. Lekauf bounced back with a grunt as if he'd run into a wall, which in effect he had. But Vader didn't want Cuis dead right then. He was still savoring rage, seeing how it had swept through him and given him the power to defeat a faster Jedi and keep the memories locked deep within. He shut down his energy blade with a flick of his thumb.

Lekauf picked himself up. "There might still be others, sir."

"There aren't," said Vader, and he stepped forward and held his arm out to Cuis. The assassin didn't take it. Vader could have raised him with the Force alone, but he didn't. He took hold of his tunic and lifted him to his feet, holding him steady.

"You'll never betray the man who sent you after me, will you?"

Cuis never took his eyes off Vader's mask. But it wasn't horror on his face. It was simply disdain. It was a novelty for Vader, who had grown used to the awe his appearance alone inspired in everyone else.

"Get one of those technicians," he said.

Palpatine sat up, distracted from his datapad, by a faint tingling ripple that filled the back of his mouth and spread into his chest. The Force shifted imperceptibly in a far corner and settled again, but it was different this time. Something had changed forever.

Vader had changed.

"How reassuring," said the Emperor to himself.

. Boots clattered on the polished floor.

"Sir, did you call, sir?" said the stormtrooper. "I heard—"

"Nothing to worry about," said the Emperor, laying the datapad on the inlaid table, screen-down. "There's nothing further to worry about at all."

Arkanian Micro was a very obliging contractor. Vader sat and watched carefully as medical technicians took buccal swabs from Cuis's mouth and passed cell-collecting devices over the skin of his arms. They were harvesting the building blocks of an army. For all the curious things Vader had seen in his life, this seemed the most extraordinary, that so much could be made from so little.

"Is that it?" said Cuis. His voice had recovered a little from the repeated choking, but he still didn't show any fear, or even that pathetic sense of hope that he might have escaped retribution. He did appear to be simply asking a question, not embarking on a plea for mercy.

In his enhanced peripheral vision, Vader noted that the technicians were now watching Cuis with more interest than they were watching him.

There were gestures and lessons and symbols that you could employ without even needing to harness the Force. Vader knew he had to choose one, or lose ground and reputation. He needed to stamp his authority on the situation and let word of mouth do the rest.

It was still a pity.

"I said, *Is that it*." Cuis was insistent. "Answer me."

"I'm afraid it is," said Vader, and took out his lightsaber. The red beam activated at the lightest of touches. "But you'll become an entire army. How many men can say that?"

He stood up and swept the saber as he had swept it so many times before in such a short life. Cuis's head hit the floor. The sound of the impact was surprisingly loud: heads were heavy parts of the human body. A technician slumped against the wall, hand pressed to his mouth. The salutary lesson would be spread by horrified gossip: Darth Vader would be obeyed, or the consequences would be unimaginable.

Sa Cuis had served everyone's purpose but his own, whatever that had been. He was timely propaganda, an excellent clone template, and the tool by which Vader had grown. It was fitting that the essence of Cuis would survive in a unique way and serve the Empire.

It was the least Vader owed a professional man, an honorable man who wouldn't betray his Master.

"But why a hired killer?"

Lekauf had relaxed a little in the seat facing Vader in the shuttle. He was curious, Vader knew, not arguing. He wanted to learn from him. That meant he would watch the man carefully, despite the self-sacrificing loyalty he had shown earlier.

"He's absolutely loyal to his ideals," said Vader. "His clones won't have his memories, but I'm confident they'll have the same courage and loyalty, and their ideals will simply be the ones I provide for them. Loyalty to the Emperor." He wondered when he might retire to the privacy of his cabin to take some nutrients. "And his Force powers will be exceptionally valuable in the field."

Lekauf gave the faintest impression of a man teetering on the brink of asking a dangerous but obvious question. He was an officer who had been around Palpatine's inner military circle long enough to know—probably—who Cuis was. Vader could almost hear his thoughts.

Was it the Emperor who sent him?

It wasn't a good idea to ask that or answer it. But if rumor ever spread, he would have to deal with any suggestion that Vader didn't have the Emperor's confidence. Ordinary men couldn't be expected to fully understand the relationship between a Sith Master and his apprentice. They would mistake the attempt on Vader's life for vengeance or rivalry, not a necessary hard lesson.

They were like regular Jedi in that respect. A Dark Jedi would understand far better. It was a shame about Cuis, but he was a more powerful tool now he was dead than he ever was in his lifetime.

Train yourself to let go of everything you fear to lose.

A Jedi philosophy: a good one, too, if providing only half of the picture, as their sanctimonious way always did. Vader realized he had feared losing Palpatine's . . . *approval.*

He no longer feared that. He'd let himself taste anger again—a reminder of its flavor was enough to refocus him—and then he was reassured that the Sith way was the reality of the Force. Anger was a *necessary path.* It could even motivate ordinary men to great things. It had its function, a reaction placed in living beings for the *purpose of survival.*

Vader examined the detail in the handle of his lightsaber, almost not seeing it. Jedi had—yet again—helped him learn more about the Sith path: it would have sickened them. But it was yet another elegant lesson, if he needed one, that the dark and the light side were inseparable, necessary to each other.

He defocused a little, surprised that he could still do such a thing with his artificially assisted eyes. The detail in the lightsaber's hilt appeared to shift, turning convex surfaces into concave ones, creating a new image.

It was all a matter of how you looked at it. The hilt had not changed at all. And that was it: that was the fundamental weakness of Jedi.

Vader thought of the optical illusion that so amused him as a child. It was the simple silhouette of a white urn that then became the black profiles of two identical people staring at each other, then snapped back to the urn again as his mental focus changed.

Some youngsters could see only the urn; others, only the faces. Vader could always see *both,* at will.

Ah, he could remember without pain now. He could recall *moments* from his past. But could no longer feel who he had *been,* and something within him said that was a mercy to be welcomed.

The Jedi would never—could never—let themselves see the whole picture. *Still* they couldn't see that the Force was an indivisible amalgam of dark and light.

But there were now very few left alive to learn that lesson, even if they could.

And soon, he would ensure that there were none.

Emperor Palpatine was waiting at the palace landing strip to welcome Vader back.

Lekauf ran down the shuttle ramp to stand like an honor guard at its foot, but Vader dismissed him with a nod. The lieutenant seemed grateful to be sent away. It was probably that he wasn't comfortable now being so close to Palpatine.

"A successful trip, I know," said the Emperor.

Vader almost enjoyed his dual layer of speech now, with its apparent meaning covering the subtext like a layer of snow, something soft and deceptive concealing hazards that might trip him if he trod carelessly.

"Yes, I think we've made progress," said Vader, meaning the clone templates, but also something else.

"I admire your ability to see both the strategic view and the operational detail. It's a rare combination."

"Will you require more staff, Master?" *You lost your Hand. You'll be proud when you see what he becomes.* "You appear to be getting *busier*."

Palpatine smiled. "I have many staff."

I know. There'll be others. "I've learned a great deal on this trip."

"Cloning is a complex and fascinating science, is it not?"

"Indeed it is."

Vader paused for a moment to let Palpatine pass into the palace vestibule in front of him, standing back between white-armored stormtroopers who were at that moment the only beings around him whom he knew for certain wouldn't make an attempt on his life.

The thought no longer bothered him. The power of the dark side was his reassurance.

"We should talk about the templates later when I've assembled the Moffs," said Palpatine.

"I'll await your call, my Master."

"I know what you will do."

But I'll do it sooner than you might expect. The thought was unbidden, and it was neither an unspoken threat nor the seed of a counterplot. It was simply a fleeting Force-vision of the future, Palpatine's death far short of the millennium he planned to reign.

"I'll rebuild your army," said Vader.

"Exactly, and you'll do it well," said the Emperor.

Vader waited for Palpatine to disappear from sight before walking to his adapted meditation chamber to feed himself and maintain and clean his suit.

He was no longer a Jedi—or even a man—but the first Jedi rule still rang true somewhere inside him.

Survive.

TWO-EDGED SWORD

Karen Traviss

What can you teach a clone in a few months that a man takes a lifetime to learn?

—Emperor Palpatine to Lord Darth Vader

IMPERIAL TRAINING CENTER, YINCHORR, THE MID RIM

For a dead man, Sa Cuis had a fine lightsaber technique. Lord Vader swung his blade and the two beams of red energy rasped off each other.

Cuis—or one of his clones, anyway—circled and Vader matched him, keeping a constant distance between them. He had no intention of killing the assassin again. Arkanian Microtechnologies had spent more than a year creating this clone of the Dark Jedi, and it would have been wasteful to destroy him or any of his five brothers simply to prove superiority.

Besides, they were *men*. Vader tried not to lose sight of that. If he had wanted mindless predictability, he would have commissioned droids for the Imperial Army.

He was aware of two people watching the duel intently from the dais set a little above the gymnasium floor: his Master, Emperor Palpatine; and one of his own aides, Lieutenant Erv Lekauf. Part of his mind could sense Lekauf's discomfort at being so close to the Emperor without Vader beside him.

"Enough," said Vader, and shut down his lightsaber. The Cuis clone snapped his blade down, too, but watched Vader cautiously until he stood back to allow the clones to continue their lightsaber drill with the instructor. Vader was satisfied. The clones had retained all the speed and sharp reflexes of the unfortunate Emperor's Hand whose genome was now theirs. He hoped they had somehow inherited his extraordinary loyalty, too.

I wonder if the Emperor knew Cuis would never reveal he was his Hand. I wonder if my Master values that kind of devotion, or just expects it.

Vader went back to the dais to watch the clones continue their lightsaber training. They ran through parry and riposte, redoublement and remise, red blades shimmering. The cavernous hall echoed with the hum of lightsabers and the clack of armor plates, a combination that Vader found oddly disturbing. Their instructor was yet another of Palpatine's many Hands—an assassin called Sheyvan, who had a taste for vibroblades as well as the more conventional lightsaber skills.

Vader paced up and down the hall, watching the sparring pairs with a careful eye. Hands often thought they were the only personal assassin in Palpatine's service, and most were unhappy if they found they were *not*. Sheyvan looked as if he was in that majority. His occasional glance at Palpatine was more accusing than adoring.

"Men need to believe they're unique," said Palpatine quietly. He always lowered his voice to make people listen carefully to him. "And women, too. We all like to think we are special and irreplaceable. It is a great motivator."

Sometimes Vader suspected Palpatine could read more than his emotions. "You made me feel I alone could help you defeat the Jedi Council, Master."

"And that was true, was it not?"

Vader had wondered just once—and no more—how his life might have unfolded had he not been seduced by Palpatine's assurance that he was the only member of the Jedi Council whom he could trust. It was true, yes. But if he had resisted, Padmé would still have died. At least now he had the power and position to remake the galaxy as he wished—*orderly.* He used it. He used it more every day.

"Not only do all men wish to be special," said Vader. "They also wish to know there is someone they can trust."

Palpatine's yellow eyes betrayed no reaction, just as he didn't seem troubled by Sheyvan's discomfort. The disappointment of those around him was of no consequence to him until they ceased to serve their purpose, and then they were discarded.

You will not discard me, Master.

"One day, I may form a legion of Dark Jedi," said Palpatine, as if the idea had just struck him. "They have great potential. This Cuis would be honored to see what's become of him."

It was as if he had never known Cuis. Vader had never mentioned that he knew Palpatine had sent Sa Cuis to kill him. *He wouldn't name you, my Master. Not even when I offered to spare his life.* That's *what I want in my troops. Loyalty.*

Vader hadn't taken the assassination attempt personally. It was part of his training. The path toward Sith mastery had to be hard because the power it yielded was not for the weak or lazy. Vader understood that. He still knew he would oust his own master one day. Palpatine knew, too, and seemed not to mind.

Lekauf—loyal, intelligent, with no special powers beyond the capacity for hard work—hovered at his elbow, radiating anxiety. Clones had been created from him, too, but he was very much alive to see them. He had even trained them. Now they were being evaluated, and they had passed inspection in all core skills except hand-to-hand combat.

"You still seem worried," said Vader.

"No, sir . . ."

Lekauf had spent six months on this miserable, barren ball of rock training his clones. If they passed muster, he could finally return to Coruscant. It was clear what his fears were.

"You haven't seen your wife and children for six

months, and you worry that if your clones don't perform well, you'll be here for another six," said Vader.

Lekauf swallowed hard and nodded. "Yes, sir. I do."

His courageous honesty was one of the qualities that made him both a good clone donor and a good instructor. Vader's memories of missing someone dear—the memories that he had learned to wrap and lock away, almost without pain now—echoed in response.

And I trusted you, too, Padmé. I'm practiced at handling betrayal now.

"You'll see your family soon," said Vader.

Lekauf looked toward the gymnasium doors. He was a strongly built man in his thirties, with an incongruously open face and scrubby light brown hair. "I always worry about disappointing you, sir. But when I see what Dark Jedi can do, I wonder how ordinary humans can ever compete."

"Stormtroopers will never have to fight Jedi," said Vader. "Only Rebels."

Lekauf inhaled and held his breath as the six clones marched in. Vader heard it, however hard the man tried to suppress it. They looked as Lekauf himself might have a few years earlier, with that same expression of permanent optimism. And, Vader hoped, they would be equally efficient soldiers.

The clones, wearing the same Imperial armor as the Cuis batch, lined up in front of the dais and saluted. They were flash-trained from decanting to make them competent soldiers who could function in any army, but Vader needed them to be *better* than that. He needed them to meet the standards of the Kaminoan-cloned troops that still made up the majority of his stormtroopers.

"No lightsabers." Vader's voice boomed across the gymnasium. "Use durasteel staffs. This is an exercise. I want no serious injury."

Palpatine turned his head very slowly to look at him. Vader hooked his thumbs over his belt, waiting for the challenge.

"How can you test their suitability if you handicap them?" Palpatine's voice was soft and insinuating, as it always was when he was planting an idea. "Is this not a concession?"

"No, my Master. It creates more realistic conditions for the test." Vader stood his ground. "They need only to perform well against Rebels, who are not Force-users. Just men."

Palpatine paused for two heartbeats, his sign of silent disapproval. "Very well."

Vader beckoned to Sheyvan to join them on the dais to clear the gymnasium floor for combat. The clones paired off, one Lekauf to each Cuis.

"Begin," said Palpatine.

Lekauf swallowed again.

The clones stalked each other, durasteel rods clasped in both hands. Then metal crashed as they smashed staff against staff, struggling to drive the other back. One Lekauf clone, the name NELE stenciled on his chest plate, brought his staff around in a low arc to upend his opponent. But as soon as the man fell flat on his back, he sprang to his feet again in one move and threw the Lekauf clone almost the full width of the gymnasium with a massive Force push. He hit the wall, the impact of his back plate making the hall echo, and struggled back to his feet, shaking his head to clear it.

The other five Cuis clones laid aside their staffs and sent their opponents' weapons spinning from their hands with a single gesture. All the Lekauf clones were knocked flat on their backs and pinned down by an invisible hand.

It had been a very brief demonstration. Lekauf looked resigned to his fate, hands clasped behind his back, eyes fixed straight ahead.

"I would not expect any man to defeat a Jedi without adequate weapons," said Palpatine.

Vader wasn't sure if that was a verdict of failure or simply an observation. He glanced at Lekauf. "No, Master," he said, addressing the Emperor but watching his aide.

"Perhaps we should now try this again without allowing use of their Force powers."

"No, I have seen enough." Palpatine pulled his cowl a little farther over his face. "I will take the Cuis clones and train them more. Your Lekauf batch may yet prove useful for *other* tasks."

We could simply clone an entire army of the Cuis template. We know what they can do. But a soldier is the product of constant training. They need to see action.

"I suggest that we put them all on active service and see how they perform," said Vader.

Palpatine paused again. "Yes. But commission a battalion of Cuis models from Arkanian Micro anyway. I'm impressed by how much the clones have retained of his Force abilities."

Lekauf's clones had picked themselves up and were waiting at *stand easy* with their hands clasped behind their backs.

"Does that mean we're returning to Imperial Center?" Lekauf asked, unable to disguise his desperation.

"Yes, Lieutenant, it does." Vader strode ahead, and Lekauf managed to match his pace. His six clones collected their helmets and weapons and followed him, as did the Cuis batch. Sheyvan brought up the rear, looking sullen.

"I apologize for our performance, sir," said Lekauf.

Vader noted the use of the word *our*. "I won't consider that failure in hand-to-hand combat until I see you fight ordinary men."

"That's very generous of you, sir."

No, it wasn't generous: it was *fair*. The test against the Cuis clones was merely an act of curiosity and no reason to judge them unfit. Vader watched them mount the ramp of his *Lambda*-class shuttle and noted that even with their helmets on, he could tell the Lekauf from the Cuis simply by their bearing and their disciplined, synchronized stride. The Cuis clones looked more like athletes than soldiers, and—he couldn't help but notice—they did *not* move like one machine.

"Smarten up," Lekauf snapped, instinctively knowing what Vader thought with his usual unerring accuracy. "You're in the Five Hundred and First now."

COMMANDING OFFICER'S DAY CABIN, SHUTTLE ST 321, EN ROUTE TO IMPERIAL CENTER

"I think I might like the Cuis battalion under my personal command," said the Emperor, leaning back in Vader's seat as the shuttle jumped to hyperspace.

Vader ignored the infringement on his own territory and simply registered the fact that his Master bothered to do it. It was another of those little tests, the constant pushing and prodding designed to make Vader hungry for supremacy and angry enough to seize it. A thousand small threats would feed the dark side within him, but sometimes it seemed more for sport than education.

I don't need you to keep me sharp, Master. I won't forget what drives me. And I'll kill you one day, yes, but the day will be of my choosing, not a reflex when you finally provoke me once too often.

"They will not form part of the infantry, then, Master?"

Palpatine's tone hardened a little. "I know how to command an army, Lord Vader."

"I mean that the Cuis clones are effectively all Hands, and so might be ideal for special operations."

The Emperor accepted a glass of water from Lekauf, who never seemed to find menial tasks demeaning. "Yes, I shall train them to carry out *many* tasks."

Vader still managed to avoid the words that always hung between them now. "Cuis was loyal to his Master to the end. He would not reveal his name."

"A commendable quality that I hope will be found in his clones."

"It may be genetic, but it can also be encouraged."

It can also be crushed. Vader thought of the man he had been—yes, there was no pain now, just a vivid and angry determination—and those whom he had loved but who had betrayed him. He could still re-create that cold, focusing sense of disappointment when he realized that Palpatine had sent Cuis, and that the only thing he could trust him to do was be a source of constant threat. Knowing how alone he truly was might have made him stronger, but it did not comfort him. He suspected it was why he surrounded himself with the Lekaufs of this world: not simply because loyal soldiers were good soldiers, but also because it reassured the small part of him that had been Anakin, the part that still seemed sufficiently useful not to suppress. Lekauf was soothing: a man who liked to know where he stood, a man who simply wanted to excel and be given clarity of purpose in exchange for his devotion.

You won't disappoint me. So many people disappoint me.

"Lieutenant," said Palpatine, looking past Vader to where Lekauf stood in patient silence. "What makes *you* loyal to Lord Vader?"

Lekauf, normally uncomfortable around Palpatine, relaxed a little. Vader could feel it. Lekauf's doubts and passions seldom showed on his face, but he had them. Vader could always taste them, and sometimes he relied on them to understand what was happening within the Imperial Army.

"With your permission, sir," said Lekauf, and looked to Vader. "It's because my lord never asks his men to do anything that he wouldn't do himself."

"Laudable," said Palpatine.

Honest, thought Vader. *He could have said that the Empire was all that was holy and I was its instrument. But he gave a soldier's answer.*

The Emperor went back to sipping his water, and Lekauf still stood motionless. He wouldn't sit unless Vader was seated. Vader was used to that now and occasionally had to order the man to sit when it was clear he needed to.

"Call your wife, Lekauf," said Vader. "Tell her when you will be arriving."

There was a brief flare of excitement in Lekauf's spirit

that illuminated the Force for a brief moment. "Thank you, sir. *Thank you.*"

Lekauf saluted and disappeared through the hatch toward the cockpit. Master and apprentice remained silent until he was out of earshot.

"You constantly surprise me with your capacity for . . . compassion," said Palpatine, somehow shaping the word into an insult

"*Motivation,*" said Vader, daring to correct Palpatine. "There would be no point in denying Lekauf such a small thing. Exercising power for the sake of it achieves nothing. Knowing when to let it go *does.*"

"Making people want to please you is an important skill," said Palpatine. "You are becoming adept at it. Fascinating, is it not? To see that desire for approval?"

Ah, he *enjoyed* it. It *was* his sport. This was more than the exercise of political power. He liked to see people, helpless lesser people, in his thrall.

I no longer wish to please you, my Master. Vader decided he was content to be a simpler man, relying on strength and clarity. *Your need for games will one day be your undoing— now I know where you weakness lies. I will use it when the time is right.*

Vader settled down in the seat opposite—normally the first officer's—and occupied his time catching up with reports from Imperial bases in the Outer Rim.

It should have been a short, uneventful flight. And it was, right up to the time when something tingled at the back of his throat and he looked up, hand reaching instinctively for his lightsaber. Then the red action stations alarm lit up the bulkhead, and the warning klaxon deafened him.

Palpatine, still all glacial calm, placed his glass carefully on the nearest table and opened up the comlink to the cockpit.

"What is the problem?" he asked.

There was nothing but the crackle of static from the other end of the link. Vader was already at the hatch, his

Force-senses tearing their way through what seemed like layers of padding and smoke to feel clearly what had been hidden from him by a concerted effort. The Dark Jedi were in revolt, struggling to screen their intentions from him, but all he needed to know was that they had no plans to be loyal to *him*.

They were probably coming for him.

Cuis clones were still on their donor's mission, it seemed.

Vader strode down the passage to the cockpit, lightsaber drawn, the pulsing red action stations light reflecting off his armor. He could hear blasterfire. He opened his comlink. "Lekauf, what's happening?"

"The Cuis clones killed the pilots and seized the entire forward section of the ship, sir." The *b-dappp* of a blaster bolt interrupted the lieutenant. "It's just me, my clones, and the navigation officer back here. We're trying to blast the hatches open at the ten-meter bulkhead."

"Wait for me."

"I don't think you should come down here, sir."

"I will deal with it. They want me."

"Sheyvan seems to want the Emperor, sir, not you."

Vader felt the shuttle lurch as if it had made a sudden course correction. He strode back to the day cabin and checked the navigation display repeater to check the heading; the shuttle was now traveling toward the Outer Rim. Palpatine was still sitting calmly in his seat, his lightsaber hilt on his lap.

A thought crossed Vader's mind. He phrased it carefully. "Is this a live-fire exercise you saw fit not to mention to me, Master?"

"It is not," said Palpatine.

Another of his games, though. Perhaps he has tasked the Cuis clones to kill me. "You are in danger, Master."

"I can handle seven Dark Jedi, Lord Vader. What neither of us can handle, however, is the vacuum of space. So let us ensure there is no hull breach."

"*Seven,*" said Vader. "You include your own Hand, then."

"Either Sheyvan is dead, or he is part of this rebellion, in which case he will die anyway."

The Lambda was a small craft, twenty meters stem-to-stern, and Palpatine could fight as well with his Force powers from the day cabin as he could within lightsaber range of an enemy. Vader took his calm reaction as tacit proof that the Emperor knew he was not at risk, but that Vader was. And suddenly he resented him for compromising his crew, who deserved better than this.

"I will deal with this, Master. There is no need for you be involved." *Don't put obstacles in my way. Don't try to test me further. Keep out of this fight.* "Lekauf and I will restore order."

Vader strode back down the passageway and came out at the hatch one compartment aft of the ten-meter bulkhead. Smoke and the smell of discharged blaster filled the air; Lekauf, the navigation officer Pepin, and the Lekauf clones had stacked crates as a defensive barrier and were alternating between blasting at the hatch and attempting to force the sections apart with a metal bar.

"If we didn't have Jedi on the other side of the hatch, this would be open by now," said Pepin, grunting with the effort as he put all his weight on the metal bar.

"It's Sheyvan, sir," said Lekauf. "He led them."

Vader walked up to the hatch, moved Pepin out of the way with an assertive hand, and struck his balled fist against the durasteel twice.

"Sheyvan, give up. You can never defeat me."

Sheyvan's voice was muffled. Vader's amplified hearing picked out the words clearly even through the heavy durasteel.

"He betrayed us," said Sheyvan. "The Emperor betrayed us all."

"Open this hatch."

"He *uses* us, Lord Vader. Don't you understand?"

Oh, yes, indeed I do. And I could rip this hatch apart with the power of my will, but I want to hear more. How did you find the strength to defy Palpatine?

"I said *open the hatch*."

"He makes us believe we're each the only Hand, and then we find—he throws away our lives, Lord Vader, and our loyalty deserves better."

Indeed it does. So did mine. Who am I still angry with—Palpatine or Kenobi? Which Master disappointed me more?

"Cuis clones!" He rapped the hatch again. "You cannot have your donor's memories. What makes *you* feel betrayed enough to threaten your Emperor?"

A dead man's voice answered with a slightly different accent, the accent of Sheyvan. "We're loyal to the man who trained us, Lord Vader."

"Terrific," said Lekauf. "Smart way to turn their qualities against us."

There was no disputing their capacity for loyalty, and Vader had been right to spot that quality in Cuis; but he hadn't known how betrayed Sheyvan would feel by finding he wasn't the only Hand, and by discovering what had happened to Cuis.

But Palpatine must have known the reaction was likely. Had he engineered this, putting a bitter man in charge of training Dark Jedi who were highly likely to take on their instructor's cause? Had he influenced Sheyvan's mind? Vader never knew how many layers there were to Palpatine's intrigue, only that he was tired of it.

Lekauf was right. Loyalty *was* a two-edged sword. It was a pity that it was working against him at the moment.

"Lord Vader," said Sheyvan. "Lord Vader, help us overthrow Palpatine. You could rule in his place."

Yes, I will oust him. But now seemed very soon, *too* soon. Vader considered it for a moment. He turned and caught Lekauf staring at him, then dismissed the thought.

"Stand back and let me open this hatch, Lieutenant."

The Cuis clones heard him. It felt as if one had moved

closer to the hatch. "If you attempt to storm the cockpit," the clone shouted, "we'll overload the laser cannons and destroy the ship."

Lekauf nodded. "They can do that, sir," he said quietly. "They have control of all weapons systems."

"Then we need to neutralize them safely."

"Safe for them?"

"Safe for us."

"If you're prepared to cope without life support for a while, my lord, I can probably cut power to the whole ship," said Pepin. "The generator is on our side of the hatch."

That would cripple the laser cannons. It meant fighting in darkness, but Vader and the clones all had helmet enhancements that enabled them to see in infrared and low light. Pepin could manage somehow.

"They still have their lightsabers, sir, even if we kill the power," said Lekauf. "They're very good at deflecting blasterfire, and any heavier ordnance might blow a hole in our hull anyway."

"I've got something they'll have trouble deflecting," said Nele, the Lekauf clone who had been thrown across the gymnasium. He hefted a large rifle with a cylindrical chamber mounted where an optical scope would have been on a conventional blaster rifle. "Instant barbecue."

Lekauf looked embarrassed for a moment. "A flamethrower, sir. He's right. Better to char the section than put a big hole in it. And it's quick."

Vader couldn't imagine his ultraformal lieutenant teaching his clones phrases like *instant barbecue,* but there was clearly a side to the man he hadn't yet seen.

"Fire is the greatest danger in a vessel."

"Not as dangerous as letting them blow up the ship, sir."

"Very well," said Vader. He could use the Force to contain damage if he had to. Feeling a presence approaching, he looked around to see Palpatine, standing serene at the end of the passageway and simply . . . *observing.* "Make ready."

Vader regretted the waste of Cuis's clones. But this was a matter of survival, and if a Hand could turn on the Emperor, the man who had originally inspired his devotion, then he had instilled in his trainees a capacity to do the same.

Clones were always fast learners. *That* was a two-edged sword as well.

Palpatine remained at the end of the passageway that ran the length of Lambda's starboard side. He had projected a shimmering field in front of him, a silent statement that he would not participate in the fight.

"I have confidence in you, Lord Vader."

That trick no longer works on me, Master.

"And I have confidence in my men." Vader could see from the tight control on Lekauf's face that he was now far from inspired by the Emperor. For once, here was someone whom he didn't appear able to imbue with the desire to please him. Lekauf seemed to feel what Vader felt. It was unsettling to see that in an ordinary man.

Pepin stood with a hydrospanner in his hand, ready to shut down the shuttle's drives and generator. Lekauf positioned the six clones on either side of the hatch with flamethrowers and blasters ready.

Vader stood back. What they needed was not so much his fighting skills as his ability to prevent the Dark Jedi from using the Force. They almost certainly had a danger sense as acute as his—and seven of them together could reach out from behind that hatch and thwart Pepin or any of the clones.

He took a breath and centered himself, shutting out almost everything around him until he was aware only of the living beings in the shuttle. He could feel Lekauf and his men; he could feel Pepin at the power controls. And he could feel the seven vortices of dark energy behind the bulkhead in the forward section as if no durasteel stood between them at all.

There was a click and whir of blasters charging and a faint hiss as three of the clones adjusted the pressure in their flamethrowers.

"Ready when you are, sir," said Lekauf.

Vader concentrated on Pepin and enveloped him in a Force-shield.

"Pepin—*now!*"

Vader felt a sense of focus from behind the hatch as seven minds seemed to sense the threat and reached out. Pepin cut the generator and the shuttle was plunged into darkness except for the shimmering red blade of his lightsaber. He raised his left hand, knowing exactly where the weakest point of the hatch was, and sent a massive Force push that swept the two halves of the hatch doors apart.

For a moment, frozen in time, Vader saw a forest of red lightsaber shafts exactly like his own. He punched a Force shock wave into the cockpit just as his field of vision erupted in hot yellow light and the loud *whoomp* of flame filled the ruptured compartment ahead of them, fire licking across bulkheads and darting into the cockpit hatchway.

He could see inside now. He heard screams. Three lightsabers had disappeared, appearing to merge with the flames. Fierce gold reflections danced on white armor. But three shafts of energy continued to glow, and he could see three of Cuis's clones enveloped in Force-shields of their own, managing to hold off the flamethrower assault.

The stormtrooper plates and bodysuit were fire-resistant, and Lekauf's men had overcome that hardwired human terror of fire to walk through the inferno and continue to shoot jets of burning gas into the compartment before them. Vader could see three bodies on the floor, matte black from charring, and three moving lightsaber blades . . . but where was the fourth?

He reached out with his mind, searching behind burning panels and control fascias. Another ball of fire rolled up to the deckhead from the muzzle of a flamethrower. Lekauf, tight at Vader's side and without a respirator, coughed as acrid smoke billowed back.

"Get clear," said Vader, and stabbed his Force reach through the shield of the Cuis clones, seizing their throats and crushing them. One yielded and Vader moved in fast, taking three strides forward and slashing his saber down to fell the clone.

Two were left, plus Sheyvan. He was still alive. Vader could feel him yet not see him. Lekauf's men fired rapid bursts of flame at the last two Cuis clones standing, pinning them against the port bulkhead as Vader moved in and they struggled to maintain the protective bubble around them. Smoke rolled from every surface. The shuttle's interior was made from fire-resistant materials, but the temperature in the confined space was now getting unbearable.

Nele fired another burst of burning gas at the Dark Jedi. Then one of the Cuis clones made a massive effort and sent the ball of flame back at Vader.

Vader's suit could withstand nearly every assault. But Lekauf, a man trained to react without pausing to debate, flung himself in front of him and took the brunt of the flame. He fell, gasping, as the clones closed in on the Dark Jedi and Vader burst apart their Force-shields with pure focused rage.

Lightsabers winked out of existence.

"Pepin, fire control, *now!*" Vader shouted.

The shuttle's power came back and a fine rain of fire retardant began falling from the conduits in the deckhead, dousing the smoldering surfaces. Vader dropped to one knee to grab Lekauf's shoulders and pull him clear.

Lekauf's action had been a foolish gesture, and one Vader didn't need. But this was a painful reminder for him. Not so long ago, he had been the one burning and desperate for help—and the Master he trusted, Obi-Wan Kenobi, had abandoned him and left him to die.

Vader would not abandon Lekauf as he had been abandoned. He supported the officer's head, not to win his allegiance as Palpatine might, but because it was what Vader believed Kenobi should have done for him.

Lekauf's skin was blackened but his eyes were open, wide and white in a shocked face. Vader called for bacta, and Nele and Pepin ran to him with medpacs. Lekauf raised an arm and looked at the blistered back of his hand as if it weren't his own. "My wife's going to be furious with me," he said in the nonsensical way that badly injured men often did.

"I bet your wife will just be glad to see you back in one piece," said Pepin. "Let's get you into the cabin."

Vader straightened up. The other clones were searching the charred and twisted forward compartment, blasters aimed.

Sheyvan had to be in there somewhere. It was too small a ship in which to hide. Vader stepped carefully through the steaming debris, now slippery with a coating of fire-retardant liquid, and gestured to the clones to leave him to the search. He felt that the Dark Jedi was alive, but with a black layer of wet ash covering everything it was hard to tell what was a body and what was simply a melted sheet of plastoid. He prodded lumps with his boot, lightsaber in hand.

He counted eight bodies: six Cuis clones and the two crew who were already dead when the assault began. Then one blackened shape yielded slightly when he kicked it.

Sheyvan sprang to his feet, a nightmare smeared in wet black ash. His lightsaber cut through the damp hot air, and Vader blocked it with an upward thrust.

"He'll betray you, too, sir," said Sheyvan, his lightsaber locked against Vader's.

"Few men will *not* try to betray me," said Vader, and swung back at him. He could focus only on Lekauf's plight at that moment, an echo of his own, and rage was a fine lens through which to concentrate his power. He drove Sheyvan back across the slippery deck, sending him stumbling. Even now, after holding back flame and surviving smoke, the Dark Jedi was still a formidable fighter. Vader genuinely regretted the final stroke that sliced him from shoulder to hip and left him dead on the deck.

Sheyvan was what Palpatine had made him. Vader had once thought he was made as Palpatine had planned, but now he knew he was his own man.

The Emperor could even have influenced Sheyvan to do this. So many layers. So many games.

The cockpit was too badly damaged to pilot the shuttle back to Imperial Center. Vader sent out a distress signal and waited for rescue. He walked back to the day cabin to check on Lekauf and found Palpatine watching the emergency first aid as if it were a demonstration.

"Will he survive?" Vader asked. *I know how this feels. I know the pain.* "Are his lungs damaged?"

Pepin took him to one side. "He's very badly burned, sir," he said in a whisper.

"I survived burns once," said Vader. "And so will he. He will have the best medical care." He leaned over Lekauf and stared into his face, seeing a fraction of the image that Palpatine must once have seen of him. "You are too loyal for your own good, Lieutenant."

"That's my job, my lord."

He might have been attempting humor. Judging by the expressions on the faces of the clones he had trained, he had created that same sense of allegiance in them. They had almost formed a defensive line around him. Nele handed Pepin a succession of bacta-soaked swabs.

"You never disappoint me," said Vader. Lekauf, face and hands swathed in wet gauze, blinked a few times. "Your apology was premature."

Lekauf would recover in time, and he might even train men again. But he would now be the progenitor of a clone battalion. His men had defeated Dark Jedi, and, even if assisted by Vader, they had still given a good account of themselves.

Lekauf could be proud. And at least he would see his family again. Scarred or not, he had certain things that others—even Vader—might envy.

IMPERIAL PALACE, CORUSCANT;
TWO DAYS LATER

"How is your lieutenant?" asked the Emperor.

Vader studied the ranks of the 501st Legion from the window overlooking the parade ground. There was a certain comfort in knowing that for most of them—those whose whole life was soldiering and who had no ambitions beyond that—life was a straightforward process of doing their job, with no thought of whom they might oust or assassinate or outmaneuver.

"He's improving, Master."

"Loyalty is a fine quality."

"I have asked Arkanian Micro to produce a battalion of Lekauf clones. I think they have proved themselves."

"Yes." Palpatine wandered across to the window to stand beside Vader as if curious about whatever had caught his attention. "Cancel the orders for the Cuis clones. For the time being."

I already have. "It will be done, my Master."

"You are still troubled. I feel it."

Vader decided to risk the question that was on his mind. Palpatine knew it was there anyway. The only issue was whether Vader would ask it.

"Master, was Sheyvan's rebellion designed to test me?"

Palpatine turned his head sharply. The cowl shadowed his eyes: once his face had seemed kindly to Vader. "If it *was* a test, Lord Vader, it was for the clones, not for you. And *if* it was, then the Lekauf batch proved the more worthy."

So that was your motive. With a little mental manipulation to turn Sheyvan's resentment into hatred. And what a poor reward for Lekauf.

Vader curbed his anger simply to deny his Master the taste of victory. "A real crisis shows what a man is made from."

"I have not ruled out more Cuis clones, of course."

How far ahead do you plan your little games? You

*waited decades to defeat the Jedi. You used trillions of lives
to achieve it. Will I ever be able to think enough steps
ahead of you?*

"I feel Dark Jedi are not suitable for the Imperial Army."

"With the right commander they would be."

"And who would train them?"

"You, Lord Vader."

"I prefer ordinary soldiers. They don't covet power. I
would spend all my time watching my back."

"Indeed you would," said Palpatine.

It had been a game at first, an annoying one, but just verbal sparring; the Emperor neither lied nor told the truth.
Now it had ceased to be a challenge, and Vader longed for
a simpler relationship. There was a very fine line between
strengthening a man through constant challenge and turning him into an enemy.

"Perhaps the solution to having to watch your back is to
make your enemy watch theirs instead," said Vader.

I will come for you one day.

"Or have others want to watch it for you," said Palpatine, and turned to leave his apprentice alone in the ante-
room.

Vader now knew there were no Force-users, dark or
otherwise, whom he could wholly trust—his own Master
least of all. Vader had no loyalties beyond himself, except
for his interest in the well-being of the likes of Lekauf, men
with no extraordinary gifts or powers whatsoever.

Unless, of course, you counted simple honesty as a gift.

At that moment he thought it the equal of any Force
power. Yes, Vader preferred ordinary men made excellent
by effort. The part of him that was Anakin Skywalker remembered the few things he had struggled to achieve—
love, excitement, freedom—and thought how much more
they had thrilled him than his prodigious and easy powers.

He had been a man himself, once. Thinking of Lekauf,
he wondered if he would ever choose to be one again.

The adventure does not stop here.

Keep reading for an excerpt from the second book
in the thrilling Legacy of the Force series:

BLOODLINES
Karen Traviss

Available now from Del Rey Books

Atzerri system, ten standard years after the Yuuzhan Vong war:
Slave I *in pursuit of prisoner H'buk. Boba Fett's private record.*

"Whatever he's paying you, Fett, I'll *double* it," says the
voice on the comlink.

They say that a *lot.* They just don't understand the nature of a contract. This time it's an Atzerri glitterstim dealer
called H'buk who's overstepped the mark with the Traders'
Coalition to the tune of four hundred thousand credits.
The coalition feels it's worth paying me five hundred thousand credits to teach him—and everyone else—a lesson
about honoring debts.

I agree with the Traders' Coalition wholeheartedly.

"A contract's a contract," I tell him. *Slave I* is close
enough on his trail for me to get a visual on him: I swear
he's flying an old Z-95 Headhunter. No hyperdrive, or he'd
have jumped for it by now. And no wonder he's surprised.
An old, old Firespray like *Slave I* shouldn't be able to catch
him on sublight drive alone.

But I've fitted a few more . . . *extras* recently. The only
completely original part of *Slave I* now is the seat I'm in.

"My laser cannon's armed," says H'buk, breathless.

"Good for you." Why they *always* want a conversation, I'll never know. Look, shoot or shut up; I *know* you'll have to come about to target me with that cannon, and in that second or two I'll take out your drives anyway. "The galaxy's a dangerous place."

The Headhunter executes a neat turn to port with its aft maneuvering jets and the *Slave*'s laser locks on to the Headhunter's drive signature, matching its turns and loops with no need for guidance from me. His engine flares in a ball of white light. The fighter begins an uncontrolled roll and I have to gun it to get the tractor beam locked and haul H'buk in.

The grapple arms make a satisfying *chunk-unkkkk* against the Headhunter's airframe as I secure the fighter against the casing above *Slave*'s torpedo launcher. The sound of that reverberating through your hull, I'm told, is just like a cell door closing behind you: the point at which prisoners lose all hope.

Funny; that would only make me fight harder.

H'buk is making the noises of panic and pleading that I hardly notice these days. Some prisoners are defiant, but most give in to fear. He makes me offers all the way back to Atzerri, promising anything to survive.

"I can pay you millions."

The contract is to deliver him alive. It's *very* specific.

"And my stock holdings in Kuat Drive Yards."

I think it's the silent routine that gets to them in the end.

"Fett, I have a beautiful daughter . . ."

He shouldn't have said that. Now I'm angry, and I don't often get angry. "*Never* use your kids, scumbag. *Never.*"

My father put me first. *Any* father should. Not that I ever felt pity—or anything—for H'buk, but I'm satisfied now that he deserves everything that the Traders' Coalition is going to do to him. If I were the sympathetic kind, I'd kill him. I'm not. And the contract says *alive*.

"Want to negotiate a landing fee?" asks Atzerri Air Traffic Control.

"Want to negotiate an ion cannon?"

"Oh . . . apologies, Master Fett, sir . . ."

They always see my point.

Landing on Atzerri is a little tricky when you're hauling a crippled fighter on your upperworks. I set *Slave I* down on the landing strip, lowering gently on the thrusters, feeling the aft section vibrating under the load. And I have an audience.

The coalition wants to show they can afford to hire the best to hunt down *anyone* who crosses them. I oblige. A bit of theater, a little public relations: like Mandalorian armor, it makes the point without a shot needing to be fired. I walk along *Slave I*'s casing to clamber up onto the Headhunter's fuselage and crack open its canopy seal with the laser housed in my wrist gauntlet. So I hit H'buk harder than I need to, and haul him out of the cockpit to rappel down ten meters to the ground on the lanyard with him.

It hurts deep in my stomach. I don't let anyone see that.

Then I deposit the prisoner on the landing strip in front of the men he owes four hundred thousand credits. It makes the point. I *like* making points. Presentation is half the battle.

"Want to keep the starfighter, too?" asks my customer.

"Not my taste." The spaceport utility loader comes to remove it from *Slave I*. I hold out my palm: I want the rest of my fee.

He hands me the outstanding 250,000 creds on a verified chip. "Why do you still do this, Fett?"

"Because people still ask me."

It's a good question. I ponder it while I sit back in the cockpit and catch up with the financial headlines on the HoloNet news as *Slave I* heads for Kamino on autopilot. My doctor is meeting me there. He doesn't like the long journey but I don't pay him to be happy.

Now I find I'm thinking of a daughter—Ailyn—who I haven't seen in fifty years, wondering if she's still alive.

You see, I'm ill. I think I'm dying.

If I am, then there are things I've got to do. One of them is to find out what happened to Ailyn. Another is to decide who's going to be Mandalore when I'm gone.

And the third, of course, is to cheat death.

I've had a lot of practice at that.